a long time gone

"Flows with the river of life....Once you have
started the journey...you will not be able to stop."
—The Huffington Post

"It's so real that it's hard to leave at the end."
—*The Herald-Sun* (NC)

Praise for the Novels of Karen White

A Long Time Gone

"This multigenerational family saga is a book you could get lost in."
—*Delta Magazine*

"A sweet Southern tale of the bond between mothers and daughters . . . emotionally satisfying."
—*Kirkus Reviews*

"White . . . crafts a story with something for almost everyone: betrayal, murder, history, family secrets, and a little romance. Readers will find it difficult to put this one down since each chapter leaves one craving more."
—*Library Journal*

"Karen White's new delta-drawn narrative is gothic gold."
—*The Atlantan*

"Karen White's best novel to date. . . . Use your vacation reading to escape and immerse in this world White has so deftly created. It's so real that it's hard to leave at the end."
—*The Herald-Sun* (NC)

"White . . . writes, plots, and develops characters to levels above the usual summer-reading fare."
—fayobserver.com (Fayetteville, NC)

"There is a rhythm to the writing of Karen White. It has a pace, a beat, a cadence that is all its own. It creates a flow of words, like a river surging forward, from the first page to the last page. This is certainly the case with White's latest novel, *A Long Time Gone*. The reader gets swept up by the story right from the start and barely comes up for breath until all has been revealed. This makes this Southern saga of life in Mississippi one of White's best, and that means it is very, very good. Once you have started the journey contained in *A Long Time Gone* you will not be able to stop. The current of words will pull you along as you glide toward the ending. When you reach the shore of your real life, you will have a feeling of being fully sated by Karen White's talent as a teller of tales."
—The Huffington Post

"Intense, riveting, and mysterious contemporary fiction—finely told."
—The Best Reviews

"An absorbing drama. . . . White consistently prevails as a shining literary star."
—Jennifer Vido

continued . . .

"Her colorful narrative is melodious and haunting, and gives a Tennessee Williams–like aura to the awesomely depicted places and all of her impeccably played and fantastic characters. Brava!"—*RT Book Reviews*

"Kept me turning the pages. . . . From the 1920s to the 1960s to the present, you will be enthralled with the lives and legacy of Walker women."
—Heroes and Heartbreakers

The Time Between

"From its mesmerizing first scene, *The Time Between* propels you into the sunbaked world of the South Carolina Lowcountry and a childhood tragedy that haunts the lives of two unforgettable sisters in love with the same man. In clear and gorgeous prose, White spins a luminous tale of love and loss, of betrayal and redemption, and of a harrowing family secret buried in the upheaval of the Second World War. This is storytelling of the highest order: the kind of book that leaves you both deeply satisfied and aching for more. No one weaves together the present and the past with greater magic than Karen White."
—Beatriz Williams, *New York Times* bestselling author of *One Hundred Summers*

"White . . . once again crafts characters who transcend their romantic roles through their frailties and weaknesses."   —*Kirkus Reviews*

"White moves smoothly between narrators as well as different time periods, crafting an intriguing and romantic family drama."—*Booklist*

"White writes complex, heartbreaking novels with just enough pathos and plenty of redemption."   —*RT Book Reviews* (top pick)

"Set in South Carolina's idyllic Lowcountry against the bittersweet notes of a piano in mourning and a prophecy spoken in Gullah, *The Time Between* weaves a story as intricate and sturdy as a sweetgrass basket, with the fresh, magnetic voices of its headstrong characters."
—ArtsATL

"*The Time Between* is a lyrically written, beautiful novel about atonement, love, and letting go. Engrossing and unforgettable."
—*New York Times* bestselling author Eloisa James

More Praise for the Novels of Karen White

"White's dizzying carousel of a plot keeps those pages turning, so much so that the book can—and should be—finished in one afternoon, interrupted only by a glass of sweet iced tea."   —Oprah.com

New American Library Titles
by Karen White

The Color of Light

Learning to Breathe

Pieces of the Heart

The Memory of Water

The Lost Hours

On Folly Beach

Falling Home

The Beach Trees

Sea Change

After the Rain

The Time Between

The Tradd Street Series

The House on Tradd Street

The Girl on Legare Street

The Strangers on Montagu Street

Return to Tradd Street

A Long Time Gone

KAREN WHITE

 NEW AMERICAN LIBRARY

New American Library
Published by the Penguin Group
Penguin Group (USA) LLC, 375 Hudson Street,
New York, New York 10014

USA | Canada | UK | Ireland | Australia | New Zealand | India | South Africa | China
penguin.com
A Penguin Random House Company

Published by New American Library, a division of Penguin Group (USA) LLC.
Previously published in a New American Library hardcover edition.

First Trade Paperback Printing, April 2015

REGISTERED TRADEMARK—MARCA REGISTRADA

NAL Trade Paperback ISBN: 978-0-451-46855-0

The Library of Congress has cataloged the hardcover edition of this title as follows:

White, Karen (Karen S.)
    A long time gone/Karen White.
        pages cm
    ISBN 978-0-451-24046-0 (hardback)
    1. Family secrets—Fiction. 2. Caregivers—Fiction. 3. Delta (Miss.: Region)—Fiction. 4. Suspense fiction. I. Title.
    PS3623.H5776L65 2014
    813'.6—dc23   2014000340

Printed in the United States of America
10 9 8 7 6 5 4 3

Set in Bembo Book MT
Designed by Alissa Rose Theodor

*To my aunts Mary Louise, Janie, Gloria, and Charlene, my mother,
Catherine Anne, and my grandmother Grace for showing me the unique and
timeless beauty of the Mississippi Delta*

Acknowledgments

Thank you to my parents, who forced me to endure the long summer car drives south to Mississippi to visit my mother's hometown in the Mississippi Delta. I grew to love that small Southern town, which became the inspiration for this book.

Thanks also to Jane Evans, Indianola city clerk, who pointed me in the right direction for further research, and a very huge thanks to Heather Burton, Sunflower County coroner, who was so generous with her time and answered every nitpicky question I had with much patience. Any errors I might have made in the translation are completely mine!

A Long Time Gone

Chapter 1

Vivien Walker Moise
INDIAN MOUND, MISSISSIPPI
APRIL 2013

I was born in the same bed that my mama was born in, and her mama before her, and even further back than anybody alive could still remember. It was as if the black wood of the bedposts were meant to root us Walker women to this place of flat fields and fertile soil carved from the great Mississippi. But like the levees built to control the mighty river, it never held us for long.

We were born screaming into this world, the beginning of a lifelong quest to find what would quiet us. Our legacy was our ability to coax living things from fallow ground, along with a desperate need to see what lay beyond the delta. A need to quell a hurt whose source was as unexplainable as its force.

Whatever it was that drove us away was never stronger than the pull of what brought us back. Maybe it was the feel of the dark Mississippi mud or the memory of the old house and the black bed into which we'd been born, but no matter how far we ran, we always came back.

I returned in the spring nearly nine years to the day after I'd left. I'd driven straight through from Los Angeles, twenty-seven hours of asphalt and fast food, my memories like a string guiding me home. The last leg from Little Rock to Indian Mound was punctuated by bright flashes of lightning and constant tornado watches on the radio. I kept my foot pressed to the accelerator as strong winds buffeted my car. It didn't occur to me to stop. I had a trunk's worth of hurts piled in the car with me that only my grandmother Bootsie could make go away. She would forgive those long years of silence because she understood doggedness. I'd inherited it from her side of the family, after all.

It was nearly dawn when the storm passed and I crossed the river into Mississippi and headed east on Highway 82 and into the heart of the delta. The hills and bluffs to the west disappeared as if a giant boot had flattened all the land between the Mississippi and Yazoo rivers, creating a landscape as rich and fertile as it was difficult to contain and control. This place of my ancestors was known to make or break a man, and I figured by now the scorecard was about even.

I've been a long time gone. Billboards and highway lights fell away, leaving behind empty fields and ramshackle structures swallowed by kudzu, turning them into hulking ghosts haunting the roadside. Sinewy cypress swamps randomly appeared as if to remind us of our tenuous hold on the land. The predawn flatscape flashed by me in shades of gray, as if the years had absorbed all the color, so that even my memories were seen only in black and white.

A therapist had once told me that my hindsight color blindness was due to an unhappy childhood. I tried to tell him that I had never considered my motherless childhood to be *unhappy*. It was more of an accumulation of years filled with absence, that perhaps black and white were simply the colors of grief.

The rising sun had painted the sky pink by the time I passed the sign for Indian Mound, the first seeds of panic making my heart beat faster. I glanced over at my purse, where I kept my pills, wondering whether I could swallow them dry again as I'd been doing for most of the trip. My throat felt sore, and my hands shook. *I'm almost home.* I turned my gaze toward the dim light outside that seemed to swallow my car as I passed through it, and pressed my foot harder on the accelerator.

I slowed down, trying to avoid the increasing amount of debris tossed across the road, the tree limbs, leaves, and roof shingles that seemed to have been scattered by the hand of a careless child. I caught up to an old, faded red pickup truck as it slowed down at the bright flashing red and blue lights of a police car stopped in front of fallen electrical lines. A large, brindled dog, his lineage as indecipherable as the vintage of the pickup truck in which he sat, stared at me with a lost expression. A police officer guided our way around the danger zone, his other hand reminding us to slow down. As soon as he had disappeared from my rearview mirror, I sped up, passing the truck and maneuvering past a mailbox that stood upright in the middle of the highway as if it were meant to be there.

My tongue stuck to the roof of my mouth and I thought of the pills again, and how easily they could take away the pit of worry that had begun to gnaw at me. I went faster, clipping a tree limb with my left front tire and hearing a crack and a thump of the split wood hitting metal. I kept going, realizing that I was prepared to drive on the rim of a flat tire if I had to. *I've been a long time gone.*

I turned off the highway onto a dirt road studded with puddles and rocks. The road bisected a large cotton field, the furrows drowning in standing water. I remembered this road and had turned by instinct. It probably had a name, one we'd never used when giving directions to the odd visitor. We usually instructed visitors to turn right about one and a half miles past the old general store, which leaned to the left and still had a Royal Crown Cola sign plastered over the doorway even though it had been abandoned long before I was born.

The store was gone now, but I still knew where to turn in the same way my hair still knew where to part no matter how hard I tried to tell it different. But the road was the same, still narrow, with the tall white oaks—taller now, I supposed—creating a green archway above. Tommy and I used to race barefoot down this road, watching our feet churn up dust like conjured spirits.

My back tires spun out, bringing me back to the present and slipping my car off the side of the road. Panicking, I gunned the engine, succeeding only in digging the wheels further in muck. Although I knew it was useless, I gunned the engine two more times. I stared through the windshield down the tree-shaded road. It had taken me nine years to come back. I figured stretching it out for a few more minutes wouldn't matter.

I began to walk, my leather flats sticking to the Mississippi mud as if reluctant to let me go again. A murder of crows sprang up out of the trees, cawing loudly and making my heart hammer as I tried counting them, recalling the nursery rhyme Mathilda had sung to me as a child.

One for sorrow,
two for mirth,
three for a wedding,
four for a birth,
five for silver,
six for gold,
seven for a secret never to be told,
eight for heaven,
nine for hell,
And ten for the devil's own self.

I clenched my teeth, wishing I'd taken another pill. I glanced over my shoulder at the car, realizing too late that I'd left my purse. I'd almost decided to go back when a flurry of wings made me look up. Seven black crows, their inky black wings seeming wet in the light of the sun, swirled and dipped over me, cawing and cackling, then took off again across the field.

My throat stung as I walked faster, feeling light-headed as I tried to recall the last time I'd eaten. And then the trees by the side of the road fell away and I stopped in a large clearing with a wide, paved drive edged with centuries-old oak trees. The old yellow house of indeterminate architecture with columns and porches and an improbable turret and at least three different roof styles stood before me in all of its confused splendor. It was an anomaly among all the Greek Revival homes of the region, as peculiar and original as the women who'd lived there for two centuries. My heart slowed as if Bootsie were already with me, letting my head rest on her shoulder. I had come home.

Despite the storm, the house appeared almost untouched except for the litter of pink azalea petals that had been stripped from their stems and scattered around the drive and yard like fuchsia doubloons from a Mardi Gras float.

Grass blades stuck their tips out of standing water in the yard as if struggling for breath, the water reflecting the sky and odd yellow house. Its windows stared down on me with reproach, as if wondering at the audacity of the return of another Walker woman, my hubris in believing it wanted me back. But I'd lived my first eighteen years inside its walls and had run through the fields of cotton that surrounded it. This house was the only spot of color in my monochromatic memories.

I listened for the songbirds, as much a part of my memory as the landscape. Except for the crows, the only sound cutting the silence was that of dripping water as it fell to the ground from the eaves and chipped paint of the old house, and from the arthritic fingers of the oak trees. I slowly walked up the wooden steps to the wide porch, pausing to take off my mud-caked shoes and leave them by the side of the door, just as I had done as a child. I placed my hand on the large brass knob of the front door before deciding to knock instead.

I knocked twice, waiting for the tread of my grandmother Bootsie's footsteps, or the glide of my mother's bare feet. Or even the heavier tread of my older brother, Tommy. But all I heard was the sound of the water leaking from the house. *Drip. Drip.*

I hesitated for a moment, then reached for the knob. It didn't turn. In all of my years growing up, the front door had never been locked. I couldn't help but wonder if they'd known I was coming after all. I stood for a moment with my hands on my hips until I remembered it was a stance my mother had frequently used, and dropped them again. The air was heavy with the scent of rain and the boxwoods that had begun to creep over the porch railings unchecked.

I slid my shoes back on and crossed the drive to walk around the side toward the old carriage house that had been converted into a garage sometime in the twenties. I recognized Bootsie's 1977 white Cadillac convertible and my heart lurched with relief. A white pickup truck with an enormous toolbox in the bed that I assumed was Tommy's sat behind it, and next to it was a dark sedan that looked suspiciously like an unmarked police car. I didn't take the time to think about why it was there. I walked quickly now, no longer caring about avoiding puddles, needing to be embraced by my grandmother until I no longer craved my pills to soothe away the hurting.

I moved to the backyard, looking toward the rear of our property, toward the forest full of sweet gums and pines, the solid land giving way to the swamp and giant bald cypress trees that Tommy had once told me were over a thousand years old. A lone cypress tree had managed to take root on higher ground halfway between the house and the swamp, standing by itself among the sparse grass and haphazard pine trees whose scraggly branches always made them look bewildered next to the corded majesty of the giant cypress. I'd called it "my tree" as a child, and I longed to sit in the comforting shade of its branches again.

But the landscape had been altered. Limbs and leaves mixed blindly with papers and other indistinguishable man-made debris. A porch swing that I remembered had once hung on the front porch sat right side up, its chains missing, in the middle of the yard. Close by, almost as if they'd been set there on purpose, were the two metal chairs that had always graced my grandmother's vegetable garden. They had once been a neon lime color, but sun and time had faded them into a disappointed green. With the swing, they formed a cohesive seating group, almost as if the wind had decided in the middle of its destruction to take a break.

I paused, feeling my equilibrium shift as if I'd just stepped off a moving sidewalk. I took in the three figures standing in the near distance, and then waited for my gaze to register what they were standing next to, blinking twice until I understood. My tree, the stalwart reminder of the best parts of my childhood, had toppled over, clipping the edge of the old cotton shed. The roots were singed black, with chunks of bark encircling the area. I imagined I could smell the burnt ions in the air from the lightning strike, still feel the atmosphere pulsating with the power of it.

"Bootsie?" I called out, my walk becoming a run. Three heads turned in my direction just as another cluster of crows flew out from the dead tree, their shiny black bodies seeming to mock me.

I stopped in front of the small group, my breath coming in gasps, as we regarded one another, all of us looking as if we'd just seen a ghost. Nobody said anything as my gaze moved from one person to another, registering my brother's face, and then another man, and then my mother. Whereas Tommy wore jeans and an untucked shirt, like he'd just been roused from bed by the sound of a lightning strike, my mother wore a silk brocade cocktail dress taken directly from the Kennedy White House, complete with rhinestone earrings and matching bracelet and ring. I recalled seeing a photograph of her mother, Bootsie, wearing the same ensemble.

My mother turned to me with mild surprise. "Vivien, I know I've told you before that you should never leave the house without lipstick."

I stared at her for a long moment, wondering if there was more to this altered landscape than just a fallen tree.

My brother hesitated for a moment, then took a step forward to embrace me. He was ten years older than me, and almost a decade had passed since I'd last seen him, but now, at nearly thirty-seven, he still looked like the gangly and awkward boy I'd grown up with. Tommy's shirt was soft and worn under my fingers, and I clutched at the familiarity of it. "It's been a while." He didn't smile.

My lips trembled as I tried to smirk at his vast understatement, as if we both believed his words could erase nearly nine years of silence. "Hello, Tommy." I forced a deep breath into my lungs. "Where's Bootsie?"

His eyes softened, and I knew then that I'd lost more than just time in the last nine years. "You've been gone awhile." His gaze drifted to our mother in her cocktail dress and high heels and something icy cold gripped the area around my heart.

Before I could say anything, the other man stepped forward. Tripp Montgomery was as tall and slender as I remembered him, short brown hair and hazel eyes that always seemed to see more of the world than the rest of us. He wore khaki pants and a long-sleeved shirt and a tie, which only added to my confusion. I looked at him, wondering why he was there and hoping that somebody would tell me this was all a dream and that I'd soon awaken in my bed in the old house with Bootsie kissing my forehead.

"Hey," Tripp said, as if he'd just delivered me to my front steps after school. As if the earth had somehow stopped spinning in this corner of the world and everything was the same as when I'd left it. Except it wasn't.

"Why are you here?" I asked, plucking at one of the random questions I needed to ask to make the ground beneath my feet stand still.

His face remained impassive, but I thought I saw a flicker of what looked like sympathy pass through his eyes. "I'm the county coroner." He stepped back, allowing my gaze to register the gaping hole in the ground that the intricate root system of the giant cypress had once inhabited. The grass around the edges was blackened, wood and bark sprinkled like confetti around the wounded earth. And there, nestled inside the dark hole like a baby in its crib, were the stark white bones of a human skeleton.

My hands began to shake, my vision marred by mottled dots of light. I struggled to focus as I stared at the skull, unable to look away.

I forced myself to look at Tripp and saw that he was staring at my hands as if he knew why, like he'd always known everything about me without my ever having to open my mouth. I tried to clench my fingers into fists, but they were shaking too hard. The dots of light had now become streaks across my vision, and I tried to focus on Tommy again, but my mother's voice broke through the pounding in my head.

"Have you taken my car keys again, Vivien? I can't seem to find them."

I looked down at the dirty white of the forehead bone, now shimmering in the bright morning sun as if it were trying to speak to me. I started to say something, but the light suddenly dimmed and I closed my eyes as I felt myself falling, still seeing behind my eyelids the glow of white bone against dark, dark earth.

Chapter 2

Adelaide Walker Bodine
INDIAN MOUND, MISSISSIPPI
JUNE 1920

Everybody has secrets. Even thirteen-year-old girls like me who nobody paid any attention to, like we were supposed to be too busy with our dolls and pretty dresses and birthday parties to notice that the judge's wife spent a lot of time alone in her house with different traveling salesmen, or that Mr. Pritchard, who owned the drugstore, always gave you free penny candy if you came in around closing, because he was too drunk from drinking bottled medicine by then to make change.

And I knew that my mama had jumped off the Tallahatchie Bridge when I was ten because my daddy had been killed in the war and she just couldn't take to life without him. I wish she'd asked me first, because I would have reminded her that she still had me. But I couldn't say that to anybody, since I wasn't supposed to know anything important. So I spent a lot of time outside halfway closed doors just so I could know what little I did.

My best friend was Sarah Beth Heathman, whose daddy was the president of the Indian Mound Planter's Bank on Main Street. I didn't have many friends on account of what my mama had done, like other parents were afraid that something like that might be catching. I was told that Mama had fallen into the river on accident, but I guess nobody else believed that either.

But it worked out, since Sarah Beth didn't have many friends, either, on account of her parents being so old. They were old when they had her, and even older now that she was fourteen. Maybe that's why Sarah Beth was so wild, or at least that's what Aunt Louise called her. But it seemed to me that whatever crazy idea Sarah Beth came up with, I was always happy to go along.

On a Wednesday in late June, I was sitting under the cypress tree in my backyard filling my lungs with the thick warm air while pretending to read a book. I'd been staring at the back of my house, wondering why it was still yellow when everybody else's house was white. I'd been told my great-grandmother had come from New Orleans, had the house painted and the odd castlelike turret added to one side, then given birth to a daughter before leaving it all behind to return to New Orleans. When the house became mine—and it would, because Aunt Louise told me that some papers meant that the house was always inherited by the oldest girl—I promised myself that I would paint it white.

I sometimes wondered if Uncle Joe—my daddy's brother—and Aunt Louise and my cousin Willie ever thought it should be their house, since they were stuck taking care of me and forced to live there. I'd hear my aunt fretting about the house needing painting or another leak in the roof, but then she'd look at me like I was a kitten drowning in a puddle and she'd get all choked up, and hug me like I was the only thing that mattered. She loved me like I was her daughter, and I appreciated that. But she wasn't my mama. My mama had walked off the Tallahatchie Bridge and left me behind.

At two o'clock in the afternoon, the men had all gone back to work after dinner, and the women were sponge-bathing themselves before collapsing onto sofas or beds in a cloud of flowery perfume and baby powder. A horn honked in the front drive, and I ran to find Sarah Beth in the backseat of the family's Lincoln, their driver, Jim, behind the wheel.

"Want to go to a picture show?" she asked, smiling sweetly through the car window.

We'd already seen *Dr. Jekyll and Mr. Hyde* three times. I should have known that she was up to no good. Jim dropped us off at the theater, and Sarah Beth waited for him to drive away before she told me her plans.

Twenty minutes later, I was wishing I'd said no. The sun was hot enough to burn the wings off a mosquito, and I could feel it prickling my scalp under my hair. Aunt Louise called it strawberry blond, but it was still just red to the Barclay twins, who always wanted to rub it for good luck before a baseball game.

I tramped through the tall grass behind Sarah Beth, keeping my face down to avoid getting more freckles. I'd be grounded for sure if Aunt Louise counted one more than I'd had the night before. She'd told me that all the women on my mama's side of the family were great beauties, and that I just needed a little more time to grow into my looks. But when I looked at myself in the mirror, I knew it would take more than just time. Aunt Louise still wore corsets and hadn't bobbed her hair, so I knew better than to listen to her about beauty.

"Are we almost there?" I asked for the third time, noticing how the pale skin on my forearms had started to turn pink.

"Almost. Stop being such a baby."

I stopped for a minute to catch my breath, feeling the sweat run down between my shoulder blades. I glared at the back of Sarah Beth's head full of dark brown hair and skin that never freckled or burned. I wondered how I was going to explain how I got sunburn sitting in a theater.

"Where are we going?" I shouted at her. We'd walked through the downtown area of Indian Mound and straight through a neighborhood of run-down houses that both of us had been promised a switch to the backside if we ever wandered into, then right through the other side, where tall Indian grass separated the town from the cotton fields. I looked down at my dusty shoes and considered for a minute that I should take them off along with my socks and go barefoot. But chigger bites on my ankles would be a lot harder to explain to Aunt Louise than dirty shoes.

Sarah Beth reached a dirt road and headed down it, and I followed, because I didn't have anything better to do. She stopped and waited for me to catch up and it took me a minute to figure out where we were.

There was a low iron fence in front of us with an open gate hanging catawampus from a single hinge like a dog panting in the heat. Somebody had tried to keep the grass cut, but long strands of it stuck out from the bottom of the fence.

I looked up, recognizing the back of the old Methodist church. People went to the new church closer to town now, and I'd never thought to wonder what they did with the old one. Which was nothing, I guess, but leave it be.

"This is a cemetery," I whispered, afraid I might wake somebody up.

Sarah Beth rolled her eyes. "Of course it is. It's the best place for secrets."

Pretending not to be afraid, I followed Sarah Beth through the gate to where rectangle-shaped gravestones sat upright in rows like teeth. In the back corner, separated from the stone markers with a low metal chain, were rough-looking wooden crosses, each with a hand-painted name and dates. Some had little messages on them like "Gone but not forgotten" or "In the hands of Jesus."

Sarah caught me looking at them. "Those are for the coloreds. They don't have money for nice markers, so they make their own." She began walking down one of the rows, being careful not to step on top of any of the graves. Everybody knew that was really bad luck, and that the angry spirit would follow you back home. I carefully placed my feet where hers had been. I figured I had enough spirits at home to worry about bringing home another.

"Why are they in the corner like that?"

She stopped, then turned around to look at me. With an exasperated sigh, she said, "Because they're *colored*."

I stared at her back as she kept walking, thinking about all those bodies buried in the ground and how once you became all bones it probably didn't matter what color your skin had been.

Sarah Beth stopped, squatting next to five tiny stones stuck right next to one another. A rosebush had been planted at the foot of the middle one. It was clipped and the dirt around it didn't have any weeds, so it looked like somebody came by pretty regular-like.

A yellow jacket lifted off a dandelion to buzz close to me and I jerked back with a little scream.

"Shh," Sarah Beth hissed, her finger across her lips.

"Bees make me sick," I hissed back. "If I get stung you'll have to carry me to Dr. Odom before I stop breathing. And then you'll be sorry you yelled at me."

She frowned, then turned back to the stones while I moved to stand behind her, avoiding the dandelions just in case there were more bees.

My eyes moved from one stone to the next. Each had the same last name—Heathman—and each of them had only one date, going from 1891 through 1897 like some kind of filing system.

"That's your last name," I said to Sarah Beth, trying to sound observant and intelligent, which was normally her job.

She rolled her eyes. "I *know*. That's why this is a *secret*."

I looked at her silently, afraid to open my mouth so that she'd know that I had no idea what she was talking about.

With the same kind of exaggerated patience that Aunt Louise showed when she was trying to tell me why I couldn't roll up my dresses on hot days or cut my hair, she said, "These are my brothers and sisters. I know it. The last one, Henrietta, died nine years before I was born. Mama always calls me her miracle baby, and now I know why."

"There're lots of Heathmans in Indian Mound. How d'you know they're not cousins or something?"

"I wrote down every Heathman in town and there are no aunts, uncles, cousins, or anybody who would have been old enough to have babies that were the ages of these babies. Except for my parents. That's why I'm the miracle baby. Don't you remember that Bible story Mrs. Adams told us in Sunday school about Abraham's wife, Sarah, who had a baby even though she was old? Just like my mama!"

"But why wouldn't your mama have told you about your brothers and sisters?"

She shrugged. "I don't know. Maybe it makes her too sad."

"Have you looked in your family Bible? Every baby born in the family is supposed to be listed in the front."

She stared at me in surprise, then shook her head, making me feel very smart. "I'm not allowed to touch it. We keep it in Daddy's study on a shelf. Mama says it's too old for me to look at it; that's why she gave me a new one for my birthday."

A slow grin formed on her face as she regarded me. "She usually takes another bath when she wakes up, and Bertha does the grocery shopping on Wednesdays. If we hurry, we could make it back and take a peek."

Without waiting for me, she took off at a run, and I followed her because it had sort of been my idea. She lived closer to town than me because of her daddy being president of the bank, but in the middle of the afternoon I was about to die of heatstroke by the time we ran up the steps onto the columned porch. Her house looked like one of the old plantation homes in Natchez, but it was new. Sarah Beth made fun of my house, saying it looked like it didn't know what it wanted to be— something I knew she'd heard her mama say. I could usually shut her up by telling her that it had been in my family for more than one hundred years and would one day be mine.

We very carefully opened the front door, then paused on the threshold. I breathed heavily as Sarah Beth put her finger to her lips, as if I needed to be reminded that if her mama caught us and told my aunt and uncle, I wouldn't be able to sit down for a week.

We tiptoed over the thick rug of the foyer and into her daddy's office. It smelled like pipe smoke, a smell I liked but one I could never separate from Mr. Heathman. Sarah Beth moved directly to a bookcase behind the large desk and pulled out a thick black leather Bible.

She placed it on top of the desk and, with a deep breath, she opened the front cover. I was a good head taller than her, so I could easily see over her head to the facing page, where two columns of names and dates were neatly filled in on the left side of the paper.

Carefully, Sarah Beth used her index finger to march down the list of names, coming to rest on the final five in the last column. *John Heathman, 1891. William Heathman, 1892. Margaret Heathman, 1893. George Heathman, 1895. Henrietta Heathman, 1897.*

Our eyes met. "See?" she said, her voice triumphant.

I glanced down at the Bible again, a thought niggling at my brain like a gnat. "How come your name isn't in here?"

Her eyes got bigger as she looked down at the page, and for the first time ever she didn't seem to have something to say. "I don't know. Old people forget stuff sometimes."

I thought of my daddy's mama, who, before she died, saw naked people in the yard all the time and kept calling me by my dead mama's name. But Mrs. Heathman was definitely not that old, and not seeing naked people yet, either.

We heard a footfall from upstairs, and we quickly scrambled to put away the Bible, making it to the bottom of the stairs before Mrs. Heathman appeared at the top of the steps, lines of baby powder already sticking to the creases in her arms. She was dressed to go out, in her hat and gloves, and barely had time to tell Sarah Beth to wash the perspiration off her face as she walked down the stairs before leaving for her bridge club. I was glad she hadn't noticed the condition of our shoes and stockings or she might have thrown a fit when she saw us standing on her Oriental rug.

We were about to sigh with relief when a sound from the kitchen doorway made us turn. Mathilda, the daughter of the Heathmans' maid, Bertha, stood watching us. She was younger than me, about ten years old, and she never spoke a word that I knew of. Her skin was dark, like coffee with just a little bit of cream, and she had big brown eyes that always seemed to be watching. Sarah Beth called her Boo because she was like a ghost, slinking around and staring at people. And she always ran away when we spoke to her.

"Hello, Boo," Sarah Beth said with a smile I didn't like, because it wasn't really a smile meant to be nice. I was pretty sure Aunt Louise would stick a bar of Lifebuoy in my mouth if I ever tried it.

Mathilda stayed where she was, watching us, and then without a word disappeared back into the kitchen. I stared at the closed door, wondering how much she'd seen and heard.

Uncle Joe came and picked me up soon afterward, so Sarah Beth and I didn't have a chance to further speculate on what we'd discovered that afternoon. But I couldn't help wondering why those dead babies had all made it into the Heathmans' family Bible and Sarah Beth had not. I looked out the car window at the cotton fields and considered all the possibilities. *Everybody has secrets,* I thought, thinking about my mother and how she'd jumped into the river, leaving me to always wonder what it was about me that wasn't enough to make her stay.

Chapter 3

Vivien Walker Moise
INDIAN MOUND, MISSISSIPPI
APRIL 2013

I woke up in my girlhood room, the sunlight shining through the pink eyelet canopy. Large butterflies the size of my head flitted around the wallpaper, the corners beginning to sag as if the insects had grown weary of flying. When I was eight and Mama left again without us, Bootsie had taken me to pick out new wallpaper, like my mother being gone was just another way of redecorating my childhood. And here it was, nineteen years after it was first stuck up on the walls, a reminder that at least on the surface, things hardly changed at all in this corner of the world.

"Here."

I turned my head to the side of the bed and saw Tripp sitting in a chair and holding out a neatly pressed linen handkerchief. He'd loosened his tie and rolled up his sleeves, looking more like the boy I'd known.

When I didn't take it right away, he said, "You've been crying in your sleep."

I closed my eyes, calling back the fading streamers of my dream, plucking at them like sticky strands of cotton candy. But they crumbled when I touched them, disintegrating until all that was left was the desolation. I took the handkerchief and held it over my face with shaking hands.

Then I remembered my mother in her odd dress, and Tommy, and the curve of a white skull against the dark earth, the ruined cypress scattered across the backyard. "The bones," I said, trying out my voice, wondering why I'd chosen the skeleton as a place to start. "Who is it?"

"I'm not sure yet. The Mississippi crime lab has sent a CSI team to assist in the recovery of the remains. You have an Indian mound on your property, which could account for the bones, but maybe not, since they were found so far away. I won't know for sure until the remains are examined, but it looks like they've been there for a while."

He spoke slowly, and I noticed it now because I'd grown used to the West Coast and how people there spoke quickly and in abbreviated sentences, like verbal texts. I hadn't realized how much I'd missed his voice and the time between words that gave you time to listen.

Tripp sat back in his chair, regarding me silently for a moment. "Bootsie's old housekeeper, Mathilda, would never go near that tree, remember? She said there were haints who haunted the tree. It's where we used to go when we stole biscuits from the kitchen, because we knew she wouldn't follow us."

I could barely focus on his words, the throbbing in my head obscuring all thoughts. "Tripp, I left my purse in my car. Would you mind . . ."

I stopped at the familiar shake of a plastic pill bottle and I pulled the handkerchief away to see Tripp holding up the bottle. "This is powerful stuff, Vivi. Not to mention the two empty bottles of other medications."

"Where did you get that?" I asked, my anger overpowering my embarrassment.

"Tommy brought up your bags and your purse, and they fell out."

"And you had to read the labels."

His steady gaze held mine, and I knew he wouldn't answer. It had always been this way with us. It's why we'd been best friends since, by the sheer virtue of our last names being alphabetical neighbors, his desk had been placed next to mine in kindergarten.

"Not that it's any of your business, but I didn't take the other two medications. I emptied them in the toilet."

"But you kept the bottles because refills are available."

I didn't argue. He'd always had a knack for pulling out the truth like a magician with a card trick.

"Who's Dr. McDermott?"

I closed my eyes. "My husband. Ex-husband," I corrected. "He's a plastic surgeon."

Tripp's eyebrows rose, making me feel defensive and pathetic all at once. As if he'd just made me admit that I was so messed up in my head that I'd blindly take narcotics for anxiety and depression prescribed by a plastic surgeon.

He shook the bottle, the pills clicking against the plastic. "These are addictive, you know. And dangerous if not taken with close medical supervision."

I shrugged, trying to pretend that I didn't care. "I've had a tough time of it these last few years. And I don't take them all the time—just when I need one to get over a rough spot." I looked away so he couldn't see the lie in my eyes. "Mark never told me. He just called them happy pills. And they are," I added defensively.

Eager to switch the subject, I pulled myself up against the head-board. "Why are you the coroner? I thought you wanted to go to medical school."

His face remained expressionless. "I did. But then I changed my mind."

"But why? All you ever talked about was becoming a cardiologist."

His silences might have been unnerving to anyone who hadn't grown up with Tripp, but to me they were plain frightening. Because they always meant that he was thinking deeply, and what he said next was never what you thought it might be.

"You left," he said, allowing me to interpret what he'd meant.

I closed my eyes, trying to focus on the meandering words ricocheting around my head, words to form questions I wasn't sure I wanted to hear the answers to. I opened them again to find Tripp staring calmly back at me.

I opened my mouth to ask about Bootsie and what was wrong with my mother, but the headache stabbed at me from behind my eyes. I wasn't sure I wanted to hear the answers to my questions, and knew that I needed a pill before I could even think about asking.

Refocusing on the bottle of pills, I said, "I need one. Just one. I need it for my nerves. I don't even need water."

He didn't give me the bottle. "When was the last time you ate?"

My head throbbed, nearly blinding me. "In Arkansas. Yesterday sometime. I don't remember."

He stood. "You're dehydrated and you need food. Tommy's making breakfast. I'll bring up a plate of eggs, bacon, and grits, and after you eat, I'll give you a pill with a glass of water."

I pressed the back of my head against the headboard, desperate to quell the throbbing. "Who died and made you king?"

Tripp shoved his hands and the bottle into his pockets, his unflinching gaze never leaving my face. Finally he said, "I'll be back."

I stared at the butterflies on the walls, wishing I could get out of the bed and storm downstairs and demand answers to all the questions that were hurtling themselves against my skull. But my whole body was shaking now, and I couldn't quite figure out how to throw my legs over the side of the bed and stand.

After what seemed like hours, Tripp appeared with a tray of food. I looked behind him, feeling disappointed when I realized he was alone. "Where's Tommy?"

Tripp took his time depositing the tray on my lap and making sure my glass of water was within easy reach on my nightstand. He waited until he was back in his chair before he answered.

"He's not ready to talk to you. You left him behind, too, remember." He indicated the tray with his chin. "Eat first and I'll give you a pill. Then we can talk."

I wanted to refuse, but the last nine years had beaten all the fight out of me. I'd learned that acquiescence was always the path of least resistance. And the smell of the food had reminded me just how hungry I was. I ate quickly, without speaking, then pushed my plate away and picked up the glass of water. Tripp removed the tray from my lap and set it on the dresser before taking the pill bottle out of his pocket and opening it, expertly spilling out one pill onto my palm. I swallowed it, then drank all of the water under his watchful eye.

He placed the nearly full bottle on my nightstand almost as a challenge. Leaning forward with his elbows on his thighs, he waited.

"Where's Bootsie?" I asked, ready to hear the answer now. It could have been my anticipation, but the pill seemed to have already begun to form its cushion around all of my nerve endings, making even the harshest blow more bearable. It was the soft bed into which I disappeared to escape the realities of what had become of my life. I had left this house at eighteen with all the hopes and dreams a young girl could stuff inside her head and heart, and returned with empty bags. Only my grandmother knew how to fill them again.

"I'm sorry, Vivi. She died last spring. Pneumonia. It was real quick. She died in her sleep."

The words skimmed over me like geese on an autumn pond, the pain blocked even as I remembered the unread letters I'd thrown away before I'd moved again, leaving no forwarding address; my unlisted phone numbers; and my constant vigilance just in case somebody from home came to find me. Shame and regret slid down my arms, and I folded my hands as if I could put those useless emotions away permanently.

"Tommy and I wrote to let you know."

I turned my head and found myself staring at a large butterfly, its wings seeming to beat slowly against the wall. "And my mother . . . ?"

"Tommy should tell you. . . ."

I shook my head. "If he's angry with me, it could take months, and I doubt I'll be here that long." Holding grudges wasn't reserved for only the females in our family.

His expression shifted. "She has dementia. We suspect she could be in the early stages of Alzheimer's, but she refuses to see a doctor and get tested. Tommy could sure use your help. He's been running the farm and the antique clock business, and he's pretty wore out taking care of your mama, too."

I felt like I was having surgery while being completely awake, sensing the pressure of the scalpel without the pain.

I shook my head. "That can't be right. She's not old enough." I closed my eyes, the beating wings of the butterfly making me dizzy. "And Bootsie can't be dead. I would have *known*. I would have felt it."

He didn't speak for a long time, and I eventually opened my eyes again to see him still sitting by the side of my bed, his expression blurred. "Tommy would have called when she first got sick if he'd known how to reach you."

I wanted to cry, but I couldn't. Numbness covered me now like a warm blanket, and I nestled further into it. I wanted to tell him that a mother's abandonment is permanent even if she comes back when it's too late to matter. That my leaving was meant to punish her and my family, who welcomed her back. If only I could have told my eighteen-year-old self that leaving home was like leaving behind a part of myself, that the pull of the land and the muddy river and the cotton fields would tether me to this place like an umbilical cord no matter how far I ran. I said nothing, inertia cocooning my body.

Tripp leaned toward me. "Tommy brought these in with your suitcases. He found them on the dash in your car and thought you might want them."

He held out two photographs, one a sonogram and the other Chloe's third-grade photo. I stared at them like a stranger would, only a vague squeezing around the heart telling me that they meant something to me. "Thank you," I mumbled from stiff lips.

He didn't ask—he wouldn't—but I could see the question in his eyes. I shrugged, burying myself further into the blanket of oblivion. "They're lost to me." I was startled to feel the sting behind my eyes. "I was wrong to think I could be different."

Tripp studied me with serious eyes. "Why did you come back?"

Because I've made a mess out of my life, and I needed Bootsie to make everything better. But now she's dead and I'm lost. "No matter where you go, there you are." I closed my eyes again, trying to remember where I'd heard those words before. I clenched my eyes tighter, realizing it had been Tripp who'd said them to my retreating back as I stepped into my Chevy Malibu, the trunk stuffed and the backseat piled high with everything I'd accumulated in the first eighteen years of my life. Bootsie, my mother, and Tommy had remained indoors, unwilling to accept my leaving. Tripp hadn't even shouted the words, knowing his calm Southern voice would stay with me longer than any words hurled at me like stones.

Tripp stood and walked slowly toward the door. "I don't know how long you're planning on staying, but don't leave just yet. I know I'll have more questions, and the sheriff will have to write up a report and might have some questions for you, too. I know it sounds redundant, but in real life the coroner just mostly handles the forensics part and the paperwork. We normally don't get involved in the actual case." He paused. "You need to make your peace with your brother. Your mama's gone back to bed, but Tommy's at his workshop trying to salvage what he can. You might as well get it over with."

I leaned back against the headboard, knowing there was something else I had to say to him. He opened the door and stepped out into the hallway just as I remembered what it was.

"I came back because I had nowhere else to go."

He kept his hand on the doorknob without looking back at me. After a brief pause, he said, "I'm sorry to hear that." He closed the door with a soft snap.

I sat up in bed and found myself facing the shelves Bootsie had hung on my wall to display my beauty pageant trophies, and the plaques and ribbons for my compositions and essays. I had once wanted to be an actress or a weather girl or a writer, and for one brief glimmering moment in time, it had all seemed possible.

I swung my legs over the side of the bed, then made my way through the old house. The walls seemed to grow and swell as I passed through the familiar rooms, as if the house recognized me and were welcoming me home. I paused near the bottom of the front stairs, at the mark in the plaster that had never been painted or wallpapered over. Or ever would be, I suspected, much like how Yankee cannonballs were preserved in the stately columns of the Vicksburg mansions like marks of pride. It was a watermark on the wall that showed the height of the water during the great Mississippi River flood of 1927. It had killed five hundred people, including a family member, an event nobody talked about anymore. The mark was the house's scar, proof that it had suffered a loss as much as the family living inside it had.

I took two steps down and stopped, placing both hands on the newel post at the bottom of the ornate stairs, remembering the day my mother had come back for the last time and everything changed.

Shaking away the memory, I began to search for my brother, hoping that he would at least remember the girl I had once been and thought I could be, but half-worried that he had forgotten her as much as I had.

Chapter 4

Vivien Walker Moise
INDIAN MOUND, MISSISSIPPI
APRIL 2013

The morning had given way to the heat of afternoon by the time I stepped outside again, finding my muddy shoes neatly tucked by the kitchen door next to the high-heeled pumps I'd seen my mother in earlier. A drainpipe hung loose from the porch roof, its paint long gone, its edges rusting. Water dripped into a large puddle from the gutter onto the corner of the porch, the wood floor buckled as if the rain had come in unchecked for more than just a single spring.

When Bootsie had lived here, flowers flourished on every walkway, by every door, and on every surface inside the house. Her vegetable garden rivaled that at any nursery, her plants green and lush, each stem hanging heavy with a bountiful harvest almost year-round. Fresh corn, watermelons, beans, okra, onions, squash, and cantaloupe were staples on our dinner plates, the taste and smell of them so pungent and authentic that nothing else would ever taste as good.

Even such a utilitarian place was beautiful to the eye, with raised sections for better drainage placed with architectural precision. I'd been told that the first Walker woman to live in the house had designed the vegetable garden, and each generation had added to it or changed it in some way, as if trying to prove to her mother before her that it could be done better. The women in my family could make things grow even in the middle of a drought, although it appeared that the gift had skipped my mother.

Ever since I could walk, I'd accompanied Bootsie while she gardened, holding baskets of seedlings and pruning shears and torn sheets. But I'd never bent next to her in the dirt, or stuck my hands in the soil. Even then I'd known not to make my mark here, to create roots I couldn't sever.

Ignoring the activity surrounding the cypress tree, I stepped off the back porch and walked toward the fenced enclosure of the garden. I felt Bootsie's loss here more than if I'd been standing by her grave. Most of the scalloped white fencing was missing, and what remained had been stripped of almost all its paint and hung listlessly, as if it couldn't summon enough interest to simply fall onto the muddy ground.

Fingerlike stalks reached up out of the earth surrounded by dead leaves and debris; the spots where the outdoor chairs had been sat empty without even weeds to keep them company. I turned my back, unable to look anymore. I found myself facing the fallen tree, saw tire tracks in the mud leading to the site and a hearse pulled near with its rear doors open. I recognized Tripp squatting down next to a man in uniform, pointing at something inside the hole. For a brief moment, I envisioned going back inside and packing my bags before heading out the front door. *I've got no place else to go.*

I looked down at my muddy shoes, the words loud inside my head. I thought of Chloe and the storybook she liked me to read to her when she was small and still enjoyed things like sitting in my lap. I hadn't seen her with anything but a cell phone in her hand in a long time, and I wondered if things might have been different if I hadn't given up trying.

Thinking of Chloe made me stumble, and I had to catch myself on the fencing. The storybook had been about a little girl who'd been given life's instruction book as a birthday gift. I wished for something like that now, something that would tell me what happened when there was no plan B, and when your only refuge had a No Vacancy sign on the door.

Squaring my shoulders, I slogged across the muddy ground, stepping over the tire grooves in the grass. The site had already been staked off with yellow tape. But even though a side porch of the old cotton shed and part of the roof had been clipped by the falling tree, the front door stood open, and I saw my brother in the doorway.

As soon as he spotted me he stepped back inside, which only made me walk faster. He was almost a decade older than I was and six inches taller than my own five foot ten, but I'd never been intimidated by him. We'd always known that we had each other no matter where our mother was. We had each other, and Bootsie, and Bootsie's cousin Emmett, the house and the farm, and that had been enough for both of us. Until my mother reappeared, reminding me that there was a world beyond the Mississippi River that must be better than what we had here.

Damp, warm air hit me as I stood inside the doorway, my eyes blinking as they tried to adjust to the darkness. When Tommy had inherited Cousin Emmett's antique watch and clock repair business, he'd moved it from the Main Street location closer to the house so he could oversee the farm and the business simultaneously. He'd taken over the old cotton shed and extended the second story beyond the attic, along with electricity, air-conditioning, and modern plumbing. He'd moved the farm's office of operations downstairs, and all the old watches and clocks found a new home upstairs. Then he'd added a small kitchen and bedroom, where he'd stay during the planting and harvest times, with their long days and short nights.

The room had been paneled in a wood laminate, a guy's interpretation of home decor, but even Bootsie wouldn't interfere with Tommy's self-expression, no matter how misguided. A basket of overflowing laundry sat by the side of the entryway, and I wondered if he now lived here permanently. The thought saddened me, not just that he lived alone, but that I didn't know for sure. I used to wonder if Tommy had gotten married and if he had children. Then the disappointments in my own life had swallowed me, and Mark began prescribing pills to calm my nerves. After that, I discovered that I didn't have to wonder or worry about anything at all.

I stared out the dirty window, toward where Tripp and the other man crouched by the roots of the old tree. I looked back at my brother's laundry basket, a sock with a hole in its toe floundering at the top. It created a mental image of our lives, like derailed boxcars sitting alongside a track where we had no idea of how to flip the switches to get us running again.

I walked past the large desk with stacks of papers spilled across the top, along with three half-filled mugs of cloudy coffee and a desktop computer that looked like it should be in a museum, then toward the stairs. The steps had been rebuilt when Tommy renovated the building, but the actual stairwell was not expanded, so the stairs were narrow and steep. Bootsie had said Tommy had done this on purpose to discourage visitors to his private sanctum, where he liked to be alone with all the antique timepieces that were sent to him from all over the world.

I paused on the landing, suddenly aware of a bright light from above. I looked up and saw a clear blue sky through the ragged edges of a hole that had spread like kudzu across the wall and toward the back of the building.

Hugging the side of the undamaged wall, I climbed the remaining stairs before stopping at the top to survey the damage. The wall and floor near the gash in the ceiling were dark with saturated water. Leaves and papers and tiny plastic bags with various watch and clock parts, their labels smeared by water, lay scattered around the room as if they'd been stirred in a pot and dumped out. Antique and contemporary clocks hung on the remaining vertical surfaces, their pendulums moving side to side and their hands pressing forward as if to remind us that time stopped for no one.

When Emmett had owned his antique clock and watch shop downtown, I'd spent hours as a child studying the different faces of all the old clocks and listening to their incessant ticking, wondering about the other lives the old timepieces had measured and marked off with each tick. For a long time I'd believed that if we wound our clocks before they stopped their measuring, we'd live forever. And I couldn't help myself from wondering whether, if I'd been here when Bootsie got sick, I could have kept her watch moving forward and stopped her from dying.

My brother stood with his back to me at the large wooden trestle table that had once been in the Main Street shop, a small stack of plastic bags in front of him. A large domed overhead light dangled above him, making his reddish-blond hair—just a shade lighter than mine—glimmer.

"Hey, Tommy," I said, taking in the slump of his shoulders as he attempted to sort through the pile. "Looks like you got lucky when that tree fell." I continued to look around the room while I waved my hand in the air, as if to erase what I'd just said. "I mean, it looks like it could have been a lot worse."

I stayed where I was, wishing he'd say something. Wishing he'd tell me it was okay, just as he had when we were children. But he kept his back to me as if I weren't even there. In another place and time, I might have been hurt by it.

I tried again. "Who do you think those bones belong to? It's a little creepy knowing they've been here all along. Remember the time we found that bone by the Indian mound and how scared we were until Bootsie told us it was a chicken bone?"

He continued to study one of the larger bags and didn't turn around when he finally spoke. "You got a death wish or something?"

My mouth dried, the only sign my body allowed to tell me that his words had skirted a little closer to the truth than I liked.

"What do you mean?"

He wrote something on a piece of masking tape and stuck it on the bag before dropping it into a box. "An old dog's got enough sense to get out of the rain. Did it occur to you to seek shelter last night or didn't you notice the weather?"

I swallowed. "I wanted to get home. I didn't really think about anything else." I almost winced at how stupid I sounded.

Continuing to ignore me, he said, "A tornado touched down in Moorhead and another near Yazoo City, and the sirens were blowing all night. There's no cure for stupid, Vivi."

This was the brother I recognized, and I found my breath slowing with relief. "It's good to see you, too."

He wrote something else on a piece of masking tape before affixing it to another bag and then dropping it into the same box as the previous bag. "Who's Chloe?"

He'd taken me off guard. "How do you know about Chloe?"

"I saw it written on the back of that picture on your nightstand. And I saw the sonogram, too."

It was warm in the old building, but an icy chill filled me from the inside, making me wonder if my pain and regret were no match for mere chemicals. "You had no right to snoop like that."

Keeping his head bent under the large domed light, he said, "I went up to talk with you, but you were sleeping. I saw the photos, so I looked. We hadn't heard from you in nine years; I figured I'd take the chance of finding out what you've been up to while I could."

"You had no right."

He shrugged. "We're family, Vivi. You might have forgotten it, but I haven't."

I remembered what Tripp had said—about how I'd left Tommy behind, too—and I softened. Even as children, Tommy had been the even-keeled one, always the cool head in tense situations. I'd always reasoned it a good thing, considering my own volatile nature, until he'd been the first person to run down the front porch steps to throw his arms around the mother I barely recognized.

I sat down on a hard wooden bench, one I remembered from the downtown shop. "Chloe was my stepdaughter," I said quietly, my mental haze allowing me to take the sting from saying Chloe's name. And to stare at the back of Tommy's T-shirt with a beer logo emblazoned across his shoulder blades, absently noticing that his hair needed cutting.

His hands paused but he still didn't turn around. "Was?"

"Her father, Mark, and I are divorced. Keeping Chloe in my life wasn't an option." I tucked the memory of her sad, angry face as I'd left under the fuzzy pillow of my pills, where I wouldn't have to look at it anymore. "Mark and I were married for seven years—since Chloe was five. Her mother moved to Australia and had another baby with her new husband and kind of forgot about Chloe. I was pretty much all she had." I swallowed. "When Mark divorced me, I didn't even get visitation. I had to leave her behind."

He stared down at the mess on the table but his hands were still. "And the sonogram?"

It sounded like somebody else speaking when I finally answered, probably because nobody had ever cared enough to ask. "I miscarried at twenty-eight weeks—a little girl. It's one of the reasons why my marriage fell apart. I wanted the baby and he didn't. But I guess everything works out in the end."

He didn't say anything for a long time, his hunched shoulders telling me that he understood what it meant for me to want a child and lose her. And what it meant to leave a child behind. Because I'd always been ~~the one to say that I'd be different.~~

Quietly, he said, "I'm sorry." He turned around, his light blue eyes from a father he never knew regarding me steadily. "You could have called, you know. Just once."

I straightened my shoulders, eager to move on from the hard pit in my stomach that threatened to break through my mental pillow. "And you could have found me if you really wanted to."

He didn't drop his gaze as we realized that we both spoke the truth, and how empty it seemed. As Bootsie used to say, if stubbornness were a virtue, we'd be shoo-ins for heaven.

"What about Carol Lynne?" I couldn't bring myself to call her Mama. Even in my memories I only thought of her by her given name. "Is she going to be okay?"

He stood and rubbed his hands through his hair. "Jeez, Vivi. Where have you been? You don't get better with Alzheimer's, okay? She's in her own little world right now, a world that's gonna get smaller and smaller, and I'm not going to recognize her anymore. Most of the time she thinks it's still the sixties and will wear some of her old clothes. Or she'll borrow something from Bootsie's closet. And you never know what's going to come out of her mouth next. I don't know if it's the disease or just age, but all filters have come off."

He moved to the side of the table, where a folded blue tarp had been placed on the floor, and began unraveling it on top of the unmarked bags and small boxes on the trestle table. That's when I noticed the stacks of corrugated boxes of all sizes leaning up against the side of the table and beneath it, all of them darkened with random water splotches. It was so much worse than I'd originally thought, and for one brief moment I really wanted to care.

"I've got to go," he said. "The water's gone down a bit, so I'm going to ride out over the fields and see how they're doing. Luckily we haven't started the planting yet, but I'm hoping the water's not too high that we've got to delay.

My brain felt sluggish, as if muddy water were running through it, too. "Can Carol Lynne take care of herself? Is she okay in the house without somebody there?"

Tommy tucked the tarp around the edges of the table and stepped back, the look on his face reminding me of the time I'd put bubble gum in my hair to see if it would stick and Bootsie had to cut it as short as a boy's. "No. Not really. I've hired Cora Smith—Mathilda's granddaughter—to do some light housekeeping and look after her. She used to come and help Mathilda some. Mama calls her Mathilda, and Cora doesn't mind. I thought that was a good sign." He glanced at his watch. "Mama usually sleeps until noon, and Cora gets here a bit earlier to get her to eat something and to make sure Mama doesn't leave in Bootsie's Cadillac."

I followed him down the stairs, a sense of urgency bursting through my numbness. "But isn't there some sort of therapy she can be doing? Like crossword puzzles or something?"

He turned around to look at me, and for the first time I saw how tired he was, how the dark circles under his eyes looked purple on his pale skin. "Have you ever known Mama to do a crossword puzzle? Me neither, but you're welcome to give it a try. Most of the time she's fixin' to leave, her bags all packed, and the rest of the time she's channeling Bootsie, about to give a big party. I've given up trying to make sense of it. Cora's good with her—has all the patience in the world."

He grabbed a baseball cap off a hook by the door and stepped outside. I rushed to catch up, trying to keep my thoughts from wandering too far before I asked the question I needed to. "But does she . . . I mean, she knows who we are, right?"

"Yeah, she does. She recognized you yesterday, although it was like she thought you were still in high school and had just been gone since morning."

I turned my head for a moment, seeing that the men were leaving, presumably to grab something to eat. I wondered if Tripp had a wife to go home to, and if she made him lunch. I'd done that in the early years of my marriage, at least until Mark stopped coming home for lunch and went directly from his plastic surgery practice to the golf course, and Chloe accused me of making her fat.

Focusing on Tommy again, I said, "But does she remember enough to tell us that she's sorry?"

He reached into his back pocket and pulled out his keys and began to jangle them impatiently. "For what?"

"For ruining our lives."

He stared back at me, the keys quiet in his hands. "I think she left that up to us." He slid the baseball cap back on his head and began walking down the muddy drive. Over his shoulder he called, "I'll be back around six for supper."

I made to follow him, then stopped, catching movement out of the corner of my eye. I turned and saw Carol Lynne, wearing familiar bell-bottomed jeans and a loose floral blouse with a drawstring tie at the neck. Her hair was down around her shoulders, thick and heavy and still the bright strawberry blond of my memory. People had always told me how much I looked like her, and I'd hated it, wanting to believe that she and I had nothing in common. But she was sixty-seven now and barely looked older than fifty. Maybe there was one good thing I'd inherited from her.

She stood inside the caution tape, her bare toes stuck into the mud on the edge of the hole. It had been dug wider in the search for more bones and any other clues, the digging instruments laid out on a square cloth just like a surgeon's instruments before an operation. More of the skeleton was exposed now, including what looked like part of a rib cage with some sort of filthy fabric still clinging to it. I looked away, not wanting to see anything that made it more real to me, made me imagine the bones as a person walking around above the ground.

Crows cried from one of the nearby pine trees, but I didn't look up. I moved to stand next to my mother, keeping my eyes averted from whatever lay in the ground just a few feet away. I tried to think about all the things I'd wanted to say to her, about all the hurts and pain her abandonment had laid at my feet as a child. How there are things you never forget no matter how far from home you run. I trembled with the anticipation of unburdening myself of all the pent-up emotions I'd carried for so long. She'd have to remember then; the force of my emotions would make her remember.

"I think she never left."

The unexpectedness of my mother's voice startled me. "What?"

With one pale, slender finger, she pointed at the exposed bones. "She never had a chance to come back because she never left."

I wanted to ask her what she meant, but her shoulders had begun to shake, and to my horror and embarrassment she started to cry in great heaving sobs. I watched her, unsure of what to do. And then she put her head on my shoulder and I had no choice but to put my arm around her.

But I kept my head turned so I couldn't see her cry, seeing instead crows flying out across the wide, flat fields. I closed my eyes to block out the image, smelling the wet earth and hearing my mother's sobs and the fading sound of the crows. *I've been a long time gone.*

I pulled my mother away and back under the yellow tape, then led her to the house. I settled her on the family room sofa to wait for Cora before flipping on what I remembered had been her favorite soap opera. Then I retreated to my room and took another pill, wondering if I would have enough to get me through until I figured out what I was supposed to do next.

Chapter 5

Carol Lynne Walker Moise
INDIAN MOUND, MISSISSIPPI
AUGUST 5, 1962

Dear Diary,

Today is my seventeenth birthday. I think it's ironic that the day I get my first diary is the same day Marilyn Monroe dies. She was my idol. I have her pictures taped up inside my closet door where Bootsie can't see them and make me take them down because she thinks it's tacky to put magazine pictures on my walls. Mathilda knows they're there, but she's good at keeping secrets.

I've decided that I'm going to smoke my first cigarette today. I'm seventeen and it's time to start acting like a grown-up. It's a real gully washer outside, but I've got all the windows open. I figure it's a lot easier explaining why the windowsills and floors are wet than why Bootsie might smell smoke.

Bootsie is my mama, but everybody calls her Bootsie, including me. She ran away from home when I was a baby, leaving me with my daddy, who'd gone crazy in the war, and my daddy's parents to take care of both of us. The war gave Daddy a bad case of nerves, making him shake all the time and not sleep much. The doctor visited a lot to give him medicine, but most of the time Daddy lay in his bed and screamed like the devil himself *was in his head. And then one day it was quiet and he was gone. Every-body said it was a blessing, but I didn't. It was wasteful, just like throwing out a piece of aluminum foil that's only been used once. I didn't cry at his funeral because I couldn't. I'd never even known him, really. I guess if you have to lose a parent, the real blessing is that you didn't know them enough to miss them.*

By the time Bootsie came back and we moved back into the yellow house, Daddy was dead and I was six and it was too late to start calling her Mama. I almost think she'd prefer me to call her Jackie, since it's pictures of Jackie Kennedy she'd be sticking all over her walls if she didn't think that was tacky. She dresses like her—even got one of those stupid-looking pillbox hats—and got her hair cut with a little flip at the bottom and a big puff on top. She's even talking about dying her red hair dark. People always tell me how beautiful she is, and how her face looks like one of those new Barbie dolls. Mathilda says that all the women in my family are beautiful, but that it takes us a while to grow into it. I'm not sure what she means, and I'm still waiting to grow into mine. I want one of those new Jackie Kennedy haircuts, too, but Bootsie wants me to keep my hair in a ponytail like a little girl. If she had her way, I'd never grow up.

I'm going to try a cigarette now. Brigitte Bardot looks so sophisticated when she smokes. I want to look like that—like I belong in some café in Rome or Paris or anyplace that's not Indian Mound, Mississippi. I'll be right back. . . .

Mathilda walked in while I was coughing on my first cigarette. She brought me one of Bootsie's ashtrays she uses for bridge club days and told me not to get ashes on the furniture or the bed and then she left. I know she won't rat on me. Like I said before, she's really good at keeping secrets.

Chapter 6

Vivien Walker Moise
INDIAN MOUND, MISSISSIPPI
APRIL 2013

I awoke to the smell of chicken frying, and for a moment I thought I'd been transported back in time, with Mathilda and Bootsie in the kitchen and Emmett in the fields, Tommy in his bedroom taking apart old clocks, and my mother somewhere far away. I opened my eyes, registering my suitcase and the bottle of pills on the table next to me, and I knew with a sinking feeling that I could never go back to that place.

When the bedside clock came into focus, I realized that I'd slept for most of the afternoon and that it was almost suppertime. I quickly washed my face and hands, then made my way slowly down to the kitchen. I studied the family pictures that filled the upstairs hall and stairway, their order and placement as random as the architecture of the house. The painted portraits of the first Walkers were hung in the living and dining rooms, filling all the wall space so that by the time the camera was invented, those family photographs were framed and hung in the hallways and stairwell. Sepia and black-and-white photos of people whose names I could never remember stared vaguely at me from wallpapered walls that had not changed since the fifties. I paused at one of the first color photographs, hung in a place of honor over the demilune table in the foyer—my mother's high school yearbook photo from 1963. She looked so normal to me, even with her bubble hairdo and thick eyeliner. Not at all like the kind of teenager who would "turn on, tune in, and drop out" and end up in a commune in California with two children whose fathers were either unknown to her or simply forgotten.

My senior year in high school I'd pulled out my mother's yearbook in the downstairs library, just to see, and read her senior quote. *There is a time for departure even when there is no certain place to go.* It was the same Tennessee Williams quote I'd already turned in for my own senior page. Tripp was on the yearbook committee and had switched it out with another quote I no longer even remembered.

I paused by the entranceway into the dining room, with its tall, corniced walls and mullioned windows—the windows an addition to the house by an ancestor who favored the Gothic style. My mother, wearing the same vintage dress I'd seen earlier, but with worn house slippers instead of heels, flitted around the table, setting it with the family china, crystal, and silver, just like in the days when Bootsie entertained.

She didn't see me and I quickly slipped away to the kitchen, unwilling to be drawn into my mother's drama. I'd already spent a lifetime avoiding it, and I wasn't ready to be sucked in right now when my own life had enough drama of its own.

A trim black woman with just a hint of gray at her temples stood at the circa-1970s avocado green stove wearing an apron over crisp khakis and a navy blue knit top. She had smooth, almost unwrinkled skin, making her look like she might be in her thirties or forties, but I figured if she was Mathilda's granddaughter she must be in her mid-sixties. She turned to me with a wide smile.

"You must be Vivien. I'm Cora Smith. I'd shake your hand, but they're covered in flour." She moved her elbows in greeting, both of her hands fully immersed in a bowl of flour and seasonings as she coated chicken parts.

"It's nice to meet you," I said, staring at a serving platter full of fried chicken as my stomach grumbled. I'd not tasted anything fried in a long time. Mark had originally been charmed by my Southern cooking, until he'd gained a couple of pounds and forbidden everything with taste from our table and hired a microbiotic chef.

When nobody was looking, I'd break the rules for Chloe in a misguided attempt to make her happy, having never encountered a more miserable child in my whole life, except for me on those days when my mother announced yet another departure. I think that's why I was drawn to her, as if my own abandonment would give me the secret to making her happy. I'd been stupid to think I could. But that hadn't stopped me from trying.

"There've been a few phone calls from the local press, wanting to know about what's going on outside in your yard. I took down their information on the pad by the phone in the front hall and told them that they'd have to wait to speak with you or Tommy." She glanced up at me. "Tommy called to tell me you'd be here, but he had to go before I could ask him about the tree and the yellow tape. I was hoping you could shed some light on the subject so I'd have something to tell your mama. She keeps looking out the window and seeing the tree and asking me what happened."

I recalled the image of my mother standing on the edge of the gaping hole. My mouth went dry, and I fumbled with the cabinets until I found the one with glasses—right next to where they'd once been kept. I took a moment filling my glass from the tap and drank some of it before I could speak.

"Lightning hit the old cypress tree, exposing the roots. It uncovered some bones that look like they've been there awhile."

Cora stopped her dipping and rolling. "Bones? As in human bones?"

I nodded. "The coroner has been here and he's working on removing the remains, but they'll probably be digging around the tree for a while longer to see if they can find any clues as to the woman's identity."

"They know it's a female?"

I stared at her for a moment, wondering why I'd said that. I quickly shook my head. "No. I was just thinking about what Carol Lynne said to me earlier today. Something about 'her' not coming back because she never left."

A small smile of understanding crossed Cora's face before she returned to her task. "I'm sorry about your mama. It's a hard thing to watch the person you knew become a stranger."

My hand gripped my glass tightly. "Well, then, I guess it should be easier, because she's always been a stranger to me." I set down my glass by the sink. "Is there anything I can help you with?"

After an appraising look, Cora indicated the refrigerator with her chin. "I have a salad and some homemade buttermilk dressing in there, and over there on the counter I've got a couple of tomatoes from my garden. If you could chop them up and then mix everything in the salad that would be great."

Memories rumbled in the back of my brain, a sort of switch on my autopilot as I set about the familiar movements of preparing a meal. There was something comforting in the familiarity of it, like becoming reacquainted with a favorite doll you'd long forgotten.

"Have you been working here long?" I asked as I opened a drawer in search of a serrated knife. Sometime over the last nine years, somebody had rearranged the entire kitchen.

"Just since Miss Bootsie passed. Tommy needed some help with your mama, and I'd recently retired from teaching—I was an English teacher at the high school for over thirty years. My children are both in Jackson and I don't have any grandbabies yet, so I figured why not. I couldn't see myself hanging around my empty house all day. I'd rather be useful."

"I'm thinking we probably met, but I'm sorry if I don't remember," I said, keeping the refrigerator door open with my knee while I balanced a jar of dressing and the large salad bowl.

She continued to coat the chicken without looking up at me. "It's been a while, so I didn't expect you to recognize me. I was busy raising my own kids when you lived here, but I sometimes helped my grandmother Mathilda. She didn't retire until right after you left. She was ninety-five, although she sure acted like she was twenty years younger. It was her eyesight in the end. Could hardly see her hand in front of her face, even though her glasses were like the bottom of Coke bottles. She broke the antique soup tureen that used to sit in the middle of the dining room table. Even though Bootsie said it was all right and just an accident, we decided it was time. Just about broke both those women's hearts. They were close. Hard for them to be separated."

She began to place the chicken in the skillet, and we were silent for a moment as the grease splattered and popped. After she replaced the lid on the pan, she said, "Grandma used to tell me stories about how sweet you were. How you used to help with the polishing and dusting when her arthritis was acting up. And she loved the little stories you would write and then read to her. She said you were pretty good. She always thought you'd be a big writer someday. Or a movie star. You had that 'sparkle' is what she called it."

I kept my back to her as I sliced through a tomato, the juice bleeding onto the orange laminate countertop. I was glad she couldn't see my face and recognize my embarrassment, or my need for another pill. The cushion from the last one was wearing thin—thin enough that Cora's words had struck like arrows to a target. My throat thickened as I waited for Cora to remind me that I'd left Mathilda behind, too. Like Bootsie, Mathilda had been one of the best parts of my childhood, a reminder that even without a mother I was worthy of love.

Clearing my throat, I said, "Are we expecting company? I saw that Carol Lynne is setting the dining room table."

Cora's eyebrows shot up as she lowered the heat on the skillet. "She does that sometimes, even when it's just Tommy and her and me. Bootsie loved using the dining room and the good china and silver, and since she passed, your mama will do that sometimes. Like she's a teenager again and Bootsie has asked her to set the table." She was silent for a moment. "Losing Bootsie was hard on all of us, but especially her. I don't care how old you get: Losing your mama is the worst kind of thing. It's like burying your childhood."

I wanted to tell her that she was wrong. That if I'd returned home and found out that Carol Lynne was already dead, I don't think I would have missed her at all.

I focused on tossing the salad, the red of the tomato blurring into the green lettuce, the edge of the salad tongs fading into the side of the bowl. I blinked, surprised to find my eyes wet. I was about to ask her where she'd like me to put the salad, when the doorbell chimed at the same time the phone began to ring.

Cora was already washing her hands in the sink. "I'll grab the phone if you'll see who's at the door."

I nodded and made my way to the front foyer, pausing momentarily at the dining room, where my mother stood in front of the fireplace. She was staring at a photograph on the mantel, a crystal glass in each hand, as if she'd been in the middle of placing them on the table and then forgotten what she was doing.

She didn't turn around as I walked past the doorway to the massive front door that somebody in the past one hundred and fifty years had had shipped over from Ireland. It had once graced a now-demolished castle, and looked as out of place on the house as the mullioned windows in the dining room and the Tiffany glass fan window over the door. But I always thought that it also gave the house an "I don't care what you think" kind of attitude. Much like the people who'd inhabited the house, for better or worse.

I unlocked the front door and pulled it open, the hinges squeaking loudly as if the front door hadn't been used in a long while.

"Looks like you could use some WD-40," Tripp said. He'd removed the tie he'd worn earlier, and his hands were jammed into his pockets, reminding me so much of the little boy I'd grown up with—minus the frogs and worms inside the pockets, I hoped—that I had to smile.

"Bootsie always kept a can under the sink. I'll go check later." I stepped back to allow him into the foyer. "It's kind of late for official business, isn't it? I'm assuming that's why you're here, since you're using the front door."

"Tommy called me and asked me for supper. Thought it would be good to talk about a few things. Seems the sheriff already interviewed him, but when he came to the house your mother told him that you were at school and sent him away. He told me to let you know that he'll be back tomorrow morning at nine o'clock to ask you some questions." He jiggled loose change in his pocket. "And I'm using the front door because you're here. You've been living in California so long that I figure you'd forgotten that friends and family pop in through the kitchen door without knocking."

I closed the door behind me, my hand clutching the knob. "How did you know I was in California?"

"Your postcard. The one you mailed from Los Angeles to let me know you'd arrived safely, and you asked me to let Bootsie, Emmett, and Tommy know."

"Oh," I said, pushing myself away from the door. I'd forgotten about that postcard until now. I couldn't remember the picture on the front, only the feeling of surprise that I was so far from home. And the weight of the memory of my mother's face as I'd left, an unexpected mixture of grief and disappointment. "Nobody else is expecting you for supper?"

A corner of his mouth lifted. "No wife or a girlfriend waiting for me with supper on the table, if that's what you're asking."

"I wasn't." I closed my eyes, sinking into the warm, fuzzy cocoon that had become my brain, and walked past him without looking up. "I was in the kitchen helping Cora. Supper's almost ready."

My mother stood outside the dining room, still holding the two glasses by their stems. She didn't seem surprised to see Tripp or me, as if we'd both just stepped out of the house for a moment and returned.

"Are we having a party tonight?" she asked.

Tripp peered into the dining room, where all the silverware and linen napkins had been placed in their appropriate spots. "Looks like it. Let me help you with those." He took the glasses from her and put them on the table.

She turned to watch him, her gaze straying to the window, where the tree and yellow tape were visible. "The tree fell."

"Yes, ma'am. It was hit by lightning in the storm last night."

"The storm?" Her brow wrinkled.

"You probably slept right through it," Tripp said, moving to stand next to her. "We found something that had been buried near the roots a long time ago. Do you know anything about that?"

Her green eyes, the exact shade as mine, went wide. "I'm not supposed to go there."

Tripp tilted his head, his eyes narrowing slightly. "Who told you that?"

Her attention drifted back to the table. "Are we having a party tonight?"

I stared at my mother, a cold breeze blowing through my insides. "No," I said. "We're just having a family supper."

"Will you eat with us?"

My breath was coming in small gasps and I had to remind myself to breathe. I had not sat at the table with my mother after she'd returned for good, eating my suppers in the kitchen with Mathilda. Bootsie and Tommy had given up asking me to join them, but my mother never had. She had somehow remembered that.

I swallowed. "Yes. I think I will tonight."

Her face brightened as she smiled the smile I remembered from the pictures in Bootsie's old magnetic photo albums, the Polaroid photographs probably now fading alongside the woman captured inside them.

I turned around and headed down the back hall toward the kitchen, almost colliding with Cora. She held the old touch-tone phone in her hand, its long, springy cord stretched to its fullest length. She had her palm pressed over the mouthpiece. "She's called twice. I hung up the first time because I thought it was a prank call. But she called back and sounded so desperate that I told her I'd go see if you were home."

"Who is it?" My tongue stuck to the roof of my mouth as I thought of how few people cared where I was. Discounting Tommy and the people in the house with me now, that left only one other person.

"She said her name is Chloe McDermott."

I stared at the phone in Cora's hand for a long moment before taking it, wishing for once that I could think clearly. I met Tripp's eyes, his appraising look suddenly conjuring my brave eighteen-year-old self. "Hello?"

Cora took my mother's elbow and led her into the kitchen, distracting me for a moment.

"Don't you ever pick up your cell phone?"

It was definitely Chloe. I pressed the phone closer to my ear as if to keep her close. I thought hard for a moment, trying to remember where my cell phone was. "I'm sorry. The battery died somewhere in Oklahoma and I threw it in the bottom of my purse." I paused, chewing on my bottom lip. "I didn't really think I had a reason to charge it again."

A heavy sigh tripped its way from the end of the line, a sigh full of all the angst of a twelve-year-old. "You told me to call you if I ever needed you. That's why you should keep it charged."

I closed my eyes, trying to remember things that I'd pushed away so I wouldn't have to think about them. "I stayed in an apartment in LA for six months, Chloe, just in case you called." I felt something soft on my arm and looked up to see Tripp handing me a soft linen handkerchief to wipe the tears I hadn't been aware I was shedding. "You needed me?"

"Yeah. And I had to hack into my dad's computer to get your phone number in Hogswallow, Mississippi, or whatever backwoods hellhole you came from."

I pressed the handkerchief to my eyes, too relieved to hear her voice to tell her not to swear. "It's Indian Mound, Mississippi."

"Whatevs. Same thing. But I figured even the middle of freaking nowhere was better than home."

I leaned against the wall, not sure my knees could continue to make me stand. "What's happened, Chloe?"

Another sigh. "Dad got remarried to some stripper bimbo and they're on some lame monthlong cruise around South America for their honeymoon. Dad hired some lady who doesn't speak English to babysit me. I figured Pigs Butt, Mississippi, had to be better than this."

Hearing that Mark had remarried didn't affect me at all. But I felt in the basement of my memories all the hurt of a twelve-year-old girl abandoned once again. "I'm so sorry, sweetheart."

There was a pause on the line and I became faintly aware of sounds behind her, people talking and a PA system making an announcement with the word "Atlanta" in it. "Where are you calling from?"

"The airport. I used Dad's Expedia account to find the closest airport to you and to book a flight with his credit card." I could hear the pride in her voice.

"Chloe, you need to go back home. I would love for you to visit, but your dad won't let you. At least, not without his permission. I'll call him and work it out, but it could take a while. And you're an unaccompanied minor—they won't let you on the plane."

"I'm at the Jackson airport. I borrowed the bimbo's heels and makeup so I'd look older, and I used my passport for my ID."

I swallowed. "You're in Mississippi?"

"Yes. At the Jackson airport. And I need you to come get me and call Imelda so she won't freak out when she finds out I'm gone. She's the babysitter. Don't waste your time calling my dad, because he won't answer. He said he didn't want to be disturbed because he was on his honeymoon."

"All right," I said, focusing on my breathing so I could keep my voice steady. "I can be there in about two hours. I want you to go to baggage claim and sit down and not talk to anybody; do you hear me? You are twelve years old, Chloe, and you should not be by yourself at the Jackson airport!"

"You're shouting. Dad would tell you to go take another pill."

I looked at Tripp to see if he'd overheard, but his face remained impassive. "Baggage claim. In two hours. I have no idea what I did with my car charger, so I'll borrow a cell phone and let you know when I get there. I'll text you the number as soon as I have it so you can call me if you need me."

"Please hurry," she said, her voice sounding like the lost and lonely young girl she actually was. She hung up without saying good-bye.

Tripp took the phone and hit the hang-up button.

"I have to go to the airport. My stepdaughter—my ex-stepdaughter—is here. Somehow. I need to go get her."

"Is that a problem?"

"It could be. I'm not supposed to see her. Mark said I was a terrible mother." Remnants of the effects of my last pill allowed me to say those final two words without choking on them.

His eyes studied me. "Then why is she here?"

I shrugged, happy for the numbness that held my nerves hostage. "Because she has nobody else."

He continued to study me for a long moment and I braced myself. "And you have no place left to go." The words were said without malice. "Seems to me you two belong together."

I pushed away from the wall. "I need to go."

"I'll drive. You shouldn't be behind a wheel. Especially not if there's going to be a child in the car."

I wanted to laugh at his calling Chloe a child. She hadn't been one for a very long time. But I also knew he was right. I'd been lucky that I'd made it from the West Coast without incident. It had been stupid and reckless, but that's what I'd become.

"Fine, then." I leveled my gaze on him. "Why are you being so nice to me?"

He didn't answer right away, and I found myself wishing that I hadn't asked. Asking Tripp Montgomery a question had always been a lot like walking across a minefield. "Because it doesn't look like you got people standing in line."

I couldn't argue with him, so without a word I led the way into the kitchen to tell Cora we wouldn't be staying for supper, then out the back door. The branches on the fallen tree seemed to move as if they were alive, the limbs heavy with black-feathered crows shifting uncomfortably. The hole had been covered with a tarp while I'd slept, but the caution tape remained.

The sun streaked its orange light across the fields and the yard, illuminating the peculiar house and the prostrate tree. In twenty-four hours, my life had gone from simply hopeless and lost to something that resembled a runaway train en route to a brick wall.

"How long is that caution tape going to stay up?" I was thinking of Chloe and her fascination with all things morbid.

"Until I decide there's nothing left of interest down in that hole."

An early evening breeze lifted my hair from my sticky neck. "What have you found out so far?"

"The remains are definitely female. And she's been there for a while. The roots have been growing around her for a long time."

I nodded, my gaze fixed on the hollowed-out ground where the unknown woman had waited to be discovered. I felt a connection to her, a bond of knowing what it was like to be buried without anybody noticing, her stories left untold, held in place by the slow encroachment of her bindings.

I tilted my head, hearing the old familiar sound of my childhood. It was a sound almost like a song, a moaning lament. Mathilda had called it the song of the cypress, made by two trees rubbing together high up in the canopy in the swamp. She'd said it was the sound of lonely spirits trapped inside the trunks invited to sing only at the whim of the wind. The music thrummed like a string instrument, melodic and haunting. It was the unique sound of home, and hearing it now made me want to cry.

Without a word, Tripp touched my elbow and led me to his car, leaving behind the cypress trees to sing their lament to the barren garden and the felled tree with the grave dug among its roots.

Chapter 7

Adelaide Walker Bodine
INDIAN MOUND, MISSISSIPPI
APRIL 1922

"M-i–crooked letter–crooked letter–i–crooked letter–crooked letter–i-humpback-humpback-i." Sarah Beth's singsong voice echoed in the front parlor of her parents' house as she hopscotched over her father's clean and pressed handkerchiefs we'd placed on the floor for makeshift stones. She'd taken them from her daddy's dresser drawer, which didn't sound to me like a good idea, but she'd told me it was okay. Mathilda sat curled up in a little ball with her arms around her knees, watching us silently, like she was wondering why two grown girls were playing hopscotch. But I saw her lips move as Sarah Beth and I sang out the way we'd been taught how to spell our home state.

Bertha had taken out the rugs to be cleaned, but she hadn't made it past the back porch because of all the rain. I was sick to death of hearing Uncle Joe talk about the crops and whether the levees would hold. He got like that every time the spring rains came, just as regular as a dog in heat.

The weather had also forced Sarah Beth and me inside and out of desperation to play little-girl games like hopscotch and jacks. We were bored silly from trying to keep quiet, since Mrs. Heathman had another one of her headaches and was resting upstairs.

I threw the large coat button we'd found in Bertha's mending basket and missed the handkerchief I'd been aiming for. "You skip a turn," Sarah Beth shouted gleefully. "I get to go again."

I figured that was one of Sarah Beth's made-up rules. I didn't really care. Sarah Beth was too competitive in any game to make it much fun. It was easier just to let her win. I stood back, noticing Mathilda again.

I turned to face her—mostly to give Sarah Beth a chance to cheat so the game could be over—and Mathilda shrank back behind the sofa like she wanted to disappear. "You go to school?"

Her large brown eyes just stared up at me, and I wondered if maybe she didn't know how to talk. I'd heard about people like that, but I figured they were all sent to the asylum in Jackson so we didn't see them walking around the streets and such.

I tried again. "How old are you?" I knew she was about eleven, but wanted to see if I could make her talk.

Then I remembered that Bertha had come with Mrs. Heathman from New Orleans, so maybe she only taught her daughter French. "Do you speak English?" I asked, very slow and loud.

"She won't talk," Sarah Beth said as she moved to stand next to me. "Not to us, anyway—although I've heard her talking to her mama. Won't say boo to any of us, though, and I've tried. Mama said she might have been dropped on her head as a baby, which is why she's so peculiar."

I frowned at her. "She can hear just fine, Sarah Beth."

Sarah Beth rolled her eyes, then tossed the large button behind her. "I'm so bored. Let's go play with Daddy's new radio music box."

As if to prove my point that Mathilda could hear just fine, she and I both stared at Sarah Beth in horror. Mr. Heathman had paid sixty-five dollars for his new radio music box—I knew because my aunt and uncle talked about it all the time—and had forbidden Sarah Beth to so much as look at it. It was kept in Mr. Heathman's study, the same place where we'd snooped in the family Bible. I would have rather set my hair on fire than be caught anywhere near that radio box.

We heard footsteps in the foyer. As quick as a cat on a fire-ant hill, Mathilda jumped up and gathered all those handkerchiefs in her arms before slipping behind the door just as it opened.

Bertha stuck her head in the doorway while Mathilda shrank out of her sight. "You girls need to hush now. Miz Heathman is feelin' poorly."

We both nodded, looking sorry. Bertha pursed her lips and nodded her head once, her eyes scanning the room before gently closing the door.

We looked at Mathilda, who'd knelt on the floor and was busy shaking out the first handkerchief and refolding it along the pressed lines. I sat on the floor next to her and grabbed a handkerchief from the pile.

"Thank you, Mathilda. You probably just saved Sarah Beth from getting herself knocked into next Tuesday by her daddy's belt. And me, too, most likely." I glared at Sarah Beth, who'd flopped down on the sofa and was fanning herself with a copy of *Ladies' Home Journal*.

"It's hotter than hell in here," she said. She thought cussing made her seem more mature. "I'm going to suffocate if I have to stay inside one more minute."

I looked up to find Mathilda watching me, but she quickly looked away as we each took another handkerchief to refold.

After another bored sigh, Sarah Beth said, "My daddy wanted me to go Peacock's jewelers downtown to get his pocket watch fixed, but it's too rainy to walk. Could you call Willie on the telephone and see if he'd drive us?"

I hadn't noticed exactly when Sarah Beth had developed a crush on my older cousin, Willie, and she hadn't admitted it to me, either. But ever since he turned sixteen and my uncle Joe had allowed him to drive the Ford, Sarah Beth had been looking for excuses to include Willie on our days off from school.

I folded the last handkerchief, placed it on top of the stack, and looked up at the mantel clock. "He should be home by now. He and Uncle Joe went to talk to Mr. Elkins about hiring out some of their field hands for the planting. I guess I could call if you really want me to."

Sarah Beth didn't bother to answer, but kept fanning herself silently.

I made the phone call and was disgusted to hear the excitement in Willie's voice. He was nice-looking enough, I supposed, and always cracking jokes, but he was like a brother to me, so I could never really understand the attraction. Still, if getting Willie to take us to the jewelry store could distract Sarah Beth from messing with her daddy's new radio, it would be worth the annoyance of having him around.

Willie said he could be at the Heathmans' in twenty minutes, and I hung up the phone. Sarah Beth was sitting up on the sofa and eyeing Mathilda, who was now standing in the same corner where we'd folded the handkerchiefs, the linen squares neatly stacked between her hands.

Sarah's voice sounded exactly like her mother's as she addressed the young colored girl. "I want you to go upstairs and stick those in my daddy's drawer before he gets home and finds them missing. And don't let my mama catch you in his dressing room or there will be hell to pay."

Mathilda silently slipped from the room, sending me a sidelong glance as she left. I wasn't sure, but I could have sworn she smiled at me before she disappeared through the doorway.

Sarah Beth and I waited outside on the columned porch, sitting on one of the iron benches Mrs. Heathman had purchased in France and shipped over to Mississippi. I liked our wooden rocking chairs, mostly because they were so much more comfortable to sit in than these metal ones. I never mentioned that to Sarah Beth, who would have been personally insulted and then would have repeated again what she'd heard her mama say about my home and how nobody should have a turret *and* columns on the same house. And having a real castle door was just tacky and low-class.

I turned to Sarah Beth. "So, have you asked your mama yet?"

"About what?"

She was always like that when she didn't want to talk about something. She and I both knew what I was asking.

I sighed. "About those graves we found. And how come your name isn't in the Bible and theirs are."

It had been nearly two years since our discovery, and each time I asked—which was about every week—Sarah Beth started acting all funny and would tell me it just wasn't the right time to bother her mama. Seems to me that the reason people don't ask questions is because they're afraid they're not going to like the answer. It's just that I couldn't figure out what Sarah Beth could be afraid of, and I wasn't about to let on that there was one more thing that I didn't know and she did.

"It's not the right time. Besides, I'll just get punished because I'm not supposed to be touching the family Bible. And then I'll have to tell them that you were with me and Mama will tell your aunt Louise. So then we'll both be in big trouble. Daddy keeps saying that one more thing and they're going to send me to Miss Portman's School for Young Ladies in North Carolina."

I stared at her, wondering what she thought might happen if her daddy caught her touching his radio box. I kept quiet, knowing how much she hated for me to point out when her thinking went as crooked as the Mississippi River.

The rain had stopped by the time Willie pulled up in the Ford, but he came out with an umbrella anyway and helped Sarah Beth to the car first so she could sit up front with him. I was stuck in the backseat, as usual.

Willie drove slowly through the muddy streets toward downtown, being careful to avoid bumps and puddles. I knew this was done for Sarah Beth's sake, since when Willie drove just me he sped as fast as he could so that I felt like I had lockjaw by the time he stopped.

He parked at the curb on Main Street right in front of Peacock's Fine Jewels and Watches. The Peacock family had originally run a general store when Indian Mound was just a one-horse town, slowly selling more and more expensive merchandise as the town got bigger and the farms and plantations that surrounded it began to run their own commissary stores. As Aunt Louise had explained to me, the Peacocks had a good eye toward seeing opportunities for making money.

Willie helped us out of the car and then held the door open for us as we entered the store. I'd only been inside once, right after my mama had walked off that bridge and out of my life. I'd come with Aunt Louise to sell some of my mama's jewelry. She'd told me to pick out a few pieces to keep, but had explained that to pay the taxes on the farm we would need to sell the rest. I hadn't wanted any of it, seeing no need to remember a mother who hadn't thought to remember me.

Mr. Peacock stood up from a large wooden desk with a tortoiseshell lamp and moved to the front of the store to greet us. "Mr. Bodine," he said to Willie. Willie took off his hat and shook his hand.

"Miss Heathman, Miss Bodine," the jeweler said, nodding to Sarah Beth and me. His hair was parted on the side and slicked back with pomade, but sprigs of curly blond hair seemed to sprout from his head like weeds in a garden.

He looked behind us as if expecting to see somebody else. "Is your daddy not with you, Mr. Bodine? I was hoping to invite him to my new establishment over on Monroe Street tonight. I got a blind pig that might interest him.

He winked at Willie, who twitched a bit in his starched collar as if it had suddenly grown too tight. "No, sir. He's back at the farm. But I'll be sure to let him know, although you know he's a strict Baptist."

"You do that," Mr. Peacock said with another wink.

I felt sorry for the poor pig and wanted to ask to go see it, but there was something in the way Mr. Peacock was smirking and the shade of red on my cousin's cheeks that made me hold back the words.

Mr. Peacock clasped his large hands together, and I noticed a heavy gold ring with an enormous diamond on one of his pinkie fingers. "And to what do I owe the pleasure of your visit today?"

Sarah Beth opened up her clutch purse. "My daddy's watch isn't working—it just stopped one day. He was hoping you might be able to fix it. His granddaddy wore it when he rode in the cavalry with General Nathan B. Forrest at Shiloh, and he's quite fond of it. Mama has no idea what she'll do to replace it if it can't be fixed."

She pulled out the gold watch on its chain, his dangling Knight Templar fob clinking against the black onyx stone of a second fob.

Mr. Peacock slipped a monocle from his pocket and placed it in his eye to see the watch more closely. "This is a beautiful piece of workmanship. Exquisite really."

"It's from Switzerland," Sarah Beth said. "My great-grandmother bought it for my great-grandfather on their honeymoon."

The jeweler popped his monocle out of his eye. "So it's very valuable in more ways than one," he said, smiling. "And you are in luck, Miss Heathman. I have just employed a young gentleman. He's originally from Missouri, but he has family here—the Scots who own the feed store. He's got weak lungs and couldn't handle the winters up north, so his family sent him down here when he was younger. His father is a clockmaker in St. Louis, and young John has been in his father's workshop since he could walk. Knows all about the inner workings of clocks and can fix anything. As the old clockmaker saying goes, he has ways of making a clock tock." He laughed at his own joke, and I smiled just to be polite.

"He's in the back right now. Let me go get him, and he can give you an estimate of how long it might take to get it fixed." His face became serious. "I will remind him that Mr. Heathman is the president of the bank and a very important member of this community, and certainly not a man who can go without his watch for any length of time. It wouldn't do for him to be late to meetings and appointments, would it? No, sir, it would not."

He smiled again, then headed toward a door at the back of the shop. We spent the few minutes he was gone admiring the jewelry in the low glass cabinets, each with a gilt-framed mirror atop the glass. In front of each cabinet sat a green velvet settee.

I was busy admiring a cabinet full of delicate women's wristwatches, leaning over the glass to get a better look at a watch on the far row.

"May I show you something?"

I started and turned around at the male voice and found myself flushing. The man, about nineteen or twenty, was tall and lean, with dark blue eyes and hair the color of wheat, a dimple in his left cheek. He was probably the handsomest boy I'd ever met, his smile making it easy to forgive his Yankee accent.

"No. Thank you," I stammered, wondering why my tongue suddenly felt thick in my mouth. "I'm just waiting for my friend over there," I said, indicating Sarah Beth, who was leaning over a case of diamond rings with Willie and pointing to ones she liked.

"That's too bad," he said, his eyes looking into mine. I bit my lip and tried to think of something clever, but I could only stand there blushing even harder.

Mr. Peacock returned from the back room. "Miss Heathman, this is the gentleman I was telling you about, John Richmond. Let's have a look at that watch again." He drew John over to his desk, where Sarah Beth was laying out the watch. I stayed back, wondering why I was so out of breath, and why the sight of John's forearms below his rolled-up shirtsleeves and his long fingers as they held the watch made my lungs seize up like I'd been stung by a bee.

They talked for a few moments, and after several assurances that John could fix the watch and have it ready for her by Friday, we left. I felt John's eyes on my back, but I didn't turn around. Only fast girls would encourage such forward behavior, and for my nearly fifteen years I'd been about as fast as a turtle running through molasses.

The rain had started again, and Willie had left the umbrella in the car. So we dashed across the street to the corner drugstore and drank chocolate milk shakes at the soda fountain while we waited for the rain to stop. Willie and Sarah Beth sat facing each other on their stools, leaving me to daydream about John and wonder at my odd reaction.

I didn't mind sitting in the backseat on the way home, happy to continue my daydreams. I was jerked out of my thoughts when Willie hit a pothole that bounced me so hard I hit my head on the car's roof. I was just settling back into my seat when I remembered something Mr. Peacock had said.

Leaning forward over the front seat, I said, "Where do y'all think Mr. Peacock keeps his blind pig?"

Sarah Beth and Willie glanced at each other, then burst out laughing. Feeling like a real dumb Dora, I sat back in my seat, thinking again about John and wondering how to ask Sarah Beth if I could go with her when she returned to pick up the watch.

Chapter 8

Vivien Walker Moise
INDIAN MOUND, MISSISSIPPI
APRIL 2013

"**P**ut your seat belt on."

I glared at Tripp across the front seat of his Buick. "I don't like seat belts. Too constricting." I didn't tell him that I'd stopped wearing one after my miscarriage, and after I'd lost Chloe. That I was too much of a coward to do anything except tempt fate.

Instead of arguing, he reached over and grabbed my seat belt before crossing it over my chest and buckling it. I caught his scent as he leaned over me, reminding me of fall football games and sneaking beers behind the movie theater.

"You've gotten bossy in your old age," I said, too numb with fatigue and the lingering effects of my last pill to argue.

He started the engine and pulled out onto the circular drive, the car rocking slightly as he hit a pothole. "And I hardly recognize you at all."

I kicked off my shoes and tried to curl up on my seat as much as the seat belt allowed. Going barefoot was the one thing I'd brought from home that was acceptable in Southern California.

After texting Chloe from Tripp's cell phone so she'd have the number and to tell her that we were on our way, I leaned my head against my seat and tried to stifle a yawn.

"When was the last time you slept?"

I stared out the window into the twilight, the tall oaks lining the driveway slipping by like watching sentinels. "I had a good nap this afternoon. Before that, I pulled into a rest stop near Amarillo and slept for a couple of hours in my car. Drank lots of coffee from there to Mississippi."

He tapped his fingers on the steering wheel. "Pills and caffeine. That's a great combo. You must feel great."

"I already have a shrink, Tripp, and I don't need another one. Do you practice psychoanalysis on your dead bodies?"

"They're extremely good listeners and never argue." I heard a smile in his voice. "I have a one hundred percent success rate—all of my patients are calm and relaxed when they leave my examining room."

I turned my head toward the window so he couldn't see my grin. "Do me a favor and try not to mention to Chloe that you're a coroner. She's very into the whole vampire/zombie thing right now—or at least she was. Wears a lot of black."

"She's a Goth?"

"She defies labels. She's only twelve but thinks she's twenty-two. She's apparently borrowed her new stepmother's clothes to look older, so be prepared."

The car slowed as Tripp navigated the turn onto the highway. "Were you close?"

I was silent for a moment, trying to define my relationship with Chloe. "Her mother lives in Australia and has nothing to do with her, and her father thinks she needs to lose weight and get a nose job. I was the closest thing in her life to normal."

Two headlights appeared in the distance, the only light for miles besides the moon. "Were you close?" he asked again. His persistence probably made him a good coroner, always asking the same question until he got the answer he was looking for.

"Yes," I said. "As much as Chloe would let someone get close to her. She'd pretty much been abandoned by her parents. I always felt like she was trying to keep her distance so she couldn't be hurt again."

"So you had a lot in common."

I jerked my head toward him. "I wouldn't say that. I wasn't alone like Chloe. I had Bootsie and Tommy—and Emmett and Mathilda. I didn't need my mother—or my father, whoever he was."

He was silent for a long time, and I worried. He never argued when he was convinced that he was right.

I continued, trying to prove my point. "In the beginning I just felt sorry for her. She didn't do a lot to make me warm up to her." I waited for him to say something, his silence compelling me to go on. "She was this lonely little girl trying to pretend that she didn't care, that she was fine on her own. I guess you could say I saw through her."

My fingers sought out the wire-and-bead ring I wore on my right hand, and I felt my lips turn upward. "She's so creative, with this wonderful inquisitive mind. Always wanting to know how things are made. I noticed this back when she was five, when I first married Mark. Her dolls and stuffed animals always had the most amazing outfits and jewelry—designed and made by Chloe. And she loves art, and loves to paint and draw. But until I came to live with them, nobody had ever had one of her pieces of art framed or even hung on the refrigerator."

I gripped the ring between two fingers. "She always made me think of a ballerina dancing her heart out to an empty theater." I shrugged. "I figured an audience of one was better than none. So I kind of made it my mission to give her a great childhood—just like Bootsie gave me. I took her to textile museums and art museums, and we took sewing classes and art classes together. We had a lot of fun. And then . . ." I stopped, unwilling to open a vein without the proper medication.

After a long silence, Tripp said, "It's a long drive, Vivi. I'm not going anywhere."

I'm not going anywhere. His words almost made me cry. It was what he'd said when I called him in the middle of the night every time my heart was broken, or my feelings hurt, or another birthday had passed without even a card from my mother. He'd wait through long silences until I was ready to speak again, reassuring me each time I asked if he was still on the line.

I took a deep breath. "And then Mark started losing interest in me. You can't hide something like that from a child. I think it scared her. It was like she needed to start preparing herself for me to abandon her, too."

"Did you?" he asked. "Did you abandon her?" His words thumped against my heart. Out of habit I opened my purse, searching for my pills, frantic as I fumbled through the contents until I remembered the bottle back on my bedside table. I didn't answer, no longer sure if he'd asked the question out loud or if it had just been my conscience.

I rubbed my temples, wishing it were possible to call back angry words hurled to mask a hurt, or to unbreak a heart. I stared ahead into the night, the thrum of tires against pavement oddly soothing.

"I got pregnant. I'm not even sure . . ." I stopped. "It was an accident. Mark didn't want any more children, and I have never wanted to be a mother. Women in my family just seem to do such a bad job of it." I shrugged. "But Chloe was so happy when I told her. It was like we both saw this new person as a chance to start over. A way to change our own lives by making sure this child had a perfect life, because we would be there to make sure she didn't make any mistakes."

My heart beat sluggishly, my memories like silt.

"I miscarried in my seventh month. It was a girl. Chloe was devastated. She accused me of doing it on purpose. I know it was because she was grieving, but I couldn't think straight and see that at the time. And Mark told me he was glad, because he didn't want another daughter like Chloe, and she was right there in front of us, listening to every word." I pressed my fists against my heart as if that could stop the pain.

"For the first time in our marriage I stood up to him and told him that he was a terrible father and that Chloe should be taken away from him." I swallowed, wondering how I'd find the words to continue. Finally I said, "That's when he kicked me out. Told me to leave, that he didn't want to be married to me anymore. I don't think anybody had ever stood up to him before, or criticized him. And so he punished me by getting a restraining order so that I couldn't see Chloe. He made up all these things about me, said I was a terrible mother." I paused. "He said that I was a drug addict."

I reached over and rolled my window down, my lungs suddenly gasping for air. I laid my head against the top of the door, feeling the air rush at my face and fill my nose and mouth with the wet spring air that smelled of lemony-sweet magnolias and rich, dark soil. *I always thought I'd be different.*

"You couldn't have been too terrible if Chloe is here."

I brought my head inside the car and studied Tripp for a long moment. "You should have been a priest. You're really good at this confession thing."

"I'll keep that under advisement if I ever decide on a career change," he deadpanned, only the flash of his teeth letting me know he was smiling.

I sighed, feeling more tired than I ever remembered being. "I'm going to try to nap before we get there. I'll need my rest so I can deal with Chloe."

I kept the window open a crack, then leaned my head against the back of the seat and closed my eyes and slept. I dreamed of running barefoot through late-summer cotton fields with two little girls whose faces I couldn't see. We ran toward the old cypress tree lying on the ground, jumping over the deep hole at its base, our bare legs pumping in the sunlight. Midair, I looked down at the skull grinning up at me, while the scent of the alluvial soil filled the air like a prayer.

❧

l woke up to the feel of the car stopping and something warm under my cheek. I blinked my eyes open, and found myself staring close-up at Tripp's shirt-covered biceps. I jerked upright. "Sorry," I mumbled.

"That's all right," he said, stretching out his arm and flexing his hand. "I didn't really need any feeling in those five fingers anyway."

I yawned, then opened my door, surprised to find Tripp opening his, too. "You're coming with me?"

"Thought you might need backup." Before I could protest, he'd already closed his door and moved to my side of the car to hold the door open for me as I climbed out.

"You know, I was going to ask you why you're not married, but now I don't have to. You're way too bossy."

He clicked the lock button on his key fob, then waited for me to walk ahead of him. "I told you in first grade there was only one girl I wanted to marry. But she moved to California and married another guy."

I stopped, my hands on my hips. "Seriously? We were seven and I'd just punched you in the nose because you didn't pick me for your kickball team during recess. And then I told you I wasn't marrying any boy from home, because I wasn't planning on staying."

He stopped in front of me. "Yet here you are."

I met his eyes for a moment, unable to read them. "Yes, here I am.

But only until I figure out what I'm supposed to do next." I pushed past him. "Besides, I'd never marry a guy who didn't pick me for his kick-ball team."

Tripp shrugged. "I like to win. And you were terrible at kickball. You couldn't hit water if you fell out of a boat."

Despite the situation, I found myself smiling and relaxing, making me wonder if that was what he'd intended all along. I quickly texted Chloe to let her know we were there, and went inside the terminal.

Travelers pulling luggage or carrying overnight bags bustled around us, their harried pace bringing back some of my anxiety. We stopped in front of the Delta baggage carousel and looked for the bench Chloe texted that she'd be sitting on. It was empty. "Maybe she went to the restroom," I said, the blunt nudge of panic digging into my ribs.

"Or maybe not. Is that her?" Tripp asked, looking at a spot behind me.

I turned toward one of the stationary baggage carousels, where a girl who looked a lot like what Chloe might look like in ten years if she became a prostitute sat necking with a boy who probably was about twenty-two.

They had identical jet-black hair, thick black eyeliner, and a lot of chains worn around their necks and attached to their clothes. They were dressed all in black, except for Chloe's red stilettos. When the boy came up for air, I saw he also had a goatee and what looked like a tattoo of a large reptile crawling out the neck of his shirt. If the two of them hadn't been involved in an intimate embrace, I might have mistaken them for siblings.

Before I could clear my head enough to figure out what I needed to do, Tripp was already walking toward them. I hurried after him, a little afraid of the look on his face.

"Are you Chloe?"

She looked up at him, her eyeliner smeared under her eyes, her red lipstick smeared on both their chins. "Who's asking?"

Tripp grabbed the boy's upper arm and drew him to his feet. Tripp was about a head taller and the boy had to look up at him, which was the intended effect.

"Dude. What's your problem? Let go of me."

Tripp pulled him a little closer, their noses almost touching. "Do you know how old she is?"

I saw a look of worry cross the boy's face. "She said she was twenty-one."

"She's twelve," Tripp said slowly and clearly, pushing the boy away so that he stumbled backward, the chains hanging from his pants *chinging* together in protest.

The kid at least had the decency to look appalled. He grabbed a black backpack from the floor and slung it over his shoulders before holding his hands up, palms facing us. "Yo, I don't want any trouble." He began backing up, barely sparing a glance toward Chloe before he finally turned around and ran toward an escalator, taking the risers two at a time.

"Who's the bouncer?" Chloe asked in greeting, jerking her chin in Tripp's direction.

"This is Mr. Montgomery. He's an old friend." I pointed toward the escalator. "And who was that?"

She smirked. "An old friend. He got on the plane when we stopped in Atlanta."

I wanted to yell at her, to let her know how stupid and dangerous her behavior had been. But her eyes were stark and empty, and only because I knew to look, her lower lip trembled slightly. When she was little, I knew this meant she needed a hug and then everything would be better. But her hurts were bigger now, too deep to be filled with mere reassurance. Especially from a woman who took pills because she couldn't find another way to make the pain go away.

Trying to ignore the curious glances of onlookers, or the fact that Chloe looked like a hooker on the other end of a long night, I tried a smile. "I'm so glad to see you. I've missed you."

I stepped forward to hug her, but she quickly shouldered a large duffel bag and nearly staggered under the weight. "Can we just go?"

"Chloe, please. I didn't have a chance to tell you good-bye last time I saw you. I've been wanting for so long to tell you that I didn't want to leave you. That it wasn't my choice."

"Right. And you tried so hard to see me that I haven't heard a word from you in six months."

I couldn't defend myself, because what she'd said was true. I stared at her, trying to think of something to say that would change how she felt. But there was nothing.

Without a word, Tripp took her duffel bag—after a brief tug-of-war—then followed us out to the car. He stowed it in the trunk, but before unlocking the passenger doors he moved to stand next to Chloe, his height towering over her.

His voice was warm and friendly, completely at odds with his body language. "Welcome to Mississippi, Chloe. I know your stepmother is happy to see you again, although you didn't give her a chance to tell you how much. I know she will do her best to make sure you're comfortable during your visit. Now, I'm not sure how you do it where you come from, but when in Rome and all that." He smiled, but it did nothing to reassure either Chloe or me. "Around here we put a lot of pride in good manners, and we respect our elders." He leaned in a little closer and I saw Chloe's eyes widen inside their thick, blackened rims. "If I ever hear or hear of you speaking disrespectfully to Vivien or any other adult, I will personally carry you onto the next flight back to Los Angeles. Do you understand?"

She tightened her lips.

"I asked you a question, Chloe, and I expect an answer." He leaned forward a little, making Chloe take a step back, bumping into the side of the car so she had no place else to go.

"Yes," she mumbled.

"It's 'yes, sir.' "

"Are you freaking kidding me?"

"Don't make me grab your bag and stick you on a plane before you've had a chance to stay a single night in Mississippi." He began walking toward the trunk. "I'll get your bag right now if that's what you want."

"Yes, sir," she mumbled, a little louder.

"Good. I'm glad we could come to this little understanding." He unlocked her door and held it open for her. After we'd all sat down and closed our doors, Tripp glanced in his rearview mirror. "And, Chloe?"

I held my breath, wondering what was coming next. I could see that Chloe was doing the same thing.

"You're a real pretty girl. I'm glad most of your makeup was rubbed off on that guy's face. He needs it more than you do." He turned the key in the ignition, shaking his head. "His face could scare a buzzard off roadkill. You can do much better. When you're thirty and ready to start dating, that is."

I looked into the backseat. Chloe's lips were clamped shut, as if she were conflicted about whether to argue with Tripp about his not being her father and keeping his opinions to himself, or to thank him for telling her she was pretty.

To save her, I said, "It's late and we've got a two-hour drive ahead of us. Why don't you try to get some sleep?"

She crossed her arms over her chest and turned her head away from me. "I never sleep in cars."

I faced forward again and glanced over at Tripp, whose fingers were tapping an unheard beat on his steering wheel. I wanted to thank him for being there and for being a good friend, but I couldn't forget what he'd said while we were arguing in the parking lot. *Yet here you are.*

I looked back again at Chloe and found her head slumped against the window; she was sound asleep. I stared out into the Mississippi night as we headed west on Interstate 20, feeling the darkness swallow me as I wondered what I was supposed to do next.

Chapter 9

Carol Lynne Walker Moise
INDIAN MOUND, MISSISSIPPI
OCTOBER 21, 1962

Dear Diary,

Bootsie's having the house painted, and the smell of the paint is like to make me sick. It was a good year for cotton, so she's throwing a big party at Christmastime to celebrate with all of our neighbors. My arms already hurt from all the silver polishing she's going to make me do.

She spent about a million hours looking at different paint color samples, and even got me and Mathilda to look at them with her and give our opinions. Not that any of it mattered. Bootsie went ahead and picked the same yellow the house has been since the Ice Age.

When I complained, she told me that in life there's a time for change and a time for holding close. That's how she talks about family traditions. Holding close is like using the same china and silver that have been in the family for years, and showing off the watermark on the stairs from the 1927 flood no matter how ratty that wallpaper gets. It means working in the garden that was started two hundred years ago, growing the same old flowers and vegetables that have always grown there, and maybe adding to what's there without making it too different. And holding close means never getting rid of the old creepy black bed in the master bedroom, no matter how many times I tell her that it gives me nightmares.

When Bootsie and I moved back into the house when I was six, I was put in the smaller room that I still have and she moved into the room with the creepy bed. She said it was a family tradition. I was only little, but I asked if leaving your child behind was another family tradition. I got my mouth washed out with soap for sassing. It made me mad, because I really did want to know.

Bootsie calls family traditions the glue that binds a family from one generation to the next. I guess she means using the monogrammed sterling silverware with the big "W"s on the handles. I'd rather just use plastic, and spare myself all that damned polishing.

She tells me the big black bed she sleeps in will be mine as soon as I get married, and my children will be born in it just like I was. Like that will ever happen. As soon as I can, I'm going off to see the world. I don't reckon I'm going to have much time for a husband and children, much less an old house and four-poster bed that looks like it belongs in a museum. I want to live in a modern house with metal furniture and bright colors. She calls traditions the glue that binds a family. I call them the things that hold us back from change.

I like change. This might be the South, where things hardly seem to change at all, but I can see it. Like all those riots at Ole Miss up in Oxford because some black boy wanted to go to school there. It makes me feel like we're all moving forward to something bigger and better. And then Bootsie goes and paints the house yellow again, making me feel almost paralyzed. I just don't see the point in holding on to something that will one day be just dust.

Even though it's Sunday and supposedly a day of rest, she dragged me out to the garden to get it ready for the winter. I moved slowly and complained enough that she told me I was getting in the way and to just sit and watch and learn. I explained to her that there are things called grocery stores where you can buy all sorts of vegetables and other foods, and I didn't see the point of her vegetable garden. She didn't say anything, probably because she knows I'm right. When she went inside for a glass of sweet tea, I saw that as a chance to escape and ran to my cypress tree. It looks like it doesn't belong right there in the yard, so far from the swamp and surrounded by loblolly pines. I think that's why I like it so much—it reminds me of me.

I sat down on the side of the tree that faces the swamp, where Bootsie couldn't see me from the garden. I knew she'd send Mathilda to come look for me just as much as I knew that Mathilda wouldn't come anywhere near my cypress. She said there was a haint near the tree, a lost and lonely soul looking for something. I wanted to see it, too, to chase it and find out what it wanted. But Mathilda warned me not to. She said that you can never catch the ghosts you chase. It made me sad, the way she said it, and I wondered if she wasn't talking about haints anymore.

I waited there until dusk, falling asleep just as the porch lights came on. I dreamed I saw a wispy figure standing by the tree and I starting running toward it, but no matter how fast I ran, I couldn't catch it. I woke up sweating and panting as if I'd been running, and I was so scared that I ran all the way to the back porch and into the house. I turned around to look out the screen door, but all I could see was the shadows of the trees and a sliver of moon in the sky.

Bootsie made me go to bed without supper for hiding when I was supposed to be in the garden, but I didn't care, because I didn't want to eat anyway. For the first time since I was a little girl, I plugged in my nightlight and then lit a cigarette. I watched the glowing end get brighter with each puff, and imagined I could hear Mathilda warning me about chasing ghosts.

Chapter 10

Vivien Walker Moise
INDIAN MOUND, MISSISSIPPI
APRIL 2013

I awoke lying across my bed in the same clothes I'd worn the night before, a bright shaft of sunlight from the uncovered window stabbing my face. My head throbbed, reminding me that I'd passed out from exhaustion before I'd thought to take a pill.

Cursing under my breath for forgetting to close the blinds, I rolled over so that I faced the wall and closed my eyes again. I was just about to drift off when my eyes popped open as I recalled why I'd been so exhausted. *Chloe.* I pictured her waking up alone and frightened in a strange house, and wondering where I was.

I catapulted from the bed, my foot tangling in the sheet and making me stumble, barely catching myself before I ran into the dressing table and tumbling a few of my beauty pageant trophies. Flinging open my door, I entered the upstairs hallway that ran in a square around the main staircase. There were three bedrooms off this hall, the fourth door leading onto a short flight of steps and another hallway with two more bedrooms and another set of stairs that led down to the kitchen.

The door to the bedroom next to mine, the guest bedroom where I'd put Chloe the night before, stood ajar. I peered inside and saw only an unmade bed and an open duffel bag with the contents strewn over the floor and every surface, as if a small tornado had managed to contain itself within the four walls of the bedroom.

I peered behind the door to make sure she wasn't hiding from me. "Chloe?" I called out, just in case. I waited a moment before heading back into the hallway.

I glanced into the empty third bedroom, then turned toward the second hallway, pausing on the threshold to the master bedroom. The tall black-ash four-poster bed dominated the large room, making the rest of the furniture appear to be shrinking back in awe. Nobody knew for sure which was older, the house or the bed, and I'd long ago stopped caring.

Guests always asked why the master bedroom wasn't in the main part of the house, and I'd had to explain dozens of times that it was thought this had been part of the original structure, the two front windows of the bedroom placed strategically in front of the oak alley that had long ago led up to the front door. It was assumed this vantage point was intended for the mistress and master of the house so they'd know when it was time to greet guests. Because it was my family, it was most likely a matter of knowing who they were avoiding.

The bed had been neatly made; two house slippers—the pair my mother had been wearing the previous evening—sat primly by the side of the bed. An antique mantel clock chimed over the fireplace and I looked at it with surprise. Nine o'clock. I remembered Tommy saying that Cora usually got to the house by noon to help my mother get out of bed, and except for school days I'd never seen Chloe out of bed before one. Even accounting for jet lag and time-zone issues, she shouldn't have been up and about.

"Carol Lynne?" I called, walking quickly toward the bathroom that had been added when my mother had come home for the last time when I was sixteen, and Bootsie had relinquished the bedroom to her. It had seemed to me at the time that Bootsie had given up her room as a way of thanking my mother for coming back, and maybe even as a bribe to get her to stay. It had driven a wedge between my grandmother and me, an unbridgeable chasm that I'd never been able to cross.

A silver-backed hairbrush and comb sat neatly on the laminate counter by the sink, surrounded by a mirrored tray where tubes of lipstick and mascara lay with precision between a powder compact and a bottle of foundation and a bottle of Youth Dew. The inside of the bottle was cloudy, the dark brown liquid viscous, and I wondered if the perfume had been Bootsie's.

Despite my growing worry as to where my mother and Chloe might be, I couldn't stop myself from staring at the orderliness of my mother's room. The Carol Lynne I had known had been disorganized and messy, a revolving hurricane of mindless, far-reaching plans that had her bouncing from one idea to the next, an indecisive bee unable to settle for long on a single flower. She was a constant revolution fueled by illegal substances and alcohol that allowed her to touch ground only sporadically. During her infrequent stays in this house while I'd been growing up, her room had more closely resembled Chloe's than Bootsie's meticulously ordered world.

I backed out of the bedroom, closing the door with a slam before racing down the hallway toward the back stairs and the kitchen. A piece of folded paper with my name scribbled on the outside sat on the counter by the sink and I snatched it up. It was from Tommy, giving me his cell number and asking me to call him.

I fumbled at my jeans pocket before I realized that I still hadn't charged my cell phone. *Damn.* My head throbbed and I thought for a moment that I could run upstairs and plug in my phone and grab another pill. But then I thought of Chloe and Carol Lynne and assumed that if the two of them were together, it couldn't be good.

Sticking the note into my pocket, I headed out the back door and into the ruined garden, barely noticing the healthy collection of weeds that seemed to have sprouted since I'd seen it the day before.

The ground was still soft from the heavy rain but not as flooded, the standing puddles shallow. Long running trenches had been carved around the cypress tree as the CSI team had searched for more evidence. Or more bones. Although the remains had been removed, Tripp had told me to expect more people today, just to make sure nothing remained. I paused, looking around me at the destruction, both manmade and not, and it unsettled me. Maybe it reminded me too much of my own life, with everything out of place and not appearing as it should. I half turned to go back inside but stopped when I heard voices.

I stepped past the broken gate and moved toward the cotton shed. The chant of a thousand cicadas came to me in waves, the sound oscillating like a song on the radio in Bootsie's old car, the red line of the tuner stuck between stations. My gaze moved toward the base of the felled tree and stopped. The blue tarp that had covered the hole had been pushed aside and a long stretch of the yellow caution tape appeared to have been ripped in half. With matching bare feet gripping the edge of a large root that bisected an edge of the hole, my mother and Chloe stood, holding hands. My stepdaughter's black hair, usually unbrushed and flying around her head in uncontrolled curls, had been smoothed back into a ponytail held back by a bright red bandanna similar to the one I'd seen my mother wearing.

I regarded them in silence for a few moments, trying to catch my breath, feeling *betrayed* somehow. As if I'd been circumvented and the two of them had found their way to each other before I could intervene.

"Chloe!" I shouted, realizing my error as both of them began to sway on their precarious perch.

I watched with relief as their momentum slowed and they were once again still. I pressed my fingers to my temple, wishing the pain would stop. "What are you doing? Do you have no clue what yellow crime-scene tape is all about?"

"Some guy named Tommy made us breakfast and told me that they found a skeleton here," Chloe said, her black-rimmed eyes—smeared from sleep—and black T-shirt giving her pale skin an ashen cast.

"I know," I said cautiously, cursing Tommy under my breath. He and my mother had been asleep when we'd arrived home the previous night, and I'd hoped to waylay him this morning to prepare him for Chloe.

"I had no idea," my mother said, shaking her head. "We should ask Bootsie if she knows about it."

I imagined I could feel my brain throbbing inside my skull. "Bootsie is de . . ." I stopped, recalling what Tommy had said: *She's in her own little world right now, a world that's gonna get smaller and smaller, and I'm not going to recognize her anymore.*

"Bootsie isn't here," I said, harsher than I'd meant to. Trying to change the subject to something less volatile, I said, "You both need to come back to the other side of the tape. The sheriff is coming here this morning and I don't want him to find you where you're not supposed to be."

Like a docile child, my mother left her perch on the root and moved to stand next to me. With a heavy sigh, Chloe followed at a much slower pace. When they were securely on my side of the tape, I reached down and grabbed both ends before tying them together in a knot, hoping the sheriff wouldn't notice.

Carol Lynne grabbed Chloe's hand and began leading her toward the garden. "You need to meet Bootsie. I'm sure she'll have some clothes with a little more color that would be appropriate for a young girl. Maybe we can go downtown after lunch to Hamlin's to find some new makeup for you that's more flattering."

I wanted to tell her that Hamlin's probably didn't sell anything that Chloe would want to wear, and remind her that I hadn't been allowed to wear makeup until I was fourteen. Bootsie had taken me to the Merle Norman store at the mall for my birthday present. I still had the lip gloss, tucked into one of my bedroom drawers. I'd never used it, waiting until I could show it to my mother when she came back. And when she finally did, it was too late for me to want to include her in any of the rites of passage she'd so easily let pass without her involvement.

Spots began to dance in front of my eyes, indicating that I was on the verge of a major migraine. "Bootsie's gone," I shouted, appalled as soon as the words left my mouth.

They both stared at me with widened eyes.

My mother drew back her shoulders. "Go to your room right now, Vivien Leigh. You will not speak to your mother in that tone of voice."

Chloe's eyebrows rose even higher.

I drew in a deep breath, then let it out slowly, counting backward from twenty, not having too much faith that it would work. It had been a technique recommended by a shrink I'd been to only once, never returning after he'd explained he didn't believe in pills.

Very slowly and as calmly as I could, I said, "Carol Lynne, it is way too late for you to start pretending to be a mother. And I'm way too old to be sent to my room."

Her eyes glazed over with confusion, and if my head hadn't been hurting so badly, I'm sure I would have felt the guilt and shame that settled in the pit of my stomach as I belatedly realized that the woman in front of me wasn't anybody I knew.

A male voice came from behind me. "But not old enough to be

speaking to your mama like that." Tommy lowered his voice. "Especially one who's ill." I turned around to see my brother's blue eyes harden. "And in front of impressionable young ears, too," he said, jerking his chin in Chloe's direction. She and my mother had begun their escape, skirting the yellow tape line, their bare feet making sucking noises as they walked, their postures and excited gestures making them look like small children playing in a sandbox.

I almost laughed, wanting to tell him that Chloe could probably teach him a thing or two, and that there wasn't an impressionable bone in her body unless your name happened to be Justin Bieber. Or Marilyn Manson. Consistent or logical—or impressionable—were three words I'd never before associated with Chloe.

I pressed hard on my temples. "They were inside the caution tape and the sheriff is supposed to be here any minute. They didn't give me a choice."

His expression didn't change.

Embarrassed, I looked down and noticed that he carried an old hatbox, what was left of a gold-cord carrying handle lying broken and frayed on top of the lid like a dead worm on a hot sidewalk.

He followed my gaze and handed me the box. "I got tired of waiting for you to call me, so I figured I'd bring this to you. It's Cousin Emmett's spare-parts box."

He shoved it at me and I took it, the old cardboard soft and rough like a favorite blanket, reminding me of the gentle old man and surrogate grandfather Tommy and I had adored. His pockets were always full of candy, and he was forever pulling quarters out of our ears and letting us keep the coins.

Whenever Emmett wasn't in the cotton fields, he'd been in the workshop and we'd be with him. It was there that Tommy learned about the intricate workings of watches and clocks while I played with the spare parts Emmett had saved in this hatbox. As somebody who'd lived through the Great Depression, Emmett believed that throwing anything away was a sin, and he'd been convinced that whatever he stored in that box would one day be useful.

It had been my childhood make-believe box; the art deco brooches with missing stones, the heavy clip earrings without a match, the broken watches and disembodied watch faces were my jumping boards to the stories I'd make up about them. I'd fashion elaborate necklaces and tiaras using one of Mathilda's headscarves or one of my mother's headbands she'd tie on her dresser mirror and never seemed to notice when one went missing.

"Where did this come from?" I asked.

"Emmett must have stuck it up in a nook in the attic, right where the tree hit the roof. It was hidden real good, because I haven't seen it since Emmett died. I was hoping maybe you could catalog everything that's inside. I'll give you some plastic bags to help you sort and organize." He shrugged. "Maybe Emmett was right and there might be something I can use in the box. But I can't find anything with everything jumbled together."

He shoved his hands into the front pockets of his jeans, something he did when he was anxious about something but didn't want you to know. I wanted to tell him no, that I wanted to hop on a plane with Chloe and fly back to California as soon as I could so I wouldn't have to see my mother, so I could continue to be angry with the woman she'd been. It would be so much easier. But there was something so hopeful in the way he avoided looking at me, and I recalled what Tripp had said: *You left him behind, too.*

"Sure. It's not like I have anything pressing right now. Maybe Chloe can help me. . . ." My voice trailed off as I saw two figures approaching from the side of the house. One I recognized as Tripp, and the other was a man in his mid-fifties wearing a uniform and a hat with a brim almost as broad as his belly.

As he approached I noticed the white skin that appeared almost translucent, sunspots the size of dimes marring his cheeks. He wore dark aviator sunglasses but I knew his eyes would be pale blue. Anybody with his coloring had no business in the Mississippi sun.

Tripp and Tommy nodded at each other while I became aware of Chloe slowly backing away from Tripp. I turned to watch as she and my mother headed toward the garden. I wondered if Carol Lynne was surprised by the state of the garden each time she saw it, if it was a shock she had to endure twenty times a day or however many times she walked out the back door.

I watched as she stopped in front of the garden gate and her hand moved to her mouth like she did when she was upset. I remembered that about her, at least. I turned back to Tripp and the sheriff, unable to look any longer.

Tripp introduced me. "Vivi, I'd like you to meet Sheriff Donny Adams. He's new to these parts, so you might need to fill him in on a little bit of your family history."

The sheriff took off his hat, revealing a completely bald pate with skin even paler than his face. He stuck out a meaty paw and shook my hand. "Not too much of a stranger to these parts—I'm from Leland, and I've been the sheriff here for about five years now. I'm surprised we haven't met."

"I haven't, I don't . . ." I paused, the throbbing in my head making it difficult to form words into sentences.

"She's been gone awhile—out to California," Tripp explained.

The sheriff nodded, replacing his hat. "Sorry to hear that."

Tripp's cell phone rang, and he stepped away to answer it as Sheriff Adams pulled a pad of paper and a pencil from his breast pocket. The end of the pencil was chewed like a beaver had gotten hold of it.

"So," he said, drawing out the word. "Any idea who might be buried in your yard? Looks like it's been here longer than you have, but maybe there're some family stories passed on down to you."

"About a dead body?"

"About anybody missing. Anybody who left and never came back."

I stared at the sheriff for a long moment, his image shot through with the kaleidoscope holes of my now full-on migraine. "Not that I can think of. For some reason, we always seem to find our way back here. My mother might know more . . ." I stopped, not really sure how to finish the sentence. I had no idea what my mother might know, or might remember. The only thing I was sure of was that she'd never said anything more meaningful to me than good-bye.

"She's having memory problems," Tommy responded for me. "Mostly short-term, so you might be able to get something useful from her."

Sheriff Adams jotted down something on his notepad. "So no family historian who keeps track of the family tree?"

Tommy and I looked at each other while I gritted my teeth, wondering how much longer it would be until I could run upstairs.

Finally, Tommy said, "Our grandmother, Bootsie, was into that kind of thing. Always talking about what this ancestor did to the house or garden, who died young, who embarrassed the family. I wasn't really into all that, so I didn't pay much attention. She didn't have anything written down that I can remember. Before Vivi left she said she would write down some of the stories, but I guess we both figured we'd have more time for that." He shrugged, his gaze traveling toward my mother and Chloe. Carol Lynne was staring at the garden while Chloe looked up at the house, taking in all of its peculiarities. I couldn't read her face from where I was, and I was glad.

Tommy continued. "The only thing that stuck with me—and she probably did this on purpose, since I'm a guy—was that the house is always left to the oldest girl. Started back two hundred years ago when the original house was built. It's sort of the family tradition."

"Interesting." The sheriff jotted something else in his notebook. He looked up, and I tried to focus on my reflection in his dark glasses, anything to distract me from the pounding in my head.

"You said family members had a habit of always finding their way back home. So no stories about somebody leaving and not coming back?"

Tommy and I shook our heads.

"So nothing specific about your family history that stands out?"

I closed my eyes and took a deep breath. "The only old story I remember is that the woman who built this house left it, her husband, and her children and went back to New Orleans, where she was from. I think Bootsie said she came back—eventually. But that was when all this was mostly swamp, and life was hard. Bootsie said the land broke her." I took another deep breath, trying to push the pain aside long enough so that I could think. "And we had an ancestor who drowned in the 1927 flood. I remember that because the waterline on the wall in the foyer has been preserved. You have to walk by it every time you go up or down the stairs, which is about as many times as Bootsie would tell me the story. It was her mother, but that's all I remember. It's probably all she knew. It happened the same year Bootsie was born."

"Interesting," he said again. "You remember her name?"

Tommy and I shook our heads in unison. "It'll come to me," I said. "I know Bootsie probably told me about a hundred times. I'll let you know if I think of it."

After a moment, Tommy said, "You might could talk with Cora

Smith. Her grandma used to work for Bootsie. I think she might have even been here before Bootsie was born. Maybe she heard something."

"Um-hmm," said the sheriff as he continued writing things on his pad. When he was writing he screwed his mouth up so that one corner was puckered. I thought the only thing missing from his country law enforcement ensemble was a half-smoked cigar dangling from his lips. "Know where I can find Miz Smith?"

"She's been helping us with our mama." Tommy glanced at his watch. "She should be here around noon, although sometimes she comes earlier if she can. She volunteers at the library some mornings."

Tripp hung up his phone and stepped toward us again. "The remains have been sent up to the lab in Philadelphia for a more extensive evaluation, but there're a few things I can take a stab at now. It's definitely female, and I'd say it's been there at least fifty years, just by looking at the roots of the tree. We'll need the forensic anthropologist to tell us for sure, but looking at the bones of the pelvis I'd say she was young—not out of her twenties, don't think. And there's some pelvic scarring, which means she'd given birth at least once."

I felt sick to my stomach. I wanted to blame it on the migraine, but his words made me think of the young woman buried under my tree, someone my age. And the child she left behind. I clenched my eyes, fighting the image of me I kept putting on the bare skull.

The sheriff stopped writing and directed his gaze at me. "I'm gonna see if they can get any DNA from the remains, and if they can, I'd like for you to give us a cheek swab just to see if there's some relation. You planning on hanging around for a while?"

He and Tommy stared at me expectantly while I just looked back like an opossum in the middle of the highway, preparing to curl up so the world would go away. "I, uh, yes. For a little bit anyway."

"She's got no place else to go," Tripp said, his expression blank.

Tripp's phone buzzed again, and he glanced at the screen. Shaking his head, he said, "I gotta get back to work. Old Mrs. Lee at Sunset Acres passed away in her sleep, so I have to head over there. And a wild hog has torn down the fence in the front yard of the house I'm supposed to be closing on in an hour, and is charging at everything that moves."

Chloe, apparently bored with the garden and her inspection of the house, had moved within earshot. "A wild hog?"

Tripp nodded. "It happens out here in the boonies sometimes."

She looked appalled. "What are you going to do with it if you catch it?"

"Eat it, I hope."

She blinked rapidly at him, trying to determine whether he was joking.

I was more fixated on what he'd said before. "A house closing?"

He pocketed his phone. "Yeah. Have my own real estate business, too. Helps to pay the bills. There aren't enough bodies to keep a coroner busy full-time."

He raised his hand and said good-bye before walking back to his car. Chloe ran toward him a little ways and then stopped. "What's a wild hog?"

Tripp stopped and faced her. "It's like a big pig but with tusks and sharp teeth. You wouldn't want to mess with one."

Her face seemed even paler than usual. "What kind of a shit hole is this place?"

Tripp stared at her as my mother approached, the bottom hem of her jeans heavy with mud. "Young ladies do not use that kind of language," she said, shaking her finger in Chloe's face. "You will apologize now, or I will have to wash your mouth out with soap."

Color returned to Chloe's face as she whipped around to my mother. "What the . . . ?"

She didn't have a chance to finish before Tripp stepped into her line of vision and cleared his throat. "Remember what we talked about?"

She closed her mouth, her eyes darting from me to my mother as if she were looking for somebody to take her side. Crossing her arms over her chest, she said, "Whatever."

"Excuse me?" Tripp said, leaning close to her.

"Yes, sir," she mumbled.

"That's better," he said. With a final wave he set off again, turning back once so we could see him put his first two fingers in a "V" shape to point at his eyes, and then he looked at Chloe before heading around the corner of the house and out of sight.

"I think Cora's here, Sheriff," Tommy said, pointing to the side yard, where a single parking slot had been added years ago to accommodate Tommy's motorcycle habit. I hadn't noticed a bike since my return, and I wondered if he still rode. We watched as a light blue Toyota sedan pulled into the space.

"Come on and I'll introduce you," Tommy said, beginning to lead the sheriff away. He glanced back at me. "Find me later and I'll get you some of those little plastic bags."

I remembered the hatbox in my hands, suddenly feeling the weight of it. I nodded, glad to have an excuse to run upstairs to my room. Addressing Chloe, I said, "Could you please bring Carol Lynne inside and turn on the TV until Cora is done with the sheriff? I've got to take this upstairs." I started walking quickly toward the house, dreading the part where we had to walk past the garden again.

Chloe ran to catch up with me. "Have you called my dad yet? He probably won't answer the phone, but you should leave him a message just in case."

Damn. "Not yet." *Not before I'm fully medicated.* "I will this morning. But I spoke with Imelda last night so she wouldn't panic." I began walking quicker.

"How come you call your mom Carol Lynne?"

The pressure cooker going off in my head was nearly unbearable by now. "The same reason bears crap in the woods. It just *is.*"

"Vivien Leigh! I raised you better than that."

I stopped, swaying on my feet from either the migraine or the anger, I wasn't sure. *You didn't raise me at all.*

Chloe wrinkled her nose, making her actually look like the twelve-year-old she was. "I thought Vivien Leigh was an old movie star. My friend Hailey's mom has a framed poster in her screening room with that name on it."

My mother beamed. "Vivien Leigh played the lead in my favorite film. But my mother thought naming my daughter Scarlett was too tacky."

"Tacky?" Chloe asked, squishing her nose again.

"Craptastic," I translated, seeing past my migraine to capture a word from her conversations with schoolmates she was desperate to be friends with in the backseat of the car I was chauffeuring.

"Vivien Leigh!"

I sighed, my whole body now vibrating from the pain in my head as I wondered what forces of nature had conspired against me to place

Chloe and my mother together in the same geographical location. With me. I wasn't handling this well. If I were being honest, I'd even say I wasn't handling it at all. I felt like an eighteen-wheeler headed downhill whose brakes had failed. But for years I'd taken the shortcut to dealing with my problems, and I was ill equipped to change gears now.

I was still thinking of something to say when my mother placed her hand on the broken gate and stared ahead of her as if she were seeing something more than just mud and weeds.

"I think we should fix this garden before Bootsie notices."

Chloe glanced behind her. "Only if you can make a fence high enough so the wild hogs can't get in."

I studied my mother for a long moment: her pale hands and braided hair, the beautiful face that I used to dream about as a child. That angry and hurt little girl was still inside me, banging her fists on my ribs every time I looked at my mother. We'd both grown older, but I was no less angry.

"That's a good idea," I told her, hoping she'd forget. But her green eyes met mine with hope and expectation, and a small part of me wanted her to remember—wanted her to remember so I could abandon her and the garden just as it started to mean something to her. As if dispensing some of my hurt would somehow lessen it.

I opened the kitchen door and held it for Chloe and Carol Lynne, then ran upstairs to my room to take as many pills as I needed to make me forget the anger and the guilt, where I was, and what had brought me here.

I shook two tablets into my palm and swallowed them dry, not wanting to take the time to refill the glass on my nightstand. I sat on the edge of my bed staring at the butterflies, wondering why they hadn't flown away by now, and thinking of the young mother buried beneath my cypress and why she'd chosen now to speak from the grave.

Chapter 11

Adelaide Walker Bodine
INDIAN MOUND, MISSISSIPPI
JUNE 1923

I stood in front of the tall, thick stems of my okra plants, clipping off the pods, while Aunt Louise waited behind me with her basket. The heat seemed to have turned on the growing clock, because if I didn't harvest the okra daily they'd just keep growing until they fell over and I'd have to stake them. It was only nine o'clock in the morning, but the sun had already begun to wilt my red dahlias, which I'd placed with a few geraniums in planters by the back porch. Aunt Louise's broad-brimmed hat flopped over her forehead, drooping just like my flowers.

Despite the heat, Aunt Louise and I found being outside preferable to being inside, where Uncle Joe and Willie argued constantly about everything—specifically about investing in land down in Florida. Willie, back from his first year at Ole Miss, said the families of his friends were making fortunes down there in land development because of this new thing called air-conditioning, but Uncle Joe said it was like burning money in the fireplace. He believed that owning land and growing crops—not building big fancy houses on good farming land—were the only real roads to financial security.

I'd ignored Willie's glance in my direction. The fact that I owned the house and land while my uncle ran the place was like the last piece of cake—everybody noticed it but nobody wanted to talk about it. I knew Uncle Joe got paid by the bank for farming the land—by somebody called a trustee, which I didn't really understand—so it wasn't like he was working for free. And he and his family got to live in the house with me.

But Willie hated farming, hated having to get up at sunrise and live for days without sleep during the planting and harvest times. He hated the dirt and the mules and the itinerant farmers who were happy to live in the shacks without plumbing or electricity at the back of the fields.

The discussion had been going on for more than six months now, ever since Sarah Beth's father had invested in a place called Boca Raton and had doubled his investment already. This morning the argument had begun at breakfast, and Uncle Joe and Willie were still at it an hour later, which meant that it was time for Aunt Louise and me to find something else to do.

I gave her a handful of okra pods, then moved on to the next plant, with my bare hands—something my aunt lamented—enjoying the crisp feel of the plants, the solidness of the vegetables as I held them in my palms. A lot of people, including Aunt Louise, were sensitive to the okra skin, breaking out in rashes, but I wasn't. It always seemed to me that it was the garden's way of telling me it liked me back.

"These are just beautiful, Adelaide. Just beautiful. I don't know how you do it. All of my friends in the garden club say this year the stinkbugs got to their okra plants before they could do anything about it. Ate up the whole plants. You definitely have a gift." Softly, she added, "Your mama and grandmama had the gift, too. They were both presidents of the Garden Society, you know. When you're a little older, I'll be happy to sponsor you for membership—not that you'll need me, of course."

I smiled at her to show my appreciation. I loved my aunt. Loved the way she tried her best to be my mother, and never said an unkind word about my mother or how she'd died. But I could tell she thought I was too much like Mama, my emotions worn too close to the surface of my skin, my way of looking at what came next with high expectations, leaving us unprepared for disappointment. I knew this by the way Aunt Louise always talked about the future, as if to reassure us both that I'd still be here.

I leaned forward to pluck a weed out of the soil. "Oh, I don't know. Your good name is bound to open all sorts of doors for me." Assuming my association with Sarah Beth wouldn't immediately close them despite the fact that her father was the president of the bank and her mother on every committee.

"You're a sweet girl, Adelaide. If it hadn't been for the circumstances that have brought us together, I'd be completely happy."

I nodded, blinking hard at the ground. I didn't like talking about my mother, and each year it just got harder. This past Christmas was the first one where I didn't accompany the family to her grave to pay our respects. It was set outside the cemetery gates, in unconsecrated ground. Sarah Beth had been the one to explain why, and I kept waiting for Aunt Louise or Uncle Joe to tell me. Maybe they just kept thinking that I hadn't noticed.

I felt closest to her in the garden, remembering being here with her, planting seeds and harvesting the fruits and vegetables we'd grown together. Sometimes I thought she'd been preparing me for her leaving, teaching me about how there was a time to reap and a time to sow, just like it says in the Bible. Every time I dug my fingers into the dirt, I felt like I was asking a question. And each spring her answers appeared in a bountiful harvest.

The sound of a car honking made us both pause. "What on earth . . . ?" Aunt Louise looked to me for an explanation.

I wiped my hands off as I stood. "Mr. Heathman bought Sarah Beth her own automobile for her seventeenth birthday and taught her how to drive. She said she'd swing around here this weekend to show me."

Aunt Louise pursed her lips. Under her breath, she said, "I don't know what her father was thinking. She's too wild as it is." She placed the basket of okra on the flagstone walkway and began patting her hair. It was braided and coiled into a neat bun at the back of her head, like she'd always worn it, and how all the old ladies in Indian Mound still did. She'd finally allowed me to bob my hair like Sarah Beth's, but I had to wear it with a barrette instead of marcelling it. Aunt Louise said that all those waves made a girl look cheap, and looking cheap always led to a fast reputation.

The horn honked again, and I began running toward the garden gate before Aunt Louise's voice called me back. "You will wait until she comes to the front door. It is very ill bred for her to think otherwise." Ever since Mrs. Heathman had blocked my aunt's membership in the Indian Mound Historical Society since she didn't own any property, my aunt used Sarah Beth's behavior as an example of the Heathmans'—especially Mrs. Heathman's—poor parenting skills.

Picking up the basket, she walked toward the kitchen door, not even bothering to look back to see if I was following. I took the chance to walk past my aunt when she paused to put the okra on the kitchen counter, only to halt abruptly when I entered the foyer.

The front door was open wide and Uncle Joe and Willie were on the front porch moving toward the bright, shiny red automobile in the circular drive. Sarah Beth was behind the wheel, a silk scarf tied around her forehead, and there was a man wearing a boater hat sitting next to her. I froze, recognizing John Richmond.

"Oh, no," I said, looking at my gardening dress and apron, my dirty hands and perspiration-soaked hat, then back to the front drive, where John was already climbing out of the car and walking over to Sarah Beth's side. She gave him a wide grin and I felt a little sick.

"What's the matter, Adelaide?" My aunt peered past me through the door and her eyebrows shot up. "Who is that young man?"

I wanted to run up the stairs before anybody could see me, but Aunt Louise was blocking the way, and Sarah Beth and John were already halfway up the porch steps. Uncle Joe stood in his shirtsleeves and vest with his hands on his hips—which is what he did when he was disappointed in someone's behavior—staring at the red car while his head moved slowly from side to side.

"Well, ain't that just the bee's knees, Sarah Beth. Is she yours?" Willie barely glanced at my friend as he rushed down the steps to inspect the vehicle more closely.

John hovered right outside the door, not noticing me yet, and I considered for a moment bolting back into the kitchen. I had seen him about half a dozen times since our first meeting—always orchestrated by Sarah Beth. She had developed a terrible habit of breaking her strands of pearls or needing them to be shortened or lengthened. And she made a habit of bringing me with her when she had to visit the jewelry shop.

He was always the perfect gentleman while also being an absolute flirt. Still, he never asked me out for a milk shake or a picture show, and I wondered if it was because I was so young. On one visit Sarah Beth had put lipstick on me and marcelled my hair to make me look more sophisticated, and loaned me a pair of her silk stockings, since I didn't own any. I felt like a Christmas goose, all trussed up and glazed, and after John's eyes had widened in surprise when he saw me, I'd left the store, waiting down the block until I saw Sarah Beth leave. I hadn't seen him since.

Sarah Beth saw me and squealed, rushing toward me with her arms outstretched as if it had been more than a day since we'd last seen each other. "Adelaide! I told Daddy that I just *had* to take the car out and get some wind blowing on my face to cool off. It's a *thousand* degrees outside. And then I remembered that John had the day off, and that it would be just ducky for the four of us to go for a swim."

I made myself turn my head and met John's eyes. They were wrinkled at the corners in a sort of secret smile meant just for me, as if he found Sarah Beth as brash as my aunt Louise did. I felt my aunt's disapproving stare and hurried to make the introductions.

John shook hands with my uncle and nodded respectfully at my aunt, his beautiful smile thawing her a little. "I apologize for this intrusion into your Saturday afternoon, but Sarah Beth barely gave me time to put on my bathing costume under my clothes before she was flying off again."

I noticed for the first time that he held one hand behind his back, and he quickly whipped out a beautiful bouquet of white lilies. I looked away so as not to laugh. I recognized the lilies from the vase in the Heathmans' foyer. They were Mrs. Heathman's favorite flower, and fresh lilies were in vases throughout her house regardless of the season.

I watched my aunt soften like butter left too long on the table. "Oh, Mr. Richmond. You are too kind. These are just beautiful. Let me go find a vase for these. . . ." Her gaze settled on my hair and she stopped speaking.

"Don't move, Adelaide. Keep perfectly still."

I did as she asked, knowing what she must be seeing. I'd been stung by a yellow jacket twice: once when I was two and I stepped on one—and my heel swelled up like the nose of a clown—and the second time when I was eleven and I nearly stopped breathing. The doctor told me that I should wear gloves and long sleeves when gardening, because any more stings could be more serious. Despite Aunt Louise's pleadings, I never did, simply telling her that I'd be careful and stay away from any stinging insect. I simply refused to believe that something as small as a bee should be so much bother.

I closed my eyes as everybody stopped talking. A rush of air on my forehead made me pop them open again to find John standing directly in front of me, squeezing his fist tightly while rubbing his fingertips against his palm. "It was just a little bee," he said, excusing himself for a moment to go dust off his hands on the front porch. He returned wiping his hands on a linen handkerchief.

Sarah Beth waved her hands in the air. "Adelaide simply gets red all over and swells up like a whale when she gets stung; isn't that right?" She turned to me for a moment, but didn't pause long enough for me to answer. "Hurry up, Adelaide. I'm just dying of heat prostration. You've got to come with us for a swim and a ride in my new car. Isn't it just divine? And your parents have to say yes because it's my birthday."

I stepped forward to see the car better, horribly aware of my shabby dress and dirty hands and John watching me. "I don't know. I've got more work to do in the garden, and I'm just filthy. . . ."

"Don't be such a silly goose. You can wash off in the pond. I was thinking of that swimming hole right by the old Ellis plantation. They say there aren't any snakes there because the ghosts keep them away."

I heard Uncle Joe behind me snort through his nose while I stared suspiciously at Sarah Beth. She knew I had an enormous fear of snakes, and it would take a bald-faced lie to get me into water so dark I couldn't see the bottom.

"I'm just teasing." Sarah Beth batted her eyelashes. "We're going to Max Greeley's house and swimming in his new pool. It's just the cat's meow—it's so clear you can see all the way to the bottom." She paused. "Unless you'd rather swim in the river," she said innocently.

I hated the river, hated the strong current that pulled you along whether or not you wanted to go. It reminded me a lot of my friendship with Sarah Beth.

Aunt Louise's lips were so tightly pressed together that they almost disappeared into her face. Her disapproval of Sarah Beth had only grown stronger in the past year. True to their word, the Heathmans had sent Sarah Beth to boarding school up in North Carolina. But I knew, even if they didn't, that you couldn't make Sarah Beth do anything she didn't want to do and that she'd be back for good before Christmas. And she was. She'd been expelled for smoking and being out after curfew with a boy—although she swore the boy didn't mean anything and that she just wanted to make Willie jealous. But she'd come back even wilder than when she'd left, like a bird who'd been let out of its cage and had no intention of returning.

As if sensing my aunt's mood, Sarah Beth said, "Don't worry, Mrs. Bodine. I've brought Bertha's girl, Mathilda, to chaperone."

I stepped forward, seeing now the entire roadster, the chrome and red paint so bright it was like I'd died and gone to heaven. A rumble seat at the rear of the car was open, and inside it Mathilda sat unprotected from the elements, clutching an enormous picnic basket on her lap. She wore a red kerchief, its edges dark with sweat, and her eyes were closed as if in prayer or misery.

"All right," I said, surprising myself. "I'll go. To the pool. I'll just go put on my bathing costume," I said, heading toward the stairs. Willie passed me, taking the steps two at a time regardless of Aunt Louise's admonishments to act like a gentleman. I assumed Sarah Beth wore her own costume under her dress and linen jacket.

After dressing in my extremely modest bathing costume—and I knew this was true because Aunt Louise had purchased one just like it—I threw a dress over my head and bolted for the door before I could change my mind.

John sat with me in the backseat while Sarah Beth and Willie sat up front. I smiled at Mathilda as John held the car door open for me, her eyes meeting mine for just a moment before glancing away.

Sarah Beth's driving and the bumpy road had me sliding and jolting into John. I'd never sat this close to an unrelated male before except in church. Every time Sarah Beth jerked me into his side, I'd scramble for my door and try to hold on. Finally John put his arm around my shoulder and held me against him. "To keep you safe," he said, smiling at me.

Willie sat close to Sarah Beth, whispering in her ear and making her giggle, which did nothing to help her driving, but at least kept me solidly at John's side. Watching them made me painfully aware of how silent it was in the backseat. There was only so much staring at the new leather I could do. Without looking up, I said, "Are you sure it's okay for you to go swimming?"

"I beg your pardon?"

I tilted my head in his direction, afraid to turn it completely because then surely my nose would touch his chin. "Because of your lungs?"

"My lungs?"

"Yes. Mr. Peacock explained to us that you moved down to Mississippi because your lungs couldn't handle the cold winter air in Missouri anymore."

He coughed, followed by a strangled noise, and I turned my head sharply, my nose colliding with the underside of his jaw. I tried to jerk back, but he held me to him while he continued to cough and choke. He smelled so good I wanted to bury my nose into his neck, but could think only of my aunt's disappointed lips disappearing into the folds of her face.

Finally I managed to pull away, distancing myself from him by grasping the back of the seats in each hand. "What's the matter?"

He'd calmed down and was looking at me the way Uncle Joe looked at Willie when he'd said something unexpectedly clever. "My lungs are fine, Adelaide."

I looked at him, confused. "But Mr. Peacock said—"

"Can you keep a secret?" he asked quietly. I glanced toward the front seat, where Sarah Beth and Willie were having their own private conversation, and then toward the small back window, where I could see the back of Mathilda's head. Sweat poured down her neck into the collar of her dress, and I imagined her eyes closed as she pretended to be somewhere other than in the rumble seat of Sarah Beth's car.

"Yes," I whispered back, trying not to stare at the soft part of his neck, where I still remembered the salty scent of him.

"My lungs are fine. It was just a story my family made up. My real name is Reichman—because my parents are German. Well, not German anymore. They've been in America for almost thirty years, and I was born in St. Louis. But during the war, ignorant people thought anybody with a German accent or last name was an open target. We had livestock shot, and our barn set on fire. So my father sent me down here when I was twelve to live with his sister and her family to be safe. They changed my name to Richmond so nobody would think twice about calling me a German spy. And because I'd lived here so long, it was just decided that I stay. I've got six brothers and they help my father run the farm, so they didn't exactly need me."

"Oh," I said, looking down at the leather seat between us. "Well, that makes sense, I suppose. You don't look sickly, I mean."

His fingers touched me under my chin, and he lifted it. "I'm as healthy as an ox," he said, something in his tone heating me more than the summer sun.

The car came to a jerking halt, and I realized where we were. "Sarah Beth! We're not supposed to be here—my uncle Joe will lock me in my room for the rest of my life if he finds out I went swimming at the Ellis plantation!"

"Oh, don't be such a baby, Adelaide. They won't find out if we don't tell them. So grow up and let's just have some fun."

I stared at her for a moment, knowing it was pointless to argue.

John came across to my side of the car to help me out. As I stood on the running board, I saw Mathilda trying to figure out how to navigate the basket and herself out of the rumble seat. Willie and Sarah Beth had already climbed from the car and were walking toward the ruins of the old plantation house while John stood, waiting patiently to help me out.

"Hang on," I said, jumping down, then heading toward the back of the car. "Here," I said, taking the basket from Mathilda. "Give that to me so you can climb down."

She looked at me with grateful eyes, eyes that were lighter than I'd noticed before, with specks of green in them.

"Thank you, Miss Adelaide," she said quietly. She climbed down from the rumble seat before retrieving the basket from my hands, then walked away quickly in the direction Willie and Sarah Beth had gone.

I found John watching me with an odd expression. "That was kind of you, Adelaide."

I shrugged, feeling embarrassed. "My mama always told me to treat all people the way I want to be treated. I don't remember much else about my mama, so I try to remember that."

He smiled at me and I suddenly became aware of just how alone we were. I knew Aunt Louise wouldn't approve, and the thought gave me an unexpected thrill, like a drip of cool water against my skin. I shivered. I'd never been alone with a boy before—not that I'd ever been given the opportunity—and I also knew Sarah Beth and I had been lectured again and again about coming out to the old plantation house. I'd heard my aunt and uncle talking about the "unsavory characters" who sometimes made their home in some of the abandoned slave cabins on the property, but all of us children in Indian Mound knew the adults wanted us to stay away because the old house was haunted.

You could just tell by the way the glassless windows stared out at you like empty eye sockets, and how sometimes you could see a shadow pass by even though the upper floor had rotted away years ago and there was nothing to stand on just in case you wanted to walk by a window.

And nobody hunted in the woods surrounding the house or in the old cotton fields that had been abandoned right after the Civil War. Men said that the animals stayed away, as if they sensed something they were afraid of.

The land had been allowed to return to forest. Uncle Joe called it a sin to waste all that good farmland, but I thought it was the natural course of things. In my sixteen years of history lessons and just paying attention, I knew that sooner or later the Mississippi River or the land that had been stolen from it would demand payment for trying to force them into doing something nature had never intended. It was just the way of things in the delta.

I started talking, trying to erase the silence that hid beneath the sound of the insects in the trees and in the clusters of weeds and grass that sprouted through the dirt road like the tail of a scairt cat. "This plantation used to belong to Sarah Beth's family—on her mama's side. Right after the Civil War they moved to New Orleans, where they had family connections." I didn't know exactly what that meant, but I'd heard Aunt Louise use the term a lot and figured it made me sound older.

I continued. "They brought some of their freed slaves with them— their Bertha is a descendant. People say Mrs. Heathman's grandfather was a blockade runner and made a fortune during the war."

"And who owns it now?" John walked with his hands respectably behind his back, but so close to me that my arm brushed his with every step.

"I think they still do. Uncle Joe says that with Mr. Heathman being president of the bank, he doesn't need to get his hands dirty with farming." I looked at him and saw that he was smiling at me in that way of his that made me feel like a child. I stopped walking. "I'm sorry," I said. "I forgot your family owns a farm, too. I only think of you as a watchmaker."

"No apology needed. Farming is a very noble profession, in my opinion. Not everybody can make things grow, or has the patience to wait for rain or pray for it to stop."

"I love to grow things in my garden," I said, feeling emboldened by how near he was to me. "I'm quite good at it. Even during a drought, I always have a good crop of vegetables. Aunt Louise says I come from a long line of brilliant gardeners."

We stopped, just now becoming aware of where we were. We'd walked around the ruins of the house and stood near the back, amid several outbuildings with missing roofs. Gnats and mosquitoes buzzed and dipped around us, but without biting, as if they, too, felt the magic that seemed to surround us. The pond was visible through the trees and we could hear Sarah Beth's scream of laughter followed by a loud splash.

John took my hand and began leading me in the opposite direction. "Let's go this way," he said, finding a path that skirted through stands of new trees and eventually led to a row of abandoned slave cabins. I should have said no, on account of not only the words of warning from my aunt and uncle about never being alone with a boy who wasn't related to me, but also from my sheer terror that we would encounter one of those ghosts I'd been hearing about all of my life.

"Where are we going?" I asked, trying to keep the tremble out of my voice.

"Here," he said, stopping, then facing me. "I've been dying to get you alone ever since I first saw you. Do you remember that? Last year in Mr. Peacock's shop?"

I nodded, breathless.

"I've been wanting to do this." He pushed his boater hat farther back on his forehead. Then gently he took my head between his hands and bent toward me, his lips gentle on mine. Aunt Louise would *definitely* not approve, regardless of how many lilies he brought her.

He pulled his head back, his eyes exploring mine. He smiled. "That was even better than I'd hoped." He moved his thumb to my lower lip and pulled it down, staring closely at it. He was about to kiss me again when I noticed smoke rising in the air from behind one of the slave cabins. I pulled away, and John followed my gaze.

"Somebody's here," I whispered, trying to imagine which was worse—ghosts or unsavory characters. Either way, I didn't want to see them.

John took me by the shoulders. "They'll leave us alone if we leave them alone."

I wanted to agree, and allow John to kiss me again, but I'd already spotted the picnic basket, set down in the scrubby grass in front of the cabin where the smoke was coming from.

Pulling away, I said, "Mathilda's there. We need to make sure she's okay."

He noticed the basket, too, and without argument, he took my hand and led me toward the cabin. I found myself praying that ghosts didn't light real fires. I prepared to stop, to sneak around the back so we wouldn't be noticed, but John simply led me around the cabin toward the sound of low voices.

He stopped, and I stopped right behind him, our hands still clasped tightly. The humid air was thick with the smell of what I thought was vinegar, and something else I recognized but couldn't name. And there was another smell I thought familiar: the scent I sometimes caught on Mr. Heathman's breath in the evenings.

I wondered if John could hear my heart thumping in my chest, or at least feel the rush of blood through my veins and into my fingertips. I just wasn't sure whether it was from discovering somebody in one of the abandoned cabins, or the fact that his fingers were wrapped around mine and I could smell his sweat mixing with my own.

"Good afternoon," he said softly, as if he'd stopped in on friends for a glass of lemonade.

I peered around his shoulder, my eyes widening. In the center of a clearing behind the shack were two large barrels, one with what looked like an upside-down copper tub stuck on top, with a copper tube connecting the barrels. A fire burned under a large copper pot, creating the column of steam that I'd seen. Surrounding the barrels were about a dozen oversize empty jars with a single finger loop near the top. And sitting in front of the smoldering tub were three upturned logs where a black man, a white woman, and Mathilda sat. Standing quietly by the barrels was a black boy about my age, barefoot and wearing torn denim pants, his dark eyes taking me in just like a butcher deciding which part of a hog to cut up first.

They looked at us in surprise, the man standing slowly before moving behind the woman, his hand on her shoulder to show us that they were together. The woman's lower lip was filled with tobacco, and I watched as she lifted a small jar, brown liquid swirling inside, and spit into it, her eyes never leaving my face. I wondered if these two people might be the unsavory characters Aunt Louise had warned me about.

I turned toward Mathilda, whose eyes had the look of a rabbit in the sight of a rifle. "You okay?" I asked, hoping I wasn't insulting anybody. The man's hair was heavily sprinkled with gray, but his hands were as big as watermelons, the muscles under his filthy undershirt pressing against the flannel like giant snakes caught in a sack. His suspenders hung down the sides of his pants, and I looked away as I realized I'd never seen a man before in such a state of undress, except Willie once by accident.

Before Mathilda could answer, John lifted his chin toward the man. "Leon," he said in greeting.

The black man nodded his head in acknowledgment and I wondered how John knew his name. And why he wasn't introducing us, although it was apparent that Mathilda already knew them.

John turned his attention to Mathilda. "You get on down to the pond, Mathilda. I'll bring the basket."

She looked at Leon as if seeking his approval, but before she could leave we heard the approach of running feet and laughter, and then Sarah Beth and Willie were standing in front of us, their hair and costumes soaking wet, their hair slicked back like a couple of models in the *Vogue* magazine that Mrs. Heathman kept by the side of her bed.

They were holding hands, and in Sarah Beth's other hand she held a flask. My aunt and uncle were teetotalers, so I'd never seen one up close, but I knew what it was. I just couldn't figure out what it was doing in Sarah Beth's hand.

They'd stopped laughing, as surprised to see us as we were to see them. Sarah Beth pulled back her shoulders as I'd seen her mother do before giving orders to one of the servants. "I'm thirsty," Sarah Beth said, using her new boarding-school voice. Her head was slightly tilted back so that she really was talking down her nose. She emphasized her words by raising her arm and shaking the flask.

Willie and John shared a glance before John took my shoulders and led me gently back to the path that wound around the shack. "Go with Mathilda. She knows the way. I'll be right behind you."

I was embarrassed and confused, and I couldn't understand why Sarah Beth didn't meet my eyes. Not knowing what else to do, I began to follow Mathilda.

"I said, I'm thirsty," Sarah Beth's voice announced again.

The man coughed, and I heard the woman say, "That girl ain't no better than she oughta be." I imagined her lifting the jar to her mouth again, spitting out the nasty brown liquid.

I started to turn back, but Mathilda tugged on my arm.

I followed, feeling silly, and useless, and like a child who was still supposed to believe in Santa Claus.

We made it to the pond, where I immediately pulled off my clothes and dived into the dark, still waters before I could remember my fear, knowing no amount of cool water could take the sting of heat from my skin.

Chapter 12

Carol Lynne Walker Moise
INDIAN MOUND, MISSISSIPPI
APRIL 3, 1963

Dear Diary,

I feel so sick inside, like black mildew is starting to spread all over my innards. I haven't really felt like this for a long time, at least not since Bootsie came back when I was six and reminded me all over again that there was something about me that made people want to leave me behind.

My friend JoEllen Parker buried her daddy last Saturday, which got me thinking about my own daddy. I knew better than to ask Bootsie, because she always just gets a funny look on her face and then tells me that the past is best left to the past. But I never really knew him, and that emptiness is part of my present. Maybe learning something about him will fill this empty hole in my heart before the mildew spreads into that, too.

I was in the kitchen helping Mathilda polish the silver and decided to ask her. I'd long since figured out that the best way to speak to adults about something touchy was to ask them when you were both busy doing something else. Mathilda was probably the best person to talk to about my family anyway. She's known Bootsie since before Bootsie was even born, helping to take care of her as a baby when my grandmother drowned in the flood. And she seemed happy to talk about the old days. At least at first.

She said my daddy was a sweet boy, growing up downtown in the rooms above his family's grocery store. From the moment Bootsie set eyes on him it was true love—not that I believe in that kind of thing, but I didn't want to interrupt Mathilda when she was being so free with her information. He was sweet to Bootsie, bringing her flowers and opening doors and taking her for long walks. And he loved her garden and this house—even with all its peculiarities. He said a home should be like the family who lived in it—and this family was apparently something he liked: each part independent and strong, yet all together something truly original and beautiful. Only a house built from love could have that kind of character.

I almost interrupted Mathilda to tell her that my daddy was a slick talker who knew what to say to get what he wanted, but I didn't. Sometimes it's best to let old people believe what they want. Memories and ancient photographs are pretty much all they've got left.

But then the war came and he joined up in 1943. They decided to get married before he shipped out, so they did. Fortunate for me, I guess, because if they'd waited, I probably wouldn't be here. Because when my daddy came back from the war and I was just a tiny baby, he wasn't the same man. Mathilda said he continued to fight the battles like he was still there, angry and yelling at people all the time, starting fights and spending the night in jail to cool off. Bootsie was afraid for him to come home, and only felt safe when she knew he was in jail.

And then one night my daddy did come home, and he beat Bootsie so bad that it just about killed her. She went to the hospital and never came back—not for six years.

I started crying, so Mathilda sat down and put her arm around me like I was still a little girl, and I remembered that—remembered how even when my own mother had gone, Mathilda was there to hold me when I cried. I wanted her to tell me why Bootsie didn't take me with her, wanting to understand what was wrong with me.

But all Mathilda could tell me is that each mother has her own language that she has to learn first before she can teach it to her children. It took Bootsie a long time to learn it, because she had a deep hole in her heart that started when her own mama had left her when she was a baby, even if she hadn't meant to on purpose. I think that it doesn't matter how or why, but not having a mama is like being born without a heart.

Mathilda said that Bootsie's hurt was more than just the bruises you could see, and she had to go away to get better. She left me with people who could love me and keep me safe and be my mother while she couldn't. A mother's love is a lot like faith, she explained, where you just have to believe something even when you can't see it. All I know is that I was practically an orphan for six years and there's not enough faith in this world that will ever make me see that any different. Mathilda told me that sometimes we need to grow up first before we stop seeing our mamas with the eyes of a child, and that I'd understand more when I became a mother myself, but I won't. Why would I have children if I'm going to just mess them up like my own mother and grandmother did?

It all made me cry harder, even though I didn't know what for. It was the biggest sadness I'd ever felt, like a hole out in Bootsie's garden without a seed in it, and I don't know how to fill it.

Yesterday at school the boy who sits behind me in English class, Jimmy Hinkle, said he and a bunch of kids from Indian Mound and a few other places were planning on doing a little freedom ride of their own, and visiting all the theaters in three towns. Blacks and whites are supposed to be sitting together in all public buildings now, but he says it's not happening down South, and the federal government isn't doing anything about it. College kids and adults around the country have already been doing it in the bigger cities, so why not here?

I said yes before I really understood why. I hadn't really given much thought about why all the colored people sat in the back of the theaters when I could sit wherever I wanted. But I figured if I could think about something other than that mildew growing inside me, even just for a day, it would be worth it.

And it was—right until we all got arrested in downtown Indian Mound for disturbing the peace. I got the feeling that Jimmy wanted the National Guard to be called out and dogs set on us, but all we got was Sheriff Oifer and two of his deputies to round us up and lock us into the two cells at the jail.

Bootsie didn't say a word on the drive home. It was only about five miles, but I swear it felt more like a hundred. She sent me to my room without any supper, which was unfair, because she's always preaching to me about doing the right thing even though it's not the most popular thing to do. I stood on the stairs right next to that hallowed watermark and raised my voice to her for the first time in my life and called her a hypocrite (that's a new word Jimmy taught me), because here she is pretending to be a caring mother by punishing me for spending a few hours in jail defending the rights of others, yet she could walk out of my life to let me be cared for by somebody else.

"But I came back," she said—as if that made up for her going away. Like her leaving was a pencil mark and her coming back an eraser. I wanted to take out my heart and show it to her so she could see that empty hole that no eraser could ever make go away. Instead I just told her that I hated her.

She slapped me so hard I was almost knocked into next week. I've never been hit by anybody my whole life, and it's not something I'd want to experience again. And not even because it hurt my cheek so much. It hurt my heart even more, made me almost sick enough to want to throw up.

I thought Bootsie might faint, because she'd lost all the color in her face, like she'd been the one who'd been hit, and it took Mathilda to calm us both down. I slammed my door and sat on my bed for a long time before Mathilda came in to make sure I was all right and brought me a little plate of supper. She put her arm around me and let me cry, the whole while repeating over and over that I just needed to give it time.

But I know there's not enough time left in this universe that will let me forget that my mother has never loved me enough.

Chapter 13

Vivien Walker Moise
INDIAN MOUND, MISSISSIPPI
APRIL 2013

I awoke the following morning with the sure knowledge that I wasn't
alone. My face was once again flooded with sunlight from the uncovered window, and I was aware of a definite pressure on the mattress
near my knee and warm breath on my cheek. I opened my eyes to find
Chloe's black-rimmed ones staring into mine only about two inches
from my face.

"Are you awake?" she asked.

She lifted her head enough so I could slide up against the headboard,
still blinking to clear my head. She smirked, then pointed her camera
phone at me and clicked. "What are you wearing?"

I looked down, vaguely remembering that I hadn't unpacked yet
and I'd just pulled something from one of my dresser drawers. "It's
called baby-doll pajamas. I think I wore these in junior high."

"It's like something Lady Gaga would wear to twerk in." She raised
her phone again but I grabbed it.

"Take another picture of me and you lose the phone."

With a heavy sigh she lowered it. "Are you going to stay in bed all day?"

I stared at the blurry numbers on my bedside clock. "What time is it?"

"It's almost noon."

I jerked myself out of the bed, feeling dizzy from the sudden movement. "Did your dad call?"

She shrugged. "How do I know? I'm not the one trying to reach him."

I grabbed my phone from the nightstand and checked it for voice mail. There were no messages, so I checked my texts and e-mails, too. Nothing. I'd already left Mark three voice mails. Either he was ignoring me, or he didn't have a signal in whatever side of the world he was in.

I scrubbed my hands over my face, needing desperately to wake up so I could say the right thing to Chloe. "I'm happy you're here; I am. I've missed you. But I also don't want to get into any serious trouble." I stopped there, unsure of how much she knew about our acrimonious divorce.

"You're talking about the restraining order, aren't you?"

I tossed the phone onto the bed, wondering why I even bothered to filter any information from a twelve-year-old. She'd already told me she'd hacked into her father's computer and Expedia account, so nothing should be a surprise. But it was.

"Yeah. I could go to jail if I don't get this straightened out with your father. But I promise I will try really hard to convince him that you're okay with me, and that you're welcome to stay." I tried to smile. "And that I won't give you any fried food."

With a heavy sigh, Chloe slid from the edge of my bed, then with a desultory stride walked over to the bookshelf that contained all of my childhood books. Like the wallpaper, the shelves had remained unchanged in my absence. The books had been my escape from an older brother who loved to put tree frogs down my shirt and cicadas in my hair, and from the constant reminder of the empty place at the dining table. Bootsie always set out a plate and tableware for my mother, as if she'd expected her return at any moment.

My gaze strayed to the bottle on the nightstand, wondering if I could take a pill without Chloe noticing.

"I'm not missing any school, if that's what you're worried about. It's spring break."

That had been the least of my worries. Harboring a fugitive child had pretty much topped that list, with going to jail for ignoring a restraining order right underneath it. "Well, that's good."

She sat cross-legged in front of the bookshelf and plucked out a book with a black-varnished fingernail. She wore her usual black T-shirt and black jeans, but her feet were bare. Even though her toes sported matching black polish, her feet were still soft and round like a child's, making me somehow grateful.

"Why does this book have so many bookmarks sticking out of it?" She held it up for me to see.

I recognized the cover and smiled. *Time at the Top.* "Because it's my favorite book of all time. I read it for the first time in sixth grade and then about a hundred times since. I got it at a used-book library sale and it was out of print at the time, so I didn't want to mark it up with a highlighter. I used the bookmarks at my favorite spots so I could go back and reread them."

"Sounds pretty boring to me. But I guess back when dinosaurs roamed the earth there wasn't anything else to do."

I rubbed my hands hard over my face again, desperate to be shaken awake. "I'm only twenty-seven, Chloe. We had computers when I was growing up, and the Internet and cell phones. We had indoor plumbing and electricity when I was growing up, too. We just didn't rely so much on all those gadgets for our entertainment, like a lot of people do today. I liked to read a lot, and to write."

She rolled her eyes, but I noticed she put the book next to her on the floor instead of reshelving it. Turning to the shelves, she focused on the sets of books with matching dog-eared spines, lined up like fence pickets.

"Those are my favorite series—sort of like Nancy Drew books."

"Who?"

I stared at her back. I knew she'd never been a big reader, but I thought the name Nancy Drew was ingrained in the brains of all young girls. "They're mystery books for girls. See the ones on the left? Those are the Penny Parker mystery stories. I liked those because the main character is a reporter who solves mysteries—kind of like Nancy Drew. Next to those should be the Beverly Gray mystery stories. Those were Bootsie's books that she'd had as a girl, and she gave them to me." I smiled to myself, nostalgic about the Saturday afternoons spent reading under the cypress tree or in Bootsie's garden while she worked.

"You're welcome to read any of them if you promise to be very careful." I was about to mention my favorite reading spot under the old cypress but caught myself in time.

"As if."

I didn't say anything as she removed two more books from the shelf and placed them on top of the first one she'd set on the floor.

She plucked a trophy from the shelf and examined it closely, seeing the cotton boll in flaking fake gold sitting on the top of the long white plastic column like an ice-cream cone. "What's this?"

I considered for a moment not telling her, but knew holding anything back from her was pointless. "It's my Little Miss Cotton Boll trophy. I won the crown in 2000, when I was fourteen."

She scrunched up her face. "Like a beauty pageant?"

"Yeah. And I had to twirl a baton, too."

Chloe stared at the cheap trophy for a long moment, her face impassive, and I wished I'd thrown out all of those stupid reminders of someone I'd once been but wasn't too proud of.

"Were you really pretty when you were my age?"

I measured my words carefully, knowing her father and his quest for perfection that Chloe could never live up to. "I was probably more cute than pretty—but only after I turned thirteen. But I sure could twirl a baton. Can't say winning that trophy made much difference in my life, though. That's a weekend in my life I'll never get back." I smiled, but she wasn't looking at me.

She shoved the trophy back on the shelf. "That's so lame."

"Yeah. I guess it is."

"Did you keep a diary?" Her voice sounded almost hopeful.

I shook my head. "No. It wasn't my thing, really." I couldn't tell her that the only reason I didn't was because my mother had kept a diary as a girl. I'd never seen it after she came back, and I figured she'd left it behind, like she did with everything else she didn't want.

Chloe started scanning my room again, scrutinizing the drooping wallpaper, the various awards and trophies. With her back turned, I reached for the bottle and shook out a pill into my palm.

"What's in here?" She held up the box of watch and clock parts that Tommy had found tucked in the attic of his workshop.

"Leftovers. My grandmother's cousin Emmett used to have a clock and watch repair shop. Those are all the extra pieces he never wanted to get rid of. Tommy wants me to sort through them. You can help me if you like."

"Right. Sounds almost as much fun as reading a book."

I rolled the pill around inside my fist as I watched her replace the box on the shelf.

"Your mom keeps calling me JoEllen."

My hand dropped to my side, my fist clenched over the pill. "That's a name I haven't heard in a long time. It was her best friend in high school. She married a man from Pascagoula who she'd met in college, and moved there. She'd come visit sometimes with her two boys when my mom was home." I smiled at the memory. "JoEllen was always telling me how much she'd always wanted a girl, and I would ask her to take me with her. It always upset Carol Lynne. I think that's why I did it."

Chloe stared at me in silence with the same concentration she'd given the wallpaper and my trophies, and I wished I'd held back that last part.

"Well, my name's Chloe, not JoEllen."

I stood and moved to my suitcase on the floor and began rooting through it for a pair of jeans and clean underclothes, wishing I knew what to tell her about why my mother couldn't remember her name. Should we correct her? Wear name tags with the day and year written on them? I was unprepared for this—unprepared for pretty much everything that had been waiting for me upon my arrival back home. But to see my mother again, without the benefit of her remembering our shared history, was like showing up for a party at the wrong house on the wrong date. My anger and hurt were my own now, a loose thread on the hem of my life, and I had no idea how to knot it or cut it off.

"I'm sorry, Chloe. She's not herself anymore. I guess we just need to learn to be patient."

I thought she would argue, but she didn't, making me feel like the child. Instead she said, "Where's Carol Lynne going today?"

I straightened, clutching a pair of clean jeans. "What do you mean?"

"She's downstairs by the front door sitting on two suitcases. I asked her where she was going and she just said, 'Away.' And she keeps asking me for a cigarette."

I dropped the clothes I'd already gathered back into my suitcase, then headed for the door, shoving the pill into my mouth when I knew Chloe couldn't see.

I stopped near the bottom of the staircase, right near the old watermark, and stared at my mother. Her hair was in braids again, circa 1966, and she wore bell-bottom jeans and the same floral top I'd seen her in before. Her long fingers plucked at the denim covering her thighs, something I'd seen her do whenever she'd decided to go cold turkey and give up her cigarettes. Her feet were clad in the house slippers, and she sat on top of an ancient mustard yellow American Tourister hardcover suitcase. I hated those suitcases, hated seeing them in the foyer, because it always meant that my mother was leaving. Or coming back.

"Where are you going?" I asked carefully, praying that the pill would work a little faster on an empty stomach.

She looked up, surprised to see me. "What are you doing here? Shouldn't you be in school?"

"It's Saturday," I said quickly, not even sure myself what day of the week it was.

She frowned as she took in the pajamas. "I think those are too small for you, Vivien. You're growing like a weed. I suppose we'll need to make a shopping trip to Hamlin's and find you something that fits."

I took another step down, wishing I'd remembered to ask Tommy what the appropriate responses would be, and praying that Cora Smith would walk through the door any minute.

"Sounds like a good idea," I said as Chloe moved down the staircase beside me.

My mother stood and walked toward us, her gaze focused on Chloe. I gritted my teeth, remembering what Tommy had said about our mother no longer having filters.

She reached up and tucked Chloe's hair behind one ear and then the other, and I watched in shock as Chloe let her. She was so prickly about her looks; any suggestions or comments I might have had for her always ended up with screaming and slamming doors. I suppose that's what happens when one's plastic surgeon father can only see you as a project to fix.

Carol Lynne touched Chloe's cheek. "You have the most beautiful skin, and I think the bluest eyes I have ever seen. I wish I could see

them, but it's hard to with your hair in your face and all that eyeliner."
She reached for one of her own braids and pulled off the rubber band
that held it in place. "I'm real good at doing French braids. Come sit
down and let me play with your hair."

Without waiting for a response, she took Chloe's hand and led her
to one of the Chippendale chairs that sat on either side of the demilune
hall table. With a backward glance at me, Chloe went with her without
comment and sat in the chair that Carol Lynne had moved from the
wall.

I sat down on the steps, mesmerized by how quickly my mother's
fingers worked through Chloe's hair, moving the strands in and out
with deftness and precision. It was odd to see, to know that she couldn't
remember Chloe's name or that I wasn't in high school anymore, but
she could remember how to French-braid hair. When I was a little girl,
she'd braided my hair as we sat at the dressing table in her room staring
into the same mirror. My mother would lean over me, letting her hair
fall over my face as if it were my own, and we'd delight in how identical the color was, and how we couldn't tell where my hair stopped and
hers began.

I looked away, happy to feel the fog of the pill begin to slip into my
memories and soften their sharp edges.

The sound of a key in the front lock brought my attention to the
door as Cora Smith let herself in, pausing for a moment to take in the
suitcases, me on the steps wearing ill-fitting pajamas, and my mother
braiding Chloe's hair on the antique chair in the foyer.

"Good afternoon," she said cheerily.

My mother glanced at her before returning to her work. "Hello,
Mathilda." Her fingers paused. "Is it time to eat? I think I'm hungry."

Cora glanced at me, as if to say that she didn't mind the mistaken
identity, and moved to stand next to my mother. "Let's go on back to
the kitchen and find something for you to eat."

Her fingers slid from Chloe's hair as she allowed herself to be led
back to the kitchen. Without thinking, I moved in behind the chair and
picked up the braiding right where my mother had left off. I recalled
which strands to hold back and which to tuck over and under, just as
much as I remembered what it felt like for my mother to stand so close
to me and touch my hair no matter how much I didn't want to.

When I was finished, I took the rubber band Chloe had been holding and wound it tightly around the end of the braid. I moved in front of her to see and smiled. Despite the fact that she still held a lot of her baby fat in her cheeks, pulling her hair away from her face made her newly emerging cheekbones more prominent. And now that she didn't have her long, lank strands hanging in her face, I could see her dark blue eyes that I'd hardly seen since she was a little girl. "You look very pretty, Chloe."

She narrowed her eyes suspiciously before jumping out of her chair to peer into the mirror over the table. She examined herself for a long moment, turning her head from side to side before leaning forward and blinking as if to make sure it really was her in the reflection.

"Do you like it?" I asked with hesitation, never knowing what sort of response I might get.

"It doesn't suck."

Emboldened by her not completely negative response, I pressed on. "Do you want me to get some eye makeup remover and see what you look like without the eyeliner?"

She turned on me with a scowl and I braced myself. I must have closed my eyes, because Tripp's voice took me completely by surprise.

"My, my. What a vision of loveliness. Your hair looks real pretty, Chloe. I only had a little inkling of how pretty you were before, but now I can see I was right."

I watched as Chloe froze, whatever she'd been about to say shrunk back into her throat.

Tripp looked at her expectantly.

"Thank you?" she said.

His expression didn't change.

"Thank you, sir?"

"Much better." He turned toward me and his gaze meandered down to my toes, then back to my face. If it hadn't been Tripp—who'd seen me wearing much less in my beauty pageant days and at the pool in my smallest bikini trying to get a tan—I might have been more self-conscious. Still, something flickered behind his eyes that made me wish I had a long jacket to throw over me.

"What are you wearing, Vivi?"

I crossed my arms over my chest. "An old pair of pajamas. Don't worry; I'm not planning on wearing them outside of the house. And I wasn't expecting company." I stared pointedly at him.

"I came in through the kitchen. Was hoping to snag one of Cora's lemon bars." He took a step toward me, looking closely at my eyes. Quietly he said, "You okay, Vivi?"

"I am now," I said just as quietly.

"I'm hungry," Chloe said loudly.

Tripp faced her. "Why don't you go on back to the kitchen. Cora's getting lunch together for Carol Lynne and I'm sure she won't mind making you a sandwich, too."

"As long as it's gluten-free and vegetarian I can eat it. My dad says everything else is poison." She glared at me as if we were both remembering the chicken-fried steak and gravy I had once served her and her father for dinner.

Tripp shoved his hands in his pockets. "Well, I'm not one to go against your daddy or your upbringing, but seeing as how my doctor says I'm healthy as an ox, I figure I can offer you some good advice. I can pretty much promise you that there is nothing in Miss Cora's kitchen that will poison you. Having been the recipient of many of her meals, I can attest to the fact that not only are they nutritious but tasty, too."

I wanted to tell him to save his breath, that Chloe would starve herself if it meant winning her father's approval. And even then he'd find something lacking.

"Whatever. Sir," she added hastily. Then she headed back toward the kitchen but not before we could see her rolling her eyes.

Facing me, Tripp just looked at me without saying anything, making me nervous, which I was pretty sure was what he intended.

"I just took one pill. Carol Lynne was waiting down here with her suitcases and asking Chloe for a cigarette. I needed something to help me deal with it."

He didn't say anything.

I headed for the stairs. "I need to go get dressed and figure out what I'm going to do with Chloe, and try to reach Mark again."

"You didn't ask me why I was here."

I paused with my hand on the newel post. "Why are you here?"

"Because I found something with the remains that I wanted to show you. See if it rings any bells." He reached into his pocket and pulled out a clear plastic bag, just like the ones Tommy used in his workshop. Un-zipping the top, he reached inside and pulled out a gold ring. It was small enough to have been meant either for a child or for the pinkie finger of an adult.

He held it out to me and I took it. "It looks like it's only one half of a ring," he said, pointing to the top, where half of a heart, separated from its invisible partner, was hacked through the middle in a zigzag.

I took it and turned it around to better read the partial inscription.

I LO

Y

FOR

"I think it's supposed to read 'I love you forever.' " I gently ran my thumb over the inscription. "Was she wearing it?" I asked, trying not to think of this ring on the dead finger of the unknown woman.

"Not on her finger. She wore it on a chain—the kind of large-linked chain you find on an old-fashioned pocket watch."

Our eyes met, both of us thinking about the coincidence of the watch chain.

Tripp continued. "The other half of the ring would fit on top of this one so that it looked like a double band. I'm hoping somebody will recognize this, or maybe have seen the other half."

I continued rubbing my thumb over the gold ring, knowing I'd never seen it before, but having a flicker of memory that made me think that I had. "I don't think so. At least, I can't think of it right now—I'll let you know if anything comes to me." I quickly gave it back to him, eager to get it out of my hand. "I'll ask Cora and Carol Lynne. Maybe it might jog a memory."

He dropped the ring back into the bag. "Would you and Chloe want to go see a movie with me this weekend? Carrie Holmes—Tommy's old girlfriend—has refurbished the old theater and she's having a *Twilight* marathon, starting Friday. Thought Chloe might enjoy that, and I'd like to support Carrie's new business venture."

"Technically, Chloe's not supposed to enjoy anything. But I'll let you ask her. She's too afraid of you to say no. And assuming she's still here. No word from her father yet."

"Will do," he said as I began to climb the stairs. "You don't need those pills, Vivi. You were always a good problem solver on your own."

Without turning around, I said, "Yeah, well, when you find that old Vivi, let me know. Until then, the new Vivi does just fine with her pills." I kept walking without turning around until I got to my bedroom door and had closed it behind me.

I lay down on my bed and stared at the butterflies on the wallpaper, hearing in my mind Bootsie's voice telling me something about life being tough but us Walker women being tougher. I closed my eyes, for the first time since my return glad that Bootsie was gone so she couldn't see how very wrong she'd been.

Chapter 14

Adelaide Walker Bodine
INDIAN MOUND, MISSISSIPPI
JULY 1923

The light of the moon and stars and the song of the swaying cypress trees filled my room. My eyes stung from reading by candlelight long after Aunt Louise had come in to turn off my lamp and remind me to get my beauty sleep. But I could not let the story go, and still clutched F. Scott Fitzgerald's *This Side of Paradise* in my arms as if to let it go would allow the characters to walk out of my life.

I wanted to talk to somebody about the book, but knew that Aunt Louise and Uncle Joe—both of whom believed in having only two books in the house, the Bible and the *Farmers' Almanac*—wouldn't approve. Especially when they found out that Sarah Beth had filched it for me from her mother's sitting room when I'd mentioned that I'd heard about the book and wanted to read it. I'd made the mistake of saying that to check the book out from the library, I needed a permission note from my parent or guardian, since I was just sixteen. I should have known that any mention of going against authority would have been like white on cotton to Sarah Beth.

I kicked off my covers, my nightgown sticking to my skin, the lace curtains moving languidly in the muggy breeze. I closed my eyes, still picturing John as the book's hero, Amory, and me as the wild and reckless Eleanor, hoping to fall asleep with the characters whispering in my dreams.

Something hard hit the wood floor, right inside the window. I jerked up, praying it wasn't a disgusting hard-shelled june bug flying into my room. The dark-wood posts of the bed stretched long fingers over the shadowed floor, and for a moment I was paralyzed with fear, wondering if I was no longer alone.

The sound came again, but this time I saw the small stone hit the floor and roll to a stop next to its shadowed sister.

"Adelaide? Are you awake?" a loudly whispering but definitely masculine voice called from the lawn below.

I ran to the window and stuck my head out to peer into the moonwashed yard. John stood in the middle of my rosebushes, looking up at me. His white shirt, rolled up on his forearms like the last time I'd seen him, gleamed with the same brightness as his hair, making me think of the white marble angels Mrs. Heathman had in her back garden. I wondered if he knew that roses had thorns, and how he was going to explain all those snags and holes in his trousers.

"What are you doing here? If my uncle Joe sees you, he's like to get his shotgun after you."

He didn't say anything right away, but stood staring up at me. "What's in your hair?"

I thought of the june bug again and quickly reached up, hitting something soft. Groaning inwardly, I flicked both hands through my hair, pulling out the twists of fabric I'd stuck in it before I'd gone to bed in the hopes of giving myself curls. Aunt Louise said I couldn't get one of those new permanent waves, but one of my friends at school had sworn this would work.

I quickly ducked back inside, ripping them out—and a lot of hair in the process—not caring to think about what my half-curled hair would look like. I stuck my head back out the window as if nothing had happened. "I'm supposed to be asleep," I said, realizing that he could have probably figured that out on his own.

"We need your help."

"We?"

"Willie and me. Mostly me. Willie is completely ossified, and can't stand up on his own." He stopped whispering and looked around as if he'd heard something. I was quiet, too, listening to the screech of a bobcat somewhere in the night. "Come down so I can talk to you."

It didn't occur to me that I could say no. I ducked under the window and ran to the bedroom door, grateful that I had the large room with the old bed near the rear kitchen stairs. As long as I avoided slamming any doors, I was home free.

Barefoot, I crept down the stairs to the kitchen, the light from the windows guiding my way toward the back door. The grass was cool beneath my feet as I lifted my nightgown so Aunt Louise wouldn't find any grass stains on my hem.

John met me at the corner of the house, his hair still glowing like a halo. I skidded to a stop, suddenly aware that all I wore was a long white nightgown. It had little-girl ruffles around the throat and at the wrists, but when I heard John's intake of breath, I knew they made no difference.

Without saying anything, he reached for my hand and I took it, then allowed him to lead me down the front drive, where I could see Sarah Beth's new car. Peering closer, I saw the forms of two people, each slumped over their respective doors. I couldn't see their faces, but I figured it had to be Sarah Beth and Willie.

"What happened?"

John opened Willie's door, catching him by his tie before he slid out onto the drive. "A little too much hooch. Don't worry—it's good stuff. Nothing that could kill them. Although in the morning they might wish that it had."

A whiff of gasoline, vomit, and summer grass mixed with something strong and pungent traveled past my nose and I gagged. "What's that smell?"

I felt John staring at me in the darkness. "We went to a new gin joint near Leland. Sarah Beth upchucked in the backseat. I tried to clean it up with an oil rag but I think I just smeared it. I need you to show me Willie's room and I'll carry him to his bed. Can't leave him passed out in the roses."

"A gin joint? But Willie doesn't drink. Uncle Joe and Aunt Louise are teetotalers." In a hushed voice, I added, "And it's illegal." I felt stupid saying that, recalling Sarah Beth and her flask the last time I'd seen her at the Ellis plantation. But she was different. Her parents drank wine with their supper, and I knew her father kept spirits locked in the bottom drawer of his desk in his study. Sarah Beth knew where he'd kept the key and had shown me.

She'd explained that it was illegal only to sell or distribute alcohol, not drink it. Because I knew she wouldn't appreciate my logic, I didn't bother pointing out that her father had to get the alcohol into their house by somebody buying and selling it.

John's teeth shone in the dark and I knew he was smiling. "Well, now, I don't like to contradict a lady, but your cousin most definitely drinks. I've seen him worse off than tonight, too." He reached in and lifted Willie from the backseat, easily throwing him over his shoulder like a sack of picked cotton.

He looked at me expectantly.

"This way," I said. "But you've got to be real quiet. My aunt and uncle have the room next to his."

"Does your uncle sleep with his shotgun?"

I couldn't tell if he was being serious. "He might," I said over my shoulder. "So you'd better hush."

Lifting my nightgown again, I led the way to the kitchen through the back door, then up the stairs. Turning to put my finger to my lips—realizing too late that he couldn't see me in the darkened hallway—I went up the short flight of stairs, then opened the door to the second hallway where the rest of the bedrooms were, then tiptoed to Willie's bedroom.

I pulled down the bedspread and sheets before John dumped my cousin on the bed, a small groan coming from Willie's open mouth. John knelt by his feet and took off one shoe, so I did the other, wanting to be helpful.

"Go get a washbasin and put it by the side of the bed."

I grabbed the bowl off Willie's dresser and put it on the floor by the bed while John flipped Willie over onto his stomach. "So he doesn't choke if he throws up," he explained, making me wonder how John knew what to do.

When he was finished, we stared at Willie's still form, only the loud sound of his breathing telling us that he was still alive.

"Will he be okay?" I whispered.

"It might take a couple of days, but he'll be fine." Putting his hand on my back, he led me toward the door. "You might want to change your clothes. I'll need you to go with me to Sarah Beth's house so I can get her inside to her room."

Letting a boy see me in just my nightgown was scandalous enough. Sneaking out of the house at night with a boy would be enough to send my aunt into heart palpitations. "Can't she just stay here?" I whispered back.

"No. Her parents are still out at a party, and if they find her gone when they get back, they're going to send her to a convent in France."

I'd heard the threat many times, but I took it seriously now after her stint at Miss Portman's school. It wouldn't be as easy for her to be expelled and come home if she was halfway across the world. "What if the door's locked?"

"We'll figure it out. Now go get some clothes on." There was something about his confidence that seemed to feed my own, and I could almost believe that he and I could will ourselves past a locked door.

He waited out in the hall while I got dressed in the dark, slipping on the dress I'd worn the day before but not bothering with stockings. Hopefully this wouldn't be a social call where I'd be seeing anybody who cared.

I'd already opened my door before I'd thought to try to run a brush through my hair, and as I led John to the kitchen door, I prayed we wouldn't be anywhere near a light, where he could get a good look at me.

As I stepped off the porch, he grabbed my hand, stopping me. "Hey, not so fast."

"What about Sarah Beth?"

He smiled at me in the moonlight. "She'll be all right for a little bit. I just never get the chance to see you alone."

He moved toward me, but I took a step back, remembering everything Aunt Louise had told me about young men.

"Are you afraid of me?"

I shook my head. A cloud passed over the moon as a breeze blew over us, bringing with it the scent of rain and the song of the cypress trees.

"What's that noise?" he asked.

"The trees. They say it's the sound of spirits trapped inside the trunks, and the wind allows them to sing."

"Could be—sounds spooky enough."

We both looked toward the swamp, where the moonlight skipped over the tops of the trees as if it were too scared to cut through the dark spaces. Even on the brightest nights, it always seemed darker in the swamp, a line drawn between the firmer earth and the soft swampland as if the world had drawn a curtain.

John and I faced each other without saying anything, listening to the night sounds of the tree frogs and the trees in the wind. "Do you believe in ghosts?" he asked, his voice soft.

I started to shake my head, then stopped. "I'm not supposed to—at least, Aunt Louise and Pastor Barclay say I'm not. But it just seems to me that sometimes a life's not really over when it ends. Maybe some people are allowed to come back to finish something. Or to say good-bye."

I thought of my mother and how I'd sat in the dark for hours waiting for her to come back and tell me good-bye. I'd heard that if you stared in a mirror in the dark for long enough, a departed loved one would come back with a final message. I couldn't admit to John that I still paused in front of a mirror if I passed one in the dark.

"I bet if ghosts were real they'd live in the swamp." He took a step closer but this time I didn't step back. "Willie says in the winter the ground goes dry and you can walk right across the swamp from one side to the other. Have you ever done that?"

"No. Aunt Louise says I can't. It's too dangerous—lots of big, poisonous spiders. And bobcats."

He reached up and touched my hair, making me think that I might have forgotten one of the strips of fabric. "Do you always do what you're told?"

I looked up into his eyes where the moon made them shine like stars, or maybe that was my imagination. "Yes," I said quietly. I wanted to tell him that I didn't always obey because I was afraid of getting in trouble, but that I was afraid of disappointing my aunt and uncle like I'd disappointed my mother. If they left me, I didn't know where else I could go. But I said nothing, any words I might have spoken swallowed by the gentle press of his lips against mine.

He pulled back. "How old are you?"

"Sixteen." Emboldened by his kiss, I asked, "How old are you?"

"Twenty-one."

I thought for a moment. "Uncle Joe is six years older than Aunt Louise."

His teeth shone again in the moonlight. "Is that a proposal?"

My cheeks felt like they were on fire, and I was glad he couldn't see me blushing. "No!" To hide my embarrassment, I added, "Is that why you didn't ask me to come out with you tonight? Because I'm too young? Sarah Beth is only a year older than me, you know."

He stopped smiling and leaned close to me, blocking out the moonlight. "No, Adelaide. I didn't invite you because I don't want to corrupt you. You're the one good, honest thing in this crazy, crooked world. I can't see you hoofing it up on a table in a gin joint, and I don't want to. You're different from all the other girls. That's what I like about you."

"I know how to dance the Charleston—Sarah Beth taught me," I protested, not really hearing his words but instead seeing myself as he did—dull and boring. A baby just out of diapers.

He threw back his head and laughed loudly enough that I worried my aunt and uncle would hear. "I'll let you show me sometime, then," he said, leaning in even closer to kiss me lightly.

I held on to his arms so he couldn't pull away. "Is that why you didn't introduce me to those people at the Ellis plantation?"

His teeth disappeared and I sensed his mood change. "Don't you be thinking about them, Adelaide. I didn't introduce you because they're not a part of your life and you won't be seeing them again."

I remembered how he'd seemed so familiar with them, and had called the man by his first name. "Are they a part of your life?"

He took both my hands and squeezed. "For now—but just for a little bit. I'm trying to earn enough money so I can start my own business and settle down. It won't be forever; I promise." Leaning forward, he kissed me gently.

I wanted to ask him what those people had to do with his earning extra money, but he was pulling me toward the front of the house. "Come on; let's go get Sarah Beth home."

I ran with him, feeling the presence of the swamp behind me, the black curtain almost pressing against my back. I held tightly to John's hand, somehow knowing that he wouldn't let go.

John drove as fast as he could, with all the windows down, hoping to create enough of a breeze to cool us off and to air out the stench coming from the backseat. I kept turning around to make sure Sarah Beth was all right, but she seemed completely unaware of the rest of the world. I placed my hand under her nose twice to make sure she was breathing, because she looked like a dead person thrown in a heap in the corner of the backseat.

Down the block from Sarah Beth's house, we passed a pickup truck with SCOTS FEED AND SEED on the side, looking out of place in the neighborhood. John caught my glance and said, "It's how you and I are going to get back home tonight."

I nodded, recalling Mr. Peacock telling that John lived with the Scots because of a family connection. I'd assumed that story had been made up, too, along with the one about John's weak lungs.

He parked at the end of the driveway and turned off the engine. "It's only about midnight, so her parents shouldn't be home yet. Sarah Beth said the front door usually stays unlocked until Mr. and Mrs. Heathman are home for the night." He leaned forward over the dash, inspecting the darkened windows and the porch with one single but huge lantern hanging over the front door. "You wait here and I'll go check."

More clouds had gathered overhead, blocking the moon and making it harder to see. I watched as John ran across the front lawn, ducking into the shadows formed by the trees. Crouching, he ran up the front steps and turned the knob. I held my breath, waiting for the door to open.

Instead, John jumped over the porch railing and into the boxwoods, ducking his head so it couldn't be seen from the front door. It was opening slowly, and I let out my breath with relief as I recognized Mathilda. She and Bertha lived in a room off the kitchen, and I was grateful that it was Mathilda and not her mother opening the door. I was about to lean over and call to her from the window, when I saw a figure standing behind her. The foyer light was on and I got a good look at the tall black boy who I recognized as the same boy I'd seen back at the Ellis plantation.

Not really knowing why, I shrank down into my seat so I couldn't be seen, but still high enough that I could see through the front windshield. Somebody flicked off the inside light, but I peered out to where the light from the porch lantern reached.

Almost as if he felt my eyes on him, he looked up and spotted the car. Without pause, he jumped down the stairs, right past where John was hidden, and ran toward it. I was so scared I almost passed out, until I figured it was because I'd been holding my breath so long, as if he could have heard my breathing from where I sat.

"Hey!"

I looked past the boy to see John coming out of his hiding spot, running awkwardly to where the boy had stopped. He spotted John and nodded, as if they knew each other, then spoke quietly for a moment before they approached the car together.

Leaning into my window, John said, "This here's Robert. I hurt my foot jumping over the railing, so he's going to help us get Sarah Beth inside."

I looked from his face to Robert's, trying not to think too hard about what Aunt Louise would say. Or Mr. and Mrs. Heathman. I figured that whatever we needed to do had better happen pretty fast or we'd have to answer to all three of them.

John opened my car door and I stepped out, glad to take a deep breath of fresh air. Robert nodded at me, then opened the door to the backseat. John made to reach inside, but I held him back.

"Wait a minute." I straightened Sarah Beth's clothes as best I could, making sure the hem of her dress was pulled as far down over her legs as I could get it. As I moved back, my hand caught on one of her long strands of pearls and I felt the string snap as the *tap-tap* sound of tiny pearls hitting the leather seat filled the quiet.

John laid his hand softly on my shoulder for a brief moment. "Don't worry. I can fix it. Just leave everything there."

I stood back and watched as John gently took Sarah Beth under the arms and slid her to the edge of the seat by the door, then stood her up where Robert was waiting. John held her upright as Robert put an arm under her knees and another around her shoulders, then lifted her as if she weighed nothing.

As much as I tried not to, I thought about what would happen if Mr. and Mrs. Heathman came home now and saw their unconscious daughter in the arms of a colored man. Men had been hanged for less. I wasn't supposed to know these things, according to Uncle Joe, who never left his newspapers lying about when he was finished reading them. Women were supposed to keep their minds focused on their homes and families and let the men worry about the rest.

But when I went to the market with Aunt Louise, or stood near the adults congregating on the steps after church, or even stopped at the sharecroppers' fruit stands on the side of the road, I'd hear whispers about lynchings and burnings for reasons that didn't make a lot of sense to me.

"Hurry," I whispered sharply, causing both men to glance behind them, as if expecting two headlights piercing the dark.

Robert walked quickly while John limped behind him. I ran to put my arm around John's waist, not minding the feel of his weight pressing down on me.

Mathilda was holding the door open as we walked inside and our eyes met for a moment. She closed the door behind us, then looked expectantly at John, as if acknowledging he was in charge.

"I'll wait here," he said, hopping over to a hall bench. "You and Adelaide go show Robert where to take Sarah Beth."

Mathilda and I led the way to Sarah Beth's bedroom, with its new modern furniture. It was sleek and smooth and shiny—all things that my old bedroom furniture was not.

Robert gently laid Sarah Beth on the bed and, after a brief glance at Mathilda, left the room. She and I didn't speak as we set about undressing the unconscious girl and putting on her nightgown. I had the foresight to grab a ceramic bowl from her dresser and place it on the floor near her head. When I straightened I saw Mathilda watching me.

"Don't tell my mama about Robert, and I won't tell yours about tonight," she said quietly. Her voice was lower than I'd thought it would be.

"I knew you could talk." The words were out of my mouth before I could call them back.

She gave me a little smile. "I only talk if'n I have somethin' to say."

I regarded her in the darkness as we listened to Sarah Beth's soft snores. "My mama's dead."

She looked at me with the same glance Sarah Beth gave me when I was stating the obvious. "Who you call mama don' have to be blood. My mama call a bunch of other chil'ren her own. It don't make her love no less special."

"Adelaide!" John's loud whisper carried up the stairs. "You need to hurry."

I turned back to Mathilda. "You're good at keeping secrets, aren't you?"

She nodded solemnly. "Are you?"

"Of course."

"Adelaide!" John's voice sounded even more urgent.

I ran toward the doorway, Mathilda's voice making me pause for a moment: "I be real good at keepin' secrets. You remember that, okay?"

I smiled back at her, then ran down the stairs to where John was waiting at the open door. Robert was nowhere in sight.

"Can you drive?" he asked.

"No. I mean, I've never tried."

He grinned that heart-stopping grin that I pictured when reading one of my novels about a handsome hero. "Well, looks like tonight is your time to learn. I can't drive with my foot banged up like this."

He took my hand and pulled me out onto the porch, shutting the front door quietly behind him. "You're not afraid to learn, are you?"

I shook my head, thinking that as long as he was with me, I could do anything.

"That's my girl," he said. He took a step forward, forgetting about his bad foot, and wobbled until I wrapped my arm around his waist. He smiled down at me and I almost tripped us both. "We're a great team, Adelaide."

I'm not sure how I managed to get us home, having only a vague memory of stalling the engine about a dozen times, but the dreamlike quality of the night stayed with me until morning, when I finally fell asleep with the rising sun, my last thought about Mathilda as we'd faced each other in the darkened room while she told me that she was really good at keeping secrets.

Chapter 15

Vivien Walker Moise
INDIAN MOUND, MISSISSIPPI
APRIL 2013

After a desultory supper in the dining room, the table set with the family silver—slightly tarnished—monogrammed china, and crystal, and with my mother, who divided her time staring at her food as if wondering what to do with it, Chloe's less-than-stellar table manners, and a silently brooding Tommy, I was happy to escape into the kitchen to help Cora with the cleanup.

I told her she could go home early, leaving me alone with my thoughts to dry and put away the dishes. I still hadn't heard from Mark, and neither had Chloe. I'd called Imelda—who was staying at the house in case Chloe came back—to tell her that if Mark called to give him my number and tell him it was urgent. I even considered calling the police to let them know where she was, but figured I had at least until after spring break before I had to deal with anybody reporting her as truant. I found myself crossing my fingers a lot, hoping Mark would call and we could sort something out before things got drastic.

Exactly what I wanted to have happen wasn't clear in my head. I was far from being an expert in child development, but it was obvious even to me that Chloe was in desperate need of parenting, and return-

ing her to LA seemed so wrong. But so did her staying with me. All I
knew for sure was that each pill I took helped me not worry so much.
Just like my namesake, I figured I'd think about it tomorrow.

From the kitchen window I could see the light folding in on the day,
and I recalled the dazzling sunsets of my girlhood that the flatland of
the delta made so spectacular. Tommy, Bootsie, and I would sit outside
in the garden and watch them together, the spill of light pressed against
the horizon gradually consumed by the encroaching night. Bootsie had
always finished the show with a pat on our knees and a reassuring
"Don't worry. It'll be back tomorrow." Her hopefulness was what
helped me sleep at night, helped me believe that some things really did
last forever.

After checking on Chloe and Carol Lynne in the den, where they
sat together on the sofa in front of an old episode of *Gilmore Girls*, I
hung up the damp dish towel on the handle of the ancient oven, then
let myself out the back door. I walked past the empty garden toward
the cypress. The yellow tape was still there, but Tripp said it would be
gone in the next day or two. Tommy was eager to begin chopping up
the tree to use the wood for various building projects, including recon-
structing his workspace in the old cotton shed. I felt oddly comforted
by the knowledge that I could revisit my old friend after it became part
of something else.

Without my being aware of it, my feet seemed to be leading me
there. The yellow tape where I'd knotted it had been torn again, and I
wondered whether Chloe or my mother was responsible. Wherever one
was, I found the other, and I wasn't sure if I should be reassured by this.
Chloe would give me a wide-eyed "help me" look every time Carol
Lynne took her hand, but I didn't intervene. Because I also saw the way
Chloe had appointed herself a sort of bodyguard for my mother, always
following her around even when Carol Lynne didn't ask.

"I don't want her to mess with my stuff," Chloe had told me when
I'd asked her about it. I knew better than to tell her that I thought it
sweet—if not downright unexpected—to discover that Chloe had a
nurturing side. I pushed aside the memory of her excitement about my
pregnancy, and how she'd put a sonogram photo on her bulletin board
in her bedroom. Some memories were too close to the hurt to be pressed
on again.

I walked through the broken tape and stood at the edge of the hole, the scent of rich, moist earth permeating the air. *I love you forever.* I wondered who'd worn the other half of the ring, and if they'd missed this unknown woman when she was gone.

Streaks of pink and orange littered the sky, casting a rosy glow on the ground like a benediction. I looked up in time to see the last sliver of light leave the sky like a sigh, and I stared at the spot for a long time, wishing I could call the colors back.

A light flicked on in the cotton shed, and I saw Tommy pass by the open window. I'd been meaning to talk with him, so I headed for the door. A blue tarp had been stretched over the broken roof, but the encroaching planting season had stalled any permanent repairs.

I knocked gently on the door, and when I didn't hear a reply, I let myself inside. The same messy desk greeted me, along with several additional mugs of half-drunk coffee with curdled cream on top.

"Tommy?" I called loudly.

"Up here."

"Are you decent?"

"Always."

I smiled as I ascended the stairs, wondering how old a sibling had to get before he stopped saying all the old stock responses from childhood.

He was sitting at the worktable, an old-fashioned pocket watch in front of him, its back removed to display its inner workings like a patient on a surgeon's table. The bright overhead light shone on Tommy's head, turning the strands of hair white.

"You come to get those little bags to sort through the hatbox?" he asked without looking up.

"I actually came just to talk. But I can get the bags now, too."

He jerked his head toward a tall tower of makeshift shelves made of plastic milk crates. "They're in a box over there somewhere."

I found the box and grabbed a handful before sitting down on a turquoise chair that looked a lot like our old high school desk chairs. "Nice chair."

He shrugged. "When they tore down the old high school they offered all the furnishings to whoever wanted them. This chair was the only thing left by the time I got there, and only because it was back behind the baseball field, buried in some weeds."

"Nice choice. Makes me feel sixteen again."

He just grunted and continued to work.

"So, how's the cotton business?" I asked.

"Horrible. Wonderful. All of the above. Answer'll be different depending on the year and the month."

"Well, what about right now?"

I didn't know if it was the chair I was sitting in or the way he was looking at me, but I suddenly felt like a kid sent to the principal's office for passing notes in class. "Three years ago, I had the trifecta of good cotton growing—perfect weather, great market price for cotton, and a crop failure in China. I harvested three bales per acre and was able to put a lot of money in the bank. Which was good, because the last two years have been piss-poor. Too much rain, too much heat, and low market prices. The only reason I'm still hanging on is because some of my neighbors aren't."

He pushed away from the worktable and faced me. "I've been doing some speculating in cotton futures and options—helped pad the coffers and pay the light bill. And it helped me buy out my neighbors, who couldn't wait to pack up and ship out after the last few years we've had. I got almost six thousand acres all together now—not really a lot when you think about how much I need to plant just to break even. I've diversified some, too—rice, corn, soybeans. I'm still a cotton farmer, though. Even if it kills me, I'll always be a cotton farmer."

I stared at him for a long time, wondering why I couldn't see any defeat in his shoulders and heard only pride in his voice. "What about this year's crop? *Farmers' Almanac* telling you anything useful about the weather?"

He gave me a lopsided grin. "Planting mostly cotton—taking over two of my soybean fields, even—because it looks like it's going to be a good year for cotton. Now all we can do is pray for good weather."

"And for China to have a crappy crop."

He smiled the first genuine smile I'd seen since my return. "You're catching on, Booger."

I picked up a piece of wadded-up paper from the top of a milk crate and tossed it at him, beaning him on the temple. "Please don't call me that. I'm not six anymore."

"Nope. You sure aren't." He gave me a sad smile, and I wondered if he was thinking about our growing-up years with Bootsie and Emmett here on the farm, our unconventional but mostly happy existence where Tommy hardly noticed that we didn't have a mother or father like the other kids at school. But I had. I felt their absence the way the fields missed the rain.

"So why do you do it?" I asked, because I really wanted to know. There was a lot of world outside the Mississippi Delta, and to my knowledge he hadn't seen any of it.

He studied the backs of his hands placed flat on the thighs of his jeans. "Because it's more than just what I do. It's who I am." He leaned back to rest his elbows on the worktable. "I can charge ridiculous amounts of money to a gentleman in Australia to fix his two-hundred-year-old timepiece, but I will never be a clockmaker. Being a cotton farmer is who I am. And I'm okay with that. Heck, I'd even say I enjoy the challenge. It's a dying industry; that's for sure. But I don't want to let it go. I can't. It's the fabric of our lives." He winked, but I could see the sadness in his eyes. I saw hope there, too. He'd always been that way, always believing that if the sun rose in the morning, it meant we'd been given another chance to try again. I'd just seen it as another day I was still stuck in Mississippi.

That had been our one fundamental difference growing up: I was always looking beyond the horizon for what was next, my heels merely skimming the surface, but Tommy was happiest in the fields with Emmett, his feet firmly planted in the fertile soil of our home.

I straightened in my chair, wondering if I'd thought the chairs were that uncomfortable when I was sixteen. "Before I forget, Tripp showed me a piece of jewelry he found with the skeleton. It's a ring—well, half of a ring. It has a heart on it that's cut in two, along with a little message. We think it's supposed to read 'I love you forever.' It was hung around her neck with a watch chain."

His eyebrows lifted.

"Yeah. I thought that was an interesting coincidence, too. We don't know where the other half is, and I'm pretty sure I've never seen the ring before. But . . ." I stopped, still not sure why it had seemed so familiar when Tripp had shown it to me.

"But what?"

"Well, it just seemed like I'd seen it before. I was hoping maybe the mention of the ring would jog your memory."

He shook his head. "Nope. But I'll ask Tripp to show it to me just in case. Although even if I'd seen it, not sure I'd remember. I'm a guy. I'm not supposed to remember stuff like that."

He turned back to the watch and picked up a tiny tweezers, and I knew he was dismissing me, wanting me to leave so he could go back to his solitude, but I had one more question for him.

"Why aren't you married? You and Carrie Holmes were practically picking out china together when I was back in high school."

Tommy shrugged. "She married Bobby Limbocker instead. His family's less crazy than ours." He stood and rubbed his hands through his hair. "She had two kids and then bam, Bobby starts running around on her and she dumps him. Guess it's been two years now."

"That's sad. I always liked Carrie. I would have liked to have her for a sister-in-law." I smiled up at him. "Still could, I guess."

He shook his head. "That train done left the station. She's only got time for those kids and her new movie theater."

Somewhere in my hazy brain, an idea sparked. "Speaking of which, Tripp is taking Chloe and me to see a *Twilight* movie marathon tomorrow. Why don't you come?"

"Naw. Not this close to planting. Got to make sure the fields are ready for some seed."

"I know you've been making sure the fields are ready since February. One night isn't going to kill you."

"It might," he said. "And I've got to make sure the soil's dry enough and not so heavy, so I can plant the seed without killing my tractors. I can't afford to buy a new one right now."

"Plant while you still need a coat," I said, quoting Emmett. "Isn't it getting a little late to start your planting?"

"Yeah, but with all the rain we've been having, things have been pushed back. There's always something to keep me up at night, and busy as a long-tailed cat on a porch filled with rocking chairs during the day. Doesn't allow me much time or energy for anything else."

"Is there anything I can do to help? It's been a while since I've been around a tractor, but I'm sure it's like riding a bicycle."

"Nah—but thanks. I don't have time right now to teach you all the new equipment. Besides, I've already hired my extra workers and they need the money."

I nodded, understanding the scarcity of workers and what the farmers needed to do to keep them happy and coming back every season. "Well, think about coming with us—you need a break. Not to mention we might need another pair of hands for Chloe."

Tommy snorted. "That's for sure. She's . . . different. Unique, you could say. But I like her. She reminds me a bit of you when you were her age."

I crossed my arms over my chest. "How so?"

"Oh, I don't know. It's like she's trying so hard to push people away and show them that she doesn't care if they like her or not. She's working so hard at it that she's got to be feeling just the opposite. I think that's why you were such a little snot. You were a real fire ant as a kid."

I narrowed my eyes at him. "You're just making that up. And people only called me a fire ant because of my red hair."

"Uh-huh," he said. He stretched. "I've got to be up at four, so I'd best turn in. Thanks for the invite—I'll think about it."

"You do that," I said, slipping out of my chair. I reached up and impulsively kissed him on the cheek. "Good night, Tommy."

He gave me a lopsided grin as I turned and headed toward the stairs.

"Good night, Booger," he called after me.

If I'd had something to fling in his direction, I would have. Instead I was left to contemplate the relationship between siblings, and how even though we would always get older, our relationship never really would.

Chapter 16

Vivien Walker Moise
INDIAN MOUND, MISSISSIPPI
APRIL 2013

"Why can't we take your Jaguar?" Chloe asked, her voice more whine than separate syllables. She stood squinting in the bright sunlight, looking overheated in her black shirt and jeans, pretending to text something on her phone. She only had one quasi-friend, Hailey, who liked to hold her adolescent power over Chloe by never responding to any of Chloe's texts. But that never stopped Chloe from trying.

We stood in front of Tripp's and Tommy's Ford F-150s, both white with double cabs, deciding who sat where. I'd convinced Tommy to at least join us for supper at Lillo's in Leland, understanding that he needed to get back early because planting started in the morning. He'd included Carol Lynne in the invitation, saying he'd drive her home after we ate.

I'd been nervous, wondering which persona she'd be in, and had felt more than a little relief when I saw her braids and jeans and leather sandals instead of her house slippers. It wasn't that I'd be embarrassed if she showed up in Bootsie's dress. It was just that it was easier to recognize her as my mother this way, to give me a glimmer of the old

Carol Lynne. And maybe it would help her recognize herself so that she could finally start answering all of my whys. Tommy had told me it didn't work that way, but I couldn't see that as a reason not to hope. At least it would give me something to justify my return to Indian Mound.

"Because I'm driving and I don't want to be seen in that," Tripp said, indicating my coupe. "Besides, all three of us wouldn't fit, and I don't think you'd want to ride in the trunk."

Chloe screwed up her face, her round, babyish cheeks completely at odds with her heavy eye makeup. Her hair was once again held back in a French braid, and I wondered if this had become a routine for Chloe and Carol Lynne. I knew enough to know that it wouldn't have been initiated by Carol Lynne, who continued to refer to Chloe as JoEllen, but the fact that Chloe would seek her out each day softened some of the hard places inside me.

"There's a small backseat if Chloe wants to sit there," I offered, preferring the car. Riding in Tripp's pickup truck brought back too many memories.

Tripp studied me and I tried to mentally prepare myself. "That's a real nice car, Vivi. I wouldn't have expected anything less from you."

He smiled, and I waited. Chloe did, too, as if she were already aware of how Tripp and I communicated.

"You always were looking for that new, shiny thing that would be better than the slightly less-than-new shiny thing you already had." *Yet here you are.* It was almost as if he'd spoken those last words aloud.

"Fine," I said. "Let's take the truck."

Chloe groaned. "How am I supposed to get inside? Aren't there supposed to be steps or something?"

Tripp moved up behind her. "If I didn't know it already, I'd say you must be from California." He winked at me above her head. "It's called a running board, and yes, some trucks have them. Mine and Tommy's don't because they get stuck in the mud when we're off-roading."

Her face remained scrunched, as if Tripp were speaking Swahili.

"Never mind. If you go dove hunting with me when the season starts in October, I'll show you what I mean."

Before I could remind him that Chloe wouldn't be here in October, he'd moved behind her to place his hands on either side of her waist. "Go ahead and grab on to that handle there. I'm going to count, and when I get to three I want you to bend your legs and jump up. I'll help you, so don't think you have to jump all the way by yourself."

She tried to pull herself free, her words of protest already on her lips. "I'm too heav—"

As if Tripp already knew what she was going to say, he started to count. "One . . . two . . . three!"

Chloe did as she'd been told and jumped, landing easily on the bottom of the doorjamb before sitting down on the leather seat.

"Light as a feather," he said. "Now scooch in—it's Vivi's turn." He faced me. "You ready?"

"I can climb in. . . ."

As if he'd suddenly grown deaf to the sound of protesting females, he put his hands on my waist and began counting. Knowing I had no choice, I grabbed the handle, then bent my legs and jumped when he got to three. I sat down on the edge of the bench seat and looked into his smiling eyes.

"Just like old times, isn't it, Vivi?"

The light in his eyes changed, and I knew he was remembering how I'd practice kissing with him in his daddy's pickup truck, so I'd be ready for the real thing when it happened. At the time I hadn't thought my request out of line. But now I could only cringe thinking about it.

Trying my best to distract myself, I fumbled for my seat belt, then helped Chloe find the buckle for hers.

It was a half-hour drive to Leland, and Tripp followed Tommy on the straight and flat ribbon of Highway 82. Tripp tuned in to a blues station on the radio, the music as rich and dark as the Mississippi River, and stirring up the ghosts of my past.

We passed only a handful of other vehicles, half of them white pickup trucks. "What's with all the white trucks?" Chloe asked.

"These Fords are the farmer's best friend," Tripp explained. "They can really take the beating a farmer's job gives them. And you'd know why they're white if you ever leaned your arm on the hood of a black or red truck in the middle of July. It's like to burn your skin right off."

"But where are all the people? It's like after a zombie apocalypse or something."

"Exactly what I was thinking," Tripp said without a glimmer of a smile. "Actually, though, farming these days is mostly done by machines instead of people. So a lot of the people who used to work the farms have left for the cities to find jobs. Not exactly the hustle and bustle of LA here, but I like it."

Chloe's expression made it clear that she thought Tripp had probably been dropped on his head at some point. "And what's this sh . . . stuff on the radio? Don't you have real music?"

Tripp frowned. "You're kidding me, right? This is Muddy Waters. Born and raised right here in the delta. He and Robert Johnson and B. B. King and a bunch of other guys from Mississippi invented the blues. Rock 'n' roll or whatever it is that you listen to these days wouldn't have ever happened if it hadn't been for the blues."

I thought if Chloe's eyes rolled any farther back in their sockets, she'd go permanently blind. "Never heard of 'em. Don't you have a station that plays regular music?"

Instead of answering, Tripp asked, "Do you know anything about Mississippi?"

She scowled for a moment before perking up. "Channing Tatum is from Mississippi."

"Who?" Tripp asked with disdain equal to that with which Chloe had dismissed his blues heroes. "You ever hear of William Faulkner?"

She stared at him blankly.

"Morgan Freeman? Jim Henson? Eudora Welty?"

Her expression didn't change.

He let out a heavy sigh. "What do they teach you in school in California?"

"Not about old dead people."

"Elvis Presley?" Tripp tried again.

"Heard of him. Wasn't his daughter married to Michael Jackson? Hailey's mom is a huge MJ fan and is always talking about him and playing his music. It's so last millennium."

It was Tripp's turn to roll his eyes. "You ever hear of Oprah Winfrey?"

Chloe actually sat up straighter. "She's from here?"

"Yep. From a little town about two hours east."

She stared out the window again, where the furrowed fields were interspersed with the occasional catfish farm. Not one to be easily impressed, she said, "I can see why they all left."

"That may be, but you can't grow cotton in the city," Tripp said, reaching over to raise the volume on the radio.

We rode without speaking the rest of the way, listening to the music, and I wondered if Tripp saw how Chloe's fingers had begun to tap with the rhythm without her even seeming to notice.

Muddy Waters crooned "You Can't Lose What You Ain't Never Had," and I sang along quietly. I knew every word from the forty-fives Carol Lynne had left behind along with her portable record player gathering dust in a closet. When I found myself missing her, I'd go listen to her records, memorizing the words as if they might have some secret message for me from her. But they never really did.

The smell of marinara sauce greeted us as we entered Lillo's, an Italian restaurant on Highway 82 that had been there since before I was born. It was run by one of the many Italian families who'd made their way from Sicily and other Italian ports into the delta at the beginning of the previous century. A girl I'd known from high school whose last name was Colotta had once invited me to Thanksgiving dinner to prove to me that they served meatballs and sauce with the turkey. I'd pretended disbelief just so I could see what it was like to be around a real family.

We were seated in the back room at a laminate-topped table. It was too early for the house band and the dancers—both circa 1950—and despite the nostalgia I felt toward the whole scene, I was a little glad that I wouldn't have to listen to Chloe's comments about old people dancing with moves that didn't involve censoring.

Carol Lynne greeted everybody with enthusiasm but without using anybody's names. It was as if she was aware that she should know them but was too embarrassed to admit it. Bootsie had been a Sunday-night regular since I was a girl, and they'd have our plates waiting on the table when we came in. But Richie, our waiter, didn't recognize Tommy or me. I was unprepared for the needle jab into my otherwise medicated pillow of comfort, feeling almost as if a large part of my childhood had disappeared without my being aware that I'd let it go.

I felt marginally better when I saw that the menu hadn't changed all that much. Chloe studied it with a look of despair, no doubt calculating the carbs and calories in her head. Leaning toward her, I said, "The house salad is really yummy. And my favorite entrée is the spaghetti and meatballs. It's a large portion, but we can halve it if you'd like."

She continued to stare at the menu, her jaw set. Tripp turned to her, "I promise it's not poisoned. And I won't tell your daddy."

"Like he's going to call." She looked up, almost as surprised as I was at her words.

My eyes met Tripp's. The fact that Chloe's father hadn't called even to speak with her hadn't escaped his notice, either.

Carol Lynne reached across the table and patted Chloe's hand. "He'll call, JoEllen. You know he will." I knew she didn't know who or what we were talking about, yet it amazed me how aware she was of the cadences of a conversation, and the proper place to interject. I watched her for a moment, wondering if this new version of her was better than the one I'd known. It scared me a little to realize that I didn't really know.

Chloe didn't jerk her hand away, surprising me. Instead she smiled at my mother. "Yeah. You're probably right."

I watched as a woman at a nearby table kept glancing our way, then finally stood, a little girl on her hip and a boy of about six clinging to her hand. She was petite, with short, curly brown hair that made her look way too young to have two kids. But her face looked vaguely familiar and I wasn't surprised when she stopped by our table.

"Hello, Tommy," she said with a tentative smile.

Both Tommy and Tripp stood, and Chloe leaned toward me. "Why are they standing? Are we leaving already?"

I choked on my sip of water, understanding her confusion. She'd probably never seen her father stand when a woman walked into a room or approached his table.

"No, Chloe. It's just good manners."

She made a face and then turned to the visitor.

"Hi, Vivi. It's Carrie—Carrie Limbocker. I mean, Carrie Holmes. I've gone back to my maiden name." Turning toward the two men, she said, "Y'all sit. I'm just taking Bo to the restroom, but I wanted to stop by and say hey."

After returning to his seat, Tripp said, "We're heading out to your theater tonight. How's business?"

"Can't complain. We're not getting first-run movies because we're so small, but it's also an hour's drive to the nearest cineplex, and I think that's winning over a lot of people. I actually broke even in my first month of business."

"Congratulations," Tommy said without meeting her eyes.

Her eyes brightened as she regarded my brother, and I wished he'd look at her so he'd see.

The little girl on her hip, who looked to be about two years old, kept staring at me with dark brown eyes, as if she saw something she recognized.

Carrie smiled at my mother. "Hello, Miz Moise. It's good to see you again."

"It's good to see you, too," Carol Lynne replied with a big smile. I wondered if Carrie could tell that my mother had no idea who she was.

Carrie turned back to me. "I haven't seen you in years, Vivi. You're still as pretty as ever. I always expected to see you on one of the major networks as a news announcer or hard-hitting journalist. I guess I still do."

I felt Chloe's eyes on me. Forcing a smile, I said, "No, not quite. I tried at first, when I got to LA, but then I met someone and got married. This is my stepdaughter, Chloe. She's visiting." I waved my empty left hand at Carrie. "I'm divorced, too."

"We should start a club," she said, laughing, although her eyes looked sad. "It's nice to meet you, Chloe. Do you babysit?"

"She's not going to be here very long," I interjected before Chloe could answer.

"What about you?" Carrie asked, addressing me. "Are you back to stay?"

"I—"

"I need to go potty," Bo said, tugging on her arm. "And I don't want to go to the ladies' room."

Tommy stood. "I'll take him to the men's room, if you like."

Carrie smiled at him appreciatively. "Yes, thank you. Bo, please go with Mr. Moise and he'll take you."

Like a monkey, the small boy took a leap at Tommy, who caught him like a pro, then shifted him onto his back for a ride to the restroom.

I felt something pulling at my hair and then the little girl slid from her mother's arms and into my lap.

"That's Cordelia. I named her after my grandmother. It's old-fashioned but I think it suits her. And she likes you, which is saying something. She doesn't like just anybody."

I tried to hand her back to her mother, to tell them both that I wasn't good with children, but Cordelia had put her arms around my neck and rested her head on my chest.

"The reason I was asking about how long you're staying here," Carrie continued, "is because seeing you reminded me of how you were the school historian back in high school, and the editor of the paper, and what a good writer you were. I don't know if you knew, but the Indian Mound Library burned down two years ago and we've just built a new one—thanks to a generous donation by the International Rubberized Products Company, which has just moved its manufacturing plant to Indian Mound. But all the archives that were saved from the fire are now stored in the basement of the town hall and need to be sorted and organized—and maybe even written about, but that's another project. The historical society—I'm a member—couldn't pay you anything except our undying gratitude. We've just been hoping that the right person would present herself." She beamed at me.

"I . . . I, um, thank you. I'll think about it and let you know." My hand was patting the baby's back as if it knew what to do.

Lowering her voice, Carrie said, "I heard about that business of the skeleton found in your yard. They didn't have much to say in the paper."

I was glad to change the subject, but wished she'd chosen another topic. I shifted uncomfortably in my seat, not wanting to disturb the child in my lap. "That's because we don't know much about it other than that she was young and had given birth. I gave a sample of my DNA to see if there's a match."

Her eyes widened. "Maybe you'll want to organize the archives so you can dig for more information about your family if it comes out as a match."

I nodded halfheartedly. "Yeah. That's a plan. But I'm not really expecting a positive result. From what I remember my grandmother telling me, all of us Walker women are accounted for."

Carrie continued. "You could always talk with Mathilda Simms, just in case there was more than Bootsie knew or remembered to pass on."

I stared at her, wondering for a moment why the name sounded so familiar. "Mathilda?" I asked. "Bootsie's Mathilda? But she must be ancient by now." Cordelia stuck her thumb in her mouth and began twirling my hair with the fingers on her other hand.

"Oh, she is. I think she just celebrated her hundred and fourth birthday. They're hoping she'll make it into the *Guinness Book of World Records*. She's blind now, but her mind's as sharp as a tack. She lives over at Sunset Acres. I volunteer there whenever Mama can watch the kids, and I like to visit with her. She's always got lots to say."

Tommy came back from the restroom with Bo riding piggyback. When they reached the table, Bo slid down to the floor but seemed reluctant to leave Tommy's side.

Tripp leaned back in his chair, a satisfied smile on his face as he regarded Carrie's children clinging to my brother and me. "Looks like you found yourself a couple of babysitters if you're ever in a pinch, Carrie."

"I know, right?" Carrie said, not taking her eyes off Tommy. She leaned forward and extricated a reluctant Cordelia from my lap, then reached her hand out for Bo. "It's good seeing everybody. Hope to see y'all at the theater later tonight—I'll be working the ticket booth." Looking at Tommy, she said, "And don't be a stranger."

He looked into his glass of water and just pursed his lips while he gave her a quick nod. I wanted to reach over and rap him on his forehead with my knuckles.

As she walked away, Cordelia lifted her hand and waved bye-bye to me, and I was unprepared for the electric jolt around my heart. I turned around to see Tripp watching me closely.

The waiter returned to take our orders, and then the conversation turned to the next day's cotton planting and Tommy's hopes and expectations for the growing season, and continued until after the food was put in front of us. I was quiet, still remembering the sweet smell of Cordelia's hair, and being almost overwhelmed by the memories that had flooded back to me at hearing Mathilda's name and learning she was still alive. She was the closest bond I had remaining to Bootsie, and I was left wondering if I could find the courage to visit Mathilda and have to answer questions I'd probably prefer to avoid.

I looked up and found Tripp watching me with unreadable eyes, but knowing he was probably thinking the same thing. I focused on my plate of spaghetti, trying to think only about the food and how nice it was to see my brother again, and how having Chloe with me somehow made my heart lighter.

"Vivien?"

I looked up at my mother. I wondered how long it would be until she couldn't remember my name anymore, the thought sending a panicked sense of urgency thrumming through me.

"I'd like to go see Mathilda." Carol Lynne's eyes were clear and focused, and I was afraid to speak and break whatever spell she was under. "I need to ask her something."

I nodded. "Okay. I'll see about bringing you tomorrow, all right?"

She was staring at me, her head tilted like a person does in an art museum. "You've cut your hair. It's real pretty. I wish you'd let me braid it for you. It lets people see your beautiful cheekbones, and it's so much cooler in the summertime. But I know you don't like me touching your hair anymore. I'd like to, though. I miss it. I miss you."

My chest stung from unshed tears, my face hot all of a sudden. I held my breath, unable to speak even if I wanted to.

"Mathilda taught me how to braid hair. She's so clever; she knows so many things." With a slow smile I barely remembered, she leaned across the table and lowered her voice. "She's real good at keeping secrets."

"Like what?" I managed to ask, recalling what she'd said while we were standing at the jagged hole where the roots of the cypress tree grew through old bones. *She never had a chance to come back because she never left.* I kept seeing my own face superimposed over the skull, and I could even imagine the sound of crows, thick in the leaves of the tree.

Richie returned to our table to refill our waters, and when I looked back at my mother, her eyes had the same distant look I'd begun to recognize. I sucked in a breath, tasting disappointment and anger, and feeling completely and utterly hopeless.

I slid back from the table and grabbed my purse. I excused myself, then headed toward the ladies' room, knowing I wasn't fooling anyone except for maybe Carol Lynne, but too desperate to medicate my growing conscience to care.

Chapter 17

Carol Lynne Walker Moise
INDIAN MOUND, MISSISSIPPI
JULY 25, 1963

Dear Diary,

Jimmy Hinkle and me and a bunch of other kids went to Tchula last weekend to swim in Horseshoe Lake. I wore my new bikini that I bought with the money I earned working at the drive-in and Bootsie has no idea I have. She thinks all girls should be covered from their necks to their ankles, even if they're going swimming and it's a thousand degrees outside. Somebody brought their transistor radio and we all danced to this song called "Surfin' USA," and I danced in my bikini and Jimmy watched me.

I was too ashamed to tell everybody that I was afraid of the dark, muddy water, and how I don't like the way the catfish swim right up to you and touch your toes and legs. Mostly, though, I don't like the way you can't see the bottom. I think it reminds me too much of where we all are in our lives right now, and how you can't see what's coming but you've got to keep swimming anyway.

I have a big crush on Jimmy, so I held my breath and jumped right in with everybody else. There was beer and funny cigarettes, and after a while I felt just fine and not so afraid anymore, and learned how to stick my head under the water with my eyes open. I could see the catfish then, but not much else. But after sharing another cigarette, I didn't seem to care anymore.

Jimmy gave me a couple of cigarettes to take home with me, to help me deal with Bootsie. And I need help. Just being in the same room with her makes me want to scream. I wouldn't even talk to her for a couple of weeks after she slapped me, even though she tried to apologize. It happened and there's no taking it back.

She's been talking about getting me ready to go to Starkville to start at State in the fall. I know she always wanted to go to college, but that was her dream, not mine. I only applied so she'd stop asking and leave me alone. But now she's talking about which sorority I want to pledge and how many sets of sheets I should take with me.

I read Betty Friedan's book and I know now that I don't have time to waste going to college. I need to start living my life. It will pass me by if I'm stuck in a classroom learning home economics and enough math so that I can balance a household budget.

The Russians just sent a woman astronaut to the moon, the governor of Alabama is promising segregation forever, and Buddhist monks are burning themselves up on street corners in some place called Vietnam. There's too much going on in the world for me to spend the next four years trying to earn an MRS degree when I don't even want to get married.

Jimmy said that he's planning on moving to San Francisco, where his older brother lives in a house he shares with ten others, where everybody shares the cooking and the shopping and everybody takes care of everybody. He said there's room for more if I was interested. And then he kissed me, which made me decide that I am definitely interested. I guess I couldn't get much farther away from Mississippi than California.

Yesterday Mathilda caught me smoking one of Jimmy's cigarettes while I was sitting at my cypress tree. She must have felt strongly about smoking grass, because she came pretty close to the tree, although I could tell she kept looking for what she calls a haint. The bottle tree she put up is still there, and I told her she was safe, but the thought of those haints being stupid enough to crawl into a bottle made me laugh so hard that I could barely breathe.

She said I'd left the Greyhound bus schedule in my jeans pocket and she'd found it when she doing the laundry, and she wanted to know exactly where I was planning on traveling and did Bootsie know.

I've never been able to lie to Mathilda, so I told her what Jimmy and I were planning on doing. She just shook her head, and told me it would break my mama's heart. When I told her that my mama didn't have a heart she got mad, and I never saw Mathilda get mad before. She said that if Bootsie didn't have a heart it was because she'd given it all to me. And that I needed to understand that it wasn't me that made her leave when I was a baby, but that I was what had brought her back.

I told her I hadn't been waiting for my mama to come back home, that I'd grown used to her being gone and wished she'd stayed gone. I wanted Mathilda to see that Bootsie didn't want me to go farther than Starkville because she didn't want me to see more of the world than she had, that she wanted all the same things for me but not more. Mathilda said that it's okay to want more or new or different, but before I ran off to find those things, I needed to know first what I already had.

Looking around me, all I can see is a crazy house, a garden I don't know how to grow anything in, and a mama who never wanted me. I know I've got Cousin Emmett and the cotton fields and Mathilda, too, but none of that matters when you weigh them against all the other stuff. But all Mathilda said was to stop chasing ghosts, because I'll never catch them.

Then she marched right up to the tree and took my cigarette and smashed it under her shoe, saying I was on the road to ruin if I thought I could find the answers I needed with a cloudy head. As she walked away, I yelled at her that it wasn't answers I was looking for, but maybe a way where the questions wouldn't hurt so much.

She turned around and looked at me with sad eyes, and said I was only keeping secrets from myself, and that keeping secrets is a lonely way to live. She looked so sad that I wanted to ask her what secrets she must be keeping, but I was too mad, so I let her leave without saying anything.

I watched her until the screen door shut behind her, thinking on what she'd said about chasing ghosts, and still not understanding what she'd meant.

Chapter 18

Adelaide Walker Bodine
INDIAN MOUND, MISSISSIPPI
DECEMBER 1923

I pushed open the door to Peacock's jeweler's, the tiny bell ringing overhead. The bell was new, introduced by Mr. Peacock to alert John to customers, since he was now spending so much time in the back room. His reputation as an horologist with the ability to repair any clock or watch had traveled quickly, and he was receiving packages from as far away as Savannah. He seemed almost driven about earning as much money as he could, and spent a lot of time working. I wanted to be with him as much as possible, but I found his ambition just another part of him that I loved. He always gave me a meaningful look when he talked about having a nest egg and some stability in his life, and it gave me hope for our future together.

"I'll be right with you," John's voice called out from the back. I knew he was alone, having checked with Sarah Beth about what time Mr. Peacock usually went home for dinner.

I made sure I was standing in the ray of sun from the large bay window, to reflect off my red hair that was curled around my face under my hat to spin it into gold, and to put my new outfit in the spotlight. It wasn't actually mine, since the skirt was midcalf on me and far too short for Aunt Louise to allow me to wear in public, and the shoes had three-inch heels.

I knew from our recent shopping trip to Jackson to purchase a dress to wear to the Heathmans' New Year's party—my first time to be invited, since I was almost seventeen—that Aunt Louise didn't appreciate any sort of heel that made me look like one of those flappers Uncle Joe was always reading about in the newspaper. Ever since women got the vote, Uncle Joe and Aunt Louise had thought we were heading for the end of the world. I thought they were both being a little shortsighted about the whole thing, since it was generally known that the hand that rocks the cradle rules the world, and whether women could vote wasn't going to change that one bit.

The air had dipped to a bitter cold, and in addition to wearing Sarah Beth's clothes, I wore one of her fur coats and matching cloche hat, feeling older and as sophisticated as the photos of the movie star Lillian Gish. I peeled off Sarah Beth's kid-leather gloves and put them in the pockets of the coat, then let the coat slip from my shoulders to the floor and waited.

"How can I help you . . ." John's voice faded as he caught sight of me, his business smile changing into something else entirely. He wore an apron over his starched white shirt, his sleeve garters exposed. An eye loupe hung from a strap around his neck, his blond hair tousled as if the apparatus had been perched there recently. A small-headed hammer stuck out from the large pocket of the apron, and what appeared to be a watch chain dangled from his hand.

"Well," he said, stopping several feet in front of me. "I was expecting a customer, but this is much better."

To hide my blush, I twirled for him so that my long strand of pearls—also borrowed from Sarah Beth—would swing and shimmy along with the hem of my dress. "Do you like it?"

He whistled, then stepped toward me, dropping the chain in the pocket with the hammer. "Of course I do. As long as it's your gorgeous face above the collar, I'm going to love anything you wear." After a quick glance toward the large front window, he leaned forward and kissed me, his lips soft and lingering.

"Good," I said. "Because I want you to take me out dancing at one of those places Sarah Beth is always telling me about. I'm a good dancer—I know I am. I can fox-trot, and I'm practically an expert at the Charleston. Well, Sarah Beth says so, anyway, and she should know."

Ever since that night when we'd had to sneak a drunk Sarah Beth up to her room, I'd been grilling her on which gin joints she went to and what she did when she was there. It was hard to believe that we were nearly the same age, yet she seemed to have lived much more than I had. She'd always had an adventurous streak in her, but since she'd been sent home from boarding school in North Carolina, there'd been almost a desperation to her wildness. Like something was chasing her and she was trying to make the most of things before she got caught.

"I suppose she would," he said, his expression suddenly serious. "I'll take you, but only if you promise you'll go with me, and not with Sarah Beth and Willie."

"Why?"

He kissed the tip of my nose. "Because I only want the best places for my girl. Ones with a dance floor, so you don't have to dance on the tables."

I smiled, blushing deeply because he'd called me his girl. "Well, I'm already dressed, so I'm thinking tonight?"

He threw back his head and laughed, and I had to laugh, too. "What's so funny?"

"You. And your eagerness. You're like a puppy. You just need to learn a little patience."

Crossing my arms over my chest, I pretended to scowl at him. "I believe you just called me a dog. And what would you know about patience, anyway?"

He considered me for a moment, then walked quickly toward the door and flipped the sign to CLOSED. He held out his hand to me, and I took it without question. "Let me show you something."

He led me to the back of the shop, a place I'd never been, although I'd visited the jewelry store many times. It was a small, windowless room lined with shelves that seemed to tick. Looking closely, I saw carriage clocks, wall clocks, watches of all sizes and types covering most of the shelves as well as the long worktable that sat beneath two large overhead lamps. A chair was pushed back from the table, with John's jacket hanging on the back. There was something so personal about seeing that, like a glimpse into the part of him he usually didn't show me, and it made my chest feel tight and warm.

"Over here," he said, pulling me toward the worktable. On top of a rectangular piece of cream linen placed over a cleared section of wood was a beautiful ladies' pendant watch. The case back was painted with daisies against a red enamel background, all within an engraved gold floral border, and when John opened the case, I saw that the design extended to the bezel. The white enamel dial had red and black markings with blued steel hands marking off the minutes.

"It belonged to a woman who was lost on the *Titanic*. Her sister sent it to me because she wants to wear it, to honor her sister." He was silent for a moment. "There's something about these old timepieces. They remind us that time is short for those of us who live each day in the present, yet interminable for those who long for what is just over the horizon."

I touched his hand, wanting to take away the sadness that clouded his eyes. "It's probably the most beautiful thing I've ever seen," I said, almost whispering, as if not to disturb the ticking clocks and the advance of time.

He flipped the watch over and opened up the back, revealing the inner workings. "To me, this is the beautiful part of it. All of those wheels and pins. They have to be so precise in their movement, so exact in their size and placement."

A long case clock leaning against the wall chimed the incorrect hour, the sound melancholy. "My mother had a bracelet watch that she used to let me play with when I was little. I don't know what happened to it—it wasn't with her jewelry that we sold to Mr. Peacock. Maybe Aunt Louise still has it."

He touched my cheek. "Ask her. You might want to wear it, to keep your mother close to you."

I shook my head. "No. I don't want to keep her close."

He gently placed the pendant watch back on the table. "I was angry with my father for a long time for sending me away. It took me many years to understand that he did it because he loved me and wanted to keep me safe and give me opportunities I wouldn't have if I'd remained in Missouri. You told me what your mother did, but maybe her reason was because she loved you. That she wanted to spare you from being raised by a mother who could never get past her grief."

I pulled away, his words echoing in my head but finding no place to settle. Eager to change the subject, I said, "So what made you decide you wanted to repair timepieces instead of farm?"

"My grandfather was a horologist in Germany, and my father has a small business up in Missouri. He taught me everything he knows, just as his father taught him. I hope I have a son someday so I can pass it on to him. There's more to a family's legacy than the color of our hair or a good head for numbers."

I wanted to tell him that he was wrong, but I stopped, recalling the memory of me following my mother in her garden, learning the names of things and the feel of soil against my bare skin.

The front bell rang, and we glanced at each other, remembering the CLOSED sign John had placed in the window. For a moment I panicked, thinking Mr. Peacock had returned early from dinner.

"Mr. Richmond?"

I didn't recognize the voice, but John must have, because an odd look passed over his face. Glancing briefly at the doorway leading to the store, he turned to me. "I need you to leave now. Quickly. Don't look at anything but the door. Do you understand? You just need to go."

"But . . ."

He had his hand on my back and was already pushing me out of the back room. I headed directly to the door, but I couldn't help taking a peek at the visitor. He was short, but built like a barrel, with massive arms and stocky, powerful legs. He kept his fedora on, but I could tell that his hair was very dark, almost black, and his skin was olive toned. His navy blue pin-striped suit fit him like Mr. Heathman's instead of loose and baggy like Uncle Joe's Sunday suit.

Just as I reached the door, he stepped in front of it, blocking my way. Taking off his hat, he smiled at me. "I'm afraid we haven't been introduced."

"I need to get home," I stammered. "My aunt is expecting me."

As if I hadn't said anything, he said, "My name is Angelo Berlini. I'm an associate of Mr. Richmond's."

John's voice held a hard edge to it that I hadn't heard before. "Let her leave, Angelo. She's got no business with you."

I didn't understand what was going on, but I wanted it to be over. "I'm Miss Adelaide Bodine. It's a pleasure meeting you, but I really must be leaving. . . ."

"It's a pleasure to meet you, too." He stepped back from the door. "Maybe next time you won't be in such a rush and we can get to know each other better."

John stepped around me, then jerked open the door, the sound of the tinkling bell as out of place as a weed in my garden.

The door shut quickly behind me, the shade drawn before I could form the word "why."

I turned my back to the store, trying to recover my breath and still my thumping heart, when I noticed a familiar figure standing on the sidewalk directly across the street from the jewelry store.

It was the man Leon, whom John had known and called by name that day at the Ellis plantation. He wasn't wearing a hat, but he put his fingers to his forelock and nodded his head, a peculiar smile on his lips, like he knew something I didn't.

I turned down the sidewalk without acknowledging him, walking away as quickly as I could, shivering and remembering too late that I'd left Sarah Beth's coat on the floor of Mr. Peacock's shop.

Vivien Walker Moise
INDIAN MOUND, MISSISSIPPI
APRIL 2013

I was up and dressed by nine o'clock, ready for the trip to see Mathilda.
Cora was scheduled to work at the school's media center, so it would just be me, Carol Lynne, and Chloe. Chloe had stubbornly insisted that she be left behind to look for more bones in the yard, which was exactly why I told her she needed to come with us.

I wasn't surprised to find their rooms empty, as the two of them had somehow gravitated into the habit of eating breakfast together and then walking outside so Chloe could report with excessive drama and adjectives the suspicious-looking places on the property where she and my mother thought other bodies might be buried. On one of their jaunts, they'd hauled the broken chair swing to the porch and re-placed Bootsie's green garden chairs in their original spots. I'd sometimes find them sitting in the barren garden, making me feel like I was the only one not seeing any plants.

I was halfway through the kitchen's screen door when my cell phone rang. I dug it out of my purse and stared at it while it rang two more times. *Slam.* The door slipped through my fingers, the vibration echoing in the still morning air.

"Hello?" I said, barely recognizing the confidence in my voice.

"What the hell do you think you're doing?"

"Hello, Mark. It's good to hear from you." It took all my control to keep my words from quavering.

"I'm *this* close to calling the police and having you arrested. You'd better have a very good reason why my daughter is with you in Pig Swallow, Mississippi."

I frowned for a moment, wondering how he and Chloe had coordinated their geographical slurs. "Because she was lonely without you there. School was out and all of her friends were gone. She just showed up—I obeyed the court order and haven't had any prior contact with her. I promise."

"Good. Then you can just put her on a plane to LA and I'll have Imelda pick her up. Then I won't have to call the police."

I took a deep breath, trying to quell the panic flushing through me. "Please, Mark. Let her stay. At least until the end of your honeymoon. She's getting along fine here. I'll put her in school, or homeschool her, if that's what you'd prefer. I know a retired English teacher, and she could help me." I bit my lip, mentally apologizing to Cora for such a presumption.

"You still taking the pills?"

She's a drug addict. The words flung across the table in his lawyer's office still stung with enough force to steal my breath. I closed my eyes, feeling for a moment as if I were standing on a boat with the water moving beneath me. I'd hated the ocean, hated the blue of it, if only because it wasn't muddy brown, hated the wild waves that pushed you out to deeper water. Mark had forced me to learn how to sail, said it was good for me to get over my fear. But I'd despised it. I remembered that now, the memory of the rolling water making me feel reckless and desperate. Before I even realized what I was thinking, I said, "I'll stop. Today. If you'll just let her stay, I'll stop."

"You know you can't, Vivien. How many times have you tried before and you failed? Chloe doesn't need a drug addict taking care of her."

Or a father who can't be bothered to call her. I forced myself to keep calm. "Please, Mark. I promise this time is for real. And if I fail, I'll send her back to LA."

"Why, Vivi? Why are you so desperate to keep her?"

I remembered something Bootsie had said to me a long, long time ago: *Everybody needs to know that they're number one on somebody's list. You and Tommy are my number one. When you're lost or alone and all give out from the road behind you or in front of you, remember that.*

I saw Chloe as the clingy five-year-old afraid to be left alone, and the eight-year-old who was afraid of thunder but who loved the rain, and the eleven-year-old who cried with me each time we watched our favorite movie, *My Dog Skip.* I didn't know how or when it had happened, but she was number one on my list. Not because there was nobody else who'd put her on the top or their list or even because every time I looked at her I saw the abandoned and bitter child I'd been, but because she'd somehow managed to make me feel as if she belonged there. I wasn't sure where I numbered on her list, but that didn't matter.

"Because I care deeply for her," I said, unable to translate my complicated feelings for Chloe into words he could understand.

He snorted into the phone. "The only thing you care about is your pills."

I put my hand over my mouth, holding in my scream. Because deep down I feared that he was right.

I heard a woman's voice in the background, and then Mark's muffled voice as he said something away from the phone. When he came back, he said, "My beautiful new wife has put me in a generous mood, so I'm willing to bend a little bit." He paused, as if he hadn't already decided what he was going to say. "Chloe can stay with you until I get back—which will be May fifteenth. We might extend our trip for a bit to see some of Europe and the Riviera, but we can play that by ear. I guess I'm going to have to deal with calling her school, but you're in charge of getting everything else sorted out. Try not to bother me too much if you need my signature on anything. And I want to hear from your doctor, who will be giving you daily drug tests and reporting back to my office, where they will inform me if there's any problems—and that needs to start right away. The first positive test, Chloe gets on a plane."

My hand was clenched so hard my fingernails bit into my palms. "Why do you care that I quit, Mark?"

"I don't. I just know you can't do it."

The woman's voice came from the background again and I just stood there and shook, waiting for him to speak. "Do we have a deal?"

"Yes," I managed.

"Good," he said.

"Do you want to speak with Chloe? I can go get her—it'll only take a minute. . . ."

I could tell from the air on the line that he was already gone.

I poured a cup of black coffee from the pot—probably made before dawn by Tommy—and drank it, not caring that it was cold but needing caffeine to wake me up and mask my need to run back upstairs and hide under the covers.

I found Chloe and Carol Lynne after some searching on top of the Indian mound that had been a part of the landscape long before the Walkers had claimed this parcel of land. A reminder of the native Indians who'd once inhabited this corner of the world, what was left of their civilizations remained in the small flat-topped hills that dotted the landscape like humps on a camel.

Over the years, student groups from several universities had come out with more and more sophisticated equipment to see if there were any artifacts that should be salvaged from our mound. But it was clear that anything of value had long since been removed or eroded away. It was called the Walker Mound, but I'd never been able to find any pride in claiming something that was all about a way of life that had been erased from the earth and wasn't coming back. It was a monument to loss, and we had enough of those in the world already, some of us still living and breathing.

They were lying on the ground with their eyes closed, facing the sky, their heads touching like Siamese twins. I was fidgety and annoyed at having had to look for them and walked with heavy footsteps.

"Shhh," said Chloe without opening her eyes. "We're trying to listen to what the earth is saying."

I rolled my eyes. "It's saying that we should have left half an hour ago, and that you'd better be in the car in the next five minutes or we're not going."

My mother didn't open her eyes. "Did you hear that, JoEllen? Did you hear the rumble?"

Chloe's eyes were shut tightly. "No, because Vivien was talking."

A soft smile lifted Carol Lynne's cheeks. "Vivien doesn't like to do this, unless she thinks she might get a tan on her legs. I could never get her to lie still long enough, like she had ants in her pants. Always too busy thinking about what comes next."

Chloe snickered. " 'Ants in her pants'?"

My mother started snickering, too, and soon they were both howling together, like the image of me with insects in my pants was the funniest thing they'd ever heard. Despite myself, my cheek trembled until it lifted in a quasi-smile. But then I remembered lying out here with my mother when I was no more than five, and Bootsie coming out to say that Carol Lynne had a phone call, and that some boy with a Yankee accent was waiting to speak with her. She'd left her sandals and I'd waited for a long time for her to come back. When Bootsie had come to get me for supper and told me that Carol Lynne had left again, I'd run with the sandals and thrown them as hard as I could into the swamp.

I pressed my fingers to my temples, feeling the beginnings of another headache. "Come on," I said. "We have to go."

Carol Lynne stopped laughing. "Where are we going?"

"To see Mathilda."

Her skin furrowed between her brows. "Did she move?"

Chloe stood, then offered her hand to Carol Lynne. "I haven't met her yet. That's why we're going."

I watched as my mother took Chloe's hand and rolled to a stand with the agility of a child. I felt an odd pang as she smiled at Chloe and I turned away, trying to remember the last time my mother had smiled at me.

As I opened the passenger door of my car and moved the front seat for Chloe to crawl in the back, Carol Lynne looked over at the old Cadillac that was splattered with dried mud and covered in dust. "Is Bootsie coming with us?"

My temples thrummed and I opened my mouth to tell her where Bootsie really was when Chloe cut me off.

"We'll meet her later." She slid into the car, then pulled down the back of the front seat so Carol Lynne could get in.

My mother stared at the seat, her brows knitted. "Where are we going?"

"To see Mathilda. She moved, so we're going to visit her." The words slid from Chloe's mouth with ease.

I met Chloe's eyes in the rearview mirror. Either she was a better liar than a twelve-year-old should be, or she was much more compassionate than anybody had ever given her credit for.

I had to remind Carol Lynne to close the door and put on her seat belt, which she did without argument. I flipped on the radio where it was set on the sixties satellite radio station that I'd been listening to for most of my drive from LA. I hadn't liked sixties music until I was in high school, when Tripp would drive me to school. He'd always had eclectic music tastes, liked most everything except for whatever was currently popular, and I had to endure listening to everything from forties big-band music, the blues, to sixties music and pretty much all types in between. I'd hate to admit to him now that after all that time when I'd scorned his music, the first three presets on my car radio were the sixties, forties, and blues stations.

The Fifth Dimension was belting out "Aquarius." I was about to flip it off, figuring music wasn't the best thing for my impending headache, when my mother started singing along. She had a clear, strong voice, perfect for the vocals of the song. And she remembered every single word.

I glanced at Chloe in the mirror again, wondering why she hadn't reached forward and changed the station to modern hits. I hadn't been allowed to listen to my own music in my car since Chloe had started first grade.

Instead, she opened her mouth and joined my mother in singing the refrain. A horn honked and I had to swerve out of the lane of opposing traffic, narrowly missing an oncoming car.

"How do you know that song?" I asked, forgetting my headache for a moment.

She rolled her eyes. "Hailey was in a production of *Hair* at the community theater last summer, remember? She made me watch it six times. I know every word by heart."

My mother continued singing and Chloe joined her, and eventually I did, too, just so I wouldn't feel left out.

Cora had given me directions to Sunset Acres, and like every business near Indian Mound, it was off of Highway 82. The fields, now accessorized with bright red or green mechanical planters that stretched across eight rows of earth, gradually gave way to strips of fast-food restaurants and chain motels. Not a lot had changed since I'd last been here, maybe one neon sign being exchanged for another, and it certainly hadn't gotten any prettier. But there was something comforting in it, too, like the scarred surface of a favorite antique chest.

The song had ended and I felt Chloe's silence as she stared out at the urban landscape of midcentury homes with new roofs and old doors with three diamond-shaped windows in a diagonal across the front. People sat in lawn chairs on porches or yards and waved as we drove by. Carol Lynne and I waved back on instinct, and I didn't even think about it until Chloe asked, "Who was that?"

"I have no idea."

"Then why did you wave?"

I shrugged. "I don't know. To be friendly, I guess. It's just what you do."

She raised her eyebrows as if the world had suddenly gone crazy, then returned her stare out the window.

Despite its name, Sunset Acres was a two-story brick building surrounded by a small square of asphalt parking lot with a slightly hipped roof that resembled an old motor lodge, but without the neon VA-CANCY sign. Cora had already warned me that it wasn't much to look at, but the staff inside more than made up for any aesthetic disadvantage.

We signed in at a front desk before being directed to an elevator. The furnishings were sparse and slightly shabby, but the white laminate floors gleamed with polish, the walls dotted with brightly framed depictions of flowers and landscapes. Examining one closely, I saw that it looked like a paint-by-numbers piece, but I chose not to judge, realizing they'd probably been made by a resident.

"What's that smell?" Chloe asked, her voice echoing off the bare floors.

It was a mixture of disinfectant and medicated skin creams blending with the cooking odors of whatever they'd served for breakfast. I gave her the look Bootsie had often given me, effectively silencing her, and allowing her to draw her own conclusions.

We walked down a long corridor with handrails along each wall and ramps instead of stairs. Pausing at a door at the end of the hallway,

I looked for the plaque that confirmed we were at room 106, then knocked on the door.

A plump middle-aged woman wearing khaki pants and a floral scrub top opened the door and smiled warmly. "I'm Johnetta Moore. You must be Vivien. Cora told us you'd be coming by this morning."

She opened the door wider to allow us to walk inside, her white sneakers squeaking on the linoleum. I introduced her to Chloe and my mother before moving forward into the room.

It was a private room with only a single bed, and although it was small I could tell that a lot of effort had been made to make it seem like home. A worn, dark green reclining chair sat in a corner next to a small table full of framed photographs. Handmade needlework hung from the walls, and rainbow-hued afghans lay across the foot of the bed and along the back of the chair. The deep windowsill was filled with pots of ivy, and in front of the window was a record player like the one in the closet of my room that had once belonged to my mother. A stack of vinyl records sat on the floor next to it, the unmistakable face of Elvis on the top cover.

"We expected you a little earlier," Johnetta said as she led us to the bed. "This is usually her rest time, but she insisted on waiting until you got here. She's been very excited. I'll let you chat and I'll be back in a little bit. Just give a holler out the door if you need me."

I watched her leave, then allowed my attention to be drawn to the head of the bed. The old woman sat against a pile of pillows, her skin dark against the bright white of her linens and the lacy nightgown she wore. She seemed to have shrunk since I'd last seen her, as if each year had demanded a piece of her in payment. Her fingers lay like brittle kindling against the sheets, her hair a steel gray bun braided at the back of her head just like she'd always worn it.

But her eyes were cloudy, as if they had been reversed so that she could only look inward. I remembered Carrie telling me that Mathilda was blind, but I somehow hadn't expected this. I thought of all the photographs and frames and bright colors and imagined Mathilda dictating what should be placed where, so that she would know what it looked like without being able to see it.

"Mathilda," Carol Lynne said, moving toward the bed like a person working herself through a maze. She knelt down and picked up Mathilda's hand. "It's me. It's Carol Lynne. I've come back."

Mathilda reached out her other hand and placed it on my mother's head. "Yes, chile. You come back to stay. Jus' like you always promise." Her voice was thin and reedy, but still held the melodious tones I remembered from being sung to at night.

"I did, didn't I?" my mother said, a child repeating something to make it true.

I wondered if she'd visited here with Bootsie, and imagined she probably had and had even already shared the same words with Mathilda. But the old woman just closed her eyes and smiled, stroking my mother's hair. Mathilda had already outlived most of her family, including her husband and a son, and maybe that was what gave her the sense of peace and acceptance, a nod toward the inevitable. Like jumping off the levee and into the river, it was pointless to pray to not get wet.

Chloe stepped back and I reached my hand out to her. She either didn't see it or ignored me, because my hand dangled in the air for a long moment before I drew it back to my side.

Mathilda turned toward us, her milky eyes searching. "Who you brung with you, Carol Lynne?"

Not wanting Chloe to be introduced as JoEllen, I spoke up. "It's Vivien. And I brought my stepdaughter, Chloe."

My mother moved to sit at the foot of the bed, and Mathilda opened her arms wide to me. I found myself moving quickly toward her and wrapping myself within her embrace, holding on to her as if she were all the parts of my past I wanted to bring back, feeling that as long as she was there it was possible.

She let go of me, and I pulled away. Her hands found my face and she stroked my cheek, her fingers wet with my unexpected tears. "You still beautiful. I always say you get prettier as you get older. And you married now."

"Not anymore. It didn't work out." I was conscious of Chloe behind me, listening to every word.

"So you come back, too." It wasn't a question, but more of a recitation of an old, familiar story. "Where you been?"

My mother let her hand fall on Mathilda's thin leg under the blanket. "She's been chasing ghosts."

The throbbing in my temples deepened as I looked between my mother and Mathilda, trying to decode her meaning.

"Um-hmm," Mathilda said as she nodded, her odd eyes closed.

For a moment, I thought she'd fallen asleep. But then her eyes popped open again, staring directly at Chloe.

"You been helpin' in Miss Bootsie's garden?"

Chloe shook her head, and then quickly said, "No. Sir. I mean ma'am."

Mathilda found my hand and squeezed. "She be gone now a year. Her garden needs tending. And you cain't chase ghosts when your fingers are busy in the dirt."

I dipped my head, wondering if her mind had started to go along with her eyesight, and wishing she could tell me what to do. I jerked my head up, remembering why we'd come. "Mathilda, you've known my family for so long. Do you remember any stories about a woman who disappeared? Maybe even a member of my family?"

Her hand felt cold in mine, but her expression didn't change. "Why you ask that, Vivi?"

"Remember that terrible storm earlier this week? Lightning struck the old cypress in the backyard, exposing the roots. There was the body of a woman found buried underneath them. We're trying to find out who she was, and how she got there."

She closed her eyes and I watched as they moved rapidly beneath her paper-thin eyelids as if scanning her memory. "There was one Walker woman, long before my time. She the one whose husband built the house. It was all wilderness then, and they say she was delicate-like, couldn't take the hard livin'. She went back to her family in New Orleans, left her husband and chil'ren. Don't know if she ever came back, though. That part of the story ain't as interestin' as the leavin' part, so people don't talk so much about that."

I thought I felt a small tremble in her hand, but it could have been from me. My headache throbbed throughout my body, and I focused on Mathilda's face so I wouldn't think about the vial of pills in my purse.

"She wore a tiny ring on a watch chain around her neck. It was half of a ring that when put together read 'I'll Love You Forever.' Does it sound familiar to you?"

She pulled her hand away and began to push her covers off. "I needs to sit in my chair so I can rest. They say more people die in bed than they do in wars."

I thought about calling for Johnetta, but she would only make Mathilda get back in bed. I figured if you'd reached one hundred and four years old, you'd earned the right to sleep wherever you wanted.

I took one of Mathilda's elbows and was surprised when Chloe took the other. We carefully led her to the chair and helped her sit. Then I laid the afghan over her and pulled the lever so that she was in a reclining position.

"So do you remember the ring?" I asked again.

"The ring," she repeated, as if to make sure she'd heard me correctly. Then she raised her hand and touched Chloe's cheek, and Chloe looked at me with widened eyes but didn't pull back. Mathilda moved her hand from one cheek to the other, tracing a thin, dark finger over Chloe's brow bone, and then her nose and chin.

"How old you be?"

"Twelve," Chloe answered, her eyes darting to me with a question.

"Hmm. You got good bones, chile. You be like Vivien and Carol Lynne. They was ugly as a naked chicken when they was knee babies— Carol Lynne 'specially. Jus' be patient. This way, you have a chance to grow your personality. It's the ones born pretty cain't barely put two words together."

Mathilda dropped her hand and closed her eyes. "Tell Johnetta that I'm already asleep so she won't bother me."

Chloe stepped back, her cheeks flame red.

I bent over the old woman and kissed her cheek, thinking she might already be sleeping. Quietly, I said, "It was so good to see you again. I'll stop back soon, all right?"

She didn't move, her only response the slow lifting of her chest as she breathed.

We tiptoed from the room, passing Johnetta along the way and letting her know that Mathilda was already asleep, but not telling her exactly where she was sleeping.

We piled into the car again, and I turned the engine, the sound overly loud to my sensitive hearing and pounding head. I felt adrift, confused for a moment as to where I should point my car. *You cain't chase ghosts when your fingers are busy in the dirt.* Mathilda's voice worked its way through the pain in my head. Facing Carol Lynne, I said, "Are Bootsie's gardening tools still in the shed?"

My mother's eyes were clear as a child's, and just as empty. I took a deep breath and let it out slowly, trying to quell the anger and frustration I felt toward her. It was almost as if I believed she'd begun to lose her memory on purpose so that she and I would never have the conversation I'd been dreaming about for years. It was unfair, and unkind, but it didn't take away the truth of it.

"Why do you need gardening tools?" Chloe asked, leaning into the front seat.

"Because we're going to grow things. Who knows? Maybe it will qualify for a science credit in your homeschooling curriculum."

"My what?"

I gave an inward sigh. I hadn't wanted to tell her that her father had called, knowing it would upset her that he hadn't asked to speak with her, but I had no choice now. "Your dad called this morning and we decided that it's okay if you stay here with me until he returns in May. Which means that we have to find a way for you to finish the school year. I thought I'd ask Mrs. Smith if she might know how to go about it, since she was a teacher for so long."

I shut my eyes, wondering if I'd made a mistake, that her being here now didn't mean she wanted to stay. Holding my breath, I waited for Chloe to speak.

Chloe leaned back in her seat, her arms clenched tightly across her chest, and I knew she was thinking about her father. She caught me looking at her in the review mirror and immediately rolled her eyes. "Whatever."

I sighed with relief as I pulled out of the parking lot back onto Highway 82. I didn't turn on the radio this time, thinking my head couldn't take it and not wanting to break my promise to Mark less than a day after I said I could stop.

"Hey, Vivi?"

I met Chloe's eyes in the mirror. "Yes?"

"When you asked Mathilda about the ring on the chain, she never answered you."

I looked back at the flat road in front of me leading into the horizon. "No," I said. "She didn't."

Despite my headache, I reached over and turned on the radio and listened to my mother singing every lyric as if she'd never forgotten them, figuring it was easier than trying to think about why Mathilda would have wanted not to talk about the ring, or why it had been buried with the woman underneath the cypress tree.

Chapter 20

Carol Lynne Walker Moise
INDIAN MOUND, MISSISSIPPI
SEPTEMBER 1, 1963

Dear Diary,

I'm leaving. For good, I think. There's nothing to keep me here and a whole world that's waiting for me. I can feel it, just like the way I can feel the change in seasons even before the cypress leaves turn the color of fire. I'll miss that the most, I think. The colors of the trees in fall and the delta sunsets. But other places have trees and horizons, too, I guess. I'll just need to get used to them.

I went down to the jewelry store yesterday to say good-bye to Emmett. He didn't know that, of course, but as long as I did it was okay. Bootsie's a couple of years older than Emmett, but he looks much younger. Bootsie once told me it's because he never had children to wear him out. I said she should look just as young, seeing as how she'd gotten a hall pass on raising her child for six years. I remember saying that, because I was twelve, and that's the last time I ever got my mouth washed out with soap. Which is better than getting slapped, I guess, but just as humiliating.

I sat and watched Emmett work for a long time, neither of us saying anything, which is the way we both like it. There's something beautiful about the only sound being the ticking of hundreds of clocks. Maybe that's why he's always so calm. He said he spent so much time there with his uncle that when he got older he never wanted to work where there was more to listen to than just the sound of time passing.

He handed me the old hatbox with all the spare parts and pieces, and asked me if I wanted to play with it. I wasn't sure if he was joking or not, or maybe he hadn't noticed that I'm eighteen now, so I took it and started going through all the watch parts and old pieces of miscellaneous jewelry. He told me that when he died the box and everything inside it would go to me. I thanked him, because he was being nice, but I couldn't imagine what I'd want with a box of old junk.

It's right before dawn now, and I'm sitting out on the front porch with my suitcases and writing this while I wait for Jimmy Hinkle. I'm also smoking a cigarette—and I'm going to leave the butt right here on the porch for Bootsie to find. I'm done with her rules. It's time I make my own.

The sky is just light enough that I can see what's around me, so I took a walk to the Indian mound and pressed my ear to the ground at the top to see if I could hear the earth talk to me. Mathilda had shown me that years ago, and I think a part of me believes that the earth and moon and sky are all living creatures. And that they speak to us if we're willing to listen. I listened real hard, waiting to hear the earth tell me it was time to leave and not come back. But no matter how hard I tried, all I heard was the wind and the sound of the cypress trees crying in the swamp.

I sat down at my cypress tree, too, opening my eyes wide just in case Mathilda's haint wanted to show itself to me. But there was nothing there except for me, and the old tree, and all the memories of me sitting beneath it. I'll miss this tree the most, even more than our weird yellow house with its creaking floorboards and peculiar style. I think I'll even miss Bootsie's garden. I'd never admit it to her, but all those hours I spent watching her have taught me something about the cycles of life and death, and how it's possible to grow something from a tiny seed pressed into the soil. Maybe it's because I think of myself as a seed, only it's taken me eighteen years to poke my head above the ground.

I'll miss Mathilda, too, and Emmett, of course, and my friends from high school. But I don't think I'll miss Bootsie. I'll do my best not to think about her, because every time I do, it reminds me that I'm not good enough, or pretty enough, or smart enough to be loved.

Jimmy loves me. He said so last month in the backseat of his daddy's

Bonneville. That's why I'm going away with him. I'm not sure what love is, or how I feel about him, but as long as he loves me, we'll be all right. I know it. Deep down, I really do.

I'd better put out my cigarette and get walking. I told Jimmy to flash his lights once when he got to the end of the drive and then to stop. I haven't seen his lights yet, but I can't wait anymore. It seems like I've been waiting a whole lifetime for this, and one more minute seems like forever.

I'm not so sure he'll remember not to come on up to the house. Jimmy's handsome and fun, but I don't know how smart he is. He blew off half of a finger last Fourth of July because he wanted to see what it felt like to have a firecracker explode from his hand. He was high, but I still couldn't think how high a person would have to be to forget to use their brain.

Bootsie's room is right in front of the house, her windows overlooking the front drive so she can spy on whoever's coming. She keeps talking about how when I graduate from college and come back home, I'll get that room and the old black bed. And she and Emmett will teach me all about cotton farming and keeping books and all those things I've never wanted to know about and still don't.

But I couldn't tell her that any more than I could tell her that I didn't want to go to college. It doesn't matter now. She saw me packing and thought it was for college, where she's supposed to be driving me tomorrow. I hope she won't be too surprised when she finds my bed empty with a note on my pillow telling her I'm gone forever.

I hear an engine, so I have to go. My future's wide-open right now, and the only thing I know for sure is that I'll be a long time gone from this place.

Chapter 21

Adelaide Walker Bodine
INDIAN MOUND, MISSISSIPPI
NEW YEAR'S EVE, 1923

Aunt Louise frowned as she examined my painted lips and rouged cheeks. Sarah Beth had forbidden me from appearing at her parents' party without any color on my face, swearing I'd fade into the wallpaper if she didn't intervene and loan me something from her makeup collection. I think it was more so that I wouldn't embarrass her in front of her parents' friends, who were important people and very fashionable, many who were traveling from the state capital of Jackson to attend.

My aunt hovered around me with a handkerchief, waiting for the opportunity to swipe off at least some of the lipstick. "Adelaide, you have so much natural beauty. I don't know why you'd want to hide it with all that paint."

I stared at my reflection in the mirror, at my reddish-blond hair that I'd been allowed to marcel, and the little hint of rouge on my cheeks that made my green eyes seem brighter. Or maybe it was the thought of dancing all night with John that made them sparkle. The bright lips made me seem older and sophisticated, and hopefully took people's eyes off the deplorably low hem of my dress. Despite my pleadings, my hem stayed where Aunt Louise thought was proper—right above my ankles. I suppose I should have been happy that she wasn't making me wear a corset and a hoop skirt.

"Are you ready yet, cuz?" Willie asked, poking his head around the door and then whistling. His hair was parted on the side and slicked back so that his cowlick didn't stick up at the back of his head. He wore a black dinner jacket with a white waistcoat and black bow tie, and I had to admit he looked handsome.

"Woo-eee, Adelaide. You're going to be the cat's meow at the party tonight. Just please don't tell Sarah Beth I said so." He winked. "I heard they've set up a tent in the back garden for the younger folks, with our own dance floor and a Negro band playing a lot of new music. Sarah Beth said all the debs in Jackson are doing it, so of course Mrs. Heathman has to have a tent and a band, too."

He smiled, then checked his wristwatch that Sarah Beth had given him for his last birthday. She'd bought it at Peacock's and John had helped her pick it out, selecting it for its quality and workmanship. Despite Sarah Beth's flashy nature, she was impressed by those things that were more than just beauty, because, she'd explained, they weren't so fleeting and temporary. The only exception was flowers, but she probably only said that because I was her best friend and the flowers in my garden were my pride and joy.

"You ready?" I asked, turning around and feeling the beady fabric swish against my body. The dress was pale pink, or "blush," as the saleslady kept reminding me, and it made my complexion glow.

"I just . . ." Aunt Louise started to say, then stopped.

"You just what?" I asked.

She pressed her lips together in a soft smile. "I just wish your mother were here to see you. She'd be very proud."

I looked down at the silver-backed brush-and-comb set that had belonged to my mother, and thought about the woman I'd barely known because she hadn't given me the opportunity. Would she have been proud of me? I had no way of knowing, and could only wish that it didn't matter so much.

"Come on, Adelaide." Willie almost twitched with excitement. "I don't want to miss anything."

I stood and kissed Aunt Louise on her cheek, trying not to notice her moist eyes. I practically had to run after Willie down the stairs, neither one of us heeding Aunt Louise's pleas to act like a lady and gentleman. Uncle Joe waited by the door, a serious expression on his face, and both my cousin and I braced ourselves for the inevitable lecture.

"Don't forget how you were raised, and how we don't tolerate alcohol or wild behavior in this household. I expect you to behave accordingly." Although he was speaking to both of us, his eyes were on Willie. I wondered how much he knew about Willie's exploits on his visits home from Ole Miss.

"Yes, Uncle Joe," I said, standing on tiptoe to kiss his sun-roughened cheek. The fact that my aunt and uncle had not received an invitation had gone unremarked, although nobody was surprised. Sarah Beth had been allowed to make her own guest list, which was how Willie and I ended up attending. Aunt Louise and Uncle Joe didn't run in the same social circles as the Heathmans, and I didn't think that bothered them overly much.

Belatedly remembering his manners, Willie helped me into my plain and serviceable wool coat, then held his arm out to me. As he escorted me to the car, I thought of Sarah Beth's fur coat. In the weeks since I'd left it at the jewelry store, I hadn't seen her, which was fine, because even though I'd reminded John often, he kept forgetting to bring it to me, and I hadn't made another trip into town. I imagined that John must have stashed it in the back room and just kept forgetting about it. Or maybe he'd given it to Sarah Beth directly, since I knew she'd been to see him about repairing the strand of pearls that had broken the night we'd brought her home. Sarah Beth hadn't asked about her coat, which was typical of how careless she was about her things, but I'd feel better knowing I'd returned it.

Willie opened the passenger door of his car, but before I could get in I watched his eyes first widen in surprise, then furtively glance at me as he reached in and grabbed what looked like a pile of white sheets wadded on the seat.

"Sorry," he said. "I brought home some laundry and left it in the car." He tightened the sheets into a large white ball, then shoved them on the floor of the rear seat.

He kept giving me funny glances and I couldn't understand why, but as I sat down, I noticed the lingering smell of wood smoke.

Willie hummed to himself on the entire drive, his hands tapping on the steering wheel, but I didn't mind. I was too busy with images of John and the anticipation of spending an evening dancing with him. I'd even decided to have a drink or two. I wouldn't get zozzled like Sarah Beth liked to, but enough that I could finally understand what all the excitement was about. And show John that I wasn't a little girl.

It had been cold enough to freeze the water in the birdbath in my garden, but we'd had a slight thaw in the last few days that brought the temperature over the freezing mark, just in time for the Heathmans' party. It would have been too cold in the tent—at least for the band members, if not for the dancers—so of course the weather obliged the Heathmans. Still, I wished I had Sarah Beth's fur coat, since the air would be cold on my sleeveless arms regardless of the temperature.

As we pulled into the large circular drive where valets were taking keys and parking cars, we were met by blinking lights sprinkled all through the trees, and windows hung with wreaths mimicking the huge one that decorated the spot over the massive front door. Cars were parked along the drive and on the lawn, and a babble of voices drifted through the open French doors on the first level, where I could see that a crowd had already gathered.

As Willie led me inside, I was caught up in the mixed scents of perfumes and cigarette smoke that swirled above the partygoers, who were swaying back and forth as if already dancing. Pine boughs mixed with magnolia leaves were festooned on all the fireplace mantels and climbing their way around the banister of the curving staircase.

Bertha, wearing a starched white hat and apron over a black dress, stepped back to allow us into the foyer, where there was already a crush of people. I waited while another servant took my coat, and then my gaze was caught by the sight of a small woman dressed just like Bertha approaching us with a silver tray filled with long glasses of a golden-colored drink.

Willie's back was to us, greeting a friend, and I smiled when I recognized her. "Mathilda! It's good to see you again."

She didn't return my smile. Instead, after quickly glancing around us, she looked down at the tray as if addressing it and said very quietly, "It be better if you don' talk to me, Miss Adelaide. Better for both of us."

Before I could ask her what she meant, Willie turned around and spotted the drinks. Without even a glance in Mathilda's direction, he picked up two glasses and handed one to me. "Your first glass of champagne! Just promise me it won't be your last. It's hard living with a saint, cuz."

I took the glass, but when I turned to thank Mathilda, she'd already disappeared into the crowd, her white cap standing out as it bobbed through the brightly colored crowd like a buoy on the water.

Willie and I turned at the sound of a squeal coming from the staircase, where we spotted Sarah Beth in a confection of feathers and fringe and a hemline that showed her knees—something Aunt Louise would definitely not have approved of.

Her hair, in marcelled waves identical to mine, shone in the lamp and candlelight like the dark fur of a mink, a dramatic backdrop for the diamonds in her hair, and at her neck and throat. My hand moved absently to my neck, where I wore Aunt Louise's good set of pearls that I had thought made me look glamorous and sophisticated. Looking at Sarah Beth, I felt like a country wife going to church in her Sunday best.

She raced down the stairs and, ignoring Willie—part of her "strategy," as she called it—flung her thin arms around me. "I thought you would *never* get here. It's so dreadfully *dull* here with all these old folks, and I've been *dying* of boredom waiting for you so we can go have a little fun. And I told Mother that we didn't need chaperones in the tent, because it's so *old-fashioned*, and besides, she and Daddy and all the other adults will be just right *here*, so we can't get into *too* much trouble." She fluttered her long eyelashes up to Willie. "You can come, too," she said with a sultry smile.

Willie downed his glass of champagne in quick swallows, two spots of color flaming high on his cheeks. "I just might," he said, his words tight. Mathilda walked by again and Willie plopped his empty glass on the tray and took two more. He eyed my untouched glass. "You'd better hurry up or I might have to drink yours, too."

I took a gulp, not wanting to seem like a first-timer and just sip it. The bubbles shot down my throat and then up to my nose, stinging my eyes and making me cough. To hide my embarrassment, I quickly took another gulp.

With a furtive look at her parents, who were busy greeting guests at the door, Sarah Beth took her own glass of champagne before grabbing Willie's elbow, causing the liquid in the two glasses he was holding to splash perilously close to the edge. "Come on—there's more juice out in the tent."

She began to lead the way toward the back of the house, but I hesitated, looking for Mathilda to discard my now-empty glass. Instead, a hand reached around from behind me and grabbed the glass. I opened my mouth in surprise, then smiled when I saw John.

He wore a black dinner jacket like Willie, but while Willie appeared to be a young man dressed up to go to a party, shifting his arms self-consciously to make the jacket fit better, John looked like a man who wore elegant evening wear all the time. His broad shoulders and tall and lean body were made for tailored clothing, and for a moment I thought he should be in the pictures. But then he wouldn't be mine.

"Hello, gorgeous," he whispered in my ear, sneaking in a quick kiss to my temple so nobody would notice.

"John," I said, breathless. There was something about him that always made me feel like the air had been snatched out of my lungs.

"I'm steamed at you, you know," he said, trying to strike a serious tone.

His sparkling eyes told me he was joking. But I pouted anyway, like Sarah Beth had taught me, hoping he'd notice my red lips. "Why? What did I do?"

"You had your first drink without me." He threaded his fingers in mine. "Come on. The least you can do is have your second drink with me."

I pulled back, making him glance at me with a raised eyebrow.

"Only on one condition," I demanded, feeling like the bubbles in the champagne had absorbed any shyness.

His eyes brightened as he stared back at me, and all the sights and the sounds of the party floated up to the ceiling with the cigarette smoke. "What's that?"

"That you dance with me, and only me."

"Deal," he said, grinning as he pulled my hand and led me the way Sarah Beth and Willie had gone.

A full moon I hadn't noticed before hung high in the sky, creating long shadows across the lawn and illuminating the giant white tent that appeared to be the moon's reflection in the dark sky of grass. Our breaths were expelled in giant cotton bolls of air that collided on their way up to heaven. I felt giddy with the feel of John's hand in mine and the moon above and our whole lives in front of us. I tugged on his hand to get him to stop. "Kiss me," I demanded.

He didn't ask why. He simply took me in his arms and did as I'd asked, softly at first and then with a passion that I thought only existed in the novels I borrowed from Mrs. Heathman or on the screen in the picture shows. As John moved his lips over mine, I could only think, *It's real! It's real!* It was like I'd discovered a secret that was all my own, not to be shared with any other soul except for John.

He finally pulled away, both of us breathing as if we'd run around the house three times. "Holy smokes," he said, his fingers trembling on my shoulders, his body leaning into me like he would fall down if I backed up. "I figure it's best if we both stop before I forget how."

John lifted his hands and stepped back, looking at me like he'd never seen a girl before. "You do things to me, Adelaide Bodine. I don't think I could imagine the rest of my life without you."

"I'm not asking you to," I said, seeing Aunt Louise's disapproving look at my forwardness. I shivered in my sleeveless dress. I hadn't even been aware that I was cold.

"It'll be warmer in the tent, but I don't want you to catch pneumonia before we get there." He shrugged out of his jacket and placed it over my shoulders. "Come on," he said, putting his arm around me and leading us toward the tent.

"I wish I had Sarah Beth's fur coat," I said. "I was hoping you'd bring it tonight."

It took him a moment to respond. "I don't have it."

"What do you mean? I left it in your store, and you keep telling me that you've been meaning to bring it by."

A tic started in his jaw. "I'm sorry. Angelo Berlini has it," John said, his clipped words and harsh tone unfamiliar.

I stopped to look up at him. "He has it? Sarah Beth is going to kill me when she finds out. She's got more than one, but I know she'll want it back."

"That might be a problem. I don't expect to see him for a while."

"I don't understand. Why would you let him just take it?"

"I thought it was his. When he left he reached down and picked it up. I thought he'd put it there when he entered the store. I didn't realize you'd brought it in until you started asking about it. I've been trying to figure out how to get it back."

"Can you telephone him and ask him to return it?"

John stopped walking and faced me, his hands in mine. "He's not somebody I can just call, Adelaide. And he's not somebody I want you to have anything to do with. You've never asked, but that's why I needed you to leave so quickly that day. I don't want him to taint you. It's just best to forget about the coat. Knowing Sarah Beth, she's already forgotten all about it."

I wasn't convinced, but I wanted the magic that had filled the air before to return to us. "Sure," I said, hoping he was right. "But why do you associate with him?"

Gently, John placed his hands on either side of my head and softly kissed my forehead. "Because I've been poor my whole life, and living in somebody else's house for most of it. There are opportunities now where a man of humble beginnings can make something of himself, make a little dough along the way, and maybe even build a nice nest egg so that he can settle down with his best girl and live a comfortable life. And sometimes that means associating with people he'd rather not, but being able to live with it because it's only for a short time."

I wasn't sure what he was talking about, but I'd heard the words "settle down with his best girl," and none of the other words seemed to matter.

I reached inside the jacket to cover my arms and move the lapels closer to cover my chest. My hand felt something hard and round, like the top half of a horseshoe, but smaller. Curious, I reached into his pocket to pull out the object, then held it up to the moonlight. "What's this?"

John threw back his head and laughed. "Your New Year's present. I didn't get you a Christmas present because I needed my bonus from Mr. Peacock so I could pay him back for the parts. I was waiting for the right moment to give it to you. I guess right now is a good time."

I turned so that my shadow didn't block my view, moving a few steps so that we stood beneath a lantern in one of the trees. Holding my breath, I looked carefully at the object in my hand. "What is it?" I asked, afraid that I already knew.

"Your mother's watch. Your aunt Louise has been keeping it for you." When I moved it in the moonlight, I saw the deep blue of the enamel, like the color of John's eyes. I didn't need the light of the moon, but saw in my memories the shimmering mother-of-pearl rectangular face with a tiny sapphire at the top for winding, the numbers and the hands in black. At the top, right under the number twelve, was the manufacturer's name: Cartier. It seemed so old and familiar, yet somehow new as well.

"Turn it over," John said quietly.

My hands were nearly numb in the cold, so I was very careful not to drop the watch. I could barely make out that there was something engraved on the back, something I hadn't seen before. "It's too dark. What does it say?"

His eyes met mine. "It says, 'I'll love you forever.' Your mother had it engraved before she died. She'd planned to give it to you when you were older. When you told me about your mother's watch that you used to play with, I asked your aunt and she told me that she still had it. And she agreed that this would be a good time to give it to you. I had to replace some of the parts and the crystal, but it's still the same."

His smile was uncertain, and it hurt my heart to see it. I stood on my tiptoes and kissed him. "It's my first gift from you, and that's all that matters."

"And from your mother. I don't want you to forget that there are two souls who have promised to love you forever."

My throat was thick with tears, strangling my words of protest, my words to explain to him that old hurts are like broken bones that never heal, the pain reappearing when you least expect it, and aching in your dreams.

He took the watch from my hands and opened it, then placed it on my wrist. It was heavy and solid, and the words on the back seemed to burn my skin like a kiss. "I know we haven't known each other that long, and you're so young. But I know we were meant to be together—I've known it since the first moment I saw you." He raised my hand to his lips and kissed it. "I'd like this to be like a promise ring. I just want to be more settled, to get my own repair shop. I want to give you the life you deserve. I just need a little more time."

I threw my arms around him, not caring that his jacket slid from my shoulders. "Yes, John. Yes. I'll wait. But we don't have to. I'd live in a shack in the woods with you if we needed to. As long as we're together, it'll be okay."

He looked at me carefully, measuring his words. "When do you turn seventeen?"

"May twenty-ninth."

"All right. That's my goal. To be a man and make you proud by the time you turn eighteen. I know that's over a year and sounds like a long time, but I want to make sure that we're both ready. I should probably spend more time with your aunt and uncle between now and then so they can get used to the idea."

"I don't know if I can wait that long," I said, my voice breathless again.

He kissed me lightly. "The wait will make it all the sweeter." Bending down, he picked up his jacket and placed it back on my shoulders. I would have been warmer if I tucked my arms inside, but I wanted to see how the watch looked on my arm, and imagine I could feel the words pressed against my skin. *I'll love you forever.*

"Come on," he said, taking my hand. "Let's go before we freeze to death." He began running and it hardly seemed as if my feet touched the ground at all.

Inside the tent a Negro band had started to play, and Sarah Beth and Willie were already kicking it up on the dance floor that had been erected in the middle of the tent. Cloth-covered tables with orchid centerpieces were placed around the floor like petals on a flower. I looked closely at the orchids, wondering if they weren't real, or if even flowers wouldn't defy Mrs. Heathman by wilting in colder temperatures.

At the far end of the tent was a bar with two servants standing behind it, both busy mixing and pouring drinks for the line of men in front of them.

"Aren't the Heathmans afraid of getting raided?" I asked John in a low tone.

He regarded me for a long moment, as if he wasn't sure if I was serious. "Didn't you see the guests? He's got the county sheriff, a state senator, and a federal judge here drinking his wine. Even if somebody's dumb enough to raid the party, I doubt anybody's going to be doing any jail time."

I frowned up at him. "How do you know who those people are? I wouldn't know any of them if they jumped in the car on the seat next to me."

He smoothed my hair over an ear, a corner of his mouth lifting. "I've done business with them."

It made sense that such important men would be customers at the jewelry store, and I smiled at John, proud to be the girl of a man with such business connections. "Let's get more champagne," I said, tugging on John's hand and leading him to the bar. The band started playing another song, the lead singer crooning the words to "The Sheik of Araby":

The stars that shine above
Will light our way to love
You'll rule this world with me
I'm the sheik of Araby

I sang along quietly, knowing the words from being forced to listen to Sarah Beth pound out the song on her piano, and watched as more couples joined Willie and Sarah Beth on the dance floor. My feet, in a pair of not-so-high heels, tapped to the music, as if they were even more eager than I was to start dancing. I'd been practicing with my pillow for months now so I could impress John.

He handed me another glass and I downed my champagne quickly, barely giving him a chance to drink his own before I dragged him onto the dance floor. The beat of the music had changed to something even faster, the singer's face now drenched in sweat that darkened the collar of his shirt. I'd left John's jacket on the back of a chair, neither one of us needing it as the crowd swelled in a gyrating frenzy stuffed onto the dance floor with no space between dancers, like a cotton field ready for harvest.

We danced the Black Bottom and the Charleston, and I kicked my legs higher than any of the other girls, holding my dress up above my knees, the champagne helping me stop considering what my aunt might think. We took infrequent breaks at our table, where servants would make sure we had fresh drinks and food that we would down quickly before heading back to the dance floor.

I saw Sarah Beth laughing and chatting with everyone, and I tried to forget my own shyness and do the same. I talked with girls from school who'd rarely paid me any attention before, but who could suddenly forget that when they saw me on John's arm. True to his word, he didn't dance with anybody but me.

It was past midnight, and the party showed no sign of slowing down, which was fine by me. Uncle Joe hadn't given me a curfew, since I was with Willie, and I knew he would most likely be one of the last guests to leave.

John had excused himself for a few moments, and I sat alone at our table. My head was spinning from either the alcohol or the loud music—or maybe both. Perspiration dampened my hairline, and I decided I needed to find a mirror to make sure I wasn't a complete fright. Slipping John's jacket around my shoulders, I stepped out into the chilly night and began walking across the lawn toward the house.

The sounds from the tent behind me seemed muffled now, almost as if the music and the laughter were already a part of an old memory. Thousands of stars, their light unfettered by clouds, sparkled like icicles slipping across the sky toward the horizon. I threw my head back in awe at the spectacle, as if it had been placed there just for me, and found myself wondering how old these stars were, and if my mother had gazed up at a moment in her life and seen the same ones. It comforted me, somehow, knowing that we shared at least this one connection to the universe.

I heard a shout from the woods on the far side of the property, and turned my gaze in time to see a woman, dressed in a maid's uniform, run between the trees, her white cap falling on the grass.

I realized it was Mathilda, and was about to call her name when I saw a white man dressed in evening wear, his tie undone and his jacket missing, run after her. She shouted again, and it sounded like the word "help."

Without thinking, I started running after them, fueled by the champagne and the music and the stars, unaware of my ankle twisting in the soft grass or the branches that slapped at my clothes and face. The moon's milky glow fell through the trees, turning the ground into a sea of shadow and light. I could hear Mathilda crying now, the sound muffled, and I moved forward without regard to what I might do once I found her.

My foot hit something soft and yielding, and I flew through the air, my palms skidding against dead leaves and pine needles. I flipped around; then, digging my heels into the ground, I skidded away until my back was pressed against a tree and stared at the two people lying on the ground in front of me.

Mathilda was flat on her back, the man's hand over her mouth as she cried, her tears reflecting the moonlight. The man—or boy, really—was lying on top of her and looking at me with an expression I'd never seen before. I started when I recognized him as one of Willie's friends, Chas Davis.

"You go away now," he said, his voice slurred and snarling. "This ain't none of your business."

I could see Mathilda struggling to get away, but she was like a fly trying to escape a spider's web.

I'd been raised around livestock and had a vague idea about what was going on, but I'd also been raised with a sure knowledge of right and wrong, and it was pretty easy to see which side of the coin holding down a person against her will fell on.

I swallowed thickly. "No," I said. "You go away. I don't think she wants you to be here."

He started to laugh but it came out as a burp instead. "And if I don't, what are you gonna do about it?"

I didn't know what I was going to say until the words were pouring out of me. "I'm going to start screaming as loud as I can, and then I'm going to tell anybody who will listen that you attacked me."

His eyes narrowed for a moment, as if deciding whether I was serious. To show him that I was serious, I opened my mouth to scream.

The boy cussed, then slid off Mathilda. He was silent for a moment while he attempted to fasten his pants and braces, then swayed and jerked until he was standing. "Wasn't worth it anyhow. Thought I was doing her a favor." He staggered toward the direction we'd come from, stopping about fifteen feet away so he could throw up. It seemed as if both Mathilda and I held our breaths until we could no longer hear him stumbling through the woods.

I crawled to her, noticing that her dress was torn and she was holding it up over her chest. I helped her sit up, then made her put on John's jacket. She protested at first, but I told her it was okay. It was like I was somebody else who suddenly knew all the answers and what to do, but I didn't stop to think about how or why.

I helped her stand, my mind somehow managing to think clearly and start planning how I was going to get her into her room near the kitchen without anybody seeing us. I placed my arm around her and began leading her forward, but she stopped and looked at me with wide eyes.

"You can't tell nobody, Miss Adelaide. Nobody, you hear? Robert can't find out nohow." She hiccuped, her eyes clenched tight. In a loud whisper, she said, "Robert will kill him, and there be hell to pay. You understand, Miss Adelaide? You understand what I say?"

I wanted to argue, but I knew that she was right almost as much as I knew that she wasn't going to let either one of us leave those woods without my agreeing. "All right. I won't tell anybody. I promise." My lips trembled into a little smile. "It'll be our secret."

She didn't return the smile, but nodded solemnly. Then she allowed me to lead her out of the woods. As we paused in the shadows at the edge of the trees and I planned our path back to the kitchen, I became aware of a lone figure standing at the side of the house. A match flared, and as he raised it to his face to light a cigar, I inhaled quickly. It was the man I'd met in the jewelry store, the man John said wasn't somebody he wanted me to associate with. As I stared across the moonlit yard, I realized that he had recognized me, too. He tipped his hat toward me in acknowledgment.

Looking away quickly, I squeezed Mathilda closer to me and began running toward the back door of the kitchen, feeling the man's eyes on my back, just like I imagined I'd feel somebody walking on my grave.

Chapter 22

Vivien Walker Moise
INDIAN MOUND, MISSISSIPPI
APRIL 2013

I parked in front of the midcentury ranch that hadn't changed much in the decade since I'd last seen it. Rocking chairs still sat on the front porch, and an old tire swing still hung from the ancient oak tree in the front of the house that shaded the structure from the hot summer sun. The house wore a coat of fresh white paint, and the lawn had been meticulously manicured with a mower and an edger. Yet there were no flowers in pots or in beds, and no seasonal wreath on the front door. It was like looking at a magazine cover where everything was perfect except for the absence of life.

Tripp answered the door and smiled without showing any surprise, as if we were still in high school and I was coming over so he could help me with my math homework. He wore old jeans that were slung low on his hips, and a Duke University T-shirt. I remembered the day he'd received his acceptance letter, and how I'd let him kiss me. He filled out his shirt and jeans a lot better than he had in high school, and I blushed when he caught me looking. He clutched a napkin in his hand and I could hear a baseball game on television inside.

"I can come back later if you're busy. . . ."

He pulled the door open wider. "I was just finishing up my supper, although I think there's plenty left if you're hungry."

I stepped inside, shaking my head. "No, but thank you. Carol Lynne and Chloe are setting the table in the dining room, so I'd better show up. I won't take up too much of your time."

I looked around the small foyer, recognizing the same furniture and faux-oil landscape paintings on the walls, the same doilies on the backs of chairs in the living room, a triple frame of a toddler Tripp spread out on top of an old-fashioned stereo console that most likely had a turntable and cassette player inside. Everything was dated and tired, a pale memory of the warmth and welcome I'd once felt here. Before I'd even opened my mouth to ask the question, a ball of dread fell thickly into the bottom of my stomach.

"How are your parents?" I asked, my eyes darting around for a pair of slippers or a stray pink hair curler.

"They passed a little over two years ago. Drunk driver hit them on Highway Sixty-one. They were coming back from a big crafts fair in Hollandale. Mama had gotten it in her head that she wanted to start making dollhouses." He grimaced. "I got the call on my radio about the accident and was at the scene to examine the two fatalities when I recognized their car. Not something you forget in a hurry."

I felt sick, remembering Mr. Montgomery's bad jokes that always made me laugh, and his wife's string of hobbies that changed almost as often as a teenage girl changed clothes. They'd been the closest thing I'd had to parents next to Bootsie and Emmett, and they'd loved me like a daughter. It hadn't occurred to me that I'd never see them again.

"I'm so sorry, Tripp. I didn't know."

"You didn't ask," he said, closing the door behind me.

I felt my chest cave with shame at his words. I'd been so lost in my fog that I hadn't even lifted my head to see past my own troubles. As if mine were the only ones worth seeing. "They were good people," I said, Bootsie's words coming back to me without prodding.

"Yes, they were."

"And your sister, Claire? How is she?" Asking Tripp these questions was all wrong. I had grown up with his family, had considered his sister one of my best friends. I should have known that his parents were gone, should have been to the cemetery to see them placed in the ground. I should know where Claire was. Of all that seemed lost to me, this was the hardest to accept. I felt my throat tightening, and the encroaching bleakness that usually sent me for a pill pulsed through me.

"She's in Michigan. Married a boy she met in vet school. They have their own practice in Lansing, and two kids—a boy and a girl."

He regarded me in his nonjudgmental way that only made me feel worse. I wanted him to yell at me, to accuse me of being self-centered and a horrible friend, anything to deflect my own self-loathing.

Instead, he led me back to the kitchen, its fixtures of a more recent vintage than my own kitchen's. He saw me looking at the stainless-steel dishwasher with envy. "Claire paid to redo the kitchen for our parents' thirtieth wedding anniversary. Mama hated it, wanted her old sink and countertops back, but never told Claire. I don't think she knows to this day."

A single plate and empty bottle of beer sat on a small table in the bay window. He switched off the television that sat on the counter, then moved the plate and bottle to the sink. "Can I get you something to drink? I made a pitcher of sweet tea. It's not as good as my mama used to make, but it's not too bad."

"Sure," I said, needing a distraction from the purpose of my visit. I sat down at the table, recognizing the scratches in the surface beneath more recent ones. I knew that if I looked closely, I could find my name in cursive where I'd forgotten to place a magazine under my homework paper when I'd signed it. I watched as he poured a glass for me, then pulled out a beer for himself. It didn't escape my notice that he hadn't offered one to me.

He set the glass in front of me before joining me at the table. I took a drink, my lips puckering from the sweetness. In the low-cal, low-sugar world of California, I'd forgotten all about real sweet tea. As I tried to adjust my taste buds, I looked around me. "It's a lot of house for a bachelor. You ever thought of selling?"

A peculiar light shone in his eyes. "Yeah, a couple of times. Being in the real estate business means I get to see a lot of available properties that might suit me better. But besides this house, there's only one other place I've ever wanted to live."

Tripp had always loved my yellow house, had even called it Dr. Seuss's house when we were in kindergarten, because of its bright color and refusal to adhere to any person's idea of what a home should look like. Since the day he'd found out that's where I lived, he'd resolutely claimed that he would live there one day, too. I would have thought it funny if he hadn't been so serious.

"Yeah, well, that house isn't for sale. If I decide to get rid of it, I'll sell it to Tommy for some nominal amount so he can live there as long as he wants."

"Buying it has never been exactly what I had in mind."

I closed my eyes, feeling the outer edges of panic begin to work through my veins. "Don't, Tripp. Please. I am not that girl you once thought you were in love with. She's so long gone I wouldn't even know how to find her. And to tell you the truth, she wasn't that great to begin with. So get over it, okay? We're not in high school. And don't tell me that you ignored all those Duke girls because of some misguided affection for somebody else."

He leaned back in his chair and put his bare feet up on another one. After taking a long pull from his beer, he said, "Nope, can't say I ignored them. But let's just say there's no comparison." What could only be described as a leer crossed his face. "You're still as fine as frog's hair, Vivi."

"Gee, thanks. I can't say anybody's ever told me that before." I leaned forward, my elbows on the table as my fingers skimmed the icy wetness of the glass. "I need a favor."

His expression didn't change as he watched me from the other side of the table.

"Do you know anybody who does regular doctor stuff? You know, like send in a urine sample to a lab for analysis even if the patient isn't dead yet?"

He took another draw from his beer. "Yep."

Knowing we would sit in silence for hours while I waited for him to ask me why, I explained. "Mark told me I could keep Chloe until the end of his honeymoon if I stopped taking the pills." *I just know you can't do it.* I bit my lip, trying to erase Mark's harsh words. "I haven't had one since yesterday."

He sat up, but his expression didn't change. "It's not good to go cold turkey, Vivi. It's doable, but not recommended. There can be some pretty serious side effects, including convulsions that could kill you. I've seen it more than once in my line of work."

I stared at the slice of lemon bobbing along the top of my sweet tea like a life preserver. "I won't have convulsions. I'll feel sick and have insomnia, and when I sleep I'll have nightmares. And I'll probably shake and have bad headaches. But nothing that I can't handle."

He continued to watch me in silence.

"I quit before. When I found out I was pregnant. I didn't want to hurt the baby."

He said nothing, his eyes empty of reproach, as if he already knew what had made me start again.

"I don't want to see a shrink."

His eyebrows lifted. "I didn't say you should."

"Not out loud. I can do this on my own. If I couldn't do it for me, maybe I can do it for Chloe. Not because I think she'll want to stay here with me on a regular basis, but because I want to give her the option."

"You're a good mother, Vivi."

I shook my head. "Don't say that. It's not in my blood to be a good mother. And God must have agreed, because he didn't even let me carry a pregnancy to term. Chloe is just . . . She needs somebody in her life to look after her, and I didn't see anybody else standing in line," I said, borrowing his own words so he couldn't contradict me.

"Did Chloe make that for you?" he asked.

I realized I'd been turning the wire-and-bead ring Chloe had made for me over and over on my finger. I'd worn the ring for so long that the gesture had become a habit, despite the green marks it left on my skin.

"Yeah. During her jewelry-making phase. The stuff I made was definitely uninspired, but she was pretty good at it. But then she discovered anime and we had to learn something new all over again."

His silence unnerved me. "So will you help me?" I prompted.

"Have I ever said no to you, Vivi? Of course I'll help you. If only because it will give me the opportunity to see you regularly to make sure you're not having any out-of-body experiences because of the withdrawal."

I drained my glass, then slid my chair back. "He wants it done every day—although that's a bit ridiculous, and I'm hoping I can convince him to go up to once a week—and we'll have to send the results to his office. Can you just make sure it doesn't say 'coroner's office' on any of the paperwork? I don't want him to think that your office is the hub of all lab-related activities in Indian Mound. He already thinks we're just a bunch of rednecks who hunt and drink all day."

"Well, he's not too far off the mark, if you think about it. Actually, you'll have to go into a doctor's office to have a witness and then they'll send it to a lab." He reached up to the counter and pulled off a pad and pen, then wrote something down on it. "Remember old Dr. Griffith? He still has his practice, although he doesn't do house calls anymore. He's been holding off on retirement, hoping I'll one day give in and go to medical school and then take over his practice. I keep telling him that dealing with dead people is a lot easier than dealing with the live ones." He tore off the top piece of paper and slid it over to me. "I'll give him a call to let him know what's going on, and then you can call and set up a schedule."

"Thanks," I said, staring down at the paper. Without looking up, I said, "What's the real reason you didn't go to medical school?"

He didn't speak for a long moment, and I found myself wishing I hadn't said anything. "I did go. But halfway through, when I realized that you weren't coming back, I sort of reevaluated what I wanted to do with the rest of my life. I wanted to do something that had no memories of you attached to it. Working with dead people sort of fit the bill."

I slumped against the back of my chair. "Don't feel you always have to be so honest with me, okay? What happened to all that Southern politeness we're supposed to be so famous for?"

"You deserve better than that." He stood and took my glass, putting it and his bottle in the sink. "I was headed toward your house this evening, but you saved me a trip. The crime lab was able to extract DNA from the remains. The lab supervisor owed me a favor and she pushed it up the priority list."

I felt a little stab at the word "she," but chose to ignore it. Judging by the calmness on Tripp's face, he had something dramatic to tell me. "It's a match, isn't it?" I didn't feel any surprise. In the medicated cloud in which I'd been living, I hadn't allowed myself to examine too deeply the implications of why a woman would be buried on my property. But now I felt the insidious fingers of real emotions nudge at my heart, and all I could do was wish I had a pill to take.

"Yes, it is. The mitochondrial DNA—that's the DNA passed down through the women in a family—was a match."

I tried to think of what that meant, but my brain remained fuzzy. "So what do we do now?"

"Sheriff Adams will probably want to come over again and chat with you and Tommy, maybe even go see Mathilda—although she always wants to go to sleep when he gets there. I'd start digging in your attic, see if there are any old letters, newspaper articles, or diaries—anything that might mention a woman who went away and never came back. I saw Carrie Holmes the other day—she told me to remind you about the archives that are waiting to be sorted and organized. That might be a good place to start. Especially since Sheriff Adams is a little shorthanded, and this is definitely a cold case. I'm afraid if you want this case solved before you're in Sunset Acres, you'll have to do some of your own sleuthing."

"Great," I said, feeling a small tremor in my hands.

"You okay to drive?" he asked, and I realized he'd seen them shaking.

"I'm fine. I've done this before, remember? The withdrawal effects will be gone within the week. Two at the most."

Without a word, he picked up my phone that I'd left on the table and pushed a few buttons before handing it to me. "True, but the reasons you reach for a pill will still be there until you confront them. You have my number now. Just call me if you need to talk to somebody."

I snatched the phone from his hand and tossed it into my purse. "I don't think that will be necessary."

He followed me out the door, his long strides keeping up with mine. "Hang on; I've got a watch for Tommy. He said he'd have a little time once the planting is over, and I was planning on bringing it when I dropped by with the DNA news."

I sighed, annoyed that he'd ruined my dramatic exit. All through my growing-up years, I'd been famous for them. I'd even once thought that it meant something.

We stopped at his car and I waited while he opened the glove box and pulled out a silver watch in a Ziploc bag. I opened my large purse for him to dump it inside and we both caught sight of the bottle of pills sitting in the bottom. Before I could talk myself out of it, I pulled out the bottle and handed it to him. "There. Even trade."

I snapped my purse shut, then got in my car and started the engine. Tripp leaned into the open window of the passenger side. I looked at him expectantly, wondering if he was going to apologize.

"No matter where you go, there you are."

I pressed down hard on the accelerator and backed out of the driveway with a squeal of tires, just like I'd done when he'd said that to me nine years before.

Almost a week later, I stood barefoot in the garden, dirt and sweat sticking to every part of my body and making me feel like a chicken leg ready for the fryer. Firmly embedded soil clung to my fingernails like polish had once done, and I wore a pair of cutoff denim shorts that could only be described as Daisy Dukes. None of my clothes from LA seemed to be good gardening clothes, and I'd been left to dig through my dresser drawers. The shorts were at least a size too small, and I prayed the zipper would stay up, since I hadn't quite managed to fasten the top button.

My sunglasses kept slipping down my nose, but my eyes couldn't take the brightness of the sun. My tremors had gotten better, as had the nausea, but the insomnia and nightmares seemed to be getting worse, the lack of sleep doing nothing to improve my mood or ever-present headache.

I leaned down to uproot yet another weed.

"Nice jorts, Booger."

Straightening, I scowled at my brother. He looked worse than me, with dark circles under his eyes, his hair sticking up around his head from him running his fingers through it one too many times, and it looked like he'd worn the same shirt and jeans enough times that they could stand up without him.

"How's the planting?" I asked. I hadn't seen more than his coming or going since he'd started to seed his fields. It was important to get all the fields seeded at the same time so everything was on the same schedule, even if it meant working sixteen- to eighteen-hour days. I'd once thought riding in the tractor next to Emmett was just this side of heaven, the hum and jerk of the motor like being rocked in a cradle. Emmett said it was because I had a connection to this land, because my family had worked it for generations. I remembered that now—

remembered how I'd regarded the long furrows of the fields like the arms of my ancestors reaching out to embrace me. But as I got older, I began to regard them as the arms that wanted to hold me down.

"Not too bad. The weather's holding out. For now." He looked up at the sky with a frown and I followed his gaze toward the high, thin clouds that Emmett had called mare's tails, and which he taught us always meant a change in the weather. "Breeze is picking up, too."

" 'Wind out of the southeast is good for neither man nor beast,' " I said, quoting Emmett's favorite phrase.

We both smiled, but Tommy's face remained grim. "I don't think I'll really sleep until harvest."

"Only five more months," I said, trying for a light tone. But I couldn't help but wonder which one of us looked worse or needed the sleep more.

"I thought you hated to get your hands dirty—that you were strictly an observation-only gardener."

"Yeah, well, I needed something to do, and I couldn't stand seeing Bootsie's garden looking so pathetic."

He nodded. "Where's Mama?"

I jerked my head in the direction of the back door. "Inside with Chloe and Cora. Cora's involved with a homeschool group and agreed to help me get Chloe up to speed so she can finish her school year here. Carol Lynne wanted to join them, and it was okay with Cora. They're supposed to be diagramming sentences this morning. I figure it couldn't hurt. Maybe jog something in Carol Lynne's brain."

Tommy's face grew serious. "It won't come back, you know. Her memory. Every once in a while you'll see a flash of it, and she'll act like she knows what's going on, but most of the time she's just somebody who kinda looks like our mother and sorta remembers who you are. Or who you were, anyway."

I grabbed a fistful of grass and yanked it from the earth, scattering dirt like confetti. "Well, isn't that convenient for her. How I'd love it if I didn't have to answer for all of my past mistakes."

"You think she did this on purpose?" Tommy's voice was low and serious, but lacked any malice or recrimination. It was simply his way of trying to find the truth of things.

I yanked up another clump of dogged weeds. "I don't know,

Tommy. I don't know anything right now except that I can't sleep, the woman they found buried in our yard is related to us, and I've pretty much lost everything I once thought I wanted, and all I want to do is take a pill so it will all go away." *Yank.* "But I can't, because I promised my ex-husband that I would stop so Chloe could stay here." *Yank.* "So, no, I don't really have an opinion one way or the other as to whether or not Carol Lynne had anything to do with her own illness."

He examined the gate with the eye of a carpenter, then spoke without looking at me.

"Before she got sick, she never stopped asking about you, or thinking about schemes to bring you back. It was Bootsie who said you'd have to come back on your own. On your own terms. I don't think Mama ever accepted that. She kept trying to convince Bootsie and me to drive out to California to bring you back. She would have done it on her own, but she'd never learned to drive."

He paused and I sat back on my heels, searching for something to say that would make him stop. But no words came, like they, too, were prisoners of the same false hope I'd had as a child that had made me rush to my bedroom window every time I heard a car pull up outside the house.

"When she first started with the symptoms, she told me it was important you knew that. Knew that she'd never stopped loving you, or wishing she'd have another chance to show you. You have that in common, you know. No matter how many times you failed at something, you always picked yourself up and tried again."

Not this time. "It's too late, Tommy. It's been too late for a long, long time."

He was silent, and I thought he'd left, but when I looked up he was watching me, his face looking as tired as I felt. "Carrie called me—not sure who gave her my cell, but whatever. She wanted me to convince you that she really needs your help with the archives. The new library opens in October, and she's afraid that the shelves in the historical reference section will be empty."

I squinted at him, seeing the fuzzy edges of an optical migraine beginning to cloud my vision. "Do you think she's really that desperate or just trying to find an excuse to talk with you?"

He gave me his boyish grin that made him look like the brother who'd taught me how to fish and ride a bike, and helped me not notice too much that our mama had left us again. "Maybe a little of both." He shrugged. "Either way, working at the library might give you something to do right now while you're waiting to figure out what's next. And you always liked to write. Carrie said they could really use somebody to write a regular column to get people excited about the opening of the library. Sounds like a win-win to me."

I'd always hated people telling me what I should do—mostly because my own ideas were usually epic failures. In hindsight I realized they were just trying to save me from myself, but it didn't make it any easier. "I might not be here in October. I'd hate to leave her high and dry."

"She said she'll take whatever she can get. She sounded kind of desperate."

The floating worms of my migraine had moved to the outer edges of my sight, obscuring my peripheral vision so all I could focus on was my brother. "I might—if I can find the time. I thought I'd restore Bootsie's garden. I even had a pipe dream that I could get Carol Lynne and Chloe to help me."

A corner of his mouth lifted. "Yeah, well, good luck with that."

I turned my head so I could view the garden better, then wished that I hadn't. It all seemed so hopeless, like I was trying to raise a person from the dead.

"I have some of Bootsie's seeds in the shed. They're all separated and labeled and should still be good. I'll go get them if you want."

"Sure," I said. "Maybe she'll have some of her magic beans mixed in with the regular seeds so that I can actually get something to grow."

"You'll manage. You always do." He leaned on the gate, making it groan. "When I get around to chopping up that cypress, I'll repair this and the rest of the fence. Don't want any of the local wildlife eating my okra and pole beans."

He waved, and I watched him leave, almost staggering in his exhaustion.

"Nice jorts," Chloe said from over the fence, Carol Lynne behind her. They both wore braids, and Chloe was wearing one of my mother's floral tops, but still had on her black jeans and heavy black combat boots. Ignoring her jibe, I said, "Are you done with your morning lessons?"

"Yeah, but I'm supposed to read now. And then I'm supposed to study science with a group of homeschool kids—or Mrs. Smith said I could ride around in the fields with Tommy and write about it. I'll do whichever is less boring."

"You might not want to mention that when you ask Tommy."

She plopped down in one of the green chairs, and I noticed she held my copy of *Time at the Top* in her lap. On her left arm she wore what appeared to be a blue enamel bracelet that was nearly buried under all of her braided leather bracelets from another jewelry craze in her recent past.

"Is that new?" I asked.

Holding up her arm, she twisted her wrist from side to side. "It's a watch. I found it in the hatbox in your room that you told me to go through and sort. It doesn't work but it's pretty."

I nodded, not remembering it from my own childhood days of playing in Emmett's hatbox.

"What are you doing?"

I blinked up at Carol Lynne, who was staring down at me as if she really wanted to know.

"I'm weeding so we can get the garden ready to plant."

She knelt down in the dirt beside me, her hands resting on the thighs of her jeans. "How do you do that?"

I waited to see if she would laugh to show me that she was joking, but she looked serious. "Do you want to help me?"

She nodded.

"Okay. Here." I took her hand and guided her to a clump of yellow Indian grass. It was the closest I'd been to her since I'd reluctantly comforted her on the day after the storm. I wanted her to be a stranger, wanted not to recognize the lemony scent of her skin, or the way her hair strands in the sun were hundreds of different colors, just like mine.

Putting my fingers around hers, I squeezed near the bottom of the shafts and pulled, tearing the roots out of the soil.

I let go as she started to clap, spraying clumps of dirt all around us. "That was fun!" she said.

I smiled reluctantly. "Great," I said. "Then do that to every single thing you see growing in this garden, then toss it in the big garbage bin behind you."

Turning to Chloe, I said, "Are you going to help?"

She scrunched up her face with a look of utter disdain. "I'm supposed to be reading."

"Fine. Then read. But read out loud. That's one of my favorite books."

Chloe gave me a sigh worthy of Hollywood, but opened the book and began to read while Carol Lynne and I dug our hands into the dark earth and began to uproot the weeds in our garden.

Chapter 23

Carol Lynne Walker Moise
NEVADA
OCTOBER 1964

Dear Diary,

I miss the autumn. I used to love to watch the sunsets from on top of our Indian mound with Mathilda, and she'd make me describe all the beautiful colors of cypress trees until I ran out of words for red. Now I only know it's October because of all the Halloween candy for sale in the gas stations and grocery stores we can go to only once. Jimmy said that once we steal from a place, we can't go back. People are peculiar that way, I guess.

I'm in the Nevada desert now, where there aren't any trees. Just our campsite and the smell of beans cooking on open fires and the scent of weed that floats over our group. Or merry band of waifs and adventurers, which is how Jimmy describes us. He's always been so creative. The thing with Jimmy is that I only saw his talent and brilliance when I was high, which was most of the time. I think he figured that out, because one morning last month when I woke up, the sleeping bag next to me was empty. I guess he's not coming back.

I don't miss him all that much, except that I'm sober a lot more now. I don't like that feeling. Because then I start thinking about Mississippi and how far from home I am. Sometimes in the morning I wake up and I think I smell Mathilda frying bacon and then I realize it's just a can of beans in a pot on the campfire. It's all Hiram knows how to cook, and I'm grateful—I am. But what I wouldn't give for Mathilda's fried catfish or Bootsie's corn bread.

Hiram's from Colorado. He was living with Jimmy's brother in San Francisco and has been traveling with us ever since we got kicked out of the apartment for squatting. He had a girl, Mary, but she got sick and decided she would go home. I can't remember where she said that was. Everything's in such a fog. I like that. I think. At least I don't have to remember all the hopes I once had about saving the world. I was in a Woolco stealing aspirin when the man behind the counter turned up his radio and told us all to hush. They were talking about three civil rights workers murdered in Philadelphia, Mississippi, by the KKK. I wanted to fall down on my knees or raise my fist to the sky for those three men who died doing what I should have been. But instead I just put three more bottles of aspirin in my purse and got high in the back of the van in the parking lot.

I wonder how far from Mississippi I have to get before I forget about the place I come from. My memories of home are like a river, and I spend a lot of time fighting the current that's always trying to take me back.

Two of the girls with us are pregnant, and there are about ten children always running about half-naked, because that's how nature intended. I'm lucky so far, I guess. I was never one of those girls who dreamed of having babies. But sometimes when I see these girls rocking their babies to sleep I wonder what it would mean to pass on all your hopes and dreams to someone, to hold a little person who completely belongs to you. I sometimes wonder if Bootsie ever felt that way about me, or if I was just another one of her plants that needed to be plucked from her garden before the bugs that were eating it destroyed the rest.

NOVEMBER 1964

I'm back in Mississippi. I've had a real bad cough for about a month, and Hiram gave me money for a doctor, but instead I bought a bus ticket. I haven't been sick a whole lot in my life, but when I am, all I want is my bed in my room in my house, with Mathilda and Bootsie bringing me chicken soup and laying cool hands on my forehead. A prissy woman was sitting across the aisle from me on the bus and kept giving me looks every time I coughed. Or maybe it was because I smelled. I'd been giving myself baths in gas station restroom sinks for a while, so maybe she had a point.

I thumbed a ride from the station from an old guy in a pickup truck going to his brother's funeral in Biloxi, and he didn't seem to mind the smell. He was nice enough and told me to take care of myself when he dropped me off on the highway in front of the long drive that led to the house. I didn't want to give Bootsie any warning. I didn't want her locking the door on me.

I went to my cypress tree first, to see if it recognized me, and when I sat down on its roots I knew I was home. I fell asleep, and that's where Bootsie found me. Emmett carried me to the big black bed in Bootsie's room, and then the doctor came and told me it was pneumonia.

I'll be here for a while, until I'm all better. But I know I won't stay. It's not in my nature. Or maybe because I heard Bootsie crying outside my door when she thought I was sleeping. There's something in the ways of mothers and daughters, I think, that makes us see all the bad parts of ourselves. Or maybe there's a part of me that wants to hurt her as badly as she hurt me. I'd like to think not.

She told me the story again of my grandmother, who was lost in the flood of 1927. She told me that when her mother left she knew the levees had been breached, but she got in her car anyway and told her friend that she had to drive to New Orleans. And then she gave Bootsie to her friend to look after before she drove away. It saved Bootsie's life, but she'd never stopped wondering why her mama didn't take her with her.

I thought of the river bursting out of its boundaries created by men, its strong-flowing current sweeping up everything in its path. I know what that's like, to feel like your destiny isn't really yours but decided upon by things that happened long before you were born.

I tried to tell this to Bootsie, but she just smiled and told me to wait until I become a mother, and then I will understand that my real destiny will be decided by those not yet born.

I know she's wrong. That's why I need to figure it all out on my own. I fell asleep trying to remember what it was I'd been looking for, and what I'd been running from. I didn't come up with any answers, but it seems to me that it doesn't really matter anymore. I need to leave again, if only to show Bootsie that I control my own life, and that I'm strong enough to swim against the current to find my own way.

Chapter 24

Adelaide Walker Bodine
INDIAN MOUND, MISSISSIPPI
MAY 1924

Sarah Beth lurched back and forth over the road, our scarf-covered hair trying desperately to escape and fly in the breeze. The earth was fuzzy with new cotton plants, making all the fields resemble the heads of balding men with swirls of thin hair on top. Uncle Joe was in a good mood, saying the *Farmers' Almanac* was predicting good weather for cotton growing and a bountiful harvest. Willie just stomped around the house, muttering about wasted financial opportunities that had once again been sunk into the soil of our farm.

Willie told me in private that the best part of going to college was missing the planting, and the best part about being home was getting a job at the bank, thanks to Mr. Heathman. Sarah Beth swore up and down that she had nothing to do with it, insisting that Willie and her father had their own association. I couldn't imagine what that would be—our families even went to separate churches, and her father and my uncle were barely acquaintances—but every morning Willie dressed in a sharp suit with a vest, tie, and pressed pocket square, then drove to the bank, where he'd work all day. "Pushing papers," as Uncle Joe would say with a frown.

And just about every night, he would pick up Sarah Beth and they would go dancing. John and I would go sometimes, too, but only to places John said weren't too low-end. Everywhere we went, the juice-joint owners knew John by name, and never asked him for money for our drinks. Which, John said, meant he couldn't be arrested, since he wasn't buying alcohol. He'd wink when he said this, and Willie would slug back another shot like they were celebrating something.

A few times, Willie would have to leave early—which got Sarah Beth real steamed—or he claimed a former commitment, and then after I'd gone to bed I would hear him sneak into the house in the early hours of the morning. The back stairs would creak, and I'd know it was him because I could smell the lingering scent of wood smoke as it crept under my door like an unwelcome visitor.

I'd asked him about it once, and he'd told me that he and other like-minded citizens would have private political meetings to discuss upholding justice in a world where justice didn't seem to have a place anymore. He'd kissed me on the forehead and told me he was making our community safer for Sarah Beth and me. And then he'd told me not to breathe a word about it to anybody, especially not to Aunt Louise or Uncle Joe. They were happy in their little world of cotton and church, and they just didn't understand the bigger complexities of life.

When I asked him if I could tell John, since he was going to be my husband and I didn't feel it right that I should keep any secrets from him, Willie had laughed, and then asked me who I thought was supplying the booze for his political meetings. I smiled as if I understood, but his words had sent a cold chill through me. Obviously John didn't feel the same as I did about secrets between husband and wife. I'd promised myself to ask John about his other business activities before our wedding, and I knew I was running out of time. I knew he loved me, and nothing I could say to him would make him love me less. But still I hesitated, afraid that by my rocking the boat, all of the unlikable things about me would lie exposed for him to see and force him to go find another girl worthy of his love.

Sarah Beth honked her horn at a mule-drawn milk wagon, making the poor animal start and run off the road, the dairy farmer waving his fist at her as she sped by, stirring up waves of dirt. She'd wrecked her other car, and her father had bought her a car with a removable top—

what Sarah Beth referred to as a breezer—which she adored, but which I thought just made it more difficult to keep my hair nice. And I always ended up with new freckles every time I rode with her. Her new car didn't have a rumble seat, so Mathilda sat in the back looking petrified. She'd been given a list of things to be picked up at the grocer's and the butcher's, all to be put on the Heathmans' account. To keep Mathilda honest, Mrs. Heathman wrote everything down on a note to be handed to the respective shopkeepers.

We were on our way to town to look at wedding gowns at Hamlin's, and Mrs. Heathman had made an appointment for me with Mrs. Hamlin herself, the epitome of good taste and fashion, according to Sarah Beth's mother. Aunt Louise had wanted me to wear my mother's gown, but Mrs. Heathman—who seemed almost more excited about the wedding than I did—had said it wouldn't do. So we'd compromised, and I'd be wearing my mother's veil. Aunt Louise had been happy, saying it would be like having my mother there with me.

Sarah Beth screeched to a stop, and as I got out I noticed that she was crooked and too far from the curb, the rear end sticking clear out into Main Street. Mathilda exited the backseat, narrowly being missed by a chauffeur-driven Cadillac barreling down the road.

"Sarah Beth!" I shouted. "I think you need to move your car— you're going to get hit."

She laughed. "Don't be silly. It's bright red—they can't help but see it. And there's plenty of room for them to go around." Her eyes flickered down my dress. "It's snowing down south."

I looked at her in confusion, but she just closed her eyes and shook her head. She began walking down the sidewalk toward Hamlin's. "Hurry, Adelaide, or we'll be late."

"Your slip be showing, Miss Adelaide," Mathilda said quietly.

I thanked her and was trying to surreptitiously pull my skirt down while standing in the middle of the sidewalk when I noticed that the car that had sped past us had stopped, and was backing down Main Street regardless of whatever other traffic happened to be on the road. I heard Mathilda suck in her breath and then I did the same as I recognized the man behind the rolled-down window in the backseat.

"Miss Bodine, Miss Heathman. What a pleasure to see you both again."

The chauffeur jumped out of the car and opened the back door to allow the man to step out onto the curb.

I stood without saying anything, unsure how to greet him. He took off his fedora and gave me a genuine smile that confused me. "Angelo Berlini," he said. "We met at the jewelry store."

"Yes," I said, my voice clipped, remembering how John had told me that Mr. Berlini wasn't the kind of man I needed to know. I glanced across the street, knowing before I did so that Peacock's was too far down the block for John to be able to look out the window and see us. "I remember you."

"Mr. Berlini. What a pleasure to see you back in Indian Mound." Sarah Beth stepped forward, holding her gloved hand out to the man, who in turn kissed it, then held it in his own hand for longer than Aunt Louise would think was proper. "The pleasure is all mine. I haven't seen you since your parents' New Year's Eve party, and may I say that you're even lovelier now?"

Color flared in her cheeks, making me want to remind her that she was practically engaged to my cousin. "You certainly know how to flatter a girl." She turned to me. "I didn't realize you knew each other."

The man's smile returned. "Actually, it was only briefly. She had just lost something." He clasped his hands in front of him like a choirboy. "And how fortunate that I ran into you this afternoon to let you know that I found what you lost. It's at my hotel right now as we speak."

Sarah Beth narrowed her eyes at me. "That's funny. You never mentioned losing anything to me."

Before I could say anything, Mr. Berlini interjected, "That's because it's a surprise for you, Miss Heathman." Turning to me, he said, "Do you have a few moments now? I'm staying at the Main Street Hotel on the square. I promise I won't take too much of your time."

I could feel Sarah Beth's curiosity and wrath almost pulsate in the air between us. "I'm afraid we're already late for an appointment for Adelaide. She's shopping for her wedding gown. Perhaps another time . . ."

Mr. Berlini looked genuinely disappointed. "That's a shame, because I'm leaving very early in the morning and I've appointments for the rest of the day. I'm afraid this is the only opportunity I have, and I don't know when I'll be back."

"Sure," I said, surprising myself. I'd been lying to Sarah Beth about her coat for months, constantly forgetting to return it, and then saying it had been sent away to be professionally cleaned. I'd begun to wonder how I was going to find the money to buy a new one. I turned to my friend. "Please tell Mrs. Hamlin that I'll be there in no more than twenty minutes, all right?"

"But, Adelaide, it's not proper. I should go, too."

I knew she cared about propriety as much as she cared that there was a law against drinking. "But that will spoil your surprise. If it makes you feel better, I'll take Mathilda."

I looked at the young girl and her eyes were wide with alarm. But she nodded her head, and I knew she was remembering the night of the party and us racing across the moonlit lawn. The chauffeur opened the doors on the other side of the car. "You get in the front," Mr. Berlini said, indicating Mathilda. "I'll sit in the back with Miss Bodine."

"What about me?" Sarah Beth said, a whine in her throat.

Mr. Berlini took his hand in hers. "You are getting a personal invitation to come to my restaurant in New Orleans. You can bring your parents, or your friends." He paused. "Or you can come alone. Either way, I promise you will have a grand time." He slid a small white card into her hand, then kissed her knuckles again. "I hope to see you soon."

Sarah Beth's nostrils flared, her lips parting slightly and reminding me of the actress Mary Pickford right before she got kissed by the hero. I slid into the car, pushing aside my misgivings. I wanted the stupid coat back in Sarah Beth's closet and out of my conscience. Besides, as Mr. Berlini had said, it would only take a few moments, and I had Mathilda to chaperone.

Mathilda sat in the front seat, glancing back at me when Mr. Berlini got into the car. We drove around the block once and stopped in front of his hotel. Leaning forward, he said to the chauffeur, "I want you and the maid to get out here. Miss Bodine and I are going for a little drive."

"I don't understand . . ." I said, reaching for the door handle.

"Stop," he said, his voice low. "I have a matter of much urgency that I need to discuss with you in private. It involves your fiancé."

"About John?" I asked, letting go of the door handle.

"Yes. I promise you that I will not take up too much of your time, and I will have you at your appointment in twenty minutes, just as you told Miss Heathman—with her fur coat. You have my word."

He exited the car and held my door open. "Come on and sit up front with me."

I glanced at Mathilda, then slid into the recently vacated front seat. "You go run your errands. I'll be fine."

The car lurched to a start and I wondered if it was because Mr. Berlini was eager to get away or because he was unused to driving his own car. We'd driven a good bit before he spoke to me.

"Congratulations on your upcoming wedding, Adelaide. May I call you Adelaide? You may call me Angelo."

"Sure," I said. I wanted to ask him what business he had with John, but I didn't want to appear naive. Sarah Beth told me it was my biggest flaw and that I needed to try to be more sophisticated.

He pulled off the road and I realized with a start that we were on the road leading to the Ellis plantation. He stopped the engine on the drive in front of the ruins of the old house and I found myself listening to the sound of my own breathing and the pulsing of the cicadas in the trees.

He didn't look at me at first, but stared out the windshield, his lips moving as if he were chewing on an invisible cigar. "Your fiancé is a lucky man."

I wasn't sure if he wanted me to respond, so I didn't say anything.

Mr. Berlini turned to me, and my palms began to sweat. It wasn't that he was so handsome, or even so intimidating. It was his aura of power and confidence that rolled off of him like sweat, and I wasn't entirely sure that it was a bad thing. He continued. "I admire him. Very ambitious. Smart, too. He wants to set himself up as a respectable man, with a nice home and his own business, so he can be a worthy husband."

I nodded, wishing I understood why he was telling me all this.

He returned to staring out the windshield and moving his lips. "There's something you should know about me, that might help you to help your husband. I came from Italy with twelve cents in my pocket and a loaf of bread, and when I'd earned enough money I sent for my mother and sister. I worked delivering groceries all day and working in a button factory at night to keep us off the streets of New Orleans. We lived in a slum, but things were still better than where we came from, because at least here we had the opportunity to make something of ourselves." He glanced briefly across the seat to me. "Your fiancé understands this well, I believe." His teeth worked his lower lip for a moment as he returned to staring out the windshield. "And then one day there's a fire in our tenement and we lose everything—including all the money I'd been saving. My beautiful little sister and my own mother started selling themselves on the streets just to eat. I got a job on a lumber barge, and when I came back I found out that they were both dead from whatever sickness takes those with nothing left to fight."

He turned to me. "My sister was sweet and kind and beautiful. You remind me of her, just like John reminds me of me, with all of his ambition and plans. That's why I'm trying to help you." His dark eyes studied me intently. "I'm having a hard time reaching him lately, so I need you to pass on a message from me. I'm hoping he's better at listening to you than he has been at listening to me." Reaching into his pocket, he pulled out a packet of Wrigley's chewing gum and offered me a stick. I shook my head and he shrugged before unwrapping a stick for himself and shoving it into his mouth.

He chewed in silence for a moment. "I think John keeps forgetting that I'm not the boss. And the guy who is isn't as nice and understanding as I am. He doesn't have the affection that I have for you and your fiancé."

He reached into his pocket and pulled out another stick of gum and shoved it into his mouth, chewing in agitation, and I wondered if he'd normally calm his nerves with a cigar but was being a gentleman since I was in the car. "I'm hoping to appeal to your female mind's ability to recognize the right thing to do. See, John and I have been business associates for a few years in what has been a very profitable venture for everyone concerned. He knows the people down here and they respect him and trust him. That's worth a million bucks to any businessman trying to make a living in a place where he's considered an outsider. You understand what I'm saying?"

I nodded, only because I knew we didn't have the time for him to explain it to me.

He continued. "So when John tells me that he wants to end our business relationship so that he can get married and settle down, it worried me. I understand his reasons, but my boss won't. And no, I haven't told him yet—I've been hoping to convince John otherwise so I don't have to." He smacked his gum, the smell of peppermint filling the space between us.

"Mr. Berlini . . ."

"Angelo."

"Yes, sorry. Angelo. I'm sure John hasn't meant to hurt you in any way. I know he plans to continue working at the jewelry store, and I don't see how that would affect your relationship. . . ."

The strangest look came over his face, and his skin turned a mottled purple color as a sound that could have been laughter erupted from his mouth. "The jewelry store?" he finally managed to spit out.

I could only stare at him, having no idea what was so funny.

His expression became serious suddenly. "Look, I need your help here. For John's sake. He needs to be straight with you about things, but you can help him by letting him know that he could be in a lot of trouble if he ends our business relationship. A lot of trouble. He'll know what that means."

"All right," I said, recalling the story of his sister and his mother. There was a deep hurt in his eyes that I recognized and understood. Maybe that was why I'd stopped being afraid of him.

He sat back, chewing on his gum. "I only want the best for both of you. Tell John that, too." He grinned. "And make sure I get an invitation to the wedding."

He put the car in gear again, driving out onto the road and back into town without another word. He pulled up at the curb in front of Hamlin's just as Mathilda was crossing the street from the grocer's. She stopped when she spotted the car and pulled back into the shadow of an awning.

"Can I have the fur coat now?" I asked, trying to make my voice sound calm and mature, even though my mind was spinning with everything he'd said and everything I didn't know.

He chuckled softly. "You are more charming than you know, Miss Bodine. But it's mixed with an innocence that's oddly alluring. I find it very attractive. Too bad John found you first."

I opened my door and jumped out of the car before he could say another word. Of all the things I was supposed to tell John, that last part wouldn't be one of them.

Mr. Berlini opened his door and slowly stood, then sauntered to the rear of the car before opening the trunk. Inside was Sarah Beth's fur coat, huddled carelessly in the corner like a sleeping fox.

I reached inside and grabbed it before he could say another word, then walked quickly down the sidewalk to where Mathilda stood, watching and waiting. I suddenly understood why he'd taken the coat, and how patient he'd been for five months. *Like a spider in a web,* I thought.

"It was a pleasure getting to know you better, Adelaide," he called after me. "Please give my regards to your fiancé."

I turned, with a tight smile and a nod, then hurried past Mathilda, my stomach roiling with uneasiness, and my arms heavy with the weight of the dead thing in my arms.

Chapter 25

Vivien Walker Moise
INDIAN MOUND, MISSISSIPPI
MAY 2013

I was having the same nightmare again, the one I'd been having since
I stopped medicating myself. I wondered how long it would be until
the bad dreams stopped or I didn't reach for the pill bottle every time I
awoke with a scream in the back of my throat.

In the dream, I was in the backyard standing at the edge of the hole,
looking down at the skeleton. While I watched, the skull smiled, and
then a bony hand reached up toward me. Before I could pull away, I
found myself lying among the roots of the old tree, and somebody was
shoveling dirt over my body.

My desire not to be terrified each night was a strong deterrent to falling asleep. Once again, I found myself throwing off my covers and then
walking through the sleeping house, my bare feet padding along familiar
corridors and avoiding the creaks I remembered from my childhood.

Slowly, I walked down the front staircase, watching the moonlight
through the fan window over the doors etch patterns on the wall. I sat
down on the steps in front of the watermark, somehow drawn to this
place during each of my midnight wanderings, regardless of where I
started or ended.

I placed my hand on the spot on the wall that had become a monument to our past, the plaster cool to my touch, and heard Bootsie telling me about her mother, who'd been lost in the flood, and how she'd saved Bootsie's life by leaving her behind. But the unanswered question of why she'd been left had haunted my grandmother her entire life. I dropped my hand and clenched my eyes, trying to block out the strength of the feelings coursing through me. Or maybe they weren't really that strong at all, but felt without filters for the first time in more years than I cared to count. I hadn't yet decided if that was a good thing or not.

I began to cry, not really sure why. But I felt Bootsie's absence like a physical thing, like a gaping wound in my chest where I couldn't make it stop bleeding. Maybe I was crying for her, like a child wanting her blanket. Or maybe I was crying for the little girls we'd all once been, sobbing for our mothers who were no longer there.

The central air-conditioning—installed after my mother's return— clicked off, and I imagined I could hear the house breathing around me, the slow inhale and exhale of all the years that had settled inside its walls. I leaned against the stair railings and was considering falling asleep sitting upright when the clinking sound of silverware came from the direction of the kitchen. Thinking it was Tommy finally home from the fields, I moved through the foyer toward the back of the house and opened the swinging door that led to the kitchen.

The only lights on were the under-cabinet light beneath the giant 1980s microwave and the small china lamp that sat on the telephone table where a collection of Yellow Pages books lay gathering dust. Sitting absolutely still at the laminate table, her face showing the same surprise I felt, was Chloe. She wore an old nightgown that had once belonged to Bootsie, with lots of lace and flounces and that was way too long. I had no idea where she'd found it, but assumed Carol Lynne had something to do with it. I was just happy to see Chloe in something that wasn't black.

My fingers fumbled for the wall switch before flicking on the overhead fluorescents, leaving Chloe and me blinking in the sudden light like moles emerging from their holes. When my vision had recovered, I was able to see what was on the table in front of her. A collection of mismatched Tupperware containers and one Cool Whip bucket, all containing leftovers carefully stored by Cora Smith, sat on the table like an audience waiting for the big show. A clean fork and spoon lay on top of an empty plate, untouched, as a despondent-looking Chloe frowned at me from one of the orange vinyl chairs.

"Go away," she said, putting her face in her hands, but not before I'd seen her beautiful blue eyes devoid of black eyeliner.

Pretending I hadn't heard her, I pulled back another chair and sat down. "I thought you might be Tommy," I said. "He's been working all sorts of weird hours. It's real nice of you to make him a plate." As I spoke, I slid the plate and silverware toward me, and then began popping open the Tupperware lids, hearing the satisfying burp of air.

She leaned back in her chair, her arms crossed over her chest, and continued scowling at me. I decided to use Tripp's trick and not speak at all, hoping I could wait her out. I began scooping out multicolored Jell-O salad, sweet potato casserole, a couple of pork chops, and fried okra, taking my time arranging everything so that the plate looked like a gastronomical work of art.

I played with the food so long, waiting for her to speak, that the Jell-O began to get runny and form a little river through the potatoes. I knew Tommy would never touch it, remembering how when we were younger Bootsie would have to serve each food item on a separate plate for Tommy, who would actually gag if two items should dare spread into each other's territory. I assumed that his being nearly forty hadn't meant that his culinary peculiarities had improved any.

"I was hungry," she said finally. "And I didn't know what was in all these container things so I had to take them all out."

I began to form tall peaks with the potatoes, sticking a fried okra on top for a final flourish. "That's fine. But you know you probably wouldn't be so hungry if you'd eat more at supper."

"But it's all bad stuff—all those carbs and nonorganic vegetables. My dad would kill me if he knew I was eating all that crap."

My eyes scanned the smorgasbord on the table as if to remind her of what she *hadn't* eaten, but I didn't comment on her flawed logic. Nor did I correct her on her language. I knew this was one of those times when I had to pick my battle.

"Chloe, you should never eat or not eat something because somebody tells you to. You're almost thirteen. You're old enough to make your own food choices."

She continued to scowl but didn't interrupt me.

"My grandmother had very simple rules when it came to eating—eat when you're hungry, don't eat until you're stuffed, eat a variety of foods, and never say no to dessert. And she was right. Once I told myself I could eat the yummy stuff, I stopped wanting it just because I wasn't supposed to have it."

"That's easy for you to say, because you're skinny and beautiful. I'm fat and ugly."

There was a sob behind her words, and I knew I had to tread very carefully. I remembered having similar thoughts about myself when I was twelve, but I'd had Bootsie and Mathilda to help me navigate the quicksand otherwise known as adolescence. Chloe had no one except me. And that thought alone scared the hell out of me. Especially now, when I had no other recourse but to tap into my remembered pain and see if I could steer her away from it.

"In sixth grade at a dance mixer, a boy I had a crush on paid his best friend to dance with me so he wouldn't have to. I wasn't one of those pretty girls who knew how to dress or flirt. It was humiliating." I didn't mention how Tripp had punched the boy in the face and made his nose bleed in the parking lot to defend my honor.

"And when I got home crying so hard that the front of my bedazzled Hello Kitty T-shirt was soaking wet, Mathilda told me what she told you—that not starting out pretty meant that I'd been given a chance to work on my personality, something those other girls never had to bother with."

I flattened out a piece of cold corn bread with the back of my spoon, then stuck okra tips in it to make a smiley face. I turned it around so she could see it, relieved to notice the corner of her cheek lift slightly. "Chloe, you're funny, clever, and curious. Don't push all of that good stuff away to try to make yourself fit into somebody else's idea of what a beautiful person is."

Her hands had dropped into her lap, and she was staring at them. Very quietly she said, "If I'm all those things, why doesn't my dad call me?"

I wanted to shout and scream and hurl all the abuse I could think of at my ex-husband. Mostly I wanted to cry over all the times I'd sat in my drug-induced fog and never said anything at all.

I moved to her chair and crouched next to her, being careful not to touch her. "I want you to listen very hard, and remember this: Your dad's issues have nothing whatsoever to do with you. If he can't see what's wonderful in you, then it's his problem, not yours. You can't live your life through his eyes or anybody else's. You need to make sure that who you see in your mirror is somebody *you* like."

I sat back on my heels, breathless at the memory of hearing those words. I'd been about seven or eight, and Carol Lynne had her suitcases by the door again. I was hysterical, trying to say anything that would make her stay. Tommy had disappeared into his room, and Mathilda and Bootsie had already given up.

Carol Lynne had knelt in front of me and told me about living my life through my own eyes, and liking who I saw each morning in my reflection. At the time, I thought she was only talking about herself.

I stood, my voice shaky. "Come on—help me clean this up so we can get back to sleep." *As if.*

Without argument, she slid from her chair and began stacking containers. I picked out two pieces of corn bread and stuck them in the microwave, then helped stack the rest of the containers before returning them to the refrigerator.

The microwave binged and I took out the corn bread, placing each piece on a napkin before handing one to Chloe. She looked at me suspiciously.

"You said you were hungry. I am, too."

She took it reluctantly but didn't move to eat it. I took a bite of my own, as if to show her how it was done. After swallowing, I said, "Have you heard the cypress trees at night? They make music."

"Right." Despite her belligerent tone, I heard a note of curiosity, too.

"Well, I'm going outside to listen. You can come if you want." I didn't look behind me as I moved toward the kitchen door, deliberately walking slowly but not holding the door open behind me. At the last moment, I felt the tension of the closing door stop and heard Chloe stepping down onto the back porch before pausing.

"Are there any wild boars out there?"

I stopped and faced her. "No—my garden doesn't have anything in it for them to eat. Besides, despite what Tripp led you to think, they're not all that common." I began walking toward the mound, satisfied to hear Chloe following behind me.

We walked past the silent garden and the old cypress tree toward the Indian mound. A half-moon smiled beneath the freckles of stars in the clear sky as the outside lights from the house lit our way toward the outline of the mound. We climbed the small hill without speaking, the chorus of night insects ringing in our ears.

I finished my last bite of corn bread, and when I looked at Chloe I saw her crumpling her napkin in her hand. I sat down on the grass, feeling the cool dampness of it beneath my baby-doll pajamas. At least Chloe in her own ill-fitting sleepwear had no room to comment. Holding my breath, I lay all the way down, the cold prickles of grass tickling my skin as I looked up at the stars. Without a word, Chloe did the same, the white of her nightgown glowing like a neon sign atop the ancient mound.

"Close your eyes," I said. "You can hear the trees better that way."

I didn't check to see if she'd closed her eyes or not. It was always easier to let her decide on her own what she wanted to do. I'd learned that, at least, trying to be her mother.

As if on cue and I the conductor, the strings of a quartet began to play, the low notes of a bass the perfect foil for the melodic duet of cellos and violins. I closed my eyes, the music overtaking all of my senses, and I felt myself beginning to drift asleep as if the symphony of the trees had the power to banish my nightmares.

"That's pretty cool," Chloe said.

My eyes popped open, and I tried not to show my surprise. Any admission above "It doesn't suck" was a big compliment coming from Chloe.

"Yeah. I think so, too." I turned to her, the grass brushing my cheek. "Is there anything else about the boondocks you find cool?"

She was silent for a moment, and I was worried that she couldn't think of anything to say. Finally she said, "The house. It's like a house you'd find in a Dr. Seuss book."

I grinned, admiring her imagination. "Mr. Montgomery has always said the same thing."

Chloe made a gagging noise. "Please don't say that we think alike. I might have to go rinse my mouth out with bleach or something."

I laughed softly, hearing the wave of sound begin on one side of the swamp and move toward the other like a giant hand brushing the tips of the trees. "Oh, it wouldn't be such a terrible thing to think like Mr. Montgomery. Don't tell him I said so, but he's a pretty neat guy once you get to know him."

"So you think he's hot?"

I stammered. "I, uh, um, I've never really thought of him that way."

"Right. Well, he's pretty old and all, but he looks a lot like Ryan Reynolds, and all my friends think he's pretty hot."

Considering "all her friends" meant Hailey and maybe one or two other girls, it wouldn't have counted as an official survey, but she wasn't that far off the mark. "I'm not looking for a relationship, Chloe. I'm just trying to figure out some things."

She was silent for a moment, staring up at the stars. "Why did we never do this in LA?"

"Because the lights of the city make the sky too bright. It's one of the advantages to living out in Pork Butt, Mississippi."

She snorted out a laugh. "It's still the most boring place on earth."

I neglected to mention that she'd chosen to be here. "You've only been here for a few weeks, Chloe. Tommy said you could spend a day with him next week in the fields, depending on if the weather holds, and there's fishing, and swimming, walking the levees. We've got museums and old plantations and the blues, and some of the best soul food in the world. As a kid growing up here, I never thought I had nothing to do."

"But you still left."

And here I am. I didn't say anything, hoping she'd be distracted by the night music.

"So why did you leave?" Chloe asked, her voice holding none of the weight of her question.

Because it was something I'd been born with, a poison in the blood I'd inherited from my mother and she from hers and way on back before anybody alive could still remember. Because I'd grown up to believe that my mother's constant departures meant that anywhere else was better than here. But every time I started to tell her, I stopped, the words suddenly as foreign to me as another language. After a few false starts, I said, "Because my mother came back here to live and I'd grown too used to living here without her. And I wanted to see the world outside of the Mississippi Delta. I figured California was a good place to start."

I felt her look at me. "That's lame."

I turned my face to her but she was back to staring at the sky. "Yeah. I wish you'd been here nine years ago to tell me that. You would have saved me a lot of trouble."

She was silent for a long moment. "In California we don't have trees that sing. Maybe if we did, I might miss being home."

"But you have the sound of the ocean." I watched a plane on its lonely trek across the sky, remembering Bootsie and me doing the same thing when I was little, making up stories about the people aboard, wondering if they were leaving or coming home.

I lifted my hands in the air, my index fingers and thumbs forming a triangle to put the plane in perspective, the metal-and-bead ring that Chloe had made for me reflecting the light of the stars. "Home means so many different things. It's more than the sounds and the smells, even though they're important, because it's what we remember most from when we're children." I thought hard for a moment, still unused to the clarity of my thoughts. "It's where your people are."

Her voice sounded very small. "But what if you don't have any people?"

I thought of her mother in Australia and her father on his honeymoon with his third wife, and how he hadn't bothered to call his only child. "Then you find your own."

She sat up and I could feel her agitation, something the pills had always made sure I was immune to. "Yeah, well, the only 'people' I found was somebody who could only stand to be with me if she was popping pills."

I sat up, too, so badly wanting to tell her that I'd stopped, that I was here with her watching the stars because I wanted to. That some deranged part of my brain thought that I might be able to make a difference in her life. But I couldn't. Because then I'd have to tell her that I'd stopped the pills only because her father told me I couldn't.

Chloe pulled herself up. "Life sucks and then you die." She stomped down the hill of the mound, her moods and hormones as winding as the path of the river.

I didn't go after her. Instead I wrapped my hands around my

drawn-up legs and pressed my forehead into my knees for a moment, wondering if shame could be fatal.

I lifted my head, watching her white nightgown make its way toward the house like a stealthy ghost. I knew there was nothing I could say to her that would make her think differently; she'd have to figure that out on her own. But mostly I didn't run after her because I wasn't sure that I'd convinced myself that she was wrong.

Chapter 26

Vivien Walker Moise
INDIAN MOUND, MISSISSIPPI
MAY 2013

My mother sat at the kitchen table with Cora, dressed like Jackie Kennedy and sipping coffee with white-gloved hands. I sighed inwardly. She was coming with Chloe and me to start organizing and sorting the historical archives from where they'd been stored in the basement of City Hall in preparation for the move to the new library building. I paused on the threshold a moment before anybody noticed me, watching my mother behave as if she were a regular person having her morning coffee—a regular person who remembered that her favorite color was red, and that her daughter wasn't in high school anymore, and that she'd spent most of her motherhood with a suitcase in her hand and an old yellow house and two children at her back.

I'd borrowed Tommy's computer to look up ways to help people with dementia and Alzheimer's, and had read in one study that looking at old photographs was good therapy, if not a cure. When Carrie told me that there were boxes full of old photographs in the archives inherited from the newspaper when it had downsized to smaller offices, I took it as a sign.

"Good morning," I said, grabbing a banana from the fruit bowl and heading for the coffeemaker. I was about to ask where Chloe was when she burst into the room. She'd reverted to the hair hanging in front of her face and her black T-shirt and jeans.

She flopped herself in a chair across from my mother and next to Cora, then glowered up at me through her heavy fringe of hair. "I'm ready."

Cora put on what I could only describe as a "teacher face" and turned toward the adolescent. "You know, Chloe, I'd be happy to stay here with you and go through the history textbook section on manifest destiny and the acquisition of Texas. Or you can go help Vivien with the archives today. It's completely up to you."

Chloe rolled her eyes. "Whatever."

I cleared my throat.

"Yes, ma'am." She didn't mumble it, but looked up at the ceiling.

I pulled another banana from the bunch and placed it in front of Chloe. "Have some breakfast. It's the most important meal of the day."

She sighed heavily, as if I'd just asked her to dig a well, but took the fruit and began to peel it with surgical precision. I wondered if she got that from her father.

"How's Mathilda?" I asked Cora.

"She's fine, thank you. Fit as a fiddle. I can only hope that I've inherited those good longevity genes."

"Good to hear it. Please tell her hello from me. I'm going to try to stop by again soon. We didn't get to finish our conversation, and the last couple of times I dropped by I was told she was too tired or feeling poorly."

Cora looked at me oddly. "Are you sure you were all talking about the same Mathilda? Because my grandmother hasn't felt poorly a day in her life."

"That's what I thought, too. No matter. Just please tell her that I'll try again soon."

"I certainly will."

I turned to Carol Lynne. "You ready?"

"Sure. Where are we going?"

"To town."

She looked over at Chloe. "Good. Because I think JoEllen needs to go shopping."

Chloe glared at me as if I had control over what my mother said. "Come on, then. I'll drive."

"Is Bootsie coming?" Carol Lynne asked, repeating the same question she'd asked each time we were about to get in a car and go somewhere.

"Not today," I said. "We'll catch up with her later."

We drove for a while without talking, listening to the sixties station while my mother sang along. Chloe glowered from the backseat, making me wish for the sweet girl in the billowing white nightgown who'd listened with me to the music of the cypress trees.

"Where are we going?" Carol Lynne asked again.

Chloe interrupted her glowering. "To shop."

I was grateful for not having to answer the same question again, but it also brought into focus that my mother needed to see a doctor whether she wanted to or not. Tommy said he'd tried, but I knew he wasn't one to push against a brick wall, especially when that brick wall was the mother he'd always worked so hard to please.

I wasn't one to push either, but I also wasn't one to give up too quickly. Whether it was persistence or sheer stupidity, I always seemed to be the person hanging on to the reins long after I'd been thrown by the horse. The pills had made me forget about that part of me, and for the first time since I'd stopped taking them, I was glad my mind was clear enough to remember something worth remembering.

"Carol Lynne, when was the last time you saw a doctor?"

She stopped singing, then looked at me as if surprised to find me sitting next to her. "Not too long ago, I think."

I nodded. "I haven't had a checkup in a while, so I was thinking if you needed one we could go together."

She frowned. "I'm not sick. I don't need to see a doctor."

My attempted smile wobbled, then fell. "That's why it's good to go now, before you need one. Then if there's a problem, it gets spotted early, when there's still time to fix it."

She crossed her arms over her chest just like Chloe did when she was getting ready to argue. "I don't want to go."

I understood why Tommy would have dropped the subject at this point. We'd inherited more than just our red hair from her, after all.

"I know. I don't like to, either. It's just that, you know, as they grow older people start having different health concerns. Like cardiovascular issues, or changes in bone density. Or memory problems."

Her voice turned almost venomous. "I do *not* have memory problems. I remember everything perfectly. Just ask Bootsie. She's always saying how I never forget a thing." She shook her head as if she were trying to convince more than just me.

She knows, I thought. In the far reaches of her mind that still worked, she knew something wasn't right. She knew enough to pretend that everything was fine, and to react defensively if somebody tried to tell her otherwise. There was hope, then. Hope that there was memory there to remember what I needed her to.

"But there are medications. . . ."

"No!" She screamed the word at me, the sound reverberating in the small confines of the car.

Chloe reached up from the backseat and put her hand on my mother's shoulder, and if my mother's screaming at me hadn't already made me want to cry, Chloe's action would have. I flicked on the signal and began to turn, but my hands shook, causing me to run onto the shoulder before jerking the car back to the road.

After a few deep breaths, I faced her again. "I didn't mean to upset you. I'm sorry."

She wore a wide smile when she turned back to me. "For what?"

Warring emotions bombarded me—relief, anger, confusion—all aimed at something I didn't understand and the woman I understood even less.

"Never mind," I said softly, driving around the main square one more time, looking for a place to park.

Carrie met us in the marbled lobby of City Hall. Bo was in school, but Cordelia sat in a baby carrier on her mother's back. At least until she spotted me and held out her arms, shouting out, "Hold me, hold me."

"Do you mind?" Carrie asked, shrugging off the shoulder straps. "If you'll just hold her for a few minutes she'll stop."

"Sure," I said, wishing I hadn't as soon as the little girl's arms were around my neck and her sweet smell wrapped around the rest of me.

"I've got to get back to the theater, but Carol Shipley—that's one of our most enthusiastic volunteers—is waiting for you in the basement to show you the ropes."

"Mrs. Shipley? As in the high school librarian who had her index finger practically glued to her lips? And who hated anybody touching any of the books and messing them up?"

Carrie gave me an apologetic smile. "The very same. After she retired, she found she couldn't quite give up bossing other people around and making people lower their voices. She's president of the Friends of the Indian Mound Library. She does a great job, and she's real nice once you get to know her."

I hesitated to remind her that I'd known Mrs. Shipley for four years in high school, and I was as afraid of her when I graduated as I was on the first day of freshman year.

She led us into an ancient elevator with a metal mesh screen for a door and pushed the B button after manually sliding the door shut. It shuddered to life like an old man jolted awake from a long nap and started to move downward with slow, arthritic jerks as Cordelia began to play with my hair.

"I think she likes the color of it," Carrie said. "Or she's jealous that you have so much of it when she hardly has any." She laughed. "Runs in the family, I'm afraid. My hair's curly, but it's fine and just frizzes in this heat." Facing Chloe, she said, "You've got pretty hair. Nice and thick. I loved the way you had it in a French braid when I saw you at the restaurant. Maybe you can teach Cordelia how to do that when she's older. Or when she grows enough hair."

As if she knew we were talking about her, Cordelia suddenly lurched sideways toward Chloe. With the quick reflexes of the young, Chloe caught her and hoisted her onto her hip. The two girls stared at each other through the thick fringe of Chloe's hair. With a *pfft* sound, Chloe blew air through her lips, pushing her hair into the little girl's face.

Cordelia chortled deep in her throat, the sound intoxicating. We all watched as Chloe did it again, creating a new waterfall of childish laughs.

"You'd make a good big sister, Chloe," Carrie said.

The old elevator ground to a stop and I was relieved to be distracted from the wounded look on Chloe's face, and the memory of me telling her that she wasn't going to be a big sister after all.

Carrie led us into a thinly carpeted room that smelled like stale wood smoke and reminded me a lot of the final scene in *Raiders of the*

Lost Ark, when Indiana Jones is shown the government storage room where the Ark of the Covenant is buried. Except this room was filled with shelves and shelves of boxes and containers that went all the way back to the far wall. A line of metal folding tables filled the middle of the room, the tall shelves looming over them.

"I know it's a mess," Carrie apologized. "When the fire broke out in the old library, firefighters and employees grabbed what they could and flung everything out the windows and doors. We were just so grateful that so much was saved, it didn't occur to us to wonder how on earth we'd be able to put it all back together."

Chloe was spinning around in a slow circle, her mouth gaping open, but before I could ask her to stop, I realized I was doing the same thing. We stopped at an old schoolmaster's wooden desk—looking suspiciously like a remnant from the high school—and I read the small sign posted on the front: UNATTENDED CHILDREN WILL BE GIVEN AN ESPRESSO AND A FREE PUPPY. Next to that was a hand-drawn sign of a frowny face next to a crude depiction of a cell phone with a line going through it.

"Isn't this a little ridiculous?" I asked. "Seeing how this isn't exactly a library down here, but a storage facility for library materials?"

"I consider this a library." The disembodied voice came from the other side of the desk. Leaning over, I found Mrs. Shipley picking up a scattered pile of small paper dots, apparently escapees from the upturned three-hole punch that lay on its side on the floor.

I wanted to point out that a vacuum cleaner would probably do a faster and more efficient job, but one gaze at her eyes behind her glasses transported me back to high school. She pulled herself up using the edge of the desk and I wondered how it could be that she looked exactly the same as I remembered. Even her stiff helmet of white-blond teased and sprayed hair remained the same. I thought the frames of her glasses had probably not changed since, either, but I couldn't be sure, since I'd spent a lot of time looking at the floor whenever she was in my presence.

"Vivien! How's my favorite student?"

I met Carrie's eyes over Mrs. Shipley's shoulder as she hugged me. "I'm fine, thank you. It's so great to see you again." The entire exchange was said in loud, exaggerated whispers, even though there was nobody else in the room but us.

I introduced Carol Lynne and Chloe, also in loud whispers, and then Carrie took Cordelia from Chloe. "I have to get back to the theater now, but you're in good hands with Mrs. Shipley. And please let Tommy know that I'm doing a *Star Wars* marathon—all six prequels and sequels—this weekend. Mama's watching Cordelia and I'm bringing Bo. I know those are Tommy's favorite movies in the whole world, and I'd love for him to join us. Tell him I'll save him a seat with us, just in case."

"I will." We said good-bye as Mrs. Shipley, in her school librarian uniform of brown vest, houndstooth skirt, ankle socks, and sneakers faced us with her hands together. Carol Lynne sat down in one of the metal chairs with her purse on her lap, then slowly pulled off her white gloves finger by finger, just like Bootsie used to do.

"Are we here to eat? I think I might be hungry."

Mrs. Shipley frowned, I assumed because we weren't whispering.

Chloe leaned toward my mother. "Not yet. We're here to help Vivien go through some pictures and papers. Then we'll eat."

"Okay." Carol Lynne smiled at her gratefully.

I looked more closely at the nearest shelf, where stacks of paper protruded over the open top of an unlabeled moving box. Continuing to speak in a loud whisper, I said, "Um, so, where would you like us to start?"

Mrs. Shipley patted her helmet of hair as if a strand would defy her by moving. "I heard about the unfortunate soul buried in your yard. Carrie told me that you would be interested in old newspaper articles about missing women. I think that's a great place to start! Because the newspapers were easy to identify, they all got separated from the rest of the papers and grouped together in the same area."

"Lucky me," I said, my eyes scanning the brimming shelves. "Did Carrie also tell you that I'm not sure how much longer I'm going to be in town? I might not be here long enough to put a dent into any of this."

Mrs. Shipley glanced back at my mother and her face softened. "I understand. My grandmother got sick like that, too, and it just about killed my mother taking care of her. But your mama has Tommy and Cora Smith, who's like a saint if you ask me, so you wouldn't have to worry about her being taken care of."

"That's not what I meant."

Mrs. Shipley regarded me, waiting for me to explain the reason I would leave again, and I stared back at her, having no idea what to say. I turned around, pretending to examine one of the shelves. "Just show me where to start and how you'd like them organized and I'll have Chloe help me. If you could bring my mother a box of photographs Carrie said originally came from the newspaper's archives, she can get started on those."

With pursed lips, she nodded. "Of course. This way." Chloe and I followed Mrs. Shipley down an aisle and watched as she pulled out a Hammermill paper box, then carried it to the table where Carol Lynne sat. "Just look through these, Miz Moise. They're probably from all time periods since the camera was invented, but if you'd like, you can put aside any photographs where you recognize a person or building, and any with something written on the back. That would be a start, anyway. I suppose we should get all the old-timers in here to look through the photos and see how many we can identify."

"Sounds like fun," my mother said with confidence, and I could only hope that Mrs. Shipley didn't have high expectations that the photographs would be sorted in any discernible way. Carol Lynne pulled a photo out of the box, examining it closely, as if she knew what she was looking for.

Mrs. Shipley had already started walking toward the back of the room. "These shelves are where we put all the newspapers. Before the fire, we had a pretty complete collection starting from about 1870. Carrie and I thought this would be a great opportunity to discover some interesting historical tidbits in these old papers to write about in your newspaper column."

"My newspaper column?"

She stopped walking to face me. "Didn't Carrie tell you? The editor of the paper has okayed a weekly column for the paper and their Web site, and I remember you from the school paper, Vivien. I know you'll be able to get people all excited about the library opening and about the history of Indian Mound and the surrounding area. We at the Friends were just thrilled when you accepted the opening."

"I actually haven't accepted . . ."

Mrs. Shipley had already turned away and was marching toward the back of the room. I heard Chloe snort behind me.

"Just grab a box and start sorting by date. I thought you could use these four tables to lay them out, starting with the oldest paper in the far left corner and then just adjusting the piles as you go through the boxes." She slid a box off a shelf and handed it to Chloe. "And both of you can read the headlines and see if anything jumps out at you that might be interesting. I already calculated that we'll need twelve columns before the library's grand opening." She beamed. "I just can't wait to see what you come up with."

I took another box from the shelf and dumped it next to Chloe's on the nearest table. A moth fluttered out of the box, as if even he wanted to get away. I started to explain that I wasn't supposed to be here, that I'd been home less than a month and nothing had turned out as I'd expected, least of all being stuck in the basement of City Hall with boxes of old newspapers, a mother with dementia, and a teenager who wanted to be there less than I did.

But then I imagined Mrs. Shipley asking me what other plans I had that would prevent me from doing this job. The embarrassment of hunting for an answer was enough to keep me quiet. The thought that I might actually find an article about a woman's disappearance seemed farfetched at best, but at least searching meant I was moving forward instead of treading water. What I'd do next wasn't something I was ready to consider.

"Well, then, that should be a place to get you started. When you find an interesting article, bring it up to me and I'll photocopy it. It's against our policy to allow any originals out of the library. And remember, no food or drink, and definitely no chewing gum."

"I'm sure that won't be a problem," I said, wanting to point out that we were volunteers and couldn't be fired for breaking the rules. But she quelled any further dialogue with her librarian look before marching brusquely to her desk to finish picking up the tiny paper dots from the floor.

I grabbed a stack of newspapers from the first box and settled them into a spot in front of me. Looking over at Chloe, I saw she was busy texting on her phone. "Seriously?" she said, her voice loud enough to cause Mrs. Shipley to poke her head above her desk from down the long hall of shelves. She rolled her eyes. "I don't have *any* bars down here. How am I supposed to text if I can't get a signal?"

"You're in a basement, Chloe. And you're not supposed to be texting anyway, because you're supposed to be helping sort old newspapers. Besides, if Mrs. Shipley sees you using your phone in here or even thinks it might be turned on, she will take it. And you might not get it back." I didn't add that I spoke from experience.

She sat back in her chair with a heavy sigh. "How long do we have to do this?"

I scanned the stacked shelves with a sinking feeling. "We have until October. But for today, I say let's work until lunch. If you get hungry, I brought a bag of almonds that Mrs. Fusselbottom shouldn't be able to sniff out."

She barked out a laugh, but quickly stifled it. "My dad says nuts are fattening and I shouldn't eat them."

I took a deep breath. "Nuts are high in fat and calories. But they're very nutritious and high in fiber, too. That means that a small handful is all you need to get a good energy boost with a reasonable amount of calories."

She looked at me as if I'd just suggested we should strip naked and run screaming through the hallowed halls of Mrs. Shipley's basement library.

I went to make sure my mother was still happily going through photographs, and then returned to my task. I didn't look back at Chloe, but after a few minutes I heard her groan and then the sound of newspapers being slid out of her box and slapped on the table.

Three hours later my eyes were bleary, I had newsprint smears all over my face and hands, my backside was numb from sitting too long, and I'd gone through only two boxes. I glanced over at Chloe, who was on the floor on her stomach, her hunger pangs of an hour ago presumably erased by a strategically passed handful of almonds. She was swinging her legs as she appeared to be absorbed in a newspaper from 1963.

She'd barely gone through half of her box, because she'd start reading a headline and then get drawn into the rest of the story, and then see another article until she'd read the whole paper—including the advertisements—before she realized it. I couldn't bring myself to get her to stop, as this was the first thing besides grunge rock, boys, and her phone that I'd seen her give this much intense concentration to.

We'd accumulated a pile of printed-out articles on a variety of sub-

jects from a good sampling of decades, including the deal with the devil
bluesman Robert Johnson made for his world-renowned guitar abilities, the two German POW camps operated in the county during the
last two years of World War II, and the yellow fever epidemic of 1888.
She didn't want to, but I made her also include the story about the famous "floating hamburger" found only at the now-defunct Labella's
restaurant near the Indianola train depot. At this rate, I'd have articles
for my column well into the next century.

I stood and stretched, ready to call for a lunch break, when my gaze
settled on the newspaper in the front of Chloe's box. I slid it out and
read the headline in bold, black letters.

MISSISSIPPI RIVER BREACHES LEVEES IN 145 PLACES—16 MILLION ACRES FLOODED IN SEVEN STATES AND NEARLY 500 SOULS LOST!

I scanned the page, looking for the date at the top, remembering the
waterline in the stairway of our house. There it was: April 22, 1927.
Thinking this would be a good topic for my first column—not that I'd
completely decided I wanted to do it—I quickly thumbed through
Chloe's box and found three more editions from 1927 and 1928. I found
another from April 1937, the tenth anniversary of the flood, then
plucked them from the box and stacked them on the table to start with
them when I returned.

Calling over my shoulder, I said, "Go ahead and finish up, Chloe.
I'll go round up Carol Lynne and see how productive she's been."

I didn't have high hopes, since every time I'd gone to check on my
mother she was either making patterns on the table with the photographs or wandering around the shelves, and once was discovered
sleeping on the floor between two shelves. Mrs. Shipley had taken her
to the bathroom a few times, but most of the time she acted as the gate-
keeper to keep Carol Lynne from wandering out of the basement.

I stopped at the table where my mother had placed stacks of photographs in a circular pattern. I surveyed them and tried to determine if
they'd been arranged with any method of organization.

After giving up hope that the stacks were intentional, I asked, "Are you hungry?"

She looked up from where she was spinning a single photograph with her short-cropped nail, flicking a corner as soon as it came around, seeing how fast it would spin. She stared at me as if needing to translate what I'd just said. She furrowed her brow. "I think so."

"Do you want to grab a sandwich and a shake at the lunch counter at the drugstore? I thought Chloe might enjoy that."

The name didn't seem to register, so I quickly corrected myself. "I meant JoEllen. She's coming, too."

She smiled the smile I was beginning to recognize as the one she used when she was unsure of a situation and didn't want anybody else to know. She hadn't made a move to slide out her chair, so I grabbed it by the sides to help her, then stopped, my gaze settling on the photograph she'd been spinning.

It was an old black-and-white studio portrait of a baby girl with light eyes that could have been green, sitting on a satin blanket, smiling up at someone or something behind the photographer, her index finger raised in a point. But it wasn't the baby or her sweet expression that captured my attention. It was the tiny gold ring she wore on her finger, with half of a heart that appeared to have an engraving on the face of it. I squinted my eyes, peering closely at the letters, but they were too small to see.

"Do you know who this is, Carol Lynne?"

She looked at me with clear eyes that looked remarkably like the baby's in the photo and smiled. "Yes." She tapped her finger on the photo at the spot where the ring was.

"Who is it?" I prodded.

She looked down at the photo, and when her eyes met mine again, they wore the familiar cloudiness that I'd begun to grow used to.

"Who is it?" I asked again, knowing it was too late.

"A baby," she said, her smile wide, as if she'd just given the right answer in a spelling bee.

I picked up the photo, staring at the ring and wishing I could read the engraving. And then, when nobody was looking, I slid it into my shirt. I'd be careful with it, but I knew Mrs. Shipley wouldn't agree to let me take it, and for some reason I couldn't explain, I didn't want a photocopy.

We said good-bye to Mrs. Shipley and made plans for our return visit, the photograph seeming to burn a hole in my chest while I tried to remember where I'd seen the photograph before, and the identity of the baby who wore the other half of the ring found in the unknown woman's grave.

Chapter 27

Carol Lynne Walker Moise
CALIFORNIA
DECEMBER 1976

Dear Diary,

I just found this journal in the bottom of my backpack, where it hasn't been touched in twelve years. I'm thinking that's a good thing, seeing as how I don't remember much about those years, and what I do remember isn't worth writing about.

I have a baby boy now. I named him Tommy, after the song from my favorite band, the Who. I was living on a ranch somewhere in northern California, and I had lots of boyfriends whose names I can't remember. Like Tommy's daddy. At least that meant I got to name him whatever I wanted, because he belonged only to me.

Tommy's the reason I'm clean now. Right when I'd figured out I was pregnant, I was real sick, and the healers at the ranch couldn't get the right medicine for me. I had to thumb a ride into the nearest town and find a doctor who would give me some medicine. The receptionist in the fourth doctor's office I tried was the doctor's wife, and she said she recognized my accent and asked was I from the South? It turned out she was from Itta Bena, not too far from Indian Mound.

I don't know if it was because I was sick or because I was pregnant or

even if it was just hearing her voice that reminded me of home, but I
started to cry. She got the doctor and he gave me some medicine to make
me feel better. But he also said I had to get clean for the baby. He said if I
thought I could do that, I could stay with them and I could work filing stuff
in the office, and when I told them I knew how to type, he said I could do
some typing work, too, to pay them for my room and board.

That meant I couldn't go back to the ranch, and I'd been okay with
that. I'd been crazy about a boy there, Michael, and he said he was crazy
for me, too, but the rules said that we couldn't have partners, so he was
with another girl every week. It wasn't supposed to, but it made my heart
hurt, and there was nobody else there to make it better. So it worked out
that I moved in with Dr. and Mrs. Kelly and got clean and got a job and
had my healthy baby boy.

Dolores—the doctor's wife—wrote to Bootsie and told her where I
was and that I was okay and that she had a grandbaby. I hadn't spoken to
Bootsie since that Thanksgiving twelve years ago when I left without saying good-bye. I didn't mean for that long to pass without sending a letter
or anything, but those years are all a blur, like pages being flipped in a book
where you can't read all the words.

Bootsie wrote back saying she would wire money for a ticket home for
me and Tommy, that now that I'm a mother maybe things will be different
for us. I wasn't so sure, but Dolores told me that I needed to at least try,
and that her house would always be open to us. They didn't have any kids
of their own, and I think me and my baby had become family to them.

I've decided that I will go home. It's funny that I still call it home even
though I haven't been there for so long. But when people ask me where I'm
from, that's where I tell them, and not because I don't remember all the
other places I've been since I left, but because it just feels right. I don't
know how long I'm going to stay, but I do want Tommy to see where his
people come from.

He's such a sweet boy, real good-natured and smiling all the time. He's
a bit shy, and always watching what's going on with those big blue eyes.
He has hair the same color as mine, too, but more curly. I thought I'd give
him up after he was born, because I was pretty sure I didn't have a moth-
ering bone in my body. But when they first put him in my arms it was like
I'd been touched by the hand of God. It was that powerful. All I could
think about was being the best mother I could, and I knew that meant not

taking him back to the ranch. I had the funniest vision of him walking through cotton fields and fishing in the lake. Maybe that means I need to take him home. Maybe Dolores is right and things might be different now between Bootsie and me.

I remembered what Mathilda told me about chasing ghosts, and I wonder after all these years if I'm any closer to catching them.

Chapter 28

Adelaide Walker Bodine
INDIAN MOUND, MISSISSIPPI
AUGUST 1924

I pressed my hand on top of my hat as I sat next to John in his truck, the windows open wide as we raced down the road, to create a cooling breeze against our clammy skin. My dress and the churned-up dust from the road clung to me, my heart racing from the speed and from how I kept bumping into John as he hugged the curves of the road.

I clung to the dash as he made a sharp turn to the right and headed down a long drive before parking. My exhilaration vanished when I saw I was once again at the Ellis plantation. "Why are we here, John?"

"I thought we'd go for a swim. Cool off a little."

"But I didn't bring my swimming costume."

He smiled, a bright light in his eyes. "I promise I won't look."

I slapped his arm, but my good mood had deserted me. "I don't like it here," I said. "Those people behind that shack—they might still be here."

"They aren't," John said with conviction. "They had to move—temporarily. I know that because I helped them. And they aren't bad people, Adelaide. They're Mathilda's kin on her daddy's side; did you know that?"

I looked at him in surprise, shaking my head. "But that woman, Velma. She's white."

He raised his eyebrows. "Yes, that's right. She's also Mathilda's aunt. Leon is her common-law husband. They can't get married because it's against the law."

I stewed on that for a while. I'd heard the terms "white trash" and "high yellow" whispered often enough, when people thought I was out of hearing range, to know that the races mixed, but I'd been sheltered enough to have never knowingly come in contact with someone of both races. At least as far as I knew. "No, I didn't know. Nobody ever told me."

"Because there's no need. But you know Mathilda and Bertha, so I figured you'd be more at ease if you knew these were their people."

"Thank you," I said. He leaned toward me to kiss me, but I put my hands on his chest. I mostly didn't like it here because it reminded me of my discussion with Mr. Berlini, but I couldn't tell John that. I'd told him that I'd run into Mr. Berlini downtown when I was shopping with Sarah Beth, and that he seemed upset that John wanted to end their business relationship. I'd never seen John so angry, so I'd left out the fact that he'd driven me out to the Ellis plantation and touched my cheek and made me feel sorry for him with the sad story of his mother and sister. It had left me so confused about what was right and wrong that I still hadn't found a way to tell John everything or ask questions I needed to. I wasn't even sure that I could, but I also knew that to have a good marriage, we needed to be honest with each other.

"What's wrong?" he asked, searching my eyes.

"I was just thinking about Mr. Berlini. About what he said. About how he wanted you to reconsider leaving the business." I lowered my gaze to hide my embarrassment. "I don't even know what business it is! I know I've been sheltered and protected, but I've learned a lot of things from Sarah Beth that my aunt and uncle probably wish I hadn't." I looked him in the eyes, no longer able to avoid the subject. I had turned seventeen in May and I figured it was time I grew up. "Are you a bootlegger, John?"

A rainbow of emotions crossed his face, and it was impossible to tell whether he wanted to laugh or be angry. But he didn't answer right away, as if he were still deciding what or how much he should tell me.

I placed my hand on my watch that had been my mother's, my love for John finally helping me to understand her a little more. It was as if the years had built a bridge on which I could now stand and look at my life from a perspective that was farther away, but with much more clarity.

"My mother was a stranger in my father's life. I see that now, the more that I'm with you. And I don't want our lives together to be like that. My father protected my mother from anything that was unpleasant, kept her like a bird in a cage. It isolated her, I think. Made her believe that she didn't need to know about the world—his world and everybody else's. When he died, it was like her life had become like quicksand, ready to swallow her up. That's not how I want our marriage to be."

He held both of my hands in his and took a deep breath. "I guess you could call me a bootlegger—in a way. I started out just as a courier for Mr. Peacock's juice joint behind Mr. Pritchard's drugstore. I'd go pick up the liquor from various moonshiners and negotiate prices. I was good at it, because I was honest, and they knew that I would give them fair market price. My deal with Mr. Peacock was that I could keep a percentage of the profits.

"But then we got a visit from Mr. Berlini. He's got some powerful friends, some say even a Chicago connection. And he said he and his group of business associates were going to take over the supply down here in the delta. We could either give him a big cut of our business, or we could stop doing it completely."

Sweat was running down his face, so I reached over and took off his boater, then smoothed his hair under my fingers. "But you were making too much money to want to stop."

He nodded. "Pretty much. Mr. Peacock decided he was okay with the cut, but that meant that I'd be taking in much less money, even though I'd be doing the same thing. So I approached Mr. Berlini directly and worked out a deal."

"Doing what?" I asked, tilting my chin up so I would appear stronger and smarter than I felt.

"I don't hurt people, Adelaide. I want you to know that. I'm what Mr. Berlini calls his account manager. I'm the contact for all the speakeasies in this part of the delta. I've grown up with most of them, so they know me and trust me. I let them know that this is Mr. Berlini's territory and that they need to be buying their liquor from me, and if anybody else disagrees with them then I let Mr. Berlini know. I work with the local moonshiners and I also set up the trucks to pick up train shipments from Canada. I make everything run smoothly. And because Mr. Peacock is one of my accounts, he looks the other way when I need to leave the store to take care of business."

He averted his eyes for a moment, his gaze following a squirrel dashing up the side of one of the old oaks. "I knew I was breaking the law. But it seemed to me the Volstead Act had become a big farce, with those who didn't want to drink conceding to the new law and the people who wanted to drink finding ways to go around it. People were making a lot of money, and I figured this was my chance to secure my future. I've been dirt poor, and I don't ever want to go back." He touched my cheek gently and gave me a soft smile. "But then I met you, and I felt that I was somehow tarnishing you with what I was doing, and I wanted to stop."

I saw the pain and uncertainty in his eyes, and I thought of Aunt Louise and Uncle Joe after a bad harvest, about how she didn't condemn or condone any actions that may have led to the failure, but just let him know that she was there by his side. I could see now that she was the stronger of the two, willing to be the backbone for both of them when her husband faltered.

I cleared my throat. "Mr. Berlini didn't seem so unreasonable when I spoke with him. Maybe I can talk with him. . . ."

"No. I don't want you speaking with him anymore." He shook his head. "Just promise me that you'll let me handle it. I'm the one who got us involved in all this, and I have to be the one to get us out."

"I'm here now, John. You don't have to do this on your own. I also respect your dreams. I'll understand if you need to stay in the business for a little longer. But I don't think Mr. Berlini is as bad as you think. He knows what it's like to love somebody and to make sacrifices for them. And he said he wanted to be invited to our wedding. I think we should. Maybe when he sees us together and so in love, he'll understand why you're ready to start a new life and let you go. Or at least convince his boss to let you go."

A look I'd never seen before passed behind his eyes. In a stiff voice, he said, "Well, if he said he wanted an invitation, I guess we'll have to send him one." He took my head in his hands and moved me forward, pressing a kiss on my forehead. "It will be all right. With you by my side, there isn't anything I can't do."

I nodded, wishing I hadn't heard the uncertainty in his voice. And then I remembered something about the day Mr. Berlini returned Sarah Beth's fur coat. "Is Mr. Berlini married?"

"No, he's not. Why would you ask such a question?"

"I'll need to know how to address his invitation. And because he seemed a little sweet on Sarah Beth and I thought she might have been interested."

John's lips thinned for a moment. "If you have any sway over Sarah Beth, tell her to stay clear. He has a certain reputation with the ladies. He's a real cake eater."

"A what?"

"A ladies' man." His eyes darkened, but before I could press him further, he jumped out of his seat, then ran around the front of the truck. After opening my door he lifted me out and swung me around twice, then set me back down on my feet. Before I knew what was happening, he went down on one knee and took my left hand in his.

"I know you've got your wedding dress already, but we haven't really made our engagement official yet. Miss Adelaide Walker Bodine, would you do me the honor of being my wife?"

He reached into his jacket pocket and pulled out a diamond ring. The small stone winked at me in the sunlight, and I spread my fingers out so he could slide it on my third finger. "This ring has been burning a hole in my pocket, and I've decided I can't wait another year to get married. So please, Adelaide, end my misery right now and say yes and let's get married as soon as your aunt Louise can pull it all together."

"Yes," I shouted. Then, "Yes," even louder as he stood and swung me around again and then kissed me so that my knees buckled and he had to lift me up in his arms.

"You ready to go swimming?" he asked, his lips brushing mine.

"I already told you, I didn't bring my swimming costume."

"That's all right. Because neither did I."

He started running with me in his arms, then stopped to let me slide down before tugging on my arm and pulling me toward the water. I threw my head back, laughing, my joy nearly erasing the seeds of doubt that all would work out the way John planned.

◈

SEPTEMBER 5, 1924

The sun shone on my wedding day, and I took that as a good omen. We were married in the abandoned Methodist church. My aunt had been horrified when I suggested it, but once I pointed out that it was where my mother and father had been married she relented, and even led the efforts to clean up the churchyard and polish the pews and floors inside.

It had been John who'd asked me about my parents' wedding and who'd suggested we marry in the same church. Theirs had been a love match, like ours, he said, and it would be a good way to honor them while we said our vows.

The stained-glass windows were still intact, their rainbow of colors glittering on the altar and pews like a blessing. It was a small gathering of family and neighbors, easily fitting into the church. And Mr. Berlini was there, too, sitting alone in one of the rear pews, his custom-made suit and expensive shoes standing out among the farmers and shop-keepers, and making even Mr. and Mrs. Heathman look like country people.

I noticed how he kept looking at Sarah Beth and how she pretended not to notice but gave herself away by the bright pink of her cheeks that wasn't from cosmetics. And I saw how Willie noticed it, too, and kept reaching for his coat pocket, where I knew he kept a flask.

After the ceremony as I stood in the receiving line on the steps of the church, I saw Sarah Beth walk into the deserted cemetery. It reminded me of that time we'd snuck out here for an adventure and found all those graves of Heathman babies. She'd never told me if she'd asked her mama about why her name wasn't in the family Bible, and I'd given up asking about it. It was so long ago, anyway, when our adventures were fueled by childish imagination. Something I liked to think we'd grown out of along with pinafores and ribbons in our hair.

Angelo Berlini was one of the first guests in line. He shook John's hand, and my new husband thanked him for coming. I wondered if I was the only one who could hear the lack of warmth in John's voice.

Angelo leaned toward me and took both of my hands in his large, warm ones, then kissed me on both cheeks.

"You are a radiant bride, Mrs. Richmond. I don't believe I have ever been to a wedding of a couple so in love. If it could be bottled, I'd put you in all of my advertisements."

I smiled, charmed by his eccentric, foreign ways. And I couldn't help but remember his story about his family and all he'd lost, and all he'd fought to regain. "Thank you, Mr. . . . Angelo. It means a lot to both of us that you came today."

He raised an eyebrow as he looked at John, then nodded before moving down the newly repaired steps.

I was greeting Mr. and Mrs. Peacock when I noticed that Mr. Berlini had followed Sarah Beth into the cemetery and that they were both pretending to study the handmade grave markers of the colored people that Sarah Beth and I had discovered and then forgotten. Their lips were moving but they weren't looking at each other. But they were both leaning toward the other, like ancient tombstones bending under the weight of time.

"Your dress is absolutely breathtaking," Mrs. Peacock was saying, drawing my attention away from Sarah Beth and Mr. Berlini. "I must remember to ask if I can study its construction when it's time to make our Lucy's dress. Not that she has a beau yet, but I'm sure it's just a matter of time."

"My Maryanne's quite the artist with a needle and thread," Mr. Peacock said with pride in his voice. "An artist—just like your husband, John. I've never seen anybody with such an understanding into the mechanics of timepieces. Most horologists study for years to attain the knowledge he seems to have been born with."

I glowed with pride, thrilling at the word "husband." "Thank you, Mr. and Mrs. Peacock. And thank you for coming. I look forward to seeing you at the reception."

I stilled when I recognized the next guest in line, Willie's schoolmate from Ole Miss Chas Davis. Willie had wrecked his car again and said he'd have to ride from school with a friend. It hadn't occurred to me to ask which friend. I'd seen Chas a couple of times since the Heathmans' New Year's party, when I'd threatened to scream my head off if he didn't leave Mathilda alone, and each time he gave no indication that he remembered any of it. I knew alcohol sometimes did that to people, but I was never sure whether he had any recollection of what had happened or if he was just pretending that he didn't. Either way, my skin crawled every time I saw him, and during his brief visits with Willie, I tried to stay at Sarah Beth's. He greeted and offered congratulations to both of us, then moved down the steps without a hint of recognition or memory of that night.

The reception was held at my house, the yellow house with the improbable turret and the cedar tree out back and my garden that I had nourished since I was old enough to dig in the dirt.

John would move into my bedroom and we would sleep in the big black bed together for our entire married lives. And our children would be born in the same bed I'd been born in, and my mother before me. It was the way of us Walker women, this connection to birth and life. Much more, I was beginning to realize, than the legacy of leaving.

The dining room table overflowed with the family crystal, silver, and china, and an overabundance of the delicate tea sandwiches and cookies that my aunt Louise had been preparing for days. A large crystal bowl was filled with punch, and pitchers of lemonade were placed throughout the dining room and parlor for parched guests to help themselves. The Heathmans had lent us Mathilda for the day, which was probably more for their comfort than anything else. I wondered if the Heathmans even knew how to pour their own drinks, but figured there were enough guests in attendance to show them how even if Mathilda wasn't there.

"Is all this borrowed from the Heathmans?" John's breath tickled my ear as he bent close to kiss my cheek.

I shook my head. "It's ours now. I hope you don't mind eating off of china with a 'W' monogram. We're quite proud of it, you know. When the Yankees came after the siege of Vicksburg, they stole everything they could carry, and destroyed everything else. My great-grandmother was sixteen at the time and pretended to have smallpox. Her daddy had taken out all the stuffing in her mattress and replaced it with all the china, crystal, and silver that would fit. She had to lie on it for three whole days, but it was worth it. The Yankees were too afraid to go near her."

John laughed. "I knew I was marrying into a family with brains."

Our eyes met, and I saw the promise of years reflected in his, as well as the promise of what was to come tonight, when my aunt and uncle went to Gulfport to visit friends and Willie went back to Ole Miss, leaving the house empty for our honeymoon. At the pond behind the Ellis plantation, John had already shown me a little of what was to come, and my skin shivered in anticipation without his even having to touch me.

I studied him closely, trying to weigh my words. "We don't have to live here. I told you before, I can live anywhere, as long as I'm with you."

He smiled, his eyes crinkling at the corners. "This is your home, Adelaide. And I love this house, and your garden, and even the fields of cotton. Your uncle Joe has promised me it's not that different from growing corn, just trading in one set of problems for another." He grinned and touched my chin. "I like farming, and I'll still be able to repair watches. Not having to buy a house means we're that much closer to getting my own shop."

I loved the sound of the word "we" on his lips, enough that I was able to overlook that he hadn't mentioned his business dealings with Angelo Berlini, which I knew had not altered. I knew he was waiting until he had enough money in the bank to start his own repair business before severing all of his ties to Mr. Berlini. John was uncomfortable with his decision, but even I had to agree with the wisdom of it. At least now Angelo had time to prepare, to put another person in place.

Not caring if anybody was watching, I stood on my tiptoes and kissed him. "It will all work out. I know it will." I hoped the tone of my voice was enough to convince us both.

We were distracted by the sound of an altercation coming from the rear of the house. We followed the rush of people toward the kitchen and through the back door. John tried to hold me back, but his hand slipped as I was caught up in the moving group of people as we fanned out onto the back porch, viewing the spectacle in the backyard.

Willie, staggering about in his shirtsleeves and with his tie undone and his hair falling over his eyes, was throwing ineffective punches in the direction of Angelo Berlini, who didn't even have a hair out of place. Every time Willie came toward him, Angelo held up his hands, not to deflect the wayward punches, but more as if to say he was refusing the invitation to fight.

I spotted Sarah Beth looking like the beautiful heroine in a Rudolph Valentino picture show, a small smile on her lips, almost as if she were enjoying the spectacle. Mathilda stood next to her, angled in such a way that it seemed she was protecting her.

Willie threw another punch, almost tripping over his own feet, and Angelo didn't even bother to back up. "Look, Mr. Bodine, I'm not sure what you're upset about. . . ."

"What d'ya mean?" Willie shouted, his words slurring together. "Everything's jake between me and my girl, and then you show up in your fancy car and your fancy clothes and stick your fat Italian nose in where it doesn't belong." He bobbed a fist in the air and this time he did trip, falling down on both knees. Angelo went to offer assistance, but Willie tried to pummel him again, looking as threatening as a cotton bale lying in a field.

"I've already given my best wishes to the happy couple, so I'll leave now and you can calm down and return to the party."

Angelo turned on his well-shod heel and began walking toward the porch, either pretending he didn't see us all crowded on it or simply planning to barrel through us. A collective gasp rose from the gathered crowd as we all turned to see Willie suddenly lurch to his feet and rush toward Angelo from behind. Before the Italian could turn around to see what we were all looking at, Chas Davis raced out from the crowd and tackled Willie, bringing them both to the ground.

Willie managed to stagger to his feet again, but Chas wouldn't let go, hanging on to him with both arms. "She ain't worth it, Will. That girl ain't no better than she ought to be."

I jerked my gaze around to Sarah Beth, realizing they were talking about her. And that I'd heard those words before. It had been at the back of the old slave cabin with Mathilda's Robert and the man Leon and the woman spitting tobacco juice into a jar. She'd said the exact same thing about Sarah Beth.

Both Chas and Willie were looking in Sarah Beth's direction, and as everybody followed their gazes, Mathilda took a step in front of her so that it appeared Willie had been speaking about her.

Willie looked at Chas with a confused expression that had nothing to do with his drunkenness. But any question he had for Chas was interrupted by my uncle Joe cutting through the crowd to come to his son's side, his expression a mixture of disbelief and anger. He yanked on Willie's arm and dragged him around to the front of the house and out of sight. I figured Willie was too old and too big for the switch, but I wouldn't blame Uncle Joe one bit for trying.

Angelo paused on the bottom step of the porch, turning around with a polite smile on his face, as if he were the host and was satisfied that everybody was having a grand old time. He turned to my aunt, who looked like she might cry, and kissed her hand.

"Thank you, Mrs. Bodine, for such a lovely party. The wedding couple is truly lucky to have you and your husband in their lives." He turned to me and kissed me again on each cheek. "And what a beautiful bride. I wish you every happiness in your marriage, and may you be blessed with many children who are as beautiful as their mother."

I blushed and thanked him, then watched as he shook John's hand, giving him a long envelope with the other, and then left. John and I stayed where we were while my aunt fluttered her hands and forced a smile, and led everybody back inside.

When we were alone, John approached me, holding the unopened envelope.

"What is it?" I asked.

He was staring at the envelope as if he weren't quite sure. "His wedding gift."

I took it from his stiff fingers, then carefully tore it open to find a note folded in thirds. I opened it up and a rectangular piece of paper slid out. As John bent to retrieve it, I read the note, each letter thick and dark and sprawling. *Cosa rara, cosa cara.*

I looked up to show John, but his face was milky white. "What's wrong?" I asked.

He held up the paper, a bank draft for two thousand dollars. He was shaking his head. "We can't accept it. It's too much money."

"But, John, don't you understand? He wants to help us start our new lives. He wouldn't have given it to us if he couldn't afford it." I threw my arms around my new husband, wanting to jump up and down and shout. "You see? He's not as bad as you think he is! We now are that much closer to you owning your own business. Isn't that wonderful?"

He just looked at me without saying anything.

His response was a lot more subdued than I expected. "John?"

The eyes that bore into mine were almost unrecognizable. But he smiled, and I saw the man I knew and loved. "Yes, darling. It's wonderful."

I held the note up to him. "Do you know what this says? I think it's in Italian."

He looked at it and then slowly nodded. " 'That thing that is rare is dear.' "

"That's lovely," I said.

John put his arms around me and we stayed like that until Aunt Louise came out to tell us that it was time to cut the wedding cake and throw my bouquet.

John's mood lightened as we celebrated our marriage with our family and friends, and then said good-bye to everyone as they left, except for Willie, who hadn't come back to say good-bye, and the Heathmans, who had left with Sarah Beth right after the scene outside.

When the front door closed, I led John through the house and out the back door before stopping at my cypress tree. I loved watching the sunset from here, seeing the sun puddle into the cotton fields that sprawled in front of us. We were nearing harvesttime and the rows and furrows resembled what I imagined to be a snow-covered field. A flutter of wings made us look up, and I could see a murder of crows gathered on the branches of the tree, their oily wings reflecting the bloodred sun.

A soft breeze blew across the evening sky, like fingers stroking the cypress trees and making them play. "I love you forever," John said, his lips in my hair.

I smiled up at him. "And I'll love you for longer."

We looked up at the sound of fluttering wings and watched as the birds lifted out of the tree and flung themselves into the sky, an inky cloud that seemed to carry our words out over the horizon. We held hands as we walked back to the house and the big black bed, and into our future together.

Chapter 29

Vivien Walker Moise
INDIAN MOUND, MISSISSIPPI
MAY 2013

I mashed the button on my phone to read the time, dropping it unceremoniously back on my nightstand, disgusted that once again I was still awake in the darkest part of the night. I'd been tossing and turning for hours, trying to count sheep or anything else that would distract my thoughts from the photo of the unnamed baby and the ring on her finger. But like a persistent gnat on a hot summer's day, the niggling thought that I'd seen a photo of the baby before kept buzzing around my head.

All thoughts of sleep long gone, I flipped on my bedside light and sat up, my gaze roaming around my room for a distraction before finally settling on the bookshelf that seemed to be getting less and less full. I knew Chloe had been borrowing my books, but I was too thrilled to know that she was reading them to tell her that she should ask first.

My gaze slid to the bottom shelf, where an assortment of old framed photographs sat gathering dust. Photos of Tommy playing baseball in high school, pictures of the dog he'd had as a little boy that he'd never had the heart to replace. And there were the photos of Tripp and me at our junior and senior proms. He'd been my date for both, since I'd had so many boys asking me that the only way I would be free to dance and flirt with all of them would be if I went with Tripp. The memory of it now made me wince.

There was a photo of Tommy and me wearing sunglasses and bathing suits on a beach trip to Biloxi, and next to that was a picture of Bootsie with the floppy hat that I'd found in the shed and had been wearing while trying to resuscitate her garden. She wore a floral-print dress and sensible shoes, and no gardening gloves. She'd never worn them, saying she needed to feel her plants to understand them better, and I had grown up to believe she'd been right. In the photo she held one of her prized tomatoes, its size and color the envy of any greengrocer or gardener. Behind her, standing like sentinels against the fence, were tall sunflowers, their faces turned toward the sun like those of teenage girls at the beach.

I'd forgotten about her sunflowers, how she loved to surround herself with their cheerful faces and would put them in a vase in the middle of the kitchen table, because she claimed it would put us on the right foot as we started our day. I made a mental note to find out if Tommy had any of her sunflower seeds.

My gaze traveled back to her face, to her warm and loving smile, and then up to her eyes. I froze. I left the bed and picked up the frame, bringing it to the lamp so I could see it better and to compare the photo with the one from the library. Even in the dim light, they seemed nearly identical. I'd once read that we are born with the same size eyes we will carry through adulthood. In the framed photo, my grandmother had creases in the corners and lines underneath, but when I held up the photograph of the baby, I had no doubt they could be the same pair of eyes.

Being as quiet as I could, I raced through the house to the downstairs parlor, carrying the frame and the loose photo. I caught the door before it slammed behind me, then flipped on the overhead light and table lamps before pulling out the old photo albums that Bootsie had assembled over the years. The older albums had the tabbed corners that made the photos easy to lift and examine any writing on the backs. The more recent albums were the magnetic ones, whose glue had long ago adhered to the photos, making it hard if not impossible to remove without damaging the photographs.

Not that I needed to look at the most recent albums, the photos of Tommy and me with our nineties haircuts and awkward phases of braces and bad skin. There were so many photos of us, but Bootsie had always wielded the camera. If somebody were to look at the albums, he would have thought we'd raised ourselves without any adult supervision.

But I remembered that there were photos of Bootsie as a little girl in the older albums. I flipped through the pages of black-and-white photos of people I didn't know and a few photos of a young Bootsie with a tall, handsome man with sad eyes who I knew was her father. There were none of her and her mother, which didn't surprise me, since I knew she'd died the year Bootsie was born. I was flipping through quickly, but stopped suddenly as I turned to two facing pages in the middle of the album. They were empty except for four black photo tabs in the shape of a rectangle on each page, and in the approximate size of the photo I held in my hands.

Balancing the album on my lap, I slipped the corners of the baby photo into the tabs, not all that surprised when the photo fit perfectly. I could only guess at what had been on the facing page.

It wasn't until I'd turned to the next page that I found what I'd been looking for. It was a photo of the same baby, in a different pose as the photo in the archives, but wearing the identical clothing, which made me assume the photos were taken in a studio at the same time. And on her chubby baby finger she wore the heart ring. I'd gone through this album dozens of times as I was growing up, seeing the baby ring but not really *seeing* it. And I'd forgotten all about it until Tripp had shown me the ring from the grave and it had jogged loose an old memory.

I carefully lifted the photo from the page and turned it over. *Bootsie Walker Richmond*. I flipped back a page, staring at the empty spot, wondering why one of Bootsie's baby photos had been used in a newspaper article, and what might have been in the missing photograph. I replaced the second photo into the album, then curled up on the sofa by the window and stared at the sky while waiting for morning, finally falling asleep just as the sky flushed pink.

*

I knelt in the soft soil of the garden, wearing Bootsie's old floppy hat and marking out sections in the dirt with the tip of my trowel. Carol

Lynne sat cross-legged in her old jeans, holding her own trowel and watching me closely, while Chloe sat in one of the green chairs, reading aloud from some of the photocopied news articles that Mrs. Shipley had made for us.

I reached over to my mug that sat on top of the hatbox Chloe seemed to bring with her everywhere. I was on my fourth cup already, but still feeling sluggish. Despite my hours of sleeplessness, I'd managed to fall asleep long enough to miss asking Tommy to use his equipment to read what was engraved on the baby's ring. Frustration at having to wait a little longer nearly eclipsed my anxiety at finding out what was written on the tiny heart.

"Here's something you can write about," Chloe shouted from behind the sheets of paper in her hands.

I sat back on my heels and looked at her. "What?"

"Did you know that President Kennedy was shot?"

It crossed my mind that she might be joking, but I dismissed the thought when I saw her amazed expression, like she'd just found out that Justin Bieber was a girl. "Yes, I might have heard that."

"Well, some guy in Indianola dropped dead when he heard about it while watching the news on TV. I guess he was a big fan."

"Cousin Emmett had a stroke when he heard the news, too. He always had a limp after that." Carol Lynne dug her trowel into the ground and twisted it just like I'd shown her.

"You remember that?" I asked softly. "You remember when President Kennedy was shot?"

She stared at the handle of her trowel that was sticking up out of the dirt, as if she wasn't sure what she was supposed to do next. She nodded. "It was really sad. I was in a bus station. With Jimmy." She smiled, as if she'd just won an award for pulling an obscure name from her past out of the ether. "There was a TV on and then people started crying. I remember that."

"Do you remember my high school graduation? When my heel got caught on my gown and I fell when I went up to get my diploma?"

She stared at me blankly, her smile dimming.

"Or how I was voted most likely to be famous? Do you remember that?"

I heard the sound of a pencil scratching across paper and saw Chloe jotting down what my mother had said about Kennedy's assassination, and I knew I'd have to use it in an article. I was jealous of those memories of a time and place that had nothing to do with me, jealous of a boy named Jimmy who played a larger part in the play that had become her past than her own daughter, whose presence had been relegated to backstage. It was almost as if the very existence of my childhood hinged on my mother's ability to remember it.

"Here's another one, Vivi. About that blues singer guy Mr. Montgomery was telling us about who made a deal with the devil and sold his soul to make him the best guitar player ever. It's a real place—at the crossroads of highways Sixty-one and Forty-nine in a lame-sounding town called Clarksdale. We should go there and take pictures."

I barely heard her as I tried to fill my empty lungs with air, each breath full of the hurt of being forgotten, of being replaced by memories of people I'd never known. I thought of my purse and the single pill I'd found at the bottom of it when looking for a pen. I'd left it there; I wasn't sure why. But all I could do right now was think about it, and think about making an excuse to go upstairs and take it so that all this pain would stop and I could forget just as easily as my mother had.

"For your *column*," Chloe reminded me. "Do I have to write it, too, or do you just want me to do all the research?"

I cleared my throat. "No, but thanks." I stuck my bare fingers in the dirt and squeezed as if that could ground me. It calmed me, and I could almost imagine it was Bootsie's hand in mine instead of a fistful of dirt. I smiled at Chloe. "You're doing a great job with the research, and I think we've got two winners there. But why don't you put that away now. It's time for your science lesson."

She actually groaned. "Just don't make me put my hands in the dirt. Do you know how many *germs* are in there?"

"That's why it's called dirt. And I didn't ask you to eat it, just dig little holes and put seeds in them. I've marked off an entire section just for you, so you can be responsible for your own plants."

With great exaggeration, she slapped the papers down onto the seat next to her and stood. "I'll work with Carol Lynne, since we're both newbies and you're the professional. That makes us even."

"I didn't realize this was a competition," I said, amused despite myself.

"Dad says everything's a competition and nobody remembers who comes in second."

I bit my lip hard to keep from blurting out what I really thought about her dad and his nuggets of wisdom. "Fine," I said, handing her a bag of Bootsie's seeds that Tommy had given me. "These are lima bean seeds. Dig your holes two inches deep and four to six inches apart so they have room to grow. I've already prepared the soil with compost and fertilizer, so I don't want to hear you complain about getting dirty, okay?"

She scowled up at me but I kept on talking. "I'll show you each day what you need to do with your plants to keep them healthy—and a lot of that depends on the weather. Cora said she was picking up a garden journal for you to keep all your notes."

She took the seed bag with an eye roll and a heavy sigh, but I could see that she was also looking at the lines drawn in the dirt with interest. "I have another trowel in the toolshed," I suggested. "Although, to be honest, I find that using my fingers is best for such a small hole. But I know how you feel about getting your hands dirty."

We both settled our gazes on Carol Lynne, who still crouched on her knees in front of the same hole she'd begun to dig, examining it as if she weren't sure about what happened next.

"That's okay," Chloe said, getting down on her knees in the dirt next to my mother. "We'll share."

She placed Carol Lynne's hands around the trowel, then put hers on top, and together they flipped the tip out of the dirt, excavating a perfectly round hole a single inch deep. She held open the bag and my mother selected a seed after picking up then putting back three, then placed it in the hole. Then they both scraped the loose dirt back over the hole and pressed it down snugly, Chloe's round hands almost completely covered by my mother's older ones.

"Don't pack it too tightly," I said. "The little shoots are very delicate and not strong enough to break through hard ground, so don't smother them. And then they have to figure out how to stick their heads out into the sunshine on their own. All you can do is watch and hope for the best, because you've done everything you know how to do."

"Like we're the mothers and these are our little babies," Carol Lynne said, her voice as clear as a child's.

Chloe laughed, a sound I hadn't heard a lot of in the last few years.

"You're right!" she said. Their eyes met and they smiled at each other like a freaking Hallmark Channel movie.

I looked away, sad yet somehow contented, too. Chloe was different here, despite all of her protestations. It had been a good thing for her to come; I could see that now. Not because of me, but because of the opportunities in compassion she could experience for the first time in her life.

By the time they were finished with the first hole, I'd already planted three seeds. I kept silent, reminding myself that it wasn't a race.

We worked side by side for about an hour in the hot sun, Chloe and my mother singing harmony to the song "Mockingbird" over and over. I had no idea where Chloe had picked up the lyrics to that, but assumed Hailey must be responsible.

At the sound of a car door slamming, I stood. "I think that's Tommy, and I need to see if he'll look at the photograph. I'll bring you both some lemonade on my way back."

I brushed off my stiff knees, then hobbled around the house instead of through it, still minding Bootsie's rule about keeping the dirt in the garden and not in her house. I was surprised to find three vehicles pulled up in the drive in front of the house, recognizing Tripp's truck and the sheriff's cruiser. Tommy stood halfway between the drive and his shed, seeming as surprised to see the two men as I was.

The sheriff tipped his hat at me as he approached. "Good afternoon, Miz Moise. Hope I'm not disturbing you. Just thought it was time we talked again, now that we know the deceased was a relative of yours."

"Yes, of course," I said, wondering what other information he thought I might have that I hadn't already given him.

"Why are you here?" I asked Tripp.

"It's always nice to see you, too, Vivi. I'm here because I'm celebrating a good closing on a house I never thought would sell, and it's a slow day for calling souls to heaven. So I thought I'd come get you and Chloe and head out to Horseshoe Lake to show her how to fish. I figure Cora could make it a science lesson, or maybe we could do a math lesson, where Chloe adds up how many more fish I catch than you."

"As if," I said, using one of Chloe's favorite expressions. "But I think Tommy's supposed to take her out in the tractor today to teach her about pesticides."

Tommy walked closer, shaking his head. "I'm having to replant my back thousand acres because the dang planter is broken again, and got the seed depth all wrong. Weather's still a bit cool for May, so the new seeds might have a chance. Came back to get more tools I didn't have on the truck to see if I can fix it." I remembered Emmett telling us that farmers spent most of their time repairing equipment, since it was always easier to figure out a way to fix something than figure out a way to pay to replace it. "Next week I've scheduled a crop duster, which might be even more interesting."

"Then fishing it is," Tripp said, rubbing his hands together. "We're going to make Miss Chloe a true Southern girl before she knows it."

"Good luck with that," I said, picturing Chloe wearing one of her black Marilyn Manson T-shirts with a pair of Daisy Dukes and cowboy boots and almost laughed. At least she wasn't wearing the thick black eyeliner anymore. One morning at breakfast Carol Lynne had simply reached across the table with a wet paper napkin and started wiping it off. I'd have liked to think that Chloe's days were too full with her schoolwork and her new chores—suggested by Cora and adopted wholeheartedly by me—that she just didn't have the time to apply it, but I knew the reason had more to do with pleasing my mother. I tried not to think of the dozens of times I'd tried to get Chloe to take it off, only to be met with a hostile stare. Maybe she'd just needed to hear it from somebody else's mother.

I turned to the sheriff. "Actually, I do have something new for you. I needed Tommy to take a look at it before I called you, so this is perfect timing. Why don't you all head to Tommy's office and I'll be there in just a minute."

I ran upstairs to my room and grabbed the photo of Bootsie before heading out the door, tripping on my own feet in my excitement as I ran to Tommy's office.

The three men were lounging in turquoise high school chairs, all three of them looking like Gulliver in Lilliput, and I was thinking that we'd all either grown a great deal since high school, or the school board had found a way to save money by buying tiny chairs. The men stood as I entered, and Tripp offered his seat to me while he dragged another one from the corner.

I thanked him, then sat down. "Where'd the extra chairs come from?" I asked, remembering the single one I'd sat on during my last visit.

Tommy looked everywhere except my eyes. "Carrie said she had some extras she'd picked up but didn't need. She said if I wanted them I just needed to go get them."

"And she just happened to have enough meat loaf and corn bread to make you a plate and have you join her and the kids for supper." Sheriff Adams winked at me.

Tommy's face, already sunburned from working outside in the fields, turned a darker shade of red. "I just needed some more chairs. . . ."

Tripp sat up. "And what's this I hear about you agreeing to coach Bo's Little League team? Have you even thrown a baseball since high school?"

"Look, I have to get back to my fields. Can we just focus on what you came here for?"

I decided to take pity on him and handed the picture to Sheriff Adams. "My mother found this yesterday in the historical archives that came from the library—it's a photograph of my grandmother, Bootsie, who was born in 1927. The photo came from the newspaper archives from when the paper moved offices and they sent all their old records to the library, since they didn't have any room for them. So I'm guessing that this photograph might have been used in an article—just haven't found which one yet."

I waited for him to notice the ring on the baby's finger, and when he did, he looked up at me. "Same one that was in the grave?" He held up the photo for Tripp and Tommy to see.

I nodded. "It sure looks like it. It has something engraved on it, but it's too hard to see from the photograph. I thought Tommy could use some of his magnifying equipment to read it."

Tommy stood and took the photo from the sheriff and placed it on his worktable. He flipped a couple of switches and the two overhead lamps spilled blue light onto his workspace. Then he opened a drawer and pulled out what looked like a pair of regular glasses, except the eyepieces were thick and round and definitely not made for street wear. He pulled over a piece of paper and a pen, then slid the glasses onto his face. Without a word, he moved the photo up and down and side to side as he tilted it in various ways to get rid of any reflection from the overhead light.

After a few moments, he picked up the pen without looking at it and wrote something down. He studied the photo one more time, then slid the glasses off his face. He stared at what he'd written, his eyebrows lifted. "Well, that's certainly not what I expected."

I took the paper as the sheriff and Tripp moved to stand behind me so we could look at it together.

VE

OU

EVER

I looked up, my eyes meeting Tommy's. "It's the other half of the ring. The other half to the one found in the grave." I brushed my fingers against the letters, as if by my touching them they'd reveal their secrets.

Sheriff Adams cleared his throat. "So if your grandmother wore the matching ring as a baby, who do you think would have the other half?"

I love you forever. The words had been engraved on a gold heart and then split in two, as if each wearer would be incomplete without the other. I remembered how I'd felt when I'd held Chloe's hand to cross the street when she was little and still allowed those things, and what it had been like to see my unborn child on a sonogram screen, the sweet perfection of the little nose and fingers splayed so I could count all ten.

"Her mother," I said, my voice too quiet to be heard. The three men looked at me. Clearing my throat, I said louder, "It would have been her mother who wore the other half of the ring."

"But she drowned in the flood the year Bootsie was born," Tommy said. "That's why we still have that mark on the wall in the foyer."

I nodded. "Bootsie said that her mother left her in the care of a friend and then tried to drive to New Orleans even though she knew the levees had been breached and it wouldn't have been safe. She always wondered why her mother hadn't taken Bootsie with her."

The silence in the room was filled with the sound of ticking clocks, each movement like the beating of a heart.

"Because maybe she never left," Tripp said, and I remembered Carol Lynne saying the same thing as we'd stood by the edge of the grave where the woman had slept for more than eighty years while her daughter wondered why she'd been left behind.

"Do you remember her name?" Sheriff Adams asked, his pad and pencil held in readiness.

I shook my head, impatient with my young self, who never thought remembering names of the dead was important regardless of how many times Bootsie told me the same old stories.

Tommy stood. "It was something like Abigail. Or Abilene. Or maybe Angelica?"

The name came to me as if somebody had just breathed it into my ear. "It was Adelaide. Bootsie's mother was named Adelaide."

Chapter 30

Carol Lynne Walker Moise
INDIAN MOUND, MISSISSIPPI
MARCH 1977

Dear Diary,

I was sitting under my cypress tree smoking a cigarette and thinking how to write about three months of nothing that have actually turned out to be so much more. My diary was lying on its back in the grass, its outspread pages like wings, but I could just look at it while I took drags on my cigarette and wished I had something stronger to smoke.

And then Mathilda came from the house to tell me that Michael had called again but that he didn't have enough dimes for the pay phone to keep waiting, but I was to call the Kellys and leave a message for him there.

He found out where I am and we've been talking since Christmas. He's still on the ranch but says he misses me, and if I come back we'll leave the ranch and do something together. He hasn't been real specific about what exactly we'd be doing, but I'd be lying to say I can't stop thinking about it.

I want to stay. There's so much in me that wants to keep me here. Like Tommy. But the more Bootsie tries to get me to stay, the more I want to leave. Maybe that's just the way of mothers and daughters, to always be at opposite ends of a rope, tugging like you'd win some prize if your oppo-

nent fell. But there're no winners in this game we play. And the more Bootsie begs, the more my demons start clamoring in my head that I need to move on and get my next fix so that I don't care so much about this place.

I can't believe that it's almost April. That's when Emmett disappears into the fields and we hardly see him again until the fall harvest. But I like April, because it's a good time to leave. Right before the farmers start seeding, there's a feeling in the air that reminds me of hope. Like somewhere beneath the soil the earth is deciding our fate. I'm thinking I need to leave now, when I can carry that hope with me the way a child carries a balloon. I just don't know how long I can keep that balloon inflated.

The fields are barren and empty and the temperatures are still low enough that we might still get a frost, according to Emmett. He knows a lot about soil and planting and weather. Emmett once cracked an egg outside just to prove that it was hot enough to fry. I might not have grown up with a daddy, but he's been a pretty good substitute. He's already started taking Tommy into his shop, where Tommy likes to just sit and watch him work. He loves the sound of the ticking clocks, and when we put a blanket on the floor at the back of the shop, he'll nap for hours.

This planting season, Emmett's promised Tommy that he can ride in the tractor. My little boy is still a baby, but he's an old soul. When you look in his blue eyes it's like he's been around forever. And maybe he has. Only one of us should be allowed to be a child.

Yesterday Emmett brought home a puppy from a litter he found in a box on the side of the road. He thinks it's got some yellow Lab and maybe a little bit of beagle, too, but I think that there's also something small and fluffy inside that dog, because he's got fur as fine as a bird's feather, and a tail that curves over his back. We've always had big outside dogs. Dogs that could hunt and jump into the back of a truck. But Emmett said that now that we have a boy in the family, we needed to get an inside dog to grow up right along with Tommy to teach him the important things about life.

As Tommy's mama, I was given the honor of naming the dog. He's got short legs—the beagle part of him, I guess—and a Lab's head, but his body is sort of round, with wispy fur that will probably grow darker as he gets older, but right now looks almost white. So I named him Cotton. Not the most original name, but I think it fits.

When we brought Cotton inside, Tommy was sitting on a blanket playing with blocks, and Cotton raced in and knocked him over. Tommy was surprised at first and then started giggling as Cotton licked his face like they'd been friends forever. Emmett was right: No boy should be raised without a dog.

A long time ago—it seems like a lifetime—Bootsie told me that I would understand her better once I became a mother. I would never admit this to her, but I think she might be right. She's so good and patient with Tommy—the only one who can get him to eat or go to sleep. When he wakes up screaming in the middle of the night, it's her name he calls. The first time it happened I was a little upset. But then I realized that I had brought the two of them together, that I had gifted Tommy with a mother who could give him what I cannot. And I gave Bootsie a second chance to be the mother I never allowed her to be. Maybe that's what she meant. That when we're mothers we have to choose what's best for our children, even when it breaks our hearts.

I love Tommy more than I ever thought it possible to love another person. But I sometimes want to walk out the front door and keep walking. I've been clean since before he was born, but I still miss the oblivion the drugs gave me. The power over my past they offer. I know that's no life for a child. I keep thinking that if I leave him here he'll have Bootsie, and Emmett, and Mathilda—and now Cotton. And this big yellow house and the cotton fields and a nice bed and lullabies each night. It will kill a part of me to leave him behind, but I keep thinking about Michael, and the things he can give me that will stop my hands from trembling and my mind from thinking too much. When I can't remember the sunsets over the fields, and the sound of Tommy laughing, I'll be okay.

Chapter 31

Adelaide Walker Bodine Richmond
INDIAN MOUND, MISSISSIPPI
OCTOBER 1925

The streets of downtown Indian Mound were decorated with scarecrows and all manner of autumn gourds and more jack-o'-lanterns than I could count. It was the annual Harvest Festival, when the sharecroppers set up stalls on Main Street to sell homemade cakes and breads, handcrafts, and selections from their vegetable patches. John had teased me that I should open up my own stall, but that it wouldn't be fair to the other gardeners, because my vegetables would put theirs to shame.

The heat of summer and the dust of the harvest had passed, leaving a day of bright blue skies and a breeze that carried on it the scent of burning leaves and the coming winter. I looked forward to the evening, when there would be music and dancing and a large bonfire to ward off the chill of a cloudless night.

I'd always loved the festival, mostly because it was the only memory I had of being with both of my parents at the same time. It was before the war, when my mother still smiled and my father was there to hold her hand and carry me on his back.

This year it held special meaning for me. After two false starts, I was in the family way again, further along than I'd made it the first two times. Aunt Louise said it was still early and that I wouldn't start showing for a while, but I felt my body changing already. John was extra careful with me, taking my elbow at every set of steps, and making sure I didn't stay on my feet longer than necessary. I told him I was expecting a baby and was not yet an old woman, but I understood his concern. I think he wanted to be a father almost as much as I longed to be a mother, the need in both of us growing stronger after the first two losses. They had been lost early in the second month, but that hadn't mattered. As soon as I missed my monthly courses, I'd felt like a mother. The losses had been no less devastating to me than if I'd had the chance to hold those babies in my arms.

We'd stopped in front of a farmer's stall, where six baby piglets snuggled up together in a pen. "It smells," Sarah Beth said from behind us, where she walked with Willie. Behind them were Chas Davis and Larissa Belmont, Sarah Beth's hall mate from Newcomb College. We'd all been surprised when Sarah Beth had announced that she'd decided to go to college after all, but I'd understood why when I'd remembered that Newcomb was in New Orleans. From Willie's placid expression, I didn't think he'd yet made the connection with Angelo Berlini.

"It's a pigpen, Sarah Beth. It's supposed to smell," Willie said, surreptitiously fishing out his flask and taking a swig before passing it back to Chas, while Sarah Beth and Larissa pretended not to notice.

I stared down at the sweet little pigs, pink and plump, and remembered the first time I'd met John at the jewelry store, when I'd wondered where Mr. Peacock kept his blind pig. I wasn't as naive as I'd once been, but sometimes found myself wishing that I were. It was so much easier believing that John was content to repair timepieces in the back of Mr. Peacock's store or help Uncle Joe with the farm. But one of the things that had made me fall in love with him was his ambition, and I'd made a vow to love and obey, and to stay by his side through sickness and in health. Everything he did was for us, and it was my duty to support him. It was only John's assurances that it was for just a little bit longer that allowed us both to sleep at night.

"Anybody up for a sack race?" Willie called out.

He'd meant it for the gentlemen, but I was feeling lighthearted. "I'd love to, but John feels I might break, so I can't. I'm just hoping that he'll let me go on the hayride later tonight." I glanced behind me. "But maybe Larissa and Sarah Beth would like to race."

They sent me matching arched eyebrows, their pencil-thinned brows in marked contrast to the natural brows of the rest of the women we passed, including mine. Sarah Beth had changed a great deal since she'd started college. I'd expected her to be wilder, but except for her new and outlandishly short dresses and bright makeup, she seemed almost subdued compared to the girl I'd grown up with.

"Fine," I said. "Then how about a horseshoe toss? We'll challenge any of you." John and I, having been raised on farms, would have no match in our four companions. Even Willie, who now worked fulltime at the bank along with Chas, liked to pretend he didn't even know what a horseshoe was.

Sarah Beth and her friend snickered, the sound erased by the sound of four Negro men in matching striped vests and boater hats singing "Shine On, Harvest Moon." They stood on the corner with a hat on the ground in front of them. John reached into his vest pocket and pulled out a coin before tossing it into the hat. One of the singers tipped his hat to John, crooning the words as if they were meant just for us. *So shine on, shine on, harvest moon, for me and my gal.*

John put his arm around me and pulled me close, then whispered into my ear, "They're just too afraid they'll lose."

I smiled up at him, pulling his arm closer. We passed a booth that had baskets of apples surrounding it, and trays of candied apples on sticks sitting on top of a wooden table. John was well aware of my sweet tooth and stopped. "Would you like one?"

I nodded eagerly, too happy to worry about the sticky mess that would cover my mouth and teeth. Larissa and Sarah Beth declined, pulling the collars of their fox-fur coats up to their necks.

We reached the town square, a tidy spot in the middle of town covered in grass and benches, with a monument in the middle to commemorate the town's Confederate dead. The man on top of the stone horse had been an ancestor of mine. He'd lost one arm and a leg in separate battles, but his likeness on the statue didn't show his battle scars. Uncle Joe said it was a disgrace to alter history like that, but I always thought that it was a lot like how people remembered the dead at funerals, with all of their warts and bad deeds whitewashed by the kind words in a eulogy.

A corner of the square had been fenced off as it was each year to showcase the foals from a Thoroughbred farm out near Olive Branch. Three colts galloped inside around the wooden corral, their eyes wide with alarm at the noises and movement around them. A man stood in the middle of the ring with a long whip, the tip barely touching their rumps, making them run in circles to show off their dark brown coats and silky manes.

"That one horse—the biggest one—is darb," said Chas. "Let's go take a look."

Larissa and Sarah Beth held back. "We'd rather not. It smells like manure. Besides, we'll get our heels all muddy in the grass just walking over."

"I'll stay with the ladies," John volunteered, although I knew he'd love to see the horses, too. He'd had his own pony as a boy on the farm in Missouri, and had missed it as much as he'd missed his family after he'd left.

I put my hand on his arm. "It's all right, John. You go on. We'll stay right here and wait for you men to return."

The two girls shrugged in bored agreement before John kissed me briefly and jogged to catch up to the other men, who'd already started making their way toward the enclosure.

I turned around in time to see Sarah Beth opening her purse and pulling out a small flask, using her fur collar to hide behind while she took a sip before passing it to Larissa. I recognized a flash of blue at her wrist and bit my lip so I wouldn't say something I'd regret later.

She was wearing my Cartier watch, the one that had belonged to my mother and that John had given to me. Despite her own jewelry box full of expensive necklaces and rings and bracelets, she'd coveted my watch from the first time she'd seen it. She'd loved that it had been my mother who'd had it inscribed, and then was given to me by John. Despite so many actions to the contrary, I knew she was sentimental, something I'm sure was the reason our friendship had survived our childhoods.

But when she'd asked if she could borrow it, I'd said no. It had taken her tearful reminder of the fur coat she'd loaned to me that I'd lost to convince me that I was being the selfish one. She'd borrowed the watch twice before for special events, and then tonight, with a promise that she would take care of it and return it to me at the end of the evening, I'd agreed. But I missed it. Missed the weight of it, and the heat of the words against my skin. *I love you forever.*

I was about to ask Sarah Beth if she'd like a bite of my candied apple, but her eyes were focused on something behind me. Turning, I saw who she was looking at.

A table made of upturned cotton bales had been set up near the curb, a large quilt, its edges fraying, covering the top. On this was set an assortment of carved figures made from long oval root growths known as cypress knees. Each one had a humanlike face carved with exact detail, the hair of the brows and lashes and beard drawn as if God had designed them. The eyes seemed lifelike, watching us with solemn intensity.

"Ooh, let's go see," Larissa said, marching forward before I could stop her, Sarah Beth and I holding back.

Standing to the side and a little behind the table was the man Leon. He was looking around as if he were part of the crowd, but I recognized the white woman sitting at the table as the same woman I'd seen him with at the Ellis plantation. I supposed it wouldn't be proper for them to be seen together at the festival, and so they had to pretend that they weren't. It didn't seem possible that either of them would have the skill or intellect to create anything of such beauty and artistry as the carvings displayed on the table.

"Who is that?" Sarah Beth asked quietly, squinting at the man and the woman as if she knew she'd seen them before but couldn't place them.

"They're just moonshiners. We saw them at the Ellis plantation," I whispered, surprised that she didn't remember. But Sarah Beth rarely noticed people who weren't in a position to do something for her or to play a part.

I started to walk away, but she had stepped forward to stand next to Larissa, too close to the table now to leave without being seen. Leon came closer to the table when he spotted her, his big beefy arms crossed over his chest, his dirty undershirt showing beneath the open collar of his shirt. "Look who here, Velma," he said to the woman. She remained seated, but her eyes widened with interest as we approached.

I noticed her eyes then, how they might have been pretty in a face

that hadn't been so weathered by the sun and circumstances. She regarded Sarah Beth with an odd expression that I couldn't decipher,
something between dislike and surprise. *That girl ain't no better than she
oughta be.* I remembered those words and the venom behind them, and
I wanted to pull my friend away, knowing she had no business with
these people.

Sarah Beth tilted her head back in the way she did when she felt
threatened and wanted to show her superiority. She picked up one of
the carvings, her kid-gloved fingers gently touching the face. "These
are quite lovely," she said, putting that one down and picking up another. "Did you make them?" She didn't look up to direct her comment
to either of them, but the woman started laughing, revealing yellowed
teeth and a gap in the front.

"I did."

We turned around to see Robert emerge from the crowd, dressed
neatly in an inexpensive suit and hat, his expression wary. Mathilda
clung to his arm, her gaze darting from Sarah Beth to the couple behind the table, and then back to Robert. I felt as if I had suddenly been
thrown onstage in the middle of a play, but somebody had forgotten to
give me my lines.

Robert removed his hat and inclined his head to us, his gaze passing
over Larissa before settling on Sarah Beth and me. "Miss Bodine. Miss
Heathman."

Sarah Beth tilted her head back again. "How do you know my
name?"

My eyes met Mathilda's briefly, and she quickly shook her head, and
it was clear that nobody was supposed to know about the night Robert
had carried a drunk Sarah Beth into her bedroom.

"He's Mathilda's beau," I said, desperate to end the awkwardness
that bounced between us like an invisible ball.

Mathilda started to say something, but I didn't hear a word. My
gaze had fallen to the neck of her dress beneath her open coat, where a
single, perfect pearl glowed from the end of a thin strand of silk. I could
almost hear the sound of Sarah Beth's long string of pearls breaking in
her car that night, and Robert carrying her from the car to her bedroom. She'd had the pearls restrung without commenting that any

were missing, but I heard Sarah Beth's intake of breath and I knew she'd seen it, too. Nobody I knew had a colored maid who owned a pearl necklace, even if it was just one.

"I see," she said, her nostrils flaring as if she'd just smelled a foul odor. "How much?" she asked, holding out the statue in her hands.

"A dollar," he said without hesitation.

"That's a little steep, isn't it?"

"No, ma'am. It take me almost a month to make 'em, and I have to go out to the swamp and cut them from the dead trees. I'd say a dollar be a right bargain."

Sarah Beth's lips pursed. "Yes, well, I'd say it's a bit too dear for my pocket money." She replaced the statue on the table and then brushed her gloves together as if to remove any dirt that might stain them.

The woman, Velma, stood, the grooves around her mouth deepening as she frowned. "You da banker's daughter, ain't ya? You got all dem pretty dresses and jewels and you strut around town like you some queen of Sheba. Well, you ain't no better than us. Ain't that right, Leon?"

Leon shook his head. "Yes, Velma. I 'spect you right. She ain't no better dan us."

She began to cackle as the large man threw back his head and guffawed, loud enough that I saw several people in the crowd look in our direction. I prayed one of them wasn't Willie, who wouldn't like Sarah Beth speaking to these people, much less being laughed at by them.

Larissa had already backed up from the table as if to distance herself from us, and I grabbed Sarah Beth's arm, pulling her away so that we stood with Larissa, the crowd now separating us from Leon and Velma and her watchful, spiteful eyes.

With a shaking hand, Sarah Beth drew out her flask from her purse and took a deep gulp. She started to cough, and when I turned to see if she was all right, I spotted what had made her choke. Mr. and Mrs. Heathman were walking toward us, followed by another couple who were walking out of view behind them. Other festivalgoers spread out like chicken feed as they approached.

Ever since Mrs. Heathman had found out that I was expecting, she'd been sending me an ever-growing assortment of Bertha's tonics, along with her own handwritten notes of advice. I remembered all those little graves in the cemetery, and wondered how she'd been able to face her grief, and if her faithfulness had been what had finally brought her a daughter. I also wondered if she'd given up on Sarah Beth and Willie ever announcing their engagement, and if I'd become a substitute daughter, expecting their first grandchild.

Mr. Heathman tipped his hat to us as his wife, still as slender as a girl and dressed in furs and diamonds, embraced each of us. "Darlings," she said, leaning close to brush her lips against our cheeks. She smelled of Tabac Blond perfume, powder, and money, her fur coat soft against my face.

"Mother," Sarah Beth said with surprise. "I thought you and Daddy were in Jackson and were going to miss the festival."

"We were, but then look who we ran into in the hotel lobby." She stepped back and I imagined I felt the air begin to pop and sizzle like water hitting a hot fry pan. Oblivious, Mrs. Heathman continued. "He was eager to come see what our famous Harvest Festival was all about."

Angelo Berlini, dressed immaculately as always in a dark striped suit and a crisp white shirt, a cashmere coat tossed elegantly over his shoulders, stepped forward. "What an unexpected pleasure," he said, taking my gloved hand and kissing it. I hadn't seen him since my wedding, but I knew through John that he remained on the outskirts of our lives. "You are lovelier than ever, Mrs. Richmond. Married life suits you."

I thanked him, then stepped back, wondering why he'd chosen me to greet first.

Mrs. Heathman continued with the introductions. "You already know our daughter, Sarah Beth, of course, and this is her college hall mate, Larissa Belmont, of the Baton Rouge Belmonts."

Larissa fluttered her eyelashes at him, and allowed him to kiss her hand before he turned to Sarah Beth. Her face seemed as calm and still as the statue's in the square, her face pale. "It's a pleasure to see you again, Mr. Berlini." Her words were stiff, as if her stone lips would crack.

"Likewise," he said, sounding as if he were reading from a script. "I understand you're at Newcomb. How are you liking it?"

"Very well, thank you." It looked like she was about to say something else when Angelo held out his hand for another member of their party who'd been hidden from view behind the Heathmans.

The woman was only slightly older than Sarah Beth and me, but she had the air of royalty, a regal glance that made me think of Agnes Ayres in my favorite picture show, *The Sheik*. Her hair was black, as were her eyes, but her skin was as creamy as fresh-churned butter and the color of sheets bleached outside in the sun. Despite her fashionable clothes, her voluptuous figure defied constraint by the straight lines of her dress. She was as perfect as a china doll, and I felt Sarah Beth stiffen beside me.

"Please allow me to introduce Miss Carmen Bianca. My fiancée."

I smiled, feeling like a hayseed despite my best Sunday dress and new wool coat. I wished I were wearing my Cartier watch, since that at least would have made me feel more elegant.

Larissa practically gushed with enthusiasm as she greeted the newcomer, but Sarah Beth was oddly silent. She smiled vaguely in Carmen's direction, but she'd gone so pale that I thought she might faint.

I touched her elbow and felt her lean into me. "What a pleasure to meet you," Sarah Beth said, regaining some of her composure. "I wasn't aware that Mr. Berlini was engaged."

The woman laughed, the sound like water burbling in a fountain. "Yes, well, it's been unofficial for several years, because my father is a diplomat who travels a great deal with my mother, and we simply have not had the time to devote to planning a wedding." She squeezed Angelo's arm into her side. "With all of my parents' friends and Angelo's family and wide-flung businesses, it will be quite large. Mother promises me that she will have time next year."

"Your accent is just darling," Larissa said, and I wondered if that was her way of saying, "You're not from around here." She smiled sweetly, seemingly completely unaware of Sarah Beth's discomfort and her desire to get away as quickly as possible. "Where are you from?"

"New York, although I was born in Paris, where my father was stationed at the time." She said this in such a languid, bored tone that she might have just told us that she'd had grits for breakfast. Not that I thought a woman like that would ever eat grits.

"How long do you plan to stay in Indian Mound?" Sarah Beth asked, her voice strong despite the tremble I felt in her arm beneath my hand.

"Only for a day, unfortunately," Mrs. Heathman interjected. "Mr. Berlini has business to return to in Jackson. He will be staying at the Main Street Hotel, but I've invited Miss Bianca to stay with us. I didn't realize you'd be home from college, dear, or I would have had your room freshened." She frowned at her daughter for her breach of etiquette. "I had the blue room made up for Miss Bianca, and I'll have them prepare the rose room for Larissa." The smile she directed at Sarah Beth was brittle, as if she couldn't imagine her daughter imposing on her with no notice. Not that she would be the one putting on the sheets or placing fresh flowers in the vases and clean towels in the bathrooms. I wondered if I should find Mathilda to let her know, so she could warn Bertha, but I didn't want to see Leon or Velma again, and I certainly didn't want to see that pearl on Mathilda's neck.

"Don't go to all that trouble, Mother. Larissa and I have to head back to Newcomb tomorrow morning, so we'll just share my room tonight. What a shame we won't have a chance to get to know Miss Bianca better."

"What a shame," Carmen repeated, her tone mimicking Sarah Beth's.

"Are you ladies here by yourselves?" Mr. Heathman asked. He was shorter than his wife, with sparse graying hair, and one usually forgot he was present, because his wife seemed to take over any room or conversation.

"No," I said, looking back toward the horse ring and wishing I could spot the men. I remembered my wedding day, when Willie and Angelo came to blows in the backyard, and I had no interest in repeating it. "John is here, along with my cousin Willie and Chas Davis."

I turned to Sarah Beth, hoping to catch her eye to let her know that she needed to get her parents to leave us before the men returned. But she was staring down at my watch, twisting it on her wrist. I leaned forward to whisper in her ear, and a sharp pain erupted from deep in my womb.

I must have groaned out loud, because Sarah Beth turned toward me, a little color flooding back to her cheeks. "Are you all right, Adelaide?"

I opened my mouth to let her know that I was fine, that I had to be fine, that all I needed was a chair to sit down in, but another searing pain shot through me, and I felt my knees buckle as something warm and thick slid down my legs. "Get John," I said, not sure if the words made it past my mouth, the world growing dim around the edges.

"It will be all right," I heard a man say, and I knew it was Angelo Berlini. And then he was picking me up in his strong arms while the world around us faded to black.

Chapter 32

Vivien Walker Moise
INDIAN MOUND, MISSISSIPPI
MAY 2013

The sunshine had awakened me before the ringing of my cell phone, which was a good thing. Otherwise I'd have been tempted to throw the phone across the room and attempt to reclaim the sleep that I'd managed to find only three hours before.

I looked at the number and groaned. I let it ring three more times so I could brace myself, then answered it. "Good morning, Mark," I said, my voice so chipper that I wondered if I should have been an actress.

"Vivien?" His voice was surprised, as if he couldn't believe that I'd be awake and alert at this hour.

"Yes, Mark. It's me. How are you?" Despite my sleep deprivation, I was rediscovering what it meant to have a clear head in the morning, with thoughts uncluttered by a drug-induced fog. It almost seemed as if the sun were brighter, the sky bluer. Like I'd parted curtains so that I could peer into a future that was still unknown but no longer seemed as frightening.

After a brief pause, he said, "What time is it there?"

I lifted the phone from my ear to look at the screen. "It's six-oh-three. What time is it where you are?"

"I, ah, it's a little after eleven in the morning." His voice was thick with sleep, and I pictured him still in bed, with the perfect body of his new wife curled up against him. The only thing I felt a pang of jealousy about was that he'd been able to sleep until eleven o'clock.

"You've been getting the drug reports?" I asked, knowing that since I hadn't been ordered to send Chloe back yet he most likely had been.

"Yeah. Twice a week like clockwork. Still can't believe it, to be honest."

"Thanks, Mark. Your vote of confidence means the world to me."

"Well, you must be taking something, because something's giving you an attitude I don't think I like."

I had to remind myself that I had to stay in his good graces to keep Chloe with me. "Is there something you need?" I braced myself, waiting for him to tell me he was coming to get Chloe, and preparing to tell him that she had a patch in my garden that needed tending, and that my mother had breakfast with her each morning, and she hadn't finished reading all of my books in my childhood bedroom. She had so many reasons to stay, but none of them could have anything to do with me, and I needed to make sure Mark believed that.

"Ah, yeah, actually." I heard a woman's voice nearby, low and suggestive. "Hang on a second," he said, and I pictured him climbing out of the bed and then moving somewhere more private. "I wanted to know if you could hang on to Chloe for another couple of weeks. We've decided to do one of those Orient Express trips through Southeast Asia. Tiffany's never been out of California and wants to see more of the world."

I bit my tongue so I wouldn't say something about how most children weren't supposed to have seen much of the world yet. "A couple more weeks," I said, as if that were a long time and I really had to think about it. "Jim's okay to run the practice alone for that long?"

"We hired a new surgeon to take some of the workload, and so I could finally have a vacation. Mike told me to take as long as I needed."

I thought of all the times I'd tried to get him to take a family vacation with Chloe and me, or to even spend a day at Disneyland, but he'd always been too busy with work—or golf. It made me sad more than angry that he'd take time off for Tiffany but not his own daughter.

"So when do you think you'll be back?"

"June fifteenth—and then we have to fly to the States. You have airports in Mississippi, right?"

"Of course. All the planes are crop dusters, but they'll get you here just the same."

"Seriously?"

For a man who could sculpt the most beautiful pair of breasts or a perfect nose, he could be pretty dense at times. "No, Mark. We have regular airports and big planes. We even have indoor plumbing."

"That's a relief."

A woman's voice in the background began singing the lyrics from Justin Bieber's song "Baby"—familiar to me only because I'd been forced to listen to the artist's songs over and over again while living with Chloe. But Chloe was twelve. Tiffany was not.

"So who's Tripp Montgomery?"

"Excuse me?" His question took me by surprise, and I couldn't at first think who he meant.

"It's the name on the letterhead attached to your lab results. I can't figure out why a note from a Realtor would be included. Is the local doctor also into real estate?"

"Oh, um, no. Not exactly."

"Well, he always includes some sort of personal note with the results, like how patient you are with Chloe and what a good mother you are to her."

I felt my face heat. "Oh. That's nice," I said, wanting to hug and punch Tripp at the same time.

"Not really. It's unprofessional and completely unwarranted. Maybe you can tell him to stop."

"Sure. And I'm glad Chloe can stay a little longer. She has a few more homeschool projects she needs to complete, and she's learning how to fish—"

I was cut off by the sound of the phone moving and then Mark's muffled voice. "Just a minute, sweetheart. I'm hanging up now."

"Anyway," I continued. "She's doing great and learning a lot and even enjoying herself. It's early and I know she's still sleeping, but she would just love to talk with you. . . ."

"Nah, I'll let her sleep. Tell her I said hi. I'll call to let you know what flight we're on so you can pick us up at the airport."

"Really, Mark, I think you should speak with—"

Once again, I knew I was talking to dead air. I ended the call and put the phone back on my night table, wondering how I was going to tell Chloe that she was staying for two more weeks without letting her know that her father had called again without asking to speak with her.

Four hours later, Chloe and I were headed downtown to the archives. I'd left my mother with Cora, along with Chloe's instructions on exactly how she wanted her lima bean seeds watered. I'd told her not to expect to see anything for five days, but she checked on her seedlings at least three times a day, and tested the soil to make sure it wasn't too wet or too dry. I'm not sure if she knew what to do if she got a positive result either way, but I applauded her enthusiasm.

Her phone sat untouched in her lap, the screen not even lighting up with reminders of Facebook posts or tweets. It was as if her former life in California had receded into the black face of her phone, and there was a part of me that was glad. She needed better friends. *Real* friends. Like Claire Montgomery and I had once been. In high school we were practically joined at the hip, both of us cocaptains on the cheerleading squad, and instigators of the senior prank where we'd locked farmer Crandall's mule, cow, and six sheep inside the high school overnight. We'd shared every secret and every dream, usually falling asleep with our phones still pressed against our ears. Until the day I'd packed up and left without saying good-bye.

"What do kids wear down here when they're going to a dance?" Chloe asked.

She was staring out her window, but I was pretty sure her question was directed at me.

"Well, that depends. What kind of a dance?"

She shrugged. "Mrs. Smith said that at the end of the school year there's a party at the middle school gym for all the kids going to high school next year. She said the homeschool kids are invited, too, and it might be cool for me to meet kids my age. It sounds pretty lame, but it's not exactly Disneyland at your house."

"What do you mean? Watching plants grow and learning how to fish isn't as exciting as riding a roller coaster?"

She speared me with a look that told me she wasn't amused. "The plants are a science experiment for *school*, which means it's not supposed to be fun. And I haven't gone fishing yet because Mr. Montgomery got called to a crash and had to leave. So, yeah, a lame dance in a school gym is like a freakin' Marilyn Manson concert in comparison."

I didn't point out that she had never actually been to a Marilyn Manson concert. Her father had been too happy to shell out the money for tickets without asking any questions, but I'd been pregnant at the time, and off of the pills and thinking clearly, and for once had put my foot down. It hadn't endeared me to either of them, but I'd been vindicated by the look of relief I'd seen on Chloe's face. It was as if she'd been testing us, wanting somebody to step forward and be a parent.

"Back in my day," I said, "there were a lot of cutoff jeans and sparkly shirts. Big hair has always been popular here, even when the rest of the world was straightening theirs. And cowboy boots. Always had to have a pair of cowboy boots all year 'round, and they're worn with everything, which, in my opinion, is what started this whole new fashion trend around the country."

She raised her eyebrows and let out a loud sigh. "Well, I guess I won't be going then."

Keeping my hands gripping the steering wheel so I wouldn't be tempted to do a fist pump, I said, "I'll be happy to take you to Hamlin's, where you can pick out an outfit or two. It's going to get really hot here and you're going to die of heat prostration if we don't get you some cooler clothing. And a bathing suit. You'll want one when you go fishing. The way Mr. Montgomery does it, you'll need to get in the water."

I'd already told her about my conversation with her father, and how she could stay with me through the middle of June. She hadn't even asked if her father had wanted to speak with her.

She slumped down in her seat. "Whatever. As long as nobody takes any pictures for my friends at home to see."

I just nodded, looking at her empty screen and knowing there was little chance of that.

"We'll have to bring Carol Lynne when we go shopping, all right? She's been dying to take you."

She was thoughtful for a moment, her brows furrowed. "Would she remember that? Or remember that she'd even been there when she got back?"

We drove in silence as I searched for answers, filtering through everything I'd read on the Internet, and everything I thought I knew about dementia, all of which could fit in a matchbox. I finally gave up trying to come up with a scientific, logical answer and instead spoke from a place inside of me that hadn't been tapped in a long time. "She probably won't. But I think she'll enjoy it while we're there, which is the point. There're a lot of things from when I was a kid that I don't remember specifically, but I do remember the overall good feeling when I think back about school, and Friday-night football games, and visiting my cousin Emmett's watch shop. Hanging out with my best friend, swimming at Horseshoe Lake, school dances, the annual Harvest Festival they have each year downtown." *And Tripp.* I shook my head, trying to clear my thoughts. "I just sort of think that if it makes her happy, then we should do it whether she remembers it or not."

She was quiet for a moment. "Is she going to get better?"

I recalled Tommy's words, the truth of them finally sinking in. *She's in her own little world right now, a world that's gonna get smaller and smaller, and I'm not going to recognize her anymore.* I shook my head. "No. I'm working on getting her to see a doctor so she can get medicine that will slow the progression of the disease, but she won't get better."

I respected Chloe too much to lie to her, and hoped that I was doing the right thing by telling her the truth. She turned her head to stare out the window and she was silent for a long time. As we passed the sign on the side of the highway that welcomed us to Indian Mound, she said, "At least she's here."

I wanted to touch her, but I knew better. Even as a little girl, she'd wanted to figure things out on her own, to pretend that she didn't need anybody else. But when she was sick or scared, she looked to me to lie down with her or to sit under a blanket with her. And that had been enough for us both. To just be there.

"Yeah. At least she's here," I said, in awe at the wisdom of children.

I swung into a parking space near the town green. I got out of the car, but Chloe stayed where she was. I walked around to her side and opened the door. "Everything okay in there?"

She pointed to the sidewalk, where a medium-size dog that looked like a cross between a Maltese and some kind of retriever sat in the shade of an awning, its tongue lolling as it panted in the morning sun. "I'm scared he might bite me."

"He's not showing any kind of aggression, Chloe, so I'm sure it's fine. His owner must have left him here while he ran errands."

With a worried expression, Chloe slowly climbed out, then went around the back of the car before making her way to the sidewalk. The dog, its tail now wagging happily, stood and began trotting behind us.

Chloe tried to move in front of me while keeping her eye on the dog. "He's following us. Are you sure he won't attack?"

"If he was going to, he would have done it already. He must just like kids."

"For lunch?" Chloe asked, only half joking.

The dog followed us up the steps of City Hall, but stopped outside the door as we entered, as if he knew he wasn't allowed. Chloe and I took the lumbering elevator down to the basement, where Mrs. Shipley, in an outfit nearly identical to the one we'd seen her in before—this one a slightly different shade of brown—waited for us at her desk.

"Good morning!" she said in a chipper voice. "I hope you're well rested for another morning of hard work." The corners of her mouth shifted slightly downward. "I was a little disappointed in the progress you made when you were here last, but I assume that was just because it was your first time and you were getting acclimated."

I somehow managed to restrain myself from reminding her that we were volunteers. Instead I smiled at her and said, "We actually have a little more direction this morning. We think we have a name to go with the skeletal remains found in our yard—Adelaide Richmond. All I know is that she was supposed to have drowned during the flood of 1927. I remembered finding a few newspapers from that year, so that's a place to start, but I hope that now that I have a name I can look for something specific."

Her lips had thinned while I was talking. "I was wondering why those newspapers were left out of place on the table, so I put them back in a box until you came back. A good library is a tidy library."

I opened my mouth to protest, but she'd already started speaking again. "I do think I can help you with the name, however. When I retired, I finally started researching my family's genealogy, which is something I never had time to do while I was employed full-time. Unfortunately, my family isn't that big, and I soon ran out of material, so I decided to turn my attention on other families in Indian Mound who have lived here for over a century."

"Do you have one for my family? My grandmother always talked about writing it all down—she swore she had the whole thing in her head—but I don't think she ever did."

"Well, seeing as how your family was one of the first to settle in Indian Mound, I would have been remiss not to include them. Your grandmother actually helped me compile a lot of the information."

"That's wonderful! Can I see it?" I wasn't exactly sure what I hoped to find other than another potential victim who wasn't my great-grandmother. Or maybe, possibly, the name of a murderer. On all the crime shows I watched, murders were rarely random acts. I didn't imagine that the motives had changed that much over the last eighty years.

"I actually put all of my family trees in a book, *The History of Indian Mound, Mississippi, 1830 to 2011*, and published it myself. I included a lot of local history along with the genealogies."

"Congratulations," I said. "I'd love to have a copy." I looked at her expectantly, waiting for her to open a desk drawer and hand one to me.

Two bright spots of color appeared on her cheeks. "I always keep a carton of books in my trunk. I'll let you have one for thirty dollars. Forty-five if you purchase two."

It was my turn to blink at her. "Do you take personal checks?"

"I usually don't, but since I know you, I will, as a favor."

"Great, thanks. I'll make sure to pick up my copy before I leave."

Chloe and I began walking down the long aisle toward the tables we'd sat at the previous day, Mrs. Shipley following. When we reached the end of the aisle, she pulled a box from the shelf and put it on one of the tables. "This is where I put those papers you left out." She smiled apologetically, either because she was sorry she'd put them away when I wasn't finished with them, or for charging me an extraordinary amount of money for her book.

"Thanks, Mrs. Shipley. I guess we'll work until lunchtime again. We won't be able to come back until the day after tomorrow, because I'm helping Chloe with a science field trip." I didn't tell the librarian that meant we were going fishing.

Chloe pulled out a box and set it on the floor, then selected a paper and began to read.

Mrs. Shipley stayed where she was, her hands clasped in front of her. "You know, if you like, I could help you. Until this gets organized and moved, I really don't have much to do."

"Thank you," I said gratefully. "Your help would be greatly appreciated."

She pulled another box off the shelves. "What dates did you say you were interested in?"

"Generally, 1927—but basically anything that has to do with the floods of that year. And any article that might mention Adelaide Richmond. I'm pretty sure that was her last name, because that's Bootsie's last name written on the back of a photo I found in an album."

She gave me a thumbs-up, something so incongruous coming from the librarian that I had to choke back a laugh. I bent my head and began to flip through the papers, focusing on just the dates and not the headlines anymore.

Two hours later, I'd found only two more papers from 1927 than I'd discovered the last time I'd been there. My neck and shoulders ached almost as much as my eyes. "You know, this would be a whole lot easier if all these newspapers were stored on a computer so at least I knew what I was looking for. This might be all of the papers from that year, but I could spend another month combing through these looking for more."

Her eyes blinked at me from behind her glasses. "Well, they were computerized at one time. But the fire and water from the hoses destroyed the computers, and even all of the floppy disks they were stored on. For some reason, the disks were kept in the same building as the actual records." She smiled. "No worries, though. We're getting a donation of ten new computers for the library from International Rubberized Products as part of their 'good neighbor' campaign. I suspect they're trying to smooth over all those ruffled feathers created from the protests by the preservationists and environmental people before IRP moved their headquarters here. Anyway, one of the computers has been earmarked for records. We'll just need someone to research the best software and learn how to use it, and then supervise all of the data input."

She was looking in my direction so intently that I turned to glance behind me to make sure there wasn't somebody else she was talking to.

"What's a floppy disk?" Chloe asked, raising her head from one of her newspapers for a moment. Before I could come up with a concise answer that wouldn't invite ridicule or create more questions, she returned to her newspaper. "Here's another good headline you should check out, Vivien. It's from April sixteenth, 1927—isn't that the year you're looking for?"

I nodded. "Yes, it is. Does it have anything to do with the flood?"

She shook her head, then read out loud, " 'Man found drowned in pond at old Ellis plantation. Suspected foul play.' "

"Sounds tragic," I said, flipping through more newspapers, my neck stiff from holding it at an odd angle for so long. "But I don't know if that would be monumental enough to make it into this column I haven't yet agreed to write."

"You didn't let me finish," she said. "The first line of the article says that the man was suspected of having ties to the New Orleans mob."

I didn't look up, reluctant to move my neck, because then I was afraid I'd never be able to move it back. "A mobster in Indian Mound. That does kind of sound interesting. Yeah, pull that one aside to be photocopied."

"What's Ellis plantation?"

I paused. "It's an old cotton plantation—it's still called the Ellis plantation even though nobody named Ellis has lived or planted anything there since before the Civil War. The house burned down sometime during the twenties and it's all overgrown now." I didn't mention how as teenagers my friends and I would go there to drink beer and make out with our boyfriends and tell ghost stories about the restless dead who still wandered the halls of the long-gone house. I'd heard stories of a supposed murder that had happened there long before I was born, but like all old legends I figured it was about ninety-nine percent myth and one percent truth. At that age I had more things to be afraid of. Like Bootsie finding out where I was, or my mother finally returning and deciding she wanted to be part of my life long after I'd decided I didn't want her back.

I finished going through the box I'd been working on, then stuck it on a bottom shelf where I'd put all the other boxes I'd gone through. I'd told Mrs. Shipley that my priority was helping Sheriff Adams in finding anything I could that might help with his investigation, and that the other papers would just have to wait. This had seemed to mollify her, at least, even though it hadn't gotten us any further in our sorting.

I turned to Chloe to see if she was ready for lunch, but she seemed absorbed in an article under the headline, "Neil Armstrong Walks on the Moon." Not wanting to disturb her, I decided to sit down at the table and thumb through the papers I'd pulled to see if there were any articles I'd need Mrs. Shipley to photocopy.

There were stories about the heavy rains that had begun to fall in the delta as early as the summer of 1926, and how at Christmas of that same year the Cumberland River in Nashville had reached historic heights. There were ads for men's hats and ladies' fur coats, and for products like the Bulova Lindbergh Lone Eagle watch and Feen-A-Mint laxatives. There were more articles about the difficult planting season in the spring of 1927 because of the rain, and one about a barn fire that killed a farmer's twenty-five mules. And on April twenty-ninth of 1927, a story about dynamiting the levee in Caernarvon, Louisiana, to save the city of New Orleans.

My stomach growled as I closed one newspaper and opened another, my eyes growing heavy. I was just thinking I should head out to the archives at night, when I wanted to go to sleep, when I stopped, my fingers still clutching the corner of the page I'd just turned. I must have made a sound, because Mrs. Shipley stopped what she was doing and came to stand behind me, looking over my shoulder. I looked down at the large, bold letters in all caps.

INDIAN MOUND WIFE AND MOTHER DISAPPPEARS, ASSUMED LOST IN RAGING FLOODWATERS OF THE MISSISSIPPI

Flush-mounted against the right side of the page were two photographs. The first was the photo of Bootsie, the one Carol Lynne had found in the box of photos from the newspaper archives. The caption read "Elizabeth 'Bootsie' Walker Richmond, infant daughter of missing Indian Mound woman."

Right beneath it was another studio photograph of a woman with the same baby on her lap, with matching eyes and smiles, their hair the same light color, although it was impossible to tell if it was red in the black-and-white photograph. The baby's hands were reaching for something, her fingers splayed wide so the viewer could see the back of a ring on one of her fingers but not the front. But around the woman's neck was a heavy chain, like that used with pocket watches, and hanging from it was a small ring with a tiny half heart on top of it. The caption read "Adelaide Walker Bodine Richmond, missing Indian Mound wife and mother."

I was breathing too rapidly, and I knew if I didn't calm down I'd faint. I slid the paper away from me and began taking deep breaths. "Can you read it out loud, please? I don't think I can right now."

Mrs. Shipley sat down in the chair next to me and began to read. "'At three fifteen in the afternoon of the twenty-seventh of April, Mrs. Adelaide Richmond, wife of John Richmond, also of Indian Mound, left in her car on an errand. The last person to have seen Mrs. Richmond, Miss S. B. Heathman, says that the unknown errand was of some urgency, and might have been to New Orleans. Miss Heathman tried to dissuade her friend, saying that the levees had been breached in several places already and that there was heavy flooding.

"'Mrs. Richmond said her errand couldn't wait, and then she handed her daughter, Bootsie, over to the care of Miss Heathman.

"'Mrs. Richmond's car was found submerged in the swollen waters on the west side of the crevasse in the levee at Greenville, where it was assumed it had been swept by the raging currents of the flooded river. Mrs. Richmond's body has not been recovered but is assumed lost, with the possibility of it making it all the way to the mouth of the Mississippi and out into the Gulf of Mexico.

"'John Richmond could not be reached for comment, although he passed on a message through Miss Heathman stating that his beloved wife could be identified by an unusual watch she would have been wearing. He described it as blue enamel with an engraving on the back, the jeweler's name, Cartier, on the face.

"'All information regarding this case should be directed to the office of the Indian Mound police.'"

Chloe had moved to the chair opposite me and was looking at me with serious eyes, her two fists propping up her chin, the blue watch she'd found in Emmett's spare-parts box peeking out from between her leather wrist straps.

She saw where I was looking and sat back. With her left hand, she moved aside the other straps and pushed open the hinges on the watch before taking it off. "I've never looked at the back," she said. "I just thought it was a pretty bracelet and stuck it on." She didn't make a move to flip it over.

"Go ahead," I said. "Go ahead and look."

Instead, she handed it to me. After only a brief hesitation I flipped it over, then brought it closer to my eyes to read the small lettering on the rectangular backing—and then I stopped breathing.

"What does it say?" Chloe and Mrs. Shipley asked in unison.

I cleared my throat. " 'I love you forever.' "

Chloe was shaking her head. "But it can't be her watch," she said. "Because wouldn't it have been found on the body, just like the ring and the necklace?"

"Or she wasn't wearing it when she died. Or it was taken from her."

Chloe frowned. "Then why was it in Emmett's hatbox?"

"I don't know. But I'm going to hang on to this for now, okay? I'll need to show it to Sheriff Adams."

I began to gather up the newspapers, my hands trembling. "I'm sorry, Mrs. Shipley. I'm not feeling well, and I really don't want to wait for you to photocopy all of these newspapers. Please trust me that I will return them intact when I come back in a couple of days."

She looked as if she were torn between bending the rules and appearing insensitive.

"I'll make sure she takes good care of them," Chloe said.

That made the librarian smile. "Fine. But please be very, very careful."

Chloe helped me stack the rest of the newspapers and then we left, Mrs. Shipley following us to get a book from her car.

"He's still here," Chloe said, and I looked to where the white dog sat in the shade of the awning, having apparently given up waiting for us by the doors to City Hall.

I frowned, realizing that we'd been inside for three hours and the dog had been there when we'd pulled up. "He might be abandoned," I said. "Do you see a collar or a dog tag?"

She shook her head. "Nope. What should we do? He might be hungry. Or thirsty."

I unlocked the doors and placed the papers carefully in the trunk, then pulled out my checkbook to write a check for Mrs. Shipley, hoping she wouldn't notice it was drawn on a California bank. "I'll call Mr. Montgomery. I'm sure he'll know of a shelter we can call."

"Will a shelter find his family?"

"Hopefully, and if not, then a new family."

"And if they can't find a new family, then what?"

My eyes met hers in one of those parenting moments we all dreaded. "Then they get put to sleep."

Her lip trembled a little as she looked back at the dog.

"Yoo-hoo. Over here!" Mrs. Shipley was waving a thick paperback book in the air as she approached our car. "I hope you enjoy it. Would love it if you'd post a review online." I handed her my check and watched her frown as she looked at the bank name.

Trying to distract her, I said, "Do you know whose dog that is?"

"It's just a stray. He's been hanging around the square for about a month or so. The drugstore keeps a bowl of food and water for him outside. We've tried to catch him but he's real fast. Friendly, though. Doesn't seem to have an aggressive bone in his body. Just doesn't want to be caught."

I thanked her and slid into my seat as Chloe opened her car door. But before she could get inside, the dog ran from the sidewalk, jumped into her seat, and looked at me with what I could have sworn was a grin.

I wanted to call after Mrs. Shipley to see if she'd been telling stories about this dog being hard to catch, but she'd disappeared back into City Hall.

Chloe laughed at the unexpectedness of it, and the sound made me smile. "Looks like he wants to come home with us." Her eyes met mine. "Can he?"

I looked at the dog, who was *definitely* grinning, so I said, "For now. We'll just foster him until we can find his family, or a new one. I won't send him to the shelter."

I saw a corner of her mouth lift as if she were fighting a smile. I continued. "We'll have to get him checked out at a vet to make sure he's healthy and to see if he's microchipped. And we'll have to put up posters with his photo so if somebody's looking for him they can find him."

She might have jumped a little, but not enough that I could accuse her of having enthusiasm, then happily got into the backseat so the dog could remain comfortably where he was.

On the drive home, I told Chloe about Tommy's dog, Cotton, and how much he'd loved him and how smart that dog had been. But the whole time I was talking, I felt the weight of the watch on my wrist, and imagined I could hear the words whispered into my ear: *I love you forever.*

Chapter 33

Carol Lynne Walker Moise
INDIAN MOUND, MISSISSIPPI
MAY 1986

Dear Diary,

I am back home. It always seems that no matter what roads I take and how far away I go, the road always brings me back to Mississippi and the old yellow house I was raised in. I wonder if we're like the birds that way. Having some sort of compass in our hearts that brings us back time and again, if only for a short while.

I've been back a few times to see Tommy, to let him know that even though I couldn't be with him all the time, I still loved him, and that I was doing the best thing I knew for him by leaving him with Bootsie. She and Emmett and Mathilda have taken such good care of him, and when I've seen him running through the yard with Cotton, I've known in my heart that I've done the right thing. Maybe by leaving him behind I have proved that I've been a good mother to him.

He has a forgiving soul. He's always on his best behavior when I'm home, saying "yes, ma'am" and "no, ma'am" and using the table manners Bootsie taught him. I know he does this so I won't leave. That he believes that there's something imperfect in him that makes me want to leave. And no matter what I say to him I can't change his mind. Yet each time I re-

turn, he's the first one out the door, him and Cotton running as fast as they can—the dog running a little slower than he used to—and Tommy throws his arms around me like I've been gone forever and I won't be staying long. Which, of course, is how it's always been. I still hope that one day I can get over this sickness of mine and stay long enough to tell him my leaving has never been about him, but my coming back always has been.

And here I am, back again. I'm forty-one years old and I'm pregnant. It's been ten years since I had Tommy and I haven't gotten pregnant. I guess I just started thinking that I couldn't.

Michael died five years ago of a heroin overdose. We'd been together all that time, sleeping in parks and getting odd jobs and searching for food from garbage cans. Every once in a while I'd go see the Kellys, and Dolores would give me money for a bus ticket home. I never used that money for anything but the ticket, and that's how I got to see Tommy. But I couldn't stay clean for too long, and before I knew it, I would leave again, the demons at my back. I'd hear Tommy's cries in my head that long bus ride back to the West Coast, and they'd only go away once I got high again.

After Michael died, I thought about going back to the Kellys and getting my old job back. But they would have wanted me to stay clean and I couldn't have done it. I was more afraid of disappointing them than myself, so I went back to the ranch, where they gave me a garden patch and told me to grow vegetables.

It's funny how all of Bootsie's teachings that I'd tried my best to ignore somehow seeped into my brain anyway. Or maybe I was born with a knack for growing things. But my vegetables were the ones that were loaded into the van and sold at farmers' markets. It was the first thing I'd ever done for myself that hadn't turned out to be a disaster, and I was proud of myself.

But then I found out I was pregnant. I could have stayed at the ranch and let my child be raised by groups of mothers and fathers, but I've known since the moment I found out I was pregnant that this baby is going to be a girl. It was nothing scientific, and I didn't even need Dr. Kelly to tell me. It was just something I knew. Maybe it was a mother's intuition— something I hadn't thought possible with me.

Dr. Kelly had been thinking about retiring, but Dolores told me that I would still be welcome in their home, and to bring my babies to see them.

It's nice to know that my children have people on the West Coast who love them and would care for them. But I've also always known that the farm in Indian Mound, Mississippi, is the best place to raise my children. I just wish I'd realized that when I was younger.

I never thought I was one for family tradition, but since I'm having a girl, I needed to be home. I want her to be born in the old black bed where I was born, and Bootsie before me. I didn't want to be the first Walker woman to break the tradition. That's why I went to Dolores and asked her to call Bootsie. And that's why I'm home in time to give birth to my baby girl.

Bootsie is nearly beside herself with happiness. She loves Tommy with all her heart, but there's something about a girl. I think we both see this precious soul as a second chance for both of us. We want to teach her everything we've learned so that she won't repeat our mistakes. I imagine that's every mother's dream for her children, but this little girl will be born with generations of mistakes she'll need to overcome.

Bootsie and I have been working hard to get the nursery ready, painting the old crib and rocking horse, and hanging on the windows pink curtains that she and Mathilda made by hand. There are little embroidered butterflies on them that they each stitched without a sewing machine. Bootsie's even hand-painted pink butterflies on the walls—a skill I hadn't known she had. I only hope that it really is a girl, or else a boy who really likes pink.

Bootsie has a lot of good advice, too, about little babies and feeding them and getting them to sleep. I guess she's always known these things, and always been an artist, and I just never bothered to know it. I guess that sometimes it's hard to see something that's right in front of you when you're too busy only seeing what you want to.

I've been thinking about names, but I haven't told Bootsie, because I know she'll want to argue about it. I remember sneaking around and reading Gone With the Wind *when I was twelve—sneaking it because Bootsie thought it was too racy for me to be reading—and I fell in love with the name Scarlett. I'm pretty sure Bootsie will have a fainting spell when I tell her, and that she'll try to talk me out of it. But we Walker women are a stubborn bunch, so I guess we'll just have to wait and see who is the most stubborn.*

My daughter is due in only three weeks, and while I'm excited, I'm nervous, too. *About the future, mostly. Worried that this contentment I feel right now won't last, and that as soon as she's born I'll feel the demons on my back again, the need for oblivion that I know I want just because I've grown used to it instead of needing it. Dolores said that's addiction, but I'm not sure. I argued that if I was addicted, I wouldn't have been able to stop when I was pregnant both times. She just smiled and told me that mothers can do extraordinary things to save their children, and how she'd known a woman who'd lifted a school bus off of her child's leg.*

I'm still not sure. And I won't know until my baby girl is born. I already love her with all my heart, right alongside there with her brother. I know I will always love her. I just don't know yet if I can be strong enough for her and Tommy to stay for very long. Or if I can love them enough to leave them behind.

Chapter 34

Adelaide Walker Bodine Richmond
INDIAN MOUND, MISSISSIPPI
JUNE 1926

The rains began sometime around the end of May, the dark clouds scuttling in like a mama bird covering her nest. It had rained just about every day since, and the *Farmers' Almanac* wasn't offering any good news. Uncle Joe and John spent a lot of time looking up at the sky and shaking their heads, the furrows in their fields now ribbons of silver spreading out toward the horizon.

But the new plants in the fields with their tops barely above water were the least of their worries. Engineers came in to look at the levee in Greenville and other places near us on the river, and they said there was nothing to worry about. Uncle Joe wasn't too sure, having never put much store in what engineers who'd never planted a seed had to say; nor had he seen that much rain for that long since he'd been farming. John tried to reassure him, reminding him that he couldn't control the weather no matter how much he looked up at the sky or clucked his tongue.

I barely noticed the weather. I was in the family way again, and Aunt Louise had made it her mission in life to make sure I gave birth to a healthy baby. I didn't tell anybody the news for the first two months, afraid to admit it even to myself. Afraid that by speaking it aloud, I'd alert whatever it was that had taken my first three babies from me.

But Aunt Louise could tell, she said, by the light in my eyes that had been missing since the Harvest Festival. She immediately put me to bed, made up the guest room for John, and called the doctor—in that order. I didn't have the heart to tell her that John came into my room each night and slept beside me, his hand resting on my stomach. And when I awakened in the morning, he was always gone, leaving behind his scent on my pillow.

I imagined it was times like that when a woman needed her mama, and I missed mine just as much as I did the day she went walking along the Tallahatchie Bridge and never came back. But she did a good thing, too, in leaving me in the care of Aunt Louise, who has always loved me almost as much as I imagined my own mother would have.

I enjoyed listening to the rhythm of the rain on the roof, finding it as soothing as a lullaby. And I read a great deal, with my feet propped up by pillows arranged by John and Aunt Louise, and even once by Sarah Beth, who visited me on her infrequent trips home from Newcomb. She brought me books, bought for me in New Orleans and borrowed from her mother. Books by Zane Grey, and Edith Wharton, and Sinclair Lewis. She'd even managed to find a copy of the banned book *Ulysses*, and although I never would have admitted it to her, I understood why it had been deemed pornographic. But I loved it, and loved all the books that broadened my life's experiences, and allowed me to have adventures outside the four walls of my bedroom and the watery world outside my window.

Every once in a while I'd find myself fretting over the vegetables in my garden, and my flowers, worried that I'd left them to the mercy of Aunt Louise's gentle but clumsy fingers. But I knew she'd tend them to the best of her abilities, whether gardening was her calling or not. She would care for them and love them because I did.

I'd fallen asleep right after Aunt Louise had removed my supper tray and closed the blinds to block out the light, although the clouds hardly made that necessary. I was still dozing when I heard the latch on my bedroom door turning. I opened my eyes and smiled when I saw Sarah Beth, looking lovelier than I'd ever seen her.

"I hope I didn't wake you. Your aunt said you were resting but that I could sit by your bed until you woke up."

She leaned over to kiss me, and I smelled cigarette smoke and liquor as she helped me push myself up in the bed, rearranging the pillows behind my back. "I spend so much time sleeping that I'm glad of any excuse to keep my eyes open." I smiled at her. "How is it that you manage to look so beautiful on such an ugly day?"

She blushed, her smile secretive, and I waited for her to tell me that she and Willie were engaged. But she said nothing, leaving me to wonder what was making her so happy, and why she wasn't telling me.

"How are you?" she asked, her voice bright. But when I looked into her eyes, I saw something there I couldn't name, something that wasn't joy at all.

"I'm doing well. So's the baby. Dr. Odom says it will be here by the end of September. Just three more months of me lying in this bed."

She shuddered. "I don't think I could do that. Lie in bed all day with nothing to do."

"You'd be surprised at what you would do to protect your children. Even those who aren't born yet."

Sarah Beth looked at me oddly, as if I'd just read her mind, and I wondered if her strange mood was from the alcohol I'd smelled on her breath. She stood and began wandering around my room, picking up framed photographs and reading the spines of books, but I had the strangest feeling that she wasn't really seeing any of it.

She was staring at her reflection in my dressing table mirror. "Can you keep a secret?"

"Of course," I said. "I've always kept your secrets."

I saw her reflection, her secretive smile. "I'm in love."

I sucked in a breath, but before I could ask who with, she stopped me with her finger to her lips. "Shhh," she whispered, then moved to sit in the chair Aunt Louise had placed by my bed for visitors.

"So tell me, what does it feel like?"

"What?"

"What it feels like to have a baby growing inside you. We've done just about everything together for so long, it feels almost wrong that you're going through this without me."

Her words surprised me, seeing as how even as little girls she hadn't wanted to play house or make-believe with dolls, or anything that might suggest something domestic. Despite her mother's desperation to have a child, once Sarah Beth was born it seemed that Mrs. Heathman's job was over, and all the day-to-day tedium of child rearing was given to a succession of nannies and maids.

"Well, you're going to college without me."

She waved her hand at me. "But this is different. You're growing another human being. You and the man you love." I blushed at the intimacy of her words, but she didn't seem to notice. Leaning forward, she asked again, "So what's it like?"

"It's wonderful," I said, placing my hands on my swollen belly. "It's like Christmas morning and my birthday all rolled into one."

I looked down at my hands, my fingers empty of rings because they had grown too tight, but the blue of my watch poked out from the long sleeve of my nightgown. I placed my hand over it, hoping she hadn't seen it. I couldn't let her borrow it. Not now, when it had become something I hung on to during the tedious days, waiting until John finished at the shop or in the fields and could come see me.

John continued on as Mr. Berlini's account manager, a job that occupied as much time as it took of his conscience. He'd been spending more time at the jewelry store, staying past closing often enough for me to comment on it. When I'd asked what he'd been working on, he'd just said he was busy with a gift for a man's beloved wife. I'd been peeved that another man's wife would keep him away from home, and deliberately had held back all of my curious questions.

"It's like the butterfly's boots," I said to Sarah Beth, borrowing one of her new phrases she'd come home from college with. I'd meant to cheer us both up, me from my ruminations regarding John and his absences, but also her. There was something in her mood that was as peculiar as snow in summer.

Sarah Beth didn't smile, and I wondered if she'd heard what I said. A flash of lightning lit the room, closely followed by a rumble of thunder.

"Can you feel it?" she asked quietly.

I nodded. "When I sing, she's like a little frog in there. Like she's trying to dance."

"She? You know it's a girl?"

"I don't know for sure, but when I dream, I see a little girl. Of course, I'd be happy with a boy who looks just like John, but a girl would be sweet, too. I think Aunt Louise would love to dress a baby girl. The next one can be a boy," I said lightly, trying to bring up her mood.

Lightning exploded in the sky again, making my bedside lamp flicker, then go out. Sarah Beth leaned forward, her eyes reflecting the light from the window. "What does it feel like? When she's moving."

I thought for a moment, never having been asked before to describe it. "It's like when you're swimming and a fish brushes up against you. Except you're not scared, because you know what it is."

She stared at my belly under the sheet, then looked in my eyes again. "Sing something. Sing something and make her dance."

I frowned, thinking hard, until my mind rested on the song sung by the four Negroes at the Harvest Festival. " 'Oh, shine on, shine on, harvest moon, up in the sky.' "

I felt the little brushes from inside my belly, and took one of Sarah Beth's hands to place on top of it. At the first little kick, she lifted her hand as if she'd been stung by a bee, then put it back to feel two more flutters.

Sarah Beth sat back in her chair and I watched as her gaze darted about the room, and I wondered if she was looking for her purse and the flask she usually kept inside. But she hadn't come in with it.

Her eyes returned to me. "I finally asked my mother."

"About what?" I asked, wondering if I'd missed part of a conversation.

"About why my name isn't in the family Bible. Remember that day when we went to the old cemetery and found all those baby graves? And you said we should look in the Bible to see if they were my brothers and sisters?"

I nodded, remembering that day clearly, as well as my wedding, when I'd seen her and Angelo Berlini talking in the graveyard in front of those same stones.

Sarah Beth continued. "You were always telling me I should ask, and I never did. And then you stopped asking. Why'd you stop?"

I shook my head, not really sure why. "Because I thought maybe you didn't want to know the answer."

Her eyes darkened. "That's an odd thing to say."

"Maybe. I've never asked anybody why my mama killed herself. Nobody ever talked about it, like I wasn't even supposed to know. But

I didn't ask, because I was afraid they'd tell me that it was because of me, because I wasn't a good and obedient enough daughter. That I didn't love her enough to make her stay. And I'm glad now that I didn't ask. Because I don't think anybody has the right answer for that. But mostly because then I'd never been able to see the answer through my adult eyes. Through a mother's eyes."

"And what did you see?" she asked, leaning forward as if my answer were important to her.

"That she thought she was doing the best thing for me. That she was only a shadow person, like a ghost who hadn't died yet. She missed my daddy something terrible, something I couldn't understand until after I met John. I think her sadness was a blackness inside her that filled her body and her mind like a cancer."

My gaze drifted to the apple on a plate on my nightstand, and the knife beside it that Aunt Louise had placed there in case I got hungry. My finger hurt where the knife had slipped and cut the tip of my index finger, and I'd only managed a single slice, because it hurt too much to press on the knife to cut more. I thought of my aunt coming in to make sure my pillows were fluffed, and that I wasn't too hot or cold. And that I had something to eat. She'd always been like that, anticipating something I needed before I did. She'd never told me, but I secretly thought that she'd always wanted a daughter of her own, how sad she'd been when there were no more babies after Willie. I'd only begun to understand how the universe had fitted us together, each of us filling the missing hole in the other like two pieces of a single puzzle.

I continued. "I think Mama believed that Aunt Louise could be the mother I needed, the mother she couldn't be because of her sickness. But she loved me with what all was left of her heart."

I regarded her in silence, letting her know that I'd wait as long as it took for her to tell me what her mother had told her about why her name wasn't in the family Bible.

"The names of those babies, all five of them, were my brothers and sisters. They were all born alive, but died right away. The doctors couldn't ever tell Mother why, so she kept trying until the doctor said she shouldn't try anymore."

"But then she had you, ten years later, so I guess the doctor was wrong."

Her eyes narrowed. "Not exactly."

Neither one of us spoke, the rain on the window and the roof filling the silence like the voices of all those lost children. I thought of my own three, and how I'd been blessed with this baby, and how I'd carried her longer than the others.

"A year before I was born, Mother went to New Orleans to stay with family and see a doctor, because she wasn't feeling well. That's what they told their friends here. But she went to a home for unwed mothers, run by the same nuns who had taught Mother in school. That's where she got me. And then she came back to Indian Mound and said I was hers, and that it was the excellent doctors in New Orleans who'd made sure her baby survived."

"But they should still put your name in the Bible, Sarah Beth. You are their daughter, same as if your mother had given birth to you."

She gave me a weak smile. "Funny. That's exactly what I said." She reached over and picked up the knife from my nightstand. "Mother said it was an oversight. But I think we both know that my mother has never overlooked anything in her entire life."

I watched as she examined the blade of the knife, running her finger over the flat side and then softly touching the tip as if to check it for sharpness.

"Careful," I said, holding up my own finger to show my wound. "It's very sharp."

She placed the knife in her lap and leaned forward. "Let me see."

I wasn't really surprised at her request. She'd always had an interest in all things bloody, from smashed frogs on the road to buzzards flying over dead animals. She'd once made me walk in the dried-out winter swamp to find a dead boar, a spiral of buzzards over the trees like a giant pointing finger. I'd had to turn away as the buzzards fought with the buzzing flies for pink pieces of flesh. But Sarah Beth had watched with fascination until the sun began to dip in the sky and I made her leave before it got dark. Even she didn't want to get caught in the swamp after night fell.

I held up my finger and allowed her to place it between her thumb and index finger and draw it closer to her face, as if she were a surgeon getting ready to suture it.

"It's not very deep. It looks bad because it just happened and it hasn't had a chance to scab. . . ."

I winced as she squeezed, and two large drops of red blood seeped from the wound. I tried to yank my hand back, but she held it tight for a moment, watching me bleed, before letting go.

"Look," she said, completely unaware that she'd hurt me. She picked up the knife and, with the sharp tip, stabbed the tip of her own finger. The knife, forgotten as soon as she was finished with it, dropped to the floor as she, too, began to bleed from the cut, the red bright against the paleness of her skin.

"See?" she said, holding up her finger. "See?" she said again, thrusting it toward my face to make sure that I did. I pushed her hand away, confused at what she wanted me to see.

She sat back in her chair, her shoulders falling as if she were feeling an enormous relief.

"See what?" I asked, angry and confused, as a drop of blood landed on my sheet, staining it red.

"It's the same color. Our blood is the same color."

I put my finger in my mouth and sucked on it, tasting copper. "Of course it is. Why wouldn't it be?"

Without answering, she stood again and moved to the window, watching the rain fall from heavy clouds. "I hope it stops raining soon. I can't put the top down on my breezer when it's like this."

I didn't say anything about all the farmers who might be losing their crops. Sarah Beth always seemed to have a way of making everything about her, whether it was good news or bad.

"Do you remember those awful people at the festival?" she asked.

"You mean Leon and Velma? The same people we'd seen at the Ellis plantation?"

She nodded, still staring out the window.

"They're kin to Mathilda and Bertha," I said.

She turned to me slowly, her lips slightly parted. "They're kin?"

I nodded, once again smug at another rare occasion when I knew something that she didn't. "Yes. They have a common-law marriage on account of it being illegal for different races to marry. John told me."

She went back to the window, the shadow of raindrops on her face making them look like tears. "Do you remember what they said? About me being no better than I ought to be?"

I nodded, wishing that I hadn't. It had been said with so much malice and mean-spiritedness and with no provocation. I also recalled those same words being said at my wedding reception by Chas Davis, and I hadn't understood the reason for that, either.

"What do you think they meant?"

I'd never seen Sarah Beth like this, questioning things she didn't understand instead of simply dismissing them with a flick of her kid-glove-covered hand.

I tried to soften the tone of my voice, the way Aunt Louise did when explaining something to me that might make me sad, like when old Saul, Uncle Joe's foreman and a man whose pockets were always full of candy, was run over by a spooked mule hauling a wagon full of cotton and got killed. As if she believed the tone of her voice would soften the blow of her words.

"I think they're just jealous of you, Sarah Beth. Because your family has money and you never have to worry about where your next meal is coming from. And you live in a big house, and wear beautiful clothes. They don't have any of that."

She nodded as if trying to convince herself. "That's what I thought, too." Turning from the window, she smiled brightly at me. "I should probably go and let you rest."

I wasn't tired, but I was ready for her to leave. She bent down to kiss my cheek, then swept toward the door.

"Sarah Beth?"

She turned, her expression like that of a child caught in the candy jar. "Yes?"

"You never told me who you were in love with. Is it Willie?"

"Shh. It's a secret."

I frowned. We'd never had secrets from each other. "You know you can tell me. I've never shared a secret." I thought of Mathilda, and Chas, and Mathilda's fear that Robert would find out, and knew that was one secret I'd be taking to my grave.

"I know. But I'm having fun keeping it to myself right now. It's like being able to eat a whole cake instead of just a piece."

I looked at her closely, wondering what was so different about her. There was a hint of danger in her eyes, something I was familiar with from our exploits as children that always got me the switch.

"Angelo Berlini is engaged to be married, Sarah Beth. I don't want to see your heart broken over a man you can't have."

She tilted her head back and sucked in her breath. "That may be. But they're not married yet."

I sat up, ready to question her further, but she'd already opened the door. With a quick wave, she closed it behind her.

I leaned back against my pillows, listening to the rain and thinking about what she'd said. My gaze fell to my sheets and to the single drop of blood. It had spread out, its color darkening to a shade of rust, and formed itself into the shape of a heart.

Chapter 35

Vivien Walker Moise
INDIAN MOUND, MISSISSIPPI
MAY 2013

Chloe and I sat in rocking chairs on the wide front porch, looking out toward the drive and waiting for Tripp's truck. Carol Shipley's history book sat closed in my lap. It was almost suppertime, and Cora and Carol Lynne were inside setting the dining table. I was just about getting used to eating from the antique dishes my family had eaten off of for generations, surrounded by my family—new and old—and conversations that meandered through all topics without settling for long on one in particular. It was a marked contrast to the silent dinners I'd had with Mark and Chloe. I'd be medicated enough that I didn't mind the tasteless food, and enough that I didn't care that Mark and Chloe spent more time texting on their phones than speaking to anyone at the table.

But the boisterous dining table was what I remembered from my childhood, where Bootsie always invited friends for supper. I'd looked forward to each evening, when Bootsie would take her time questioning Tommy and me about our days, and when we'd solve the problems of our small worlds over ham and biscuits. At least until my mother returned, and I'd started eating up in the kitchen with Mathilda.

Since my return home, suppertime had managed to once again become something I looked forward to each day, something that grounded me despite the fact that I still felt like the epicenter of the tornado that had become my life. With Bootsie's spirit in mind, I'd called Carrie Holmes and invited her and her two children for supper. It was so painfully obvious to all but the blind and stupid that Carrie and Tommy still had feelings for each other, and that left to their own devices they'd never work their way toward any kind of relationship that involved more than bashful glances from across a room.

"What should we name him?" Chloe asked from the rocking chair next to mine. The dog hadn't left her side except when she'd gone into the house. I'd told them both that he wasn't allowed inside until he'd been given a flea bath. He'd waited patiently on the porch, next to a bowl of water and dog food that we'd purchased on the way home, along with a collar and leash and other things that Chloe claimed were necessities, until she came back outside again.

"I don't think it's a good idea to name him yet. He probably already has a name, and it might confuse him to call him something else."

"What you really mean is that you're not going to let me keep him."

"Chloe, you don't live here, remember? And your dad has always said no to pets, because of the germs and their fur over everything, and because he thinks he might be allergic."

"But I could leave him here with you, and then he'd be here when I came to visit."

If only the world worked in the way of a child's logic. "I understand what you're saying. But I have no idea how long I'm going to be here, or if your dad will let you visit me."

Her hand stilled from where it had been stroking the dog's head. "But he's letting me stay with you now. Doesn't that mean he's going to let me stay with you sometimes from now on?"

I forced myself not to blurt out that her father was a vindictive jerk, the real truth of just how much somehow eluding me until I'd stopped medicating myself and was able to look back in retrospect. I couldn't remember a lot about the divorce proceedings, and I was glad. Because what I did remember made my skin crawl with shame. For him to have been able to allow no visits and a restraining order, what was in the record must be very shameful indeed.

"I don't know, Chloe. I really don't know."

"But you're going to ask, right? Because now I have a dog and a garden that I need to take care of."

I gave her a sidelong glance, wondering if she was aware that in a roundabout way she'd told me that she liked it here and wanted to come back. Or that she hadn't mentioned that I'd be here, too. Maybe because, like me, she wasn't that sure I would be.

"Yes, I'm going to try. But remember, too, that we'll have to take the dog to the vet to see if he's been microchipped, and if he hasn't, you're in charge of making flyers to post on telephone poles, just in case he has an owner looking for him. He's well trained, so chances are somebody's looking for him."

She crossed her arms over her chest. "Well, they don't deserve him if he's been gone this long and they haven't tried that hard to find him."

I spotted Tripp's white pickup truck down the long drive, then watched as it pulled up in front of the house, a country music ballad about beer and guitars drifting from the open windows.

He was waving a bottle of what I hoped was a flea wash as he walked toward us. He paused with one foot on the bottom porch step. After greeting us, he said, "I called the best vet I know—my sister, Claire, and she says hello, by the way—and she recommended you give the dog a bath outside with this." He placed the bottle on the floor of the porch. "There's a hose on the side of the house by the garden, and if you ask Cora real nice, I'm sure she'll give you a bucket and a sponge."

Chloe slid from her chair and ran to the door before stopping abruptly and turning around to face Tripp. "Thank you. Sir." She opened the door and ran inside before anybody could comment on how she hadn't needed to be reminded.

"Thanks," I said, admiring his form as he walked up the steps and sat down in the chair just vacated. The dog lay down and offered its belly to him, and Tripp obliged.

"Apparently that dog has been evading capture downtown for over a month. I'm thinking they've either got the wrong dog or they didn't try very hard."

Tripp grinned. "Or he was just waiting for the right family to come along."

"Well, we're hardly a family. There's no way Mark's going to allow any dog in his spotless house, much less one without a pedigree."

Tripp gave me one of his silent stares that I chose to ignore.

"I'd be careful about petting that dog, or I'll have to give you a flea bath in the backyard, too."

His mouth broadened into a wide grin. "I'm confused. Would that be a bad thing?"

I shook my head and picked up the book from my lap. "Here's the book I was telling you about—it's sort of all the local history of the county, as well as the genealogies of the oldest families, including mine. Mrs. Shipley said that Bootsie helped her with it."

He took the book from me and opened the front cover. "Well, isn't this handier than a pocket on a shirt."

I snorted, then covered my mouth.

"What's so funny?"

"I'm just glad you didn't say that in front of Chloe. She already thinks you're a redneck. If she knew what *Deliverance* was, she'd be expecting to hear 'Dueling Banjos' every time you showed up."

He looked affronted. "There is absolutely nothing wrong with banjo music."

I elbowed him and took the book back. I'd stuck in a piece of paper to mark the spot, and used it to open up to my family tree.

"Sheriff Adams was here earlier, and I showed him the watch and the photos from the paper. He told me I could hang on to the watch, seeing as how it's a family heirloom. He wanted my copy of this book, but I told him to see Carol Shipley. The thing cost me thirty bucks."

He whistled. "Good thing you're divorced from a doctor, with all that extravagant spending."

"Yeah, right. We had a prenup—which is good in retrospect, because otherwise Mark would probably try to take the farm just to be nasty—but it meant that I took nothing from the marriage that I didn't bring into it. Just a different car. I think my lawyer felt sorry for me and somehow managed a decent alimony settlement. It doesn't make me rich by any means, but I won't starve."

He didn't say anything, which meant that he wouldn't until I spoke out loud what we were both thinking.

"And no child visitation. Once he brought the drug stuff up, I didn't have a leg to stand on."

"Do you have plans to fight it?"

I blinked at him, his words surprising me. "How could I? What do I have to offer her? I own a house, sure, but I don't have a job, or career, and all I have to show for twenty-seven years is a road full of mistakes. Besides, I have no legal claims to her. I was only married to her father for seven years. I could never win."

"But what if you took it out of a court of law and just appealed to him as a father who wants the best for his daughter?"

"I don't think he cares. All he cared about was punishing me, regardless of what it did to Chloe. It's not even worth trying."

He rocked in silence, that space between words something I'd grown used to but now hated with a certain dread.

"What?" I demanded.

He kept rocking. "I didn't say anything."

"I know. That's why I want you to stop." I shook my head, realizing how stupid I sounded.

"We all make mistakes, Vivi."

"Oh, please, Mr. Perfect. Your life is exactly as you wanted it to be. You haven't taken a wrong turn since you learned how to crawl."

"That's not true."

I waited during the long silence, expecting a hammer to fall.

"I let you go."

He'd said the words softly, but they felt like a slap to my chest.

He didn't wait for me to figure out a response. "You never quit, Vivi. All those years I knew you while we were growing up, you never quit. Whether it was for some cause, or making a team, or becoming editor of the school paper, you'd always keep trying a thousand times, even when you heard 'no' nine hundred and ninety-nine times."

I stared down at the open book in my lap, at all the names of the people who'd brought me here, and who must be so disappointed. "Yeah, well, as I told you before, that Vivi is gone."

He kept rocking, not saying anything, and I cursed myself for giving him the opportunity.

"She is," I said again, trying to fill that silence.

After a long moment where I forced myself to remain quiet, Tripp said, "Since we were little kids and all the way through high school, you would always cry whenever we sang 'Silent Night' during the nativity play at Christmas. I think that says a lot about a person. And that doesn't change."

A shriek from Chloe made us look out toward the side of the house, where a drenched Chloe was being chased by an equally wet dog who looked about twenty pounds smaller with his fur stuck against his body.

Tripp stood, and I could see that he was trying not to laugh. "Stop running and he'll stop chasing you."

Chloe ran in a large circle, glancing at Tripp to make sure she was hearing him right. When he nodded, she stopped abruptly, so that the dog ran into her and knocked her over. Too stunned to move, she lay where she'd fallen while the dog proceeded to shake the water off of his fur, spraying it all over Chloe, and then licked her face in apology.

The book slid to the floor as I stood in alarm, and I was halfway off the porch when Tripp grabbed my arm. It was then that I realized that the high-pitched sounds coming from Chloe were simply squeals of delight. I stopped to watch, knowing with all certainty that my stepdaughter had never made that sound before. Or had never had reason to.

When she finally managed to sit up she looked at us with a wide grin, completely unaware that her hair was sticking up in a wild tangle, with grass and soapsuds clinging to the wet strands.

Tripp leaned against the porch railing. "You might could go around to the kitchen door and ask Mrs. Smith for some more towels—for both of you. And remember to walk—don't run."

She stood slowly, then began to walk with exaggerated slowness toward the side of the house. Stopping suddenly, she backed up a few steps. "Yes. Sir."

We returned to our rocking chairs, and Tripp resumed rocking in silence.

"Don't say anything," I said, his lack of words unnerving me.

"I didn't."

"I know!" I leaned down and picked up Mrs. Shipley's book, frowning at a crease in one of the pages from its tumble to the floor. I found the right page again, then smoothed the book open on my lap.

Without looking up at him, I said, "Mark has requested that you stop putting personal notes on my lab reports. He finds them unprofessional and annoying."

"He really said that?"

"Yes."

"Good." He kept rocking.

I smiled to myself, picturing Mark's face when he got the next report. "Are you staying for supper?"

"Are you asking?"

I let out a heavy sigh. Conversations with Tripp were never easy. "Sure. Since you're already here and all. And I need a sounding board to figure out a few things."

"About Adelaide?"

I nodded. "Yeah. Sheriff Adams said that with the DNA evidence, the newspaper articles, and the ring, he's confident that the remains are hers—although we're still waiting for the rest of the lab results, including a probable cause of death. I just don't want to bury her until we know what happened. And who's responsible."

"It was over eighty years ago, Vivi. That might not be possible."

"I know," I said, recalling what he'd said about how I'd never been able to take no for an answer. At least in the years before I'd discovered that the pills had taken away my desire to care if I won or not.

I studied the family tree on the pages in my lap. "I remember Bootsie talking to me about my ancestors, but I never paid attention. I think I always thought that I'd have time later to write things down so I could remember for later. When you're young, you never think that you're going to run out of time."

My finger moved down the lines on the page, past Adelaide's name, to Bootsie's and Carol Lynne's, and then to mine and Tommy's, where the family tree abruptly ended. "I've even found myself wishing that I'd bothered at some point to hear Carol Lynne's story. There's so much I wish I understood, and it's too late now."

"Hindsight . . ."

"I know," I said. "It's always twenty-twenty."

"Of course, I'm a firm believer that it's never too late," he said.

"Where my mother's concerned, it definitely is. She still calls Chloe JoEllen, her best friend's name from high school. And she thinks I'm sixteen."

"That's not what I meant."

He fell silent and I fought an internal battle between asking him what he meant and self-preservation. Not able to take it anymore, I asked, "What do you mean?"

"That it might be too late to hear your mother's story. But I'm also a firm believer that nobody's past is written in stone."

I turned to face him, feeling more than a little irritated. "Of course it is. You can't change things that have already happened."

I focused again on the book on my lap, hoping he'd see my body language as an indication that that part of the conversation was over. He remained silent, of course.

I cleared my throat. "Looking at my family tree, I find it kind of remarkable that we didn't die out several generations ago. Lots of mothers dying young and lots of only children, too. Tommy's a real peculiarity, being not only a boy but also being the first of two children."

"I'm sure you can't wait to tell him that."

"You bet. And I'll be sure to remind him each time he calls me Booger."

I tapped on a name near the top of the tree. "This is Rosemary, my great-great-grandmother and Adelaide's mother. She died when Adelaide was ten. I remembered Bootsie saying it was a sad story, but it wasn't until I read Mrs. Shipley's history that I understood why. Apparently Rosemary killed herself because she couldn't get over her husband's death in World War One. Bootsie always said she believed her mother had left her because of what Adelaide's own mother had done. Like it was in the blood. And it's not like my own mother was one to break the mold."

Tripp didn't say anything, and I hadn't expected that he would. My finger traced small circles on my own name, on the empty space beneath it, and I thought of Chloe and how I'd left her behind in the divorce. "I've always believed Bootsie was right, you know. About it being in the blood. And I pretty much proved it."

His answer was the slow creaking of his rocker against the old floorboards of the porch. *I'm also a firm believer that nobody's past is written in stone.* I ran my fingers over names I didn't recall hearing before, but who were on my family tree as proof that they'd existed. John. William. Joseph. Louise. They all had a connection to me, and I'd never bothered to pay attention. And until I'd read the news account of Adelaide's disappearance, I hadn't even realized that Bootsie's real name was Elizabeth.

My gaze fell on the watch that I hadn't wanted to remove, even though the time was frozen at two fifty. "Here's a clue," I said, holding up my wrist for Tripp to see. "Adelaide's husband said she always wore it, that if her body was found this is how she could be identified. There's an inscription inside that reads, 'I love you forever.'"

I rocked back and forth a few times, thinking. "But Chloe found it in the spare-parts hatbox that Emmett used to keep and that Tommy inherited."

"When was Emmett born?"

I looked at the family tree. "Nineteen twenty-seven. He was a year younger than Bootsie. They were first cousins once removed—I only know that because I called Carol Shipley and asked. Emmett's father, William, was Adelaide's first cousin."

"So Emmett wouldn't have known Adelaide, or have had any reason to have her watch. So who put it in there?" Tripp asked.

"Exactly. I'm beginning to think that Sheriff Adams was right and that we'll never find out, because it happened so long ago."

Tripp stared at me with raised eyebrows.

"I know," I said. "I've never been known as somebody who takes no for an answer."

"I'm just sayin'."

"Actually, I said it, and I'm not necessarily agreeing. It seems that there are more questions we could be asking, and just one answer might open the doors to a lot more of them. For instance—where is Bootsie's half of the baby ring? Chloe and I went through the hatbox twice and it's definitely not in there. I went through all the drawers in the house, and nothing."

"Did you check the attic?"

"Not yet. It's on my list. I've been kind of waiting, seeing as how I'm petrified of spiders, and I remember once when I went up with Bootsie to put away some Christmas decorations that there were some pretty impressive webs in the corners and in the rafters. And Tommy screams like a little girl whenever he sees one, so he's no help."

"I'm not afraid of spiders." Tripp grinned.

"Are you offering to help?"

"Are you asking?"

I tried to sigh, but it came out as a laugh. "Sure. Would you help me go through the attic, please? I need you to do some heavy lifting and to scare the spiders away."

"I'd be more than happy to. I suggest we wait until it's brighter out so we can see better. I believe there's a fan window up there."

"Thank you. And I need to go see Mathilda. I think I'll just go into her room and wait until she awakens or stops feeling so poorly. I've tried to see her about four times since I've been back and I keep getting sent away."

"Or you could invite her for supper. I've never known that woman to turn down a meal. She's as skinny as a zipper but eats like a horse."

"She's allowed? I mean, it's okay for her to leave the nursing home?"

"Sure. Cora brings her to church and then Sunday dinner just about every week. If you like, I'll invite her and even drive her. Which means I'd have to stay, too."

"By all means," I said. "How about Wednesday? That will give me time to go through the newspapers, too, which might give me a few more questions to ask. She's been around for one hundred and four years. She knew Adelaide. Maybe she'll know who might have wanted to harm her."

A beep sounded and Tripp pulled a phone from his pocket and looked at the screen. "Duty calls. Light plane crash near the regional airport." He stood.

"Does every call you get mean somebody's already dead?"

"Or close to it. And it's something you never get used to."

I remembered what I'd asked him when I'd first come back, about why he'd decided not to be a cardiologist like he'd always planned. *I wanted to do something that had no memories of you attached to it. Working with dead people sort of fit the bill.* I looked away, confused at the waves of emotion that shimmied through my veins: shame, embarrassment, and an indescribable sense of loss.

He shoved his hands into the pockets of his khakis. "So you, me, Chloe. Tomorrow morning at nine o'clock sharp. I'll pick you up. My deputy coroner will be on duty, so it's time to teach that city girl how we fish down here."

I groaned. "Can you be here three hours early to start coaxing her out of bed?"

He raised a suggestive eyebrow. "Is that an invitation, Miss Vivien?"

I felt my face turning all shades of red. "Good-bye, Tripp. I'll give your regrets to Cora but tell her that you'll be back on Wednesday with her mother. And I'll see you tomorrow at nine. Hopefully with a fully functioning Chloe, or you'll have to toss her over your shoulder and carry her."

"Yes, ma'am," he said, tipping an imaginary hat and walking away with that saunter he'd been walking with since third grade. It did something to a girl. Made her have all sorts of crazy thoughts.

I watched him until he got in his truck and drove away, remembering what he'd said about how I used to cry at "Silent Night," too embarrassed to admit to either of us that I still did.

Chapter 36

Carol Lynne Walker Moise
INDIAN MOUND, MISSISSIPPI
JANUARY 1992

Dear Diary,

I've been back home now for two months. I thought maybe I would stay here until my baby girl's sixth birthday, but I see now I was just being foolish. I've always had big dreams and big plans, and the belief that I could make them all happen. And you would think that I'd be old enough now to stop. But I kept picturing me in that old yellow house surrounded by my children and I forgot that I wasn't strong enough, that I'm no good at facing life without the buffer of a pill or another hit. I only wish the universe gave brownie points to those of us who at least try.

I've tried to come back each Christmas since Vivien was born—although I call her Scarlett in my head—and stay until her birthday. I've only missed two times, and boy, howdy, did I hear about it from Bootsie. She told me I needed to either come back and stay or go away forever, because this going and coming is giving my children emotional whiplash. She actually said that. She doesn't understand that each time I return it's because I think I'm ready to stay for good, that I'm ready to start over and be the good mama they deserve. It's just that I can't make the demons in my head understand. And Bootsie doesn't seem to care. She wants to put me in some program, says she'll pay for it and keep me there as long as I need to be there. That's just another prison, but one on the outside. I need to find a way out of the prison in my head, and each time I see my beautiful children, a brick is taken out and I can see a little bit of the light.

My Vivien calls me Mama and reminds me of the best parts of me when I was a child and saw the world through a child's eyes. I want her to stay this way forever, and I know she won't if I take her with me or if I stay here longer than I should.

But I've been a long time gone from this place. I think I stayed away for so long this last time because for days after I left, I heard the sound of Vivien's crying for me to come back. She's cried for me each time I've left, but when I returned again she wasn't angry or resentful. I wonder how many times more before she'll stop crying when I leave and instead start crying when I come back.

Tommy doesn't cry at all anymore, like he's accepted things. And I don't know if that's a good thing or not. He's the same sweet boy he's always been, although he's a senior in high school now. He says he wants to go to State and study agriculture so he can come back and be a better farmer. I know I have Emmett to thank for that. Emmett says that Tommy's got the touch when it comes to watch repairs, too, and has the patience and understanding it takes. Knowing that Tommy's doing so well takes the sting out of missing him growing up. Because it means that I've done the right thing.

Tommy's so tall and handsome, but really shy with the girls. Emmett says it's because he's afraid if he gets too attached to a girl, she'll leave him, since that's been his experience so far with women. I wanted to point out that he's always had Bootsie, but I didn't, because I knew he was right. I asked him why he never married. I've always wondered if it was because of being raised by his mama, who Bootsie said was known as a wild flapper who suddenly became a pious, churchgoing woman after her marriage. Something pretty serious must have happened to make her have a come-to-Jesus meeting, and I wondered if maybe she took it out on Emmett.

He didn't answer me. Instead he reminded me about the hatbox of spare parts he's been keeping for years, and told me again that when he died it would go to me, especially now that I have a daughter to give it to. I don't know why that's so important to him, but I could tell it was, so I didn't say anything. I didn't have the heart to tell him that he might want to make other plans, because I'm already starting to feel the need to leave again.

Vivien is a plump little girl with bright red hair and splotchy skin. I hope Mathilda's right and she'll grow into her looks. But if she doesn't she'll be fine. It's either the red hair or her laugh, but people always seem drawn to her. She's so smart and funny, and always laughing. Except when I tell her it's time for me to go.

Last night I took Vivien to the Indian mound in the backyard to hear the song of the cypress trees. I wanted Tommy to come, too, but Emmett had just received a box of antique pocket watches to be repaired from a jeweler in Connecticut, and Tommy wanted to stay and work on them. And that's fine. I'm glad he has his passions. Besides, I think it's important for mothers and daughters to share some time together before things change between them forever.

After Bootsie came back to me when I was six, she would take me up to the mound on warm evenings to watch the stars and listen to the trees. It was our special time together, and she told me about the lonely spirits who were trapped in the trees for all eternity and who waited for the wind so they could sing to their lost loves.

Vivien thought it was magical, and I was the magician who made the trees sing. I love that about her. How she sees such beauty in all things, the good in people. She'll be the popular girl in school not just because of her looks or her cleverness, but because she will genuinely like everybody she meets, and they'll know this. She's a nurturer, too, and you can tell by the way she watches Bootsie in the garden, how she makes sure each plant is strong and healthy even though she says she doesn't want to stick her hands in the dirt because it might tie her down to this place. She's nurturing with people, too—it's like she feels what they feel, and will do what she needs to do to make them happy. I just hope the wrong person won't take advantage of this part of her and yank it out like a weed.

We stayed up on the mound for a long time, identifying constellations in the sky, and listening to the sounds of the trees in the swamp. I'm not much of one for prayer, but I said a prayer then: that Vivien would always remember this, that when she heard the sound of the trees she would remember how much I love her and how the only way I know to tell her is by saying good-bye.

Chapter 37

Adelaide Walker Bodine Richmond
INDIAN MOUND, MISSISSIPPI
DECEMBER 1926

The rains that started in the summer continued through the fall and winter, making for an abysmal cotton harvest. They even canceled the Harvest Festival on account of the weather, but I don't think any of the county's farmers were much in the mood for celebration.

Despite Uncle Joe's grumblings, and Willie's increased pressure to invest in something other than the land, John and I hardly noticed the gloominess in the air. I was safely delivered of a baby girl on September twenty-sixth. We named her Elizabeth Walker Richmond, and right away I realized that her name was too serious for such a tiny and sweet baby. I started shortening it to Betsy, but Aunt Louise said she'd grown up with a dog named Betsy and that it just seemed wrong. But her little sister couldn't say "Betsy" and called her "Bootsie." So Bootsie it is. I think it suits our little bundle of joy.

Our baby girl weighed six pounds and eight ounces and was blessed with good health. She had pale skin and red hair, like me, and I knew she and I—and Aunt Louise—would be battling those freckles her entire life. She gained a good deal of weight in the first three months, with cheeks so fat that Mathilda accused her of storing nuts for the winter.

Mrs. Heathman was appalled that I didn't have a nursemaid to help me with the new baby, and despite protests from Uncle Joe that we didn't need charity, Aunt Louise and I gratefully accepted her offer of giving us Mathilda for the first year.

I wasn't sure at first that I needed help, but I found that after being confined to bed for so long, I'd grown weak and could barely walk and hold the baby. So I was appreciative, especially so because it was Mathilda. I remembered the quiet girl who'd hide in corners of the Heathmans' house, silent but always watching. It was only later that I realized that it seemed to be the ones who didn't speak who saw the most.

Mrs. Heathman and Sarah Beth gifted us with boxes of little-girl baby clothes, with lots of pink and ribbons and bows. Sweet Bootsie will be the best-dressed baby in the delta. Mrs. Heathman also gave me a new electric vacuum cleaner. I think she'd been horrified to see Aunt Louise beating the nursery rug outside, and said that it was very important to keep the nursery as clean as possible, and that the vacuum cleaner was the best choice. Aunt Louise hates it, because it's so noisy, but Mathilda is the only one who uses it. Bootsie loves it, and will fall asleep when Mathilda vacuums under her crib.

Mathilda sleeps on a small bed we set up in the baby's room so that she can hear her at night when she cries. Although Uncle Joe and Aunt Louise accepted Mathilda's presence in the house, Willie did not. He made it clear that she was supposed to use the back stairs at all times, and that if he should walk into a room where she was, she was expected to leave unless she was serving food.

I hadn't seen much of Sarah Beth since the baby's birth, and I'd given up on waiting for an engagement announcement between her and Willie. I think Willie had, too, as he seemed to be drunk most of the time, the late-night scents of wood smoke mixed with liquor more frequent than before.

The week before Christmas, we had a brief respite in the weather, and even the temperature cooperated with the bright sun to allow Bootsie and me to venture outside without fear of catching our deaths. Uncle Joe drove me downtown with the baby carriage in the back of his truck, and said he'd pick me up in two hours, which is all I thought I had the strength for. But I knew walking in the sunshine with my little girl and surprising John would restore me.

I took Bootsie to the park first, sitting her up so she could see me feeding the birds with stale bread crumbs, loving the way her small, perfect hands reached out each time a bird flew past her and then upward toward the sky. She was still a little baby, but no longer a newborn, and I felt almost nostalgic for those first few weeks when John and I figured out how to be parents. It was as if we'd moved into an unfamiliar house with a demanding stranger, and we all had to learn the new rules. It had been frightening, and intoxicating, and wonderful, and very, very hard. Still, I missed those early days and I couldn't help but wonder if I'd long for each passing phase of Bootsie's life the way the harvested fields missed the farmer.

I walked down the sidewalks of Indian Mound, stopping frequently as friends and acquaintances bent to look inside the carriage. Bootsie was in high spirits and smiled at them all. I was pleased to see this, as I'm a firm believer that a good attitude is the most important thing to have to get along in life. Aunt Louise said I was a happy baby, too, and that I brought cheerfulness to every room. When they came to live with me, she said she made it her duty to make sure that any of life's unpleasantness didn't affect my goodness, and that she wished she'd tried harder to protect me from people who didn't appreciate my good nature as much as they should. She didn't tell me who she was speaking of, but I knew she meant Sarah Beth. I wanted to tell her that I thought that influence worked both ways and that maybe my good nature softened some of the sharp edges in Sarah Beth's. And maybe that's why we'd been friends for so long.

I still had an hour to go by the time I wheeled Bootsie up to the front door of Peacock's and went inside, the sound of the bell over the door announcing our presence. I stopped in the same spot I had the day I'd borrowed Sarah Beth's fur coat, and waited in the stream of sunlight from the window.

"Please give me one moment, and I'll be right with you," John's voice called from the back room. It was dinnertime, and I knew Mr. Peacock always went home to eat.

With a quick kiss to Bootsie's forehead, and pressing my finger to my lips as if she knew what that meant, I tiptoed to the back room as quietly as I could. I spotted John at his worktable, but the lights were off despite different clock pieces strewn across the surface. He was staring straight ahead at the blank wall, his hands holding tightly to the edges of the worktable as if without their support he might fall off his stool.

"John, what's the matter?"

He swung around in surprise, and I saw that his face was pale, his eyes bloodshot. He hadn't been sleeping well at night, but with a new baby that was to be expected. Mathilda brought the baby to me during the night if she awoke to be fed, but I'm sure it disturbed John's sleep as well.

He smiled, but it wasn't one I recognized. "I'm fine," he said. "Just tired."

"Oh, sweetheart," I said, moving toward his side. "I'll move into the baby's room until she starts sleeping through the night so you can sleep. . . ."

He was shaking his head before I'd finished speaking. "No, Adelaide. I'd hate that. The one thing I look forward to each day is sleeping beside you each night." He stood and took my hands into his, kissing me gently.

A bit of the weariness seemed to leave his eyes as he looked into mine and smiled a real smile. "I'm so glad you're here. What a nice surprise. Did you bring my little girl, too?"

"Of course. You know I couldn't bear to leave her behind. Come on out and say hello."

"You go ahead. Please give me a minute. I have my Christmas gifts for both of you that I just finished with and I'm too impatient to wait five more days to give to you. It's the reason I've been working so late. I hope you like it enough to forgive me."

His spirits seemingly restored, I kissed him lightly, then returned to Bootsie, who was watching the light show on the ceiling caused by the sun's reflection from a display of emerald jewelry.

I waited only a few moments before I heard John call out, "Close your eyes and don't open them until I say you can."

I loved surprises. I remembered how my mother would pick a random day each year, a regular day that wasn't tied to any holiday or birthday, and surprise me with a small gift or favorite dessert, or a meal in a restaurant. It was something my aunt had continued, and until I'd had Bootsie I hadn't appreciated it.

I closed my eyes and listened as he walked toward us, heard Bootsie kicking her legs at the sound of her father's voice. With my eyes still closed, I said, "I told her not to look, but I don't think she's very good at surprises."

"That's all right, isn't it, pumpkin?" John said, and I heard him loudly kissing the baby and making her coo.

I wrung my hands with impatience. "Please hurry, John. You know I don't like waiting for surprises."

I felt him kiss my cheek, but not move away. His breath brushed my cheek as something was clasped around my neck. "You can look now."

Blinking open my eyes, I looked down at my chest, where a heavy gold chain, just like the one Uncle Joe wore on his pocket watch, hung like a necklace. And hanging from it was a tiny gold ring with half of a heart on its top.

I lifted the ring to see it better, then looked at John, not understanding. "What does it say?"

He opened up his other hand, where another small ring sat on his palm. He put it up next to mine, then pressed them together, the ring parts overlapping so that they made a little heart. And in the middle were the words *I Love You Forever*.

"See?" he said with the excitement of a little boy on Christmas morning. "It's a gift for both of you." He bent down and carefully placed it on Bootsie's thumb. "It's a little big for her now, but once it fits her ring finger, we'll have her photo taken in it at the studio down the street. And as she gets bigger, I can make the ring part larger—for yours, too, so you can both wear them on your hands if you like."

Bootsie brought her hand to her mouth, but John was quicker. "That's not to eat, pumpkin. It's jewelry. You'll learn what that is soon enough." He straightened and gave me a silly grin.

I placed both of my hands on his face and kissed him deeply. "It's a beautiful gift. For both of us. Thank you."

He wrapped me in his arms, pressing my cheek against his chest, where I could hear his heart beating. "Thank you, Adelaide, for making me the happiest man on earth. And the way you love our daughter makes my heart fuller than I ever thought it could be."

The bell over the door rang and we turned around to see Angelo Berlini entering the store. I hadn't seen him since the Harvest Festival the year before, when he'd carried me to his car and had his chauffeur take John and me to the hospital. It had been too late for our baby. The doctor had said that I'd lost a lot of blood, and that if I had not received immediate care, I would have died, too. I'd sent a note of thanks to Angelo for his help, and for the lovely bouquet of yellow roses he'd sent to my hospital room, but I hadn't heard from him since.

"Angelo," I said, walking toward him to greet him. "It is so good to see you again."

A brief look of surprise crossed his face, as if he hadn't expected to find me there, and I noticed that he'd already flipped the OPEN sign to CLOSED.

He took my hands in his, then kissed me on both cheeks in the elegant and romantic way I'd begun to associate with him. "The pleasure is all mine, as always. You are as lovely as ever."

"You must come meet Bootsie," I said, leading him into the store, where John was lifting the baby into his arms. "Since you're the reason she and I are both here."

"I am only glad that I was there to help. Anybody would have done the same. I'm just sorry I wasn't able to save your child."

"You did what you could, and now we have our precious girl." John remained unsmiling as we approached.

"Hello, John," Angelo said in a friendly voice. "I haven't seen you for a while. I thought it might be time for a visit to talk about business."

With clipped words, John replied, "I wish you had called or sent word. I have a lot of work to do here."

"I'm sure you do. That's why I promise to keep my business short, and then purchase something wildly expensive from your shop. It seems I need an engagement present for Carmen for a party her parents are throwing tomorrow evening in New Orleans. Our nuptials are planned for May. Things were pushed ahead when Mr. Bianca decided to run for Louisiana state senator. If we wait until after the campaign and his election, it might never happen, so my lovely bride-to-be put her delicate foot down and set a date."

"You're quite sure he's going to win?" John asked, and I looked at him sharply, wondering at the angry tone of his voice.

"Nothing is ever guaranteed, is it?" Angelo asked, putting a dark knuckle against Bootsie's soft cheek. "But he does have important supporters. He's being quite brave and running on a platform to repeal Prohibition. That might make even the non-Catholics vote for him."

Bootsie cooed at Angelo as he smiled at her, her little mouth forming itself into a perfect rosebud. John stepped back, taking the baby out of Angelo's reach. "That's bad news for you, isn't it?" John asked with a note of satisfaction.

The visitor rested his dark gaze on my husband. "On the contrary. I think it would be very good news for both of us." He began to examine one of the display cases, but his eyes remained fixed, as if he could see only his thoughts. "Like you, I don't want to be doing this forever. If we are patient, you see, this will all come to its natural end. It might not be this year, or the next, but it will happen. And then you—and I—will no longer be needed. Will no longer be valuable. And will have thick bank accounts to show for our sacrifices and hard work."

Bootsie began to fuss, and I wondered if she could sense her father's growing unease, his impatience with the words "this year or the next." I took her from John, and he barely seemed to notice.

John lowered his voice. "I told you, this is the last year. I want to start the new year with a clean slate." He glanced over at me and the baby as if seeking courage, then turned back to Angelo. "I've given you plenty of time to make other arrangements. I'm done as of the end of the year."

As if he hadn't heard John, Angelo used his pinkie to point at something in the jewelry case. "That's a lovely pair of emerald earrings. May I see them, please?"

With tightened lips, John retrieved the keys from behind the counter, then opened up the case. Angelo reached in and held up the earrings, his head moving from side to side as if he were picturing them on his bride-to-be. His eyes moved to me.

"Would you mind, Adelaide? Perhaps if I saw a beautiful woman wearing them, it would give me a better idea of what they would look like."

I didn't dare look at John. Instead I placed Bootsie, who'd fallen asleep, back in her carriage and reached for the earrings. Using one of the mirrors that sat atop each case, I clipped on the earrings, then shook my head to allow the sunlight to sparkle through them.

I faced the men. "What do you think?" I asked, smiling brightly to lighten the mood. John's lips tightened even more, but Angelo nodded appreciatively.

"Lovely," he said. "Just lovely. A beautiful woman should have beautiful things to complement her loveliness. And those emeralds match your eyes as if they were made for you. Don't you think, John?"

John didn't look at him as he replied, "My wife is beautiful enough."

Angelo seemed to notice for the first time the necklace I wore. "That's an interesting piece," he said with a raised eyebrow.

"Thank you," I said, lifting the ring to show him. "Bootsie has the other half." When I saw his furrowed brow, I said, "When they're put together it reads, 'I love you forever.' John designed it for us."

"Your husband is a very talented young man. He'll go far in life." Angelo's face grew serious. "He just needs to learn a little more patience."

John's eyes snapped with anger and his fists clenched. I'd never seen him like this, and it frightened me. "Take those off," he said, indicating the earrings. "I think we're done here."

I began taking off the earrings while Angelo pulled his wallet from his pocket, fanning out a large amount of money. "I'll take them," he said, counting out bills before laying them on the counter. "Do you have a box?"

Without speaking, John took the earrings from me, then went into the back for a Peacock's box, sliding it in Angelo's direction without even counting the cash. The Italian pocketed the earrings, smiling again.

"I'm here as your friend, John. I hope you know that. Nobody sent me. I just thought it important that somebody spoke with you about having patience. I've said it before—I'm not the man in charge. I'm like you—just a workingman trying to make everybody happy. I cannot protect you if you do something that upsets the apple cart. If you tip it, I can't promise you that I'll be there to pick up all the apples."

He turned and headed for the door, stopping to admire the sleeping Bootsie in her carriage before facing me. "You are an intelligent woman, Adelaide. I hope you will speak with your husband to make him understand the wisdom of my words." He took my hands in his and kissed the tops of each.

He reached for his hat that he'd left on one of the cases and slipped it on his head. His hand was already on the doorknob when he spoke again. Turning slightly in my direction, he said, "You might also tell your cousin William that he and his Klansmen would be better off focusing on philanthropic causes rather than busting up my stills. Besides being hypocritical on his part, it's upsetting to those businessmen who rely on a steady supply from our associates in this neck of the woods. For your sake, I'd hate to see him hurt."

He tipped his hat to me, then opened the door and left, the cheery jingling of the bell jarring in the heavy silence.

I stared at the closed door for a long moment, listening to my daughter breathe and thinking on Angelo's parting words. I'd long been suspicious of Willie's activities, of his odd hours and secretive behaviors. How he kept his bedroom door locked now, with strict instructions that nobody, especially Mathilda, have entry. But ever since my mother's death, I'd been afraid of facing the truth—either real or imagined—and had chosen to look the other way so I wouldn't be forced to confront something unpleasant.

"Is what he said true?" I finally asked. "About Willie being involved with the Klan?"

John walked over to me and put his hands on my shoulders. "He's more than involved, Adelaide. He's a kleagle, responsible for recruiting members in this area. He's been pressuring me to get involved, too, but I want nothing to do with it. That's why he's started messing with my local moonshiners, because I've refused." He pressed his forehead against mine and I heard his exhausted exhale. "I'll talk to him. Again. If that doesn't work, maybe we need to speak with your uncle Joe."

He drew me into his arms. "I'm sorry you were here and had to listen to all that."

I pulled back, meeting his eyes. "Angelo is our friend, John. He wants you to wait a little longer. If that's what it takes to keep us safe, I'm willing to wait."

"Maybe we should move to Missouri, where I still have family. Leave all of this behind us and start anew. We can do it. Together."

I touched his face, looked into his weary eyes. "I'll go anywhere with you, John. And if you want to move to Missouri, I'll go without a glance back." I swallowed, trying to find the right words. "But this is Bootsie's home, too. She has family here who love her. The house and farm will be hers one day, the same house and farm that's been lived in by her family for generations. If she wants to leave when she's older, I'd let her, because then it will be her choice. But I think it would be the wrong thing to take her away now."

Emotions warred in his eyes. I gently reached up and smoothed his eyelids with my thumbs. "If you still want to leave, we'll leave. But I'm willing to wait it out, too. It can't be that long, can it? And like Angelo said, then we'll be free to have the lives we want. With Bootsie, and any other children God will give us."

His eyes opened, making my breath stop with the bleakness I saw there. But then he leaned forward and kissed me, the look gone so quickly that I wondered if I'd imagined seeing it at all.

"You're right, my sweet Adelaide. How could I think of taking you and Bootsie from the only place where your roots are so deep. Forgive me. Sometimes I just need to be reminded about how you make me stronger, and how we can face all of this together and come out on the other end better for it."

I glanced up at one of the large clocks on the wall, set to the exact time. "Uncle John will be here to pick me up any minute, and I told him I'd wait outside so he wouldn't have to park. Come say good-bye to your baby. Just don't wake her up. It's almost time for her to eat, and I don't want her to wake up just yet to be reminded."

He waited with us until Uncle Joe pulled up to the curb, then loaded the carriage into the bed of the truck. I held Bootsie in the front seat and looked back at John as we pulled away. He waved. But as I watched, his smile fell with his hand, and from a distance he looked like a lonely old man with no more choices in front of him.

I faced forward, the image haunting me long past the time we returned home to the yellow house and the saturated fields, and despite the warmer temperature and bright sun, I felt very, very cold.

Vivien Walker Moise
INDIAN MOUND, MISSISSIPPI
MAY 2013

I was on my second cup of coffee when Tommy entered the kitchen, doing an exaggerated double take when he spotted me at the kitchen table. A stack of old newspapers was spread around me, a notebook and pencil to my side with my chicken scrawl exploding diagonally across the page. Despite what my teachers had claimed—that my imagination and creativity made me a great writer—I'd always made less than stellar grades in English because of poor penmanship. It ground my grits to know that they weren't even teaching penmanship in the schools anymore. If I had any say about Chloe's education, I would make sure she learned proper penmanship.

"What're you doing up so early, Booger?"

I put down my coffee mug. "Did you know that you're a peculiarity in our family? You're like the only male and one of only a very small handful of siblings. Obviously you were a mistake."

He raised his eyebrows. "Right. And you were planned."

I lifted my mug and took a sip so I wouldn't have to concede that he had a point.

He shook the nearly empty coffeepot. "Should I make another full one or are you about done?"

I looked at the clock. "Might as well make a full one. I've got a few more hours before Tripp gets here to take us fishing."

He started filling the pot with water from the tap and glanced over at my outfit. "What's with that?" He indicated with his chin.

I'd decided that since I was already awake at five thirty in the morning, I might as well do something productive, so I went for a run—which quickly turned into a walk. I'd had to rummage through my closet to find my old running shoes and an Indian Mound High School Cheer Squad T-shirt with cutoff sleeves. I refused to wear the Daisy Dukes out in public and had instead found a pair of old sweatpants that I'd made into long shorts with the help of a pair of scissors.

I'd thought about going to the high school track, where I used to run, but didn't want to be seen or, even worse, recognized. So I'd headed up to the highway, planning to run on the shoulder for one mile and then turn back. But I'd been stopped so many times by motorists asking me if I needed help or a ride somewhere that I'd just given up about a quarter mile into my first leg and come home and made a pot of coffee.

"Long story that involves a thwarted desire to exercise. I've been cooling my heels while waiting for Tripp by looking at these old newspapers." I spun one of the newspapers around so he could read it and see the photo. "Look what I found. It's Adelaide's wedding, in 1924." When I'd turned a page and seen it, I'd been startled to see her face again. She'd been so happy in the photo, her husband looking at her with such love. But even as I looked at this reminder of such a happy day, I couldn't help but remember that in three short years Adelaide would be dead, her body in the arms of the cypress roots. I had stared at her for a long time, my fingers touching her face. *Who killed you, Adelaide? And why?*

I wasn't even sure why the answer was so important to me. It had happened more than eight decades ago, and somebody had gotten away with the perfect crime. But I kept thinking about the heart ring, and how much she'd loved her daughter. And how Bootsie had died believing her mother had intentionally left her behind. I felt the need to prove that Bootsie had been wrong. That maybe we'd all been wrong.

Tommy leaned in, studying it closely. "She looks like you. And Mama. Although it's pretty grainy and in black and white. But I'm sure she was much prettier than you."

"Thanks, Tommy. It's so nice to have a brother." I leaned forward and pointed to the people in the photo. "Look at the woman standing next to her, holding the bouquet. The caption says it's a Miss S. B. Heathman. That last name sounds so familiar to me—any idea why?"

He shook his head slowly, then stopped, frowning. "There's a plaque over at the bank with the name Heathman—can't remember the first name, but I'm pretty sure it's a guy. He was the first president or something. But that was back before the big crash in 'twenty-nine. Probably lost everything, or killed himself, because that's what they did back then."

I frowned, confident that the name I'd seen hadn't been in reference to the bank. I took another sip of my coffee, hoping the caffeine would jog my memory banks.

"Off to the fields?" I asked.

He seemed to be concentrating a lot more intently than needed to scoop coffee into a filter, and didn't answer right away.

I leaned back in my chair, a smug smile on my face. "I remember Carrie last night saying something about Bo having a baseball game this morning. You're coaching, right?"

With deliberate precision he placed the carafe into the coffeemaker and mashed the "on" button. "Just until they can find a permanent replacement. Guy they had got a job transfer and had to bail."

"Uh-huh," I said, enjoying watching him blush. "I never thought that red was a good color for you, but I'm starting to think I like it."

He shook his head, then turned to get a mug from the cabinet. "You're one to talk. I've seen a lot of Tripp Montgomery sniffing around ever since you got back."

"He's the county coroner, and we found a dead body on our property. He's supposed to be sniffing around."

"Uh-huh," he said, mimicking me. "I think he's being waiting around all this time for you to come back."

"Right. Do you mean to tell me that he hasn't dated anybody in the last decade?"

Tommy shook his head. "Nope, wouldn't say he's been living the life of a monk. I think he had a serious girlfriend at Duke, and one during his short stint in med school. And there've been a couple of girls around here since he moved back. But they never seemed to stick."

He leaned his elbows back on the counter, waiting for the coffee-maker to finish. "Did I tell you I dated Claire for a bit? Right after she graduated from vet school she came home for a summer—before she decided that she wanted to marry the guy who's now her husband and moved to Michigan."

"Ew, Tommy. She was my best friend! Besides, she's almost ten years younger than you."

He shrugged. "I always liked her, once she stopped being my little sister's best friend. She's real nice, and smart. Funny thing is, we mostly just talked about you." The light blinked on the coffeemaker, and Tommy poured himself a cup before bringing it over to the table. I brushed the newspapers out of the way, petrified of what Mrs. Shipley would do to me if coffee dripped onto any of them.

I looked down into my mug, at my reflection in the coffee, too embarrassed to look up and meet Tommy's eyes.

"We talked about Tripp, too, and about his string of girlfriends and why none of them ever lasted. You know what she said?"

Our eyes met. "No, what?"

"Because none of them were you."

"I wish you hadn't told me that."

He shrugged. "Yeah, well, I figured you needed to hear it." He slapped his hands against the table. "I should get goin'." After pulling back from the table, he went to the coffeemaker and refilled his cup.

"Don't leave that mug on your desk, Tommy. We were running out in the cabinet, and when I went over to the shed I found seven half-filled mugs. Either return them or I'm going to forbid you from using them and make you buy Styrofoam cups."

He surprised me by crossing the room, then bending to kiss the top of my head. "It's good to have you back, Vivi. I missed you."

"I missed you, too, Tommy." I looked up at him, trying very hard to tamp down the prickle of tears behind my eyes.

He ruffled my hair as if I were eight years old again, then headed for the door. "See you later, Booger." I heard him laughing long after the door had slammed shut.

Two hours and three and a half cups of coffee later, I was still in the kitchen, having read through the majority of the newspapers I'd brought from City Hall. I'd filled three sheets of paper from corner to corner with headlines and names, all great ideas for future newspaper articles, should I decide to write them. But except for the photograph from Adelaide's wedding and the article regarding her disappearance, I'd found nothing new that might help me figure out why she'd been buried in her own yard. And who'd put her car in the river so that it looked like she'd been just one of the many flood victims.

There were still three newspapers I hadn't read yet, but as I reached for one of them Chloe entered the kitchen, dragging both feet, with her eyes nearly closed as if they were still asleep even if the rest of her was upright. I hid my smile as I admired her outfit.

We hadn't had a chance to go shopping yet, but in a fit of inspiration, I'd dug into the back of my closet for the clothes I'd worn when I was Chloe's age. Bootsie, having lived through the Depression, had never thrown anything away that had any chance—no matter how small—of being used again. But I'd been about the same size and shape as Chloe when I was twelve, and I knew there'd be a selection of one-piece bathing suits and soft cotton shorts with elastic waists—my summer uniform. I'd felt not just a little satisfaction at her shock that not only did the clothes fit her, but that they'd once fit me.

She'd chosen the bright blue bathing suit that I'd worn on the summer rec swim team the summer between seventh and eighth grade. I was laughed at on the first day, because I was chubby and slow and could barely swim. I'd hated the cold water and the mean girls, but I'd shown up every day just so I could get better. I'd even stay after practice, doing hours of laps on my own while Bootsie waited patiently in the stands for me to finish. And it had been my turn to laugh when I was winning ribbons by the end of the summer. As an added bonus, I'd also lost fifteen pounds.

The unnamed dog pranced in by Chloe's side, with Carol Lynne right behind them, wearing one of her jeans-and-floral-shirt outfits. She stopped in the middle of the kitchen, looking like she wasn't sure what she was supposed to do next, while Chloe slid into the chair vacated by Tommy, the dog lying at her feet.

"Can I have some coffee?" Chloe asked, her voice muffled because she was facedown on the table.

"No. It'll stunt your growth." I had no idea if that was true, but it was something Bootsie had said regularly. I stood and pulled out a seat for my mother. "Come sit, and I'll get you both breakfast."

Carol Lynne did as she was told, but when I put two bananas on the table, she asked, "Am I hungry?"

"It's time for breakfast. I'm going to make scrambled egg whites and wheat toast for Chloe and me. Would you like some?"

She smiled the same vacant smile I was becoming used to. I patted her shoulder. "I'll make you some, too."

I pulled a carton of eggs and a loaf of bread from the fridge. "Did the dog like his new doggy bed?"

Chloe quickly took a bite of her banana so she wouldn't have to answer.

I put my hand on my hip, sensing an uncanny resemblance to a memory I had of Bootsie standing by this same stove. I dropped my arm. "I told you no dog on the bed—or any of the furniture. It's a bad habit you don't want to start."

She swallowed. "Yeah, but you said he might not be here for long, and I figured if he slept on my bed a few times it would be okay. Besides, every time I put him in his bed he'd jump right back onto mine."

I cracked an egg. "Did he at least stay at the foot of the bed? It's not sanitary to let the dog sleep on your pillow."

She took another big bite from her banana and I rolled my eyes. I supposed this would be just another battle best left unfought.

I was in the middle of chopping a red pepper—trying to get as many nutrients into Chloe as possible without her knowing it—when Tripp knocked on the back door and entered the kitchen. He stopped when he saw me. "Nice outfit, Vivi. I wasn't aware the circus was having auditions today."

I took in his own outfit of flip-flops, camouflage hunting pants cut off above the knees, and a Charlie Daniels concert T-shirt that fit nicely over a muscled torso and tanned arms. "*Duck Dynasty* just called. They said either grow a beard or they want their clothes back."

Chuckling, he stepped into the kitchen and kissed my mother on the cheek before greeting Chloe and the dog.

"This was Vivien's bathing suit," Chloe announced.

Tripp nodded appreciatively. "I was going to say it looked familiar. She looked pretty fine in it, as I recall. But may I say that the blue brings out the color of your eyes?"

Chloe's face underwent a contortion as she fought between scowling and smiling. In the end, she took the last bite of her banana so she couldn't do either. I speared her with a look, and with her mouth full she said, "Thank you, sir."

I turned back to making breakfast so I wouldn't roll my eyes at both of them. "You're early," I said.

"I know. But I ran out of coffee and thought I could grab a cup here."

I nodded toward the coffeemaker. "Help yourself. I think my head might spin off my shoulders if I have another." I turned toward my mother. "Carol Lynne, would you like a cup?"

She looked at me with vacant eyes. "Do I like coffee?"

I stared back at her, and I imagined my eyes were as vacant as hers. "I don't know," I said truthfully. "Why don't I get you both some orange juice?"

Tripp sat down at the table, sliding the newspapers out of the way so he could put down his mug.

"Tripp, if you don't mind, could you move those papers off the table? They're from the archives, and Mrs. Shipley will probably have me arrested if anything happens to them."

"Sure." He pushed back his chair, but before he could grab them, my mother noticed the one I'd left on top, opened to the studio photograph of Adelaide and Bootsie.

"Pretty baby," she said, pointing at Bootsie, unaware that she was pointing at her own mother.

I poured the whisked egg whites and red pepper with a little bit of low-fat cheese into a bowl and began mixing it. Carrying it over to the table while I stirred, I looked down at the photograph. "Yes, she was."

Carol Lynne continued staring at the photo, tilting her head to the side as her finger drifted up toward the necklace Adelaide wore, and the ring hanging down from the chain in the middle of her chest.

"That's pretty, too," she said.

The spoon stilled in my hand as I watched her finger continue to tap the photo. "Have you seen it before?"

Tap-tap. "Oh, yes. Of course."

My eyes met Tripp's over the top of my mother's head. "Where? Where did you see it?"

Her finger stopped. "I wasn't supposed to. I was snooping in her room and she found me and told me I needed to give it back, because it was a secret."

"Who said it was a secret?" I asked gently, almost afraid to breathe.

She shook her head. "She said she was good at keeping secrets."

Tripp placed a gentle hand on her arm. "Who is, Carol Lynne? Who said they were good at keeping secrets?"

She leaned back in her chair, her face expressionless, as if she were lost in concentration. Finally, she smiled up at us, and we all seemed to hold our collective breath. "I think I'm hungry. Is it time to eat?"

I closed my eyes for a moment, wishing I knew how much of my mother's memories was real and how much was just her imagination. "Sure. I'll have your breakfast ready for you in just a minute."

I poured the contents of the bowl into the warmed pan, the loud sizzling noise almost obliterating the sound of my own disappointment.

The sun had just begun its descent by the time we climbed back into Tripp's truck at Horseshoe Lake, the large cooler in the bed of the truck conspicuously empty of any catfish.

Chloe hadn't known to question the absence of rods or reels when she and the dog had climbed into the truck, nor had any idea what was in store for her when Tripp began wading into the brown waters of the lake without goggles and told her to watch him so she'd know what to do.

It was only after he'd disappeared into the opaque water and emerged a little bit later with a catfish in his hands that she understood. And quickly began screaming and running out of the water faster than I'd ever seen her move. With a shrug Tripp had gone to his cooler and opened it, only to be stopped by new shrieks from Chloe.

"But if you put him on that ice without any water, he'll *die!*"

Tripp tried to look as sympathetic as he could with a flapping catfish in his hands. "Sweetheart, that's kind of the point."

A look of horror passed over her face, and I had visions of her screaming, "Fish murderer!" and scaring away the bass and other fish that the men on a nearby dock were hoping to attract to their baited lines.

He'd returned the catfish to his home in the water, and instead of fishing we'd had a long picnic that I'd brought with us, then did a little hiking along the shore of the lake and a lot of dock sitting, spotting fish we weren't allowed to catch. And, despite generously slathering on the sunscreen, we all ended up with pink noses and cheeks, and I knew if I looked in a mirror I'd find new freckles. I couldn't remember a time when I'd been so relaxed, or had so much fun doing absolutely nothing, or seen Chloe in such a prolonged pleasant mood. It had all been worth a few freckles.

The truck stopped in the front drive under the shade of an oak tree, and we both looked into the backseat, where Chloe slept soundly, her head on top of the dog like a pillow. The dog lifted his head to look at us, then lay back down, content to be a pillow as long as Chloe needed him.

"She looks like an angel," Tripp whispered.

"Hard to believe, but yeah, she does. Makes me not want to wake her."

"I'm in no hurry to get home. I could hang out here a bit if you want."

"Sure. And you might as well stay for supper. I'll go in and grab a couple of beers and let Cora know. I'll meet you on the porch."

I quietly let myself out of the truck while Tripp lowered all of the windows, allowing in a cool breeze that had begun blowing from the west.

He was waiting for me when I returned and handed him a beer, his attention focused on a black swirl of birds that shifted from tree to tree like an impatient child and then took off over the house. "Come on," he said, stepping off the porch steps and heading around the corner toward the back of the house and to the prone cypress tree.

The birds—crows, I could see now—had settled in the old limbs, calling to one another, mocking us. "I've never seen crows behave like that. Sparrows, sure, but not crows," he said, taking a long pull from his bottle. He turned to me. "You know that old nursery rhyme, right? 'One crow for sorrow, two for mirth'?"

"Of course. Mathilda taught it to me when I was little. There are too many to count, though, and I'm glad. I don't need a bunch of crows to tell me things look bad."

"Do they?" he asked quietly.

I took a drink from my beer, thinking. "Things don't seem as bad as when I first arrived, but I don't feel like I've won the lottery, either."

"You're off your pills," he said, watching the crows begin to lift their wings.

For now, I thought. "Yeah. And I've got Chloe for a couple more weeks. That's all good. But my mother still can't remember things, and now I'll never know why she kept leaving."

"She came back, though. For good. Doesn't that count for something?"

I shook my head. "It was too late."

He didn't say anything and I sighed. "It was," I said again for emphasis.

"I didn't argue."

I took another drink from my bottle. "You didn't have to. I could hear your disapproval in your silence."

He laughed softly. "I deal with enough dead people to know that it's only too late once you're in the ground."

I frowned, thinking of Adelaide in the roots of the tree. "I wish Bootsie had known what had happened to her mother. That she didn't leave her on purpose."

"Do you think that would have changed anything?"

I thought hard, believing that the answer should be a lot simpler than it was. "Of course. If I understood why my mother left me, I think I'd be a different person today."

He watched me carefully, and I thought for a moment that it would be another one of his silences. Instead he said, "Sure, you'd be different. But I don't think you'd be better. An easy life makes for very boring people."

The birds settled onto their limbs, the cawing silenced by a rustling of black wings. I drained my bottle, then stared down at the empty hole where Adelaide had been for all those years. "I dream about her. Most nights. Like she wants to tell me something. And then other times I dream that I'm in the hole and somebody's shoveling dirt on top of me. Like I'm being buried alive."

Tripp drained his own bottle. "Do you want me to interpret that, or can you figure it out on your own?"

He grinned, and before I could tell him that he didn't know the first thing about me, he leaned over and kissed me. His lips tasted of cold beer and warm sunshine, and we seemed to fit together perfectly, our lips meeting with just a tilt of our heads. I wondered why I'd never noticed it before. I moved closer, liking it, wanting more, pressing myself into him, touching him, running my hand through his thick hair. I heard his empty bottle drop to the ground and then both of his arms were around me, his hands stroking my back, then moving up until he cupped my face like a treasure.

This is Tripp. I ignored the little voice in my head, the rest of me enjoying the kisses too much to pay any attention. *This is Tripp.* The voice came again, louder this time, and my eyes popped open as if to verify that I'd heard correctly.

I stepped back, seeing the green specks in his eyes that I'd always known were there but never bothered to really notice. "What are we doing?"

I watched half of his mouth turn up. "I don't know what you call it in California, but here in Mississippi we call it kissing."

"You know what I mean," I said, torn between wiping off his kisses with my arm or never washing my face ever again. "You. And me. It just . . ."

"It just what?" he asked, his voice innocent-sounding. As if he were unaware of how wrong it was for the two of us to be kissing.

I tried to think of all the reasons I'd given him while growing up, but none of them seemed to fit anymore. "Because I'm not the girl I used to be. I haven't been her for a long time."

We stared at each other in the blue light of the coming evening, neither of us saying anything.

Finally, he said, "I know that, Vivi. You're nothing like that girl I used to know. The girl I knew I wanted to marry the first time I saw her. The girl who strutted around in her bikini in front of me because she didn't think it mattered, and who went with me to all the dances so she could flirt with all the other boys. The girl who was so hell-bent on leaving this place that she didn't bother to say good-bye to the people who loved her most. You're right, Vivi. I don't see that girl anymore."

I stared at him, wanting to cry, wanting to grieve for somebody we both had once known. To say a eulogy for a girl I was glad was gone.

"Great," I forced out. "Glad we're on the same page." I began walking back toward the house, unable to name the emotions that I was finally allowing myself to feel.

A loud fluttering erupted from the branches behind me, and I looked back in time to see the cloud of black crows emerge from the dead tree, then begin their erratic path toward the fields.

"You didn't let me finish, Vivi," Tripp called after me, and I began to walk faster. "I wanted to say that I'm glad that girl is gone. Because I like the new Vivi a whole lot more."

I kept walking without turning around, my response the slamming of the screen door.

Chapter 39

Carol Lynne Walker Moise
INDIAN MOUND, MISSISSIPPI
MAY 2002

Dear Diary,

I almost died five months ago. From an overdose, same as Michael. I remembered how peaceful he'd looked and I think that's why for a long time I didn't think I'd mind if I died. But I was found in time and taken to the hospital. I just kept thinking about Tommy and Vivien and that's when I knew I didn't want to die. I had two reasons to live, and I'd never seen it that way before. Maybe it's only when we're faced with losing everything that we finally get to see what we've had all along. I remembered what Mathilda had said about chasing ghosts, and when I was lying in that hospital bed fighting for the life I never valued, I finally understood. I've spent so much time looking for something more, and bigger, and better, that I never stopped to see how much I already had.

So now I'm home for good, and I'm clean and finally ready to stay that way. Tommy was the first out of the house, not running—because he's a mature college grad of twenty-six—but his hug was just as big as when he was a little boy. Bootsie and Mathilda were next, moving a lot more slowly than when I'd seen them last. Vivien stayed in her room, and I was okay with that. I understand; I do. And I will wait as long as it takes until she's ready to forgive me and let me be the mother I want to be, and that she needs me to be.

I looked at the steps, waiting for Emmett and Cotton, somehow knowing that I'd never see them coming out to greet me again. I suppose human nature makes us believe that those we love will be around forever, or at least long enough for us to tell them how much they mean to us. That's something else I want to teach my children.

I thought of Emmett's hatbox, and how it had been so important for him to give it to me when he died. But Bootsie didn't know what had happened to it, thinking it might have been lost during the store's move from downtown to Tommy's new shop in the shed. I can't help but wonder if he'd left some message there for me, and if I'll ever find out what it was. I asked Mathilda, but she just shook her head. I remembered what she'd told me all those years ago when I'd been snooping in her room and taken something that belonged to her. When she asked for it back, I told her not to tell Bootsie. And she said not to worry, because she was good at keeping secrets. So I guess I'll never know. Or maybe Mathilda's just waiting until it's the right time for me to learn something new.

I've been watching Vivien garden, taking over for Bootsie, whose knees and back bother her too much for her to do any kneeling or lifting. Vivien never liked getting her hands in the dirt, but now that she sees Bootsie needs her, she doesn't seem to mind. She's so nurturing and gentle, making sure all of her plants are strong and healthy. I know she doesn't think so now, but she'll be a wonderful mother one day.

This will be my last diary entry. I started it when I was seventeen and I think that it's time to put it away. I've been a child up until now, but it's time—I need to be an adult. I cleaned up my room, packing up books and childish mementos of a person I don't want to remember, and put the box in the attic. While I was up there, I thought it would be a good place to store this diary. Maybe Vivien and I can look at it together sometime, and maybe she will finally understand all that I was never able to tell her.

When I came down from the attic stairs to get the diary, Mathilda was waiting for me, and she asked me if I was done chasing ghosts. I told her I was, and that I wished it hadn't taken me so long to figure out what she'd meant. I guess we all figure things out in our own time. Maybe that's why I didn't die out there in California—because I still had so much to learn. I told the Kellys that I had to get back to Mississippi to teach my children what I'd learned so that they wouldn't make the same mistakes I have. Especially my baby girl. She's the one I've hurt the most, I think. And I will spend the rest of my life trying to make it up to her. If she'll let me.

Mathilda laughed in that way she has that's loving and tender but tells you that you're being foolish, too. Then she said that Tommy and Vivien will have their own way of learning things, and in their own time, and that I have to do what all mothers have done since the beginning of time: wait. As long as it takes. And, when they're finished chasing their own ghosts, be there to welcome them home.

Chapter 40

Adelaide Walker Bodine Richmond
INDIAN MOUND, MISSISSIPPI
FEBRUARY 1927

The rains continued, swelling the river's banks to record levels in Louisiana, Arkansas, and Mississippi. But the levees held, and the engineers expressed confidence that modern technology could defy Mother Nature. I could only think that the engineers should have talked to more delta farmers who'd been fighting the river for generations, and have understood that the river has eternally sought its home in the sea, regardless of the boundaries humans have made. Uncle Joe kept talking about the *Titanic*, and how it had been created by expert engineers, too, and he started making evacuation plans for his family and field-workers.

Bootsie continued to grow and thrive, my love for her stronger each day. She could even make John laugh, something for which I was grateful. He'd come home each day, his face drawn and his eyes empty, with an anger surging under his skin that could be erased with only a look at our smiling girl.

He was working longer and longer hours, and I was never sure if he was at the jewelry store or making his rounds for Mr. Berlini, whose territory had grown to include neighboring LeFlore County and parts of Arkansas. And the more he worked, the angrier he became. I tried to remind him that this was temporary, that he was thinking of our well-being and doing what was right for his family. But my words drowned in his well of anger and frustration toward a situation that was no longer in his control to manage or change.

On another typical rainy Friday night, I called Sarah Beth—who was back in Indian Mound on a rare trip home from New Orleans— and asked her to come over and keep me company. Mathilda had already put Bootsie to bed, and Aunt Louise and Uncle Joe had gone to a community meeting to discuss emergency preparedness in case the levees broke. Willie hadn't come home after work, and I assumed he'd gone to one of his political meetings. I knew in the morning I'd read about a man tarred and feathered or horsewhipped, or a disappearance. The Klan made a big show of their financial donations to churches and hospitals, but their vigilante justice was kept from the newspapers, their deeds known only to those they wanted to warn. I needed to tell Uncle Joe what his son was involved with, because my uncle was a man who'd never shown any tolerance for bigotry of any kind, but John held me back, saying Uncle Joe had other things to worry about right now. When the rain finally stopped, I'd have time then.

I didn't know where John was, or when he'd be home, and the sound of the incessant rain against the roof and the windows of the old house was beginning to unnerve me. I was about to call Sarah Beth again to find out what was taking her so long, when headlights flashed across the parlor, and I heard the sound of doors shutting.

I ran to the front door to open it so that the doorbell wouldn't awaken Bootsie or Mathilda. I watched, surprised, as three figures ran from the car and up the front steps, laughing. I could smell the alcohol and cigarettes before they'd even reached me.

"Darling," Sarah Beth crooned with a mouthful of smoke. "I hope you don't mind, but I brought Willie and Chas. They're both too drunk to drive, so I thought I'd be doing a community service by delivering them here. I'd say go ahead and make up a room for Chas, but he'll probably be happy sleeping on the floor."

"I'm perfectly fine," Chas said, stumbling forward past me and into the foyer. Willie came up from behind Sarah Beth and put his arm around her, then tried to kiss her. She pulled away from him, and he almost fell as she quickly walked past me.

When I'd closed the door and joined them in the parlor, Chas was already looking in all the drawers and cabinets. "Where d'ya think they keep the booze?" he asked. Both he and Willie were dressed in their business suits, but with their unkempt hair and slurred speech, neither looked like the respectable bankers they were supposed to be.

"My aunt and uncle are teetotalers. You won't find any liquor," I said quietly, hoping they'd give up and leave before either Bootsie or Mathilda awakened.

Willie pulled out a flask from his jacket pocket before tossing the jacket on the floor, then threw himself down in my uncle's wing chair. "Don't worry, old man. I've got you covered."

Chas made his way to my aunt's chair opposite, but missed and landed on the floor. "I meant to do that," he said, resting his head against the front of the seat and reaching up for Willie's flask.

"Put some music on, will you, doll?" Willie called out to Sarah Beth, who stood with her long, elegant cigarette holder between two fingers, looking at the men with curled lips.

"Do it yourself," she said, then sauntered toward the velvet love seat, where she dropped her fur coat before elegantly draping herself onto the thick cushions.

"We've got a radio," I said, moving toward the window, where my aunt's pride and joy sat. After the good harvest of two years before, my uncle had given in and bought one for his wife. Although he wouldn't admit it, he enjoyed listening to a baseball play-by-play as much as Aunt Louise loved *Sam 'n' Henry*. I didn't want anybody else touching it, knowing that my uncle needed to sell it if this year's crop was lost. Which, although nobody was admitting it, was already a foregone conclusion.

I turned on the radio and moved the dial until I found a station playing dance music, making a mental note to change it back before Aunt Louise or Uncle Joe turned it on again. Nobody made a move to stand, and I was grateful, having no interest in dancing with either Willie or Chas. The men sat sharing a flask while Sarah Beth lit another cigarette. If it hadn't been raining so hard, I would have opened the window to air out the room.

I was about to suggest a game of cards when we all turned to the sound of somebody coming down the stairs and walking across the foyer. I saw Mathilda the moment she saw my three guests, and she froze.

"I'm sorry, Miss Adelaide. I heard noises and wants to make sure you was okay. . . ."

"I'm fine. Thank you, Mathilda."

"I'm hungry," Willie said. Holding his flask upside down, he shook it. "And I could go for a Co-Cola."

"Yes, sir," Mathilda said quietly, and began to back up into the foyer.

I stood. "That's all right. You go on up to be with the baby. I'll get us something from the kitchen."

Willie sat up and I watched as his face darkened. He was a mean drunk, and I found myself hoping that Uncle Joe or John would come home soon.

"No, Adelaide. You're not the maid here. You, girl," he said to Mathilda. "Go get us something to eat and some Co-Colas. And don't take your sweet time about it, neither."

Mathilda left and I glowered at Willie. "That was uncalled-for, Willie."

Chas snickered, his head lolling back against the seat of Aunt Louise's chair. He hadn't bothered to get up off the floor where he'd landed.

We listened to the music and the sound of the rain, and felt the tension thicken in the air like molasses in winter. About five minutes later, Mathilda entered the room with a tray of four glasses filled with Coca-Cola and a plate of cheese and crackers. I hurriedly stood and took it from her, eager for her to leave. But before I'd had time to turn around and place the tray on the coffee table, Chas had pulled himself to his feet and was moving toward her.

"Hey, I know you," he said, managing to reach her without tripping.

I quickly put down the tray, preparing to step between them. I noticed that Mathilda's cotton dress wasn't buttoned to the top like she normally wore it, and I imagined she'd thrown it on in a hurry to come downstairs. And there, tied around her neck by a single silk cord, was the pearl I'd seen her wearing at the Harvest Festival, but which she'd kept carefully hidden ever since.

"No, sir," she said, taking a step back.

"You calling me a liar?"

"I think she is," Willie announced from his chair, either unwilling or unable to stand.

"Stop it," I said. "You've both had too much to drink. Why don't you sit down and have something to eat and Mathilda can go back to Bootsie—"

"Well, isn't this pretty," Chas said as he reached up to Mathilda's throat to tug at the pearl. Using the necklace to pull her forward, he moved her so that Willie could see. "Look—she's got a pearl. You ever seen such a thing on a colored girl?"

Willie looked at Mathilda with bleary eyes, a low whistle on his lips. "Where'd you steal that from, girl?"

"I gave it to her."

We all turned toward Sarah Beth, who was blowing out smoke from the side of her mouth. "She didn't steal it." She stood, and I noticed for the first time the earrings that swung from her ears. They were made of emeralds, and were identical to the earrings Angelo Berlini had purchased from Peacock's jeweler's. I sucked in my breath at the recognition, and she gave me a sharp glance. And when I looked at Willie, I knew he'd noticed them, too.

Chas dropped the necklace and Mathilda quickly stepped back, pausing at the threshold as if wondering if it would be worse to run away or stay.

Chas turned on Sarah Beth with a leer. "Well, well. Can't say I'm surprised to hear you're a nigger lover. I've heard things about you. From somebody who ran one of them stills up by the Ellis plantation."

Willie threw himself at Chas, knocking them both over and making the radio wobble. I held my breath, unable to do anything except wait for something horrible to happen. Sarah Beth had gone completely white, the ash at the end of her cigarette threatening to drop onto Aunt Louise's rug.

They scuffled on the floor, drunken blows flying and most of them missing. Willie managed to drag Chas up by his collar and pull him toward his face so he could shout at him, spittle flying, "Don't you say that about the woman I'm going to marry. You hear? Don't you say that! Those people at Ellis were white trash, pure and simple. They'd say anything to make a well-bred lady look bad. You hear?"

He shook Chas, then threw him back into my aunt's chair, landing him on the seat. "Get out," Willie said.

Chas swiped at his cut lip with the sleeve of his jacket. "I'm sorry. It was only a joke. She just made me mad, is all."

"Get out," Willie said again, taking a step toward his friend.

Chas backed up a step. "But I don't have my car. . . ."

"Get out," Willie shouted again, shoving him in the chest. "Get out of my house and I don't want to see your face here again."

Chas stumbled toward the front door and I heard him fall as he reached the porch, and then nothing more. I imagined he'd passed out where he fell and would walk home as soon as he awoke, or Uncle Joe would have to load him into his truck and drive him.

Willie glanced back at Sarah Beth and then at me. With a sickly smile, he said to Sarah Beth, "Nice earrings. I don't remember buyin' those for you."

Sarah Beth sucked in her breath. "You didn't. My father bought them for me. An early birthday present."

He stared at her for a long moment, then managed to make it to the steps. "I'm going to bed. G'night, ladies." He hoisted himself up each step, leaning heavily on the banister.

Neither of us said anything as we watched him until he reached the top.

"I'm going home." Sarah Beth grabbed her fur and headed for the door.

I ran to catch up with her. "Wait, please. What was Chas saying? About the people we saw. He meant Leon and Velma, didn't he?"

"You heard what Willie said, how they're all trash and the Klan did a good deed when they cleaned them out. Good riddance."

"Then why did you lie about the necklace? We both know where that came from, and you didn't give it to her."

She was standing very close to me, and when she spoke, her breath was hot and smelled like cigarettes, making me want to gag. "Don't ask questions you don't want to hear the answers to."

She tugged open the door, then left, emerald earrings swinging. When I turned back around, Mathilda was gone, Sarah Beth's words lying heavily on the air.

Chapter 41

Vivien Walker Moise
INDIAN MOUND, MISSISSIPPI
MAY 2013

Brushing my hands against my apron, I peeked into the dining room, where my mother and Cora were busy setting the table. Mathilda was joining us for supper, along with Tripp, who would be in charge of getting Mathilda here from Sunset Acres. I counted the place settings, allowing myself to smile when I realized that once again Carol Lynne had included a setting for Bootsie. Just like Bootsie had done for her all those years my mother had been gone. I'd never thought to ask, but I wondered if they'd done the same thing for me and imagined they probably had.

Tonight was the night of the dance, and I hadn't seen Chloe all afternoon as she'd been primping. I'd brought Carol Lynne up to Chloe's room to help with her hair, and she'd stayed for over an hour before she came back down. When I'd asked her how it was going, she'd already forgotten.

The three of us had gone to Hamlin's, as promised, and after a few tussles with Chloe as to what she should try on, Carol Lynne had intervened and pulled clothes off of racks. Chloe actually agreed to not only hold the hangers but to put the clothes on her body. She'd ended up with an eclectic mix of seventies throwbacks and lots of bright colors, but I didn't care as long as they fit, were age-appropriate, and weren't grungy T-shirts and black jeans.

I even managed to find a couple pairs of respectable shorts for me, and I made my mother try on a pair, too, thinking they'd be cooler for her to wear than jeans in the summertime. We stood staring at our reflections in the mirror, at our identical hair and eyes and matching grins.

"Your legs sure are pretty, Vivien."

I looked down at her legs, which didn't look like they belonged on a sixty-seven-year-old woman. "I guess I know where I got them from. You could win a swimsuit competition with those."

She laughed so hard that Chloe stuck her head into the dressing room to see what all the commotion was about, and she started laughing, too, just because.

On a whim, I'd suggested getting a hair trim—which Chloe agreed to only after Carol Lynne promised that with her shorter bangs and evened-out length she'd still be able to wear it in a French braid.

As I stepped back into the foyer, I saw Chloe coming down the stairs looking so beautiful I had to press my hands against my mouth so she couldn't see my lips trembling as I tried not to cry. She was wearing a new pair of bell-bottom jeans and a beautiful, flowing floral blouse with a scooped neck and scalloped hem. Her hair was French-braided, and there wasn't a sign of thick black eyeliner or red lips anywhere.

She stood on the bottom step, watching me, biting her bottom lip, the dog sitting at her side while both of them waited for me to speak.

"You look amazing, Chloe. I love what my mother did to your hair."

"She did my makeup, too. She had to keep asking me how old I was. I guess she didn't want to put too much on."

"She did a terrific job—I can see your beautiful eyes now. But she had a great canvas, too. And you're really rocking those clothes. Good choices."

"Whatever," she said, stepping past me, but not until I'd seen her smile. "I'm going to grab a snack before I go to the party. I'm starving and I don't want to stuff my face when I get there."

I silently patted myself on the back for teaching her that little gem and followed her into the kitchen. I'd been slicing carrots and celery and keeping them in handy plastic bags in the fridge for easy snacking, and I watched with satisfaction as she reached in and grabbed a handful of carrots.

With her mouth full—something I still needed to work on—she said, "I already met a friend who's going to be at the dance tonight. Her name's Wendy. She went on a field trip to the B. B. King museum with me and Mrs. Smith. She likes to read, too, and so we traded some books. Have you read *The Hunger Games*?"

I was too happy that she'd made a friend to point out that I hadn't known she liked to read until she'd discovered the shelf in my room, and that the books she'd lent to her new friend were actually mine. "I've heard of it, but haven't had a chance to read it. Maybe I can borrow it when you're done?"

"Sure. Or maybe we could read it together. That's what Wendy and her mom did, because there were some scary parts."

I kept my face neutral and resisted yet another urge to do a fist pump. "That sounds great."

She put a few more carrots into her mouth and said, "I need to show you something in the garden."

"Sure," I said as she picked up her gardening journal from the kitchen table. She surprised me by grabbing my hand, then leading me outside, where tiny shoots were sticking out of the dark earth like green spaghetti. "This one isn't growing," she said, squatting down in the back corner of her little plot.

I knelt next to her, and saw not even a small tip of green emerging from the spot. I looked around and grabbed a stick, then began gently scraping away the top layer.

"I thought you said we weren't allowed to help them poke through the dirt," she said.

"Technically, no. If we've done everything right they should just shoot up. But sometimes," I said as my scraping revealed a tiny glimpse of green, "our babies need a little nudge to get them going." I continued to scrape away until the tiny sprout was sticking out above the soil.

I sat back on my heels. "There," I said. "It should be fine now."

She was busy writing in her journal, her face pinched in concentration.

"Is that part of your grade?"

She shook her head. "No—Mrs. Smith just checks to make sure that we're keeping up with it. But I thought maybe I could do a vegetable garden back home and that these notes could help me."

I thought of her not here, tending a garden without me, and my chest felt hollow, a barren field in winter.

"Are you okay? Your freckles look darker."

I smiled, liking the way she said I was pale. "Yeah, I'm fine." We both turned our heads at the sound of a car driving up out front.

I took the journal from Chloe and tucked a stray hair behind her ear. "That's probably Mr. Smith. I've got your ticket money on the hall table—come on." Cora's husband would be driving the homeschooled kids and chaperoning the dance. I'd offered to move the supper with Mathilda, but Cora had said that she was just fine missing an entire evening spent with a bunch of middle schoolers.

I'd made it to the kitchen door before I realized that Chloe wasn't behind me. Turning around, I saw her looking at the cypress tree, her eyes narrowed. "You should plant another one in the same place. I mean, it was here for so long that it doesn't seem right that it's gone. Where are you going to sit with your kids and grandkids if there's no tree there?"

"Good point," I said, not really understanding her logic, but seeing how empty the backyard seemed. How somebody returning home might not recognize it.

Chloe said good-bye to Cora and my mother—the latter asking her where she was going for the third time—and then I walked her out to the front porch, where Cora's husband, Bill, was waiting in the car with three other girls about Chloe's age. One of them squealed when she saw Chloe, and I figured it had to be Wendy. She opened the back door and moved over on the bench seat, patting the vacated spot next to her. "Sit here—I want to talk about *Time at the Top*."

Chloe leaned down to hug the dog and scratch him behind the ears. "I'll be back soon."

As if he understood, he trotted to the porch and lay down by one of the rockers, where I knew he'd stay until Chloe returned.

"Thanks, Bill—I owe you," I said, leaning into the open window.

"And I'll hold you to it," he said with a laugh.

He waited to back up as Tripp's car pulled into the drive, then moved to park in front of him.

"Make good choices!" I called out, only half joking, and knowing Chloe heard me when I saw her roll her eyes.

Tripp had stepped out of his car and was helping Mathilda from the passenger seat, and I understood why he'd brought the car instead of his truck. It practically took a pole-vaulter to get in and out of the pickup.

" 'Make good choices'?" he said as I approached.

I shrugged. "I didn't know what else to say. I heard it in a Lindsay Lohan movie once."

He raised an eyebrow. "And see how well that worked."

Ignoring him, I turned toward the car. "Hello, Mathilda. May I help you out?"

"Thanks, but I've got it," Tripp said. He let his gaze rest on my lips for a moment, and I blushed, remembering the last time I'd seen him, when he'd kissed me. And I'd kissed him back.

Tripp held one of Mathilda's arms while she walked, her other hand leaning heavily on a cane. She wore slip-on athletic shoes with little white socks, her ankles so thin it looked like they might snap if she stepped down too hard. The two paused when they got to the bottom step, and I could tell that Tripp wanted to just pick her up—all eighty pounds of her—and lift her to the porch. Instead he waited patiently as he helped her negotiate each step.

When they made it across the threshold and into the foyer, it was as if the old house sighed in recognition, and I imagined the shadows welcoming back Mathilda, who had helped raise four generations of Walker women.

Cora rushed into the foyer to take over, kissing her grandmother's cheek and then removing her shawl before escorting her into the parlor. Which left Tripp and me alone.

"You're not going to run off or anything, are you?" he asked.

"Of course not. Why would I?"

"Oh, I don't know. Just seems to be your knee-jerk reaction when you start feeling hemmed in, is all."

Without responding, I turned my back on him and headed toward the parlor.

"Exactly like that," he said to my departing back.

"Can I get anybody something to drink?" I asked, ignoring him.

Cora scooted a chair up to her grandmother's. "You sit down here, Vivien; let me worry about that. I know you two have a lot of catching up to do."

I thanked her and sat down next to Mathilda, taking her hand in mine. "I'm glad to see you're feeling better and could come to supper."

She looked confused for a moment and then nodded. "Oh, yes, I'm feelin' much better. Even have a bit of an appetite."

Tripp, who'd come in and sat on the sofa, covered a cough with his hand, and I remembered how he'd compared her appetite to that of a horse.

"I'm glad to hear that. Cora and I have been cooking up a storm all day—all your favorites."

"And peanut-butter pie for dessert?" she asked.

"With whipped cream even. I used Bootsie's pie recipe, so although it most likely won't be just like hers, you might still enjoy it."

"I know I will," she said, patting my hand. "But first you want to hear my stories. I ain't gettin' any younger, so I guess I needs to start talkin'. That ol' Shipley woman—she already asks me things, but I don' like her, so I pretends I don' remember nothing. But I likes you, Vivien. I likes you a lot."

I raised my eyebrows and met Tripp's amused gaze.

We made small talk about the weather, and a little gossip about the nurses at Sunset Acres, and how everybody was excited that a male resident—a rarity in nursing homes—had recently moved in. He still had his own teeth—another rarity—and was fought over on bingo night for the various all-girl teams.

I waited for a lull in the conversation before I decided to bring up the questions that had been running through my mind all day. "I don't know if Cora told you, but we're pretty sure of the identity of the body found in our yard."

She tilted her head, her sightless eyes staring at something I couldn't see.

"We believe it was my great-grandmother Adelaide. Bootsie's mother."

She nodded, as if she wasn't surprised to hear it, and I was wondering if she'd understood.

I pressed on. "Adelaide was supposed to have drowned during the flood of 1927. But it now appears she didn't."

Cora entered and brought us glasses of sweet tea and lemon, pressing a napkin-covered glass with a straw into her grandmother's hands.

I waited for her to take a sip before asking my first question. "Did you know Adelaide?"

Mathilda nodded. "Everybody know Miss Adelaide. She just a little bit older than me. Sweet girl. Kindhearted." She leaned down to take a sip of her tea from the straw. "I works for Mr. Heathman—he the president of the bank. I works for the family, and Miss Adelaide she be friendly with the Heathman girl. That how I knows her."

I sat back, confused. "But I thought you worked for my family."

She looked in my direction, doing an exact imitation of Carol Shipley when I asked if I could take those newspapers home with me. "Let me finish my story. When Miss Adelaide had her baby, Miss Bootsie, I lives with her here in this house to take care of they both. I stays on when Miss Adelaide got drowned, to help Mrs. Bodine—that be Adelaide's aunt—raise Miss Bootsie. I never did go back to the Heathmans on account of them losing everythin' in the crash."

"S. B. Heathman—is that their daughter?" I asked, remembering the name in the news accounts of Adelaide's disappearance, as well as from the wedding announcement.

"Sarah Beth. They was best friends they whole lives. But Sarah Beth was as wild as Adelaide was sweet. Maybe that's why they was friends. She settled down, though. After she got married and had her baby. Became a proper churchgoer, she did. Even ran a soup kitchen from her own home until her daddy killed hisself and the bank took the house."

I closed my eyes, trying to remember where I'd seen the Heathman name besides the newspapers. It seemed important, somehow, but I couldn't remember other than that it had been recently.

My mother entered the room and Tripp stood and offered his seat, but she sat down at Mathilda's feet, and the old woman reached for her hair, stroking it. She hadn't needed to ask who it was, as if they were both fifty years younger, and Carol Lynne was sitting at her feet like she'd done as a girl.

Tripp leaned forward, his elbows on his knees, his hands clasped.

"Do you remember if Adelaide had any enemies—anybody who'd want to hurt her?"

Mathilda shook her head. "Not Miss Adelaide. She was an angel. Her husband, John, they was so in love made your heart hurt to see 'em. He was a real good man—he run the jewelry store on Main Street till he die. Such a nice man, an honest man—even though he was buyin' and sellin' liquor."

"He was a bootlegger?" I asked, surprised. Even I had no idea we had any skeletons in the family closet. Just one in the yard.

"In a way, yes. And he loved Adelaide more than I ever seen a man love his wife. But everybody loved her. And I never seen a mama love her baby so much as Miss Adelaide loved her Bootsie. Maybe Carol Lynne and the way she loved you and Tommy, but it was close."

I watched as the dark fingers stroked my mother's hair, and I wanted to tell her that she was wrong, that my mother had never loved anybody but herself. But I caught Tripp's eyes and something in them made me stop.

"The little ring she wore around her neck, do you remember that?" I held my breath, remembering the last time I'd mentioned it and how she'd feigned exhaustion. But maybe now—now that we knew it was Adelaide in the grave—she'd have no reason to hold back.

She leaned down to take a sip from her iced tea, then nodded. "Her husband, he made that for her. He gives the other one to Bootsie. I remember she cry happy tears when she show it to me. I went with her and the baby to get they picture taken. Bootsie lookin' at me in they photo."

I recalled Bootsie's face, how she was smiling at someone and pointing her finger, wearing the little ring.

"Do you know what happened to her ring? I've looked for it all over, and can't find it."

She sat back in her chair and sighed, her hand still stroking my mother's hair. "It been a long time. I don' think I can remember the last time I see it."

Tripp straightened. "When was the last time you saw Adelaide?"

The old woman laughed, her chest almost concave with the exertion of it. "I be an old woman and you expects a lot from this brain of mine. But I do remember seeing her the day she die. I remember it 'cause it the day the levee broke and the water started coming in." She was silent, her eyes moving back and forth as if she were watching a movie of the muddy waters of the Mississippi flooding the streets and houses.

"I remember later that day, when the water finally reach us up near the huntin' cabin on account of it bein' on high ground. The sound, you never heard such sound. Like a roar, and then theys people cryin' out and shoutin' and everybody runnin' for the higher ground. Mr. Bodine, that be Adelaide's uncle, he had it all planned so we be safe."

"But Adelaide and Bootsie didn't evacuate with the Bodines, right?" I asked.

"No. She got a phone call and said she had to go meet John. She took the baby with her; she ain't gonna be separated from her baby. And she knows she got an hour, maybe two, 'fore the water comes in."

Tripp cleared his throat. "And Sarah Beth? How did she get the baby? Because in the newspaper they say she was the last one to see Adelaide alive."

Mathilda didn't answer for a long moment, and I thought maybe she hadn't heard him.

"I don' know for sure, 'cept John never saw her again, and Sarah Beth just say Adelaide come to her house and gave her they baby, sayin' she gots to go to New Orleans in a hurry, and nothing Sarah Beth could say would stop her." Her old hand stopped moving and my mother lifted her head.

"And Bootsie had on the ring when she left with her mother?" Tripp asked.

"No," the old woman said. "I don' think she did."

An odd smile crossed my mother's face, making her look like a little girl caught doing something bad. She looked up at Mathilda, put her finger to her lips, and said, "Shhh."

Tripp leaned forward and grabbed a handful of peanuts from a dish on the coffee table. "So nobody would have wanted to hurt Adelaide, but we know that's not true, because she didn't bury herself under the tree." He popped the nuts into his mouth and chewed thoughtfully.

"No, there wasn't nobody," Mathilda said, her gaze directed at Tripp, and for a moment I thought she was trying to tell him something. And then I remembered she was blind.

I thought of the watch, and how Adelaide's husband said she'd been wearing it when she died. "When you last saw her, was she wearing her blue watch? The one her husband gave her?"

"Oh, yes. Never saw her without that or her necklace—'cept a few times she let Sarah Beth borrow it."

Tommy came in then, wearing a clean shirt and his hair wet at the hairline as if he'd just washed his face. He greeted Mathilda with a kiss on her cheek, then pulled my mother to her feet. "Cora said supper's ready and we can get started."

He escorted my mother to the table while Tripp and I escorted Mathilda, her hand as delicate as a bird's foot perched on my arm. We sat her at the place of honor at the head of the table, and listened as she identified all the food using her sense of smell—collard greens made with fatback, butter beans, fried okra, and pulled barbecue pork from the Hopson Commissary that I'd driven for more than an hour each way to get. She had some of everything, and I watched in amazement as she ate all that was on her plate and asked Cora for seconds of the candied yams that I had made using Bootsie's recipe. It came from the tattered and worn "receipt" box—that's what she'd called it—that had been used for generations of the women in my family. I'd thought of it often while I'd been away, how Bootsie knew them all by heart but used the recipe anyway, and was already thinking about how I should pull out the crumbling recipes and digitize them for future generations. Assuming there would be any.

I found I had no appetite, my mind too full of everything Mathilda had said, of my great-grandfather being a bootlegger, and how Adelaide had been wearing the watch the last time Mathilda had seen her on the day she'd died.

My mind drifted away from the conversation Mathilda and Tripp were having about the food, and how she liked the new pastor at her church. I looked down at the watch, twisting it slowly on my arm. Where was the ring? We already had the watch, but why had it been in Emmett's box?

I looked up to find Tommy watching me. "Not hungry?"

"Not really. And I want to make sure that Mathilda doesn't leave hungry."

I smiled as I looked over at Cora dipping another spoonful of candied yams onto her grandmother's plate.

He grinned, then pointed his chin at my watch. "If you want, I can see if I can make it work, though if it was in Emmett's box he probably already tried."

"Sure—thanks." I took it off my wrist, then slid it across the table toward him.

We finished the meal while Mathilda asked me about Chloe and what I'd been doing in the last ten years, and I told her without going into any of the thorny details. We talked about her grandkids and great-grandkids, and even the price of cotton.

After we'd cleared the dessert dishes and packed several Tupperware containers with leftovers for her to take back with her, Tripp announced it was time for them to leave, because he was too old to stay up late.

Cora settled her shawl around her shoulders, and then Tripp and I escorted her back to the car. I buckled her seat belt around her, then kissed her cheek. "Thanks so much for coming. I hope you got enough to eat."

She patted the stack of Tupperware on her lap. "Not to worry. I gots these if I get hungry in the middle of the night."

I laughed and pulled back, but she touched my arm. "You done chasin' ghosts?"

I remembered what my mother had said when we'd visited Mathilda at Sunset Acres. *She's been chasing ghosts.*

"I don't . . ." I stammered. "I don't understand."

"Good night, Vivien. We talks some more later."

I stood. "We will," I said. "And I'll remember to bring food," I said to the closed door.

I stopped to pet the dog on my way in, then moved to the kitchen to help Cora with the dishes. My hands were deep in dirty water when I recalled where I'd seen the Heathman name.

Quickly drying my hands, I pulled Mrs. Shipley's book off from the top of the refrigerator, where I'd stashed it. Tommy walked in, reaching into the cookie jar despite the huge meal he'd just eaten. He was as slim as a boy, yet ate everything in sight. It wasn't fair.

I placed the book on the counter and opened it, the pages falling open to my family tree.

"What is it?" Tommy asked, a cookie crumb dropping on the page.

I wiped it off, my finger running down the lines of the tree. "I remembered where I saw the Heathman name—it's on our family tree." My finger stopped. "Right here."

He leaned down and read out loud. " 'Sarah Beth Heathman Bodine. Married William Henry Bodine May 1927; son Emmett John Bodine born November 1927.' "

"She was Emmett's mother. Adelaide's best friend married her cousin, William, and their son was Emmett. I wonder why Mathilda didn't mention it."

"Maybe because she figured we already knew that. Or not." He reached into the jar and grabbed another cookie. "Sarah Beth as in the same Sarah Beth who was the last person to see Adelaide alive?"

"Yep." I nodded as he chewed, dropping more crumbs on the page.

"That's not all," he said, eyeing the family tree again.

"What?"

He tapped his finger on Emmett's name. "Looks like Sarah Beth and William had a shotgun wedding."

"What do you mean?" I asked, staring down at the page, not sure I knew what he was pointing at.

"Emmett was born only six months after they were married."

"Wow. You're right." I stared at it for a few moments, wondering if it meant anything besides two people not wanting to wait until their wedding night.

Tommy grabbed another cookie, then left the kitchen. I closed the book and returned to the dishes, glad to have something to keep my hands occupied as my brain ran in circles. I brought the book out with me onto the porch to wait for Chloe, the dog happy to keep me company.

I rocked in the chair, trying to read the history of Indian Mound, to channel my thoughts, but I kept returning to my conversation with Mathilda as she'd left, and wondering what she'd meant about chasing ghosts.

Chapter 42

Adelaide Walker Bodine Richmond
INDIAN MOUND, MISSISSIPPI
APRIL 2, 1927

I sat underneath the cypress tree, reading a novel and enjoying the cool breeze and a rare day without rain. I could feel the moisture creeping through the blanket, the water no longer far from the earth's surface. Here in the delta we were used to the river's vagaries, how for years it would flow where the farmer wanted it to, slipping dutifully between the levees like a snake, waiting for its moment to strike. We were due for a major flood. We just didn't know when.

Bootsie sat in her carriage, playing with her little feet the way babies do. I'd given up on putting shoes on her, as she always pulled them off. I had enough blankets tucked around her to keep her warm, and she didn't seem to mind the breeze on her bare toes. The cool wind made her laugh and show off her new tooth, and dried the drool on her chubby chin. Even while teething, Bootsie had remained cheerful and content, making me feel as if I must be the best mother ever.

I caught a movement from the back of the house. Mathilda stood at the kitchen door, watching as a figure approached me, walking quickly. I couldn't tell immediately who it was, or recognize the hurried gait.

But I could tell from Mathilda's wringing hands that it was an unwelcome visitor.

I stood, relaxing only as I recognized Angelo Berlini. But my smile fell as he came nearer, and I saw that the man approaching me wasn't the Angelo I'd come to know. He was dressed only in shirtsleeves and a vest, his trademark fedora discarded along with his jacket and tie. His usually neatly combed hair fell over his forehead, and when he stopped in front of me, his black eyes burned. Perspiration dotted his upper lip despite the cooler temperature, and I noticed that the corded muscles of his exposed forearms were covered in dark hair. He looked dangerous, and I quickly stepped between him and the baby carriage.

"Good morning, Angelo. I'm sorry, but John's not here. . . ."

He shook his head impatiently. "I didn't come here to see John. I needed to speak with you."

My mouth had suddenly grown dry and I had to try two times to speak. "Would you like to come inside for a glass of tea or lemonade—"

He cut me off. "There's no time. I've been driving all night. And I have to go back to New Orleans right away so nobody knows I've gone. What I have to tell you can't be said over a phone. There are ears everywhere."

I placed my hand on the handle of the baby carriage. "Angelo, you're scaring me."

"Good. Because I can't seem to scare your husband enough to make him listen. That's why I needed to speak with you. Did John tell you that he's stopped working for me?"

I sucked in a lungful of cool air. I wanted to deny it, to tell him that we had no secrets in our marriage and that John told me everything. But I was a terrible liar, my face always giving me away.

"I didn't think so," he said softly. "He's made some people very upset, the kind of people you don't want to anger. I'm doing what I can, but I might not be able to help him now. You need to leave this place just for a little while, until things settle down."

I glanced over at Bootsie, who was showing her dimples to Angelo, reaching toward him to get him to lift her into his arms. "How much time do we have?"

"Not much. John said he has family in Missouri. I've already started working on arrangements to get you safely there, and I'll transfer some funds so you'll have something to live on at first. You just need to promise me that you'll start preparing to leave now. But you can't tell anyone. Do you understand? Not your aunt and uncle or even Sarah Beth. You will put them in danger if they know anything."

I picked up Bootsie, holding her close, needing to feel her safe against me.

He continued. "I know how much you love you husband and your daughter, and how you want to keep them safe. So do as I say and everything will be fine."

"But what should I tell John?"

"Nothing. Yet. Don't tell him I've been here—not until you hear back from me with the arrangements."

I shook my head. "I can't lie to my husband."

"Even if it's to save his life? And your life? And the life of your baby?"

I clenched my eyes, wishing I could tell him no, but I knew he was right.

He softened his voice. "You and I both know it's best if he doesn't have time to think about all of this. Your husband is a very stubborn man, Adelaide, and you're the only one I know who can get through to him."

"He asked me before if I would move to Missouri, and I said no. He stayed because of me."

Angelo reached up and touched Bootsie's cheek, making her smile. "You were thinking of your daughter, and didn't understand the dangers. But now you do, and you know it will be temporary. Prohibition will be defeated, if not in the next election, then the one after that. None of this will matter anymore, and you and your family will come back."

Bootsie leaned toward Angelo and he lifted her from my arms, closing his eyes for a moment and breathing in her sweet baby scent, his smile erasing years from his face.

"Why are you doing this, Angelo? If you had to sneak away to warn us, then you could be putting yourself in danger. Why would you risk it?"

His black eyes softened as he regarded me. "Because you are one of the truly good people in this ugly world that tries its hardest to erase all good. But your love for family and home shines light into even the darkest corners. Like my sister before life beat her down and stomped her out. That's why."

Before I even knew what I was doing, I leaned forward and kissed him on his cheek. "I don't know if I agree, but thank you."

He looked down at Bootsie, who was trying to chew on her baby ring that had just begun to fit her. Angelo took her little hand in his, and gently tugged off her ring. "I'm going to take this with me. I probably won't be able to come back, so I'll send somebody I trust as a messenger with instructions. He'll show you this ring so you'll know the message is from me."

I nodded. "All right." I gave him a halfhearted smile.

We both looked up at a sudden rustling from the tree above us. Oily black crows sat four in a row on three limbs, their large round eyes staring at nothing. "Twelve crows," I said. "The old nursery rhyme only goes up to ten."

He looked at me with a confused expression.

"It's an old nursery rhyme that Mathilda sings to Bootsie." I hummed the tune at first, to help me remember the words, then began to recite them.

> *One for sorrow,*
> *two for mirth,*
> *three for a wedding,*
> *four for a birth,*
> *five for silver,*
> *six for gold,*
> *seven for a secret never to be told,*
> *eight for heaven,*
> *nine for hell,*
> *And ten for the devil's own self.*

"Not very cheerful for a nursery rhyme," he said.

"No, it's not. But none of them are. Even 'Ring around the Rosy' is about the plague."

He looked down at his hand, rolling Bootsie's ring between his large fingers. "I have to go now. Remember, don't tell anybody I was here, or that you're getting ready to leave. Wait until you hear from me. Wait until my messenger shows you this ring." He paused, his eyes looking steadily into mine. "If John is in imminent danger I will let you know, so be prepared to leave at a moment's notice."

I nodded. "I will."

"Good-bye, Adelaide. I hope we see each other again soon in happier circumstances."

"Me, too," I said, hugging Bootsie closer to me. "And thank you."

I watched him walk away toward the side of the house and the front drive. I almost called after him to ask him why he'd given Sarah Beth the emerald earrings instead of his fiancée, but I kept hearing Sarah Beth's words: *Don't ask questions you don't want to hear the answers to.*

I watched him until he rounded the corner of the house out of sight. A fluttering of wings forced my gaze upward as seven of the birds flew down from the tree and into the sodden yard, looking for the worms flooded out of their homes by the constant rains. The sky had gone suddenly dark, heavy rain clouds erasing the sun.

I tossed my book into the baby carriage and, while carrying Bootsie, began to run toward the house, rolling the carriage behind me. The first fat drops of rain began to fall as I made it to the back porch, only noticing the figure watching me from the doorway when I'd reached the bottom step.

It was my cousin, Willie, and I wanted to ask him what he was doing home in the middle of a workday, but didn't. There was something in his expression that stopped me, that made me feel as if people were walking over my grave. We stood staring at each other for a long moment as the rain began to pelt the soft earth and the metal roof of the porch. And before I could ask him to bring up the carriage, he'd walked back into the kitchen, letting the screen door slam in my face.

❦

APRIL 14, 1927

I waited for almost two weeks to hear back from Angelo. Two weeks of nearly sleepless nights and tense meals. Even Bootsie grew restless, and I wondered if mothers could ever hide their emotions from their children. I told no one about Angelo's visit, not even my husband. It seemed we were both good at keeping secrets from each other. John was too distracted to notice that Bootsie's ring was missing, but Mathilda did, and asked me about it. I told her that it was still too big and I'd put it away until Bootsie had grown a little more. But I recalled Mathilda watching Angelo and me when I gave him the ring, and suspected she knew I was lying. I rarely saw Willie, and when I did he barely spoke to me and never mentioned Angelo at all.

John went to the jewelry shop each day, the tension between us making our kisses brittle. The only thing that made me allow John to leave my side was Angelo's promise that he would let me know if my husband was in imminent danger. We seemed to all be dancing on a precipice of our own making, unaware of the hazards if we missed a step.

I began to fill two suitcases with clothing and other necessities— mine, Bootsie's, and John's—not taking enough to be noticed, but enough that would sustain us after a sudden departure. I found Mathilda in the nursery once, opening all the dresser drawers and searching for a particular bonnet. I told her that Bootsie had lost it during an outing. But from the look on Mathilda's face it was obvious that my skills at lying had not improved with use. For once I was happy for John's distraction, knowing that was the only reason he didn't notice my mood or question why his supply of socks had dwindled.

We all watched the rain continue to fall, the sweet gums and loblolly pines all leaning over like old men burdened by life. The farmers kept one eye on their crops still growing on their highest ground and not yet underwater, and another eye trained on the levees, where the mighty Mississippi flicked its muddy tongue, threatening to find a way through.

On Thursday morning, nearly two weeks to the day since I'd seen Angelo, I was sitting at the dining table, having breakfast with John, with Aunt Louise in the kitchen making more eggs. Uncle Joe had ridden out to see what was left of his crops after a heavy night of rain, and Willie had just come in for a cup of coffee before heading out to the bank. It was unusual for him to be there that late in the morning, as he usually preferred to have his breakfast and coffee with Mr. Heathman downtown.

Uncle Joe had left the morning paper folded up and unread on the server, having left before sunup with no time to read it. Willie flopped down into Uncle Joe's chair and opened the newspaper to the front page and kept it there, slowly sipping his coffee, his eyes scanning the page.

"Well, lookee here," he said. "Isn't that a friend of yours, John?"

He slid the paper over so John could look at it. John's face paled, coffee sloshing out of his cup as he set it down hard.

"What is it?" I asked, putting down my fork.

He didn't respond, didn't even seem to have heard me.

I glanced at Willie, hoping he'd be able to provide more information, but froze. He was smiling: a smug, self-satisfied smile that stilled the blood in my veins.

"What is it, John?" I asked again, louder this time.

He looked up at me, his eyes empty, his face even paler. "Angelo Berlini. He was found dead last night. In the pond at the Ellis plantation."

I sat back in my chair, my hand pressed against my heart to keep it from beating out of my chest. "Drowned?" I asked, feeling sick to my stomach, and wondering why Angelo would have been in Indian Mound, and why he hadn't contacted me.

"Appears so." John's eyes met Willie's across the table. His voice was thick when he spoke again. "It says here that he must have been there fishing and slipped in."

The thought of Angelo Berlini in his fedora and expensive suit fishing in the pond at the Ellis plantation was almost laughable. "But . . ."

John looked at me and gave me a quick shake of his head. I fell silent.

"Was anyone with him?" Willie asked, a smile behind his question. He took a sip of coffee to hide it.

John just stared at him, not answering.

I reached over and slid the paper toward me, seeing the photograph of a smiling Angelo in white tie at a party. Carmen stood beside him, decked in jewels, tall and elegant. My eyes slid over the article, reading what John had already said, then stopped. *Mr. Berlini appears not to have been alone, as fresh tire tracks from vehicles other than his own were discovered nearby. An anonymous source stated that the area was well-known by illegal moonshiners, who might have seen something or even have been involved in Mr. Berlini's death, but so far no one has stepped forward to corroborate that story. Mr. Berlini was a New Orleans businessman with ties to several area businesses. Repeated calls to his fiancée, Miss Carmen Bianca, daughter of Louisiana senatorial candidate Louis Bianca, have been unreturned as of this printing.*

My hands were shaking so badly that I had to put the newspaper down. How could Angelo be dead? I wasn't naive enough to believe that it had been an accident. Had it been the same people Angelo had been trying to protect us against? Had they found out that he'd tried to warn us? I needed to speak with John, but I had to wait until we were alone.

The door to the dining room swung open. "Look who's just had a bath," Mathilda said, holding a smiling and damp-haired Bootsie. Mathilda stopped in the threshold when she saw Willie, as surprised as I had been that he was there. I stood, eager to have my child in my arms, somehow the weight of her making all seem right in the world even when everything was off-kilter.

"Thank you, Mathilda. I'll take her. If you could go ahead and hang her laundry in the kitchen today—I'm afraid nothing's going to get dried outside."

She nodded, but I saw her gaze settling on Angelo's photograph in the paper, and then moving to the headline. I knew she could read, that she'd gone to the colored school until she was twelve, and I watched as her gaze moved upward and settled on Willie.

We all turned at the sound of the front door opening, and then Uncle Joe was standing behind Mathilda, his hat dripping from his hands. He was drenched through his overcoat, and his shoes were darkened with water. He shivered with cold, and I could tell he was clenching his teeth together to keep them from chattering. I handed the baby back to Mathilda so I could pour him a cup of coffee.

"Willie, John. I need you to go change your clothes and come with me. All able-bodied men are being asked to start sandbagging just in case there's a crevasse in the levee. It won't do no good, but this way we can all feel like we're doing something. But I'm on the levee guard and I have to do what I'm told."

I gave my uncle his coffee and he nodded with appreciation. John stood, the newspaper forgotten for now. Willie rose more slowly, and I expected him to argue, but instead he left the room to go change, telling his father he'd be back shortly.

Aunt Louise entered the dining room with a steaming plate of eggs meant for John, and began fussing at Uncle Joe for dripping on her rug. "Stop it, woman," he said, but I could tell he was more distracted than annoyed. "Are those eggs for me?"

With an apologetic glance at John, she set the plate in front of her husband, then helped him shuck his overcoat before he sat down. With his mouth full of eggs, he said, "I need you women to listen for the fire whistle. That means there's a crevasse and you need to head toward high ground just like we talked about. Don't wait. The water's so high right now that if there's a break, it's going to rush through here like Niagara Falls. Depending on where the break is, we could have three hours or less than thirty minutes to evacuate."

I nodded, hugging Bootsie close to me, the possibility of a flood becoming a reality for me. I'd been so distracted by other concerns that the more imminent threat of the river bursting through the levees had completely passed me by.

John turned to leave, and I followed him upstairs, waiting until the door was shut behind us. Without speaking, he took us in his arms, and the three of us stood there in the middle of the room feeling one another's warmth.

"Angelo . . ."

"I know," he said, kissing my forehead, and then Bootsie's.

"Who would have killed him?"

He shook his head. "I don't know."

"John, we need to leave Indian Mound. Angelo came to see me, before. . . . He told me that we needed to leave right away, and that he would help make arrangements. . . ."

John pulled back, his eyes questioning. "You didn't tell me."

"No, I didn't. But he told me that you'd quit, and that you were in danger and we needed to go away for a while. He was planning on getting us to Missouri. And he didn't want me to tell you until the last minute, because you're stubborn and would have fought it if you'd had time to consider it. Only, I never heard back from him." I clenched my eyes shut. "What if he was killed because he tried to warn us?"

"You can't think that way, Adelaide. Angelo's dead and we can't bring him back." He closed his eyes and exhaled deeply. "But he was right. I would have fought to stay. After I'd made the split with him, and even though I'd tried to get you to move to Missouri before, I don't think even you could have persuaded me." He moved to the window and looked out at the flooded fields and sodden yard. "As soon as I get back from sandbagging, we'll make our plans to leave for Missouri. But just for a while, all right? Just for a while."

"I'm afraid, John."

He turned around and touched my watch. "I love you forever, remember? We'll get through this, and when we're old and gray with Bootsie's children on our knees, we'll look back and remember how strong we were together."

He hurriedly changed his clothes, then kissed Bootsie on her nose and cheeks before kissing me deeply. "I love my girls," he said, his old smile on his face again.

"We love you, too," I said.

We watched the men leave on horseback—the mud too thick for trucks where they were heading—from the bedroom window, but even as I waved good-bye, I kept thinking of the last time I'd seen Angelo Berlini alive, and of the seven black crows that had flown out of the cypress, their oily feathers shining dully in the gloom.

Chapter 43

Vivien Walker Moise
INDIAN MOUND, MISSISSIPPI
JUNE 2013

On a night about a week after Mathilda's visit, I was doing another nocturnal wandering through the house, listening to the way it breathed at night, the sighs of the rafters and the creaks of its old floors like ghosts passing by. As a child, I'd thought the creaks were a memory of the muddy water that had filled the first floor during the flood, like a baptism to ward off future disaster. Until the body had been found under the tree, it seemed to have worked.

My mind was full of what Mathilda had said: how Adelaide had been beloved, and how she in turn had loved her husband and daughter. How nobody had wanted to harm her. Yet the fact remained that she'd been presumed drowned, yet had somehow been buried in her own yard, her story buried with her for more than eight decades. I kept seeing her face from the wedding photo and the studio photo with Bootsie, her eyes seeming to be asking me a question. I knew what the question was. I just wasn't sure if I wanted to know the answer. What if, by finding out the truth, I'd finally have to confront the past we'd all clung to, a belief that would disintegrate like a dandelion in a strong wind? Then who would I be, and how would I justify my life thus far?

I thought of Adelaide's friend Sarah Beth, Emmett's mother. She'd been pregnant when she'd married Adelaide's cousin. Back then it would have been quite the scandal. I hadn't returned several of the newspapers when I'd gone to sort through and organize the archives. I'd bring them back—just not yet. But I had decided to keep the photo of Bootsie, tucking it into the album from where it had been taken, knowing that was where it belonged. I just wasn't ready to give back the newspaper containing the wedding photo of Adelaide and Sarah Beth together. Wondering what secrets they'd shared. What secrets they'd kept.

I passed the attic door. I'd yet to go up there to search for the ring. Tripp had promised to help, but I hadn't seen much of him since he'd brought Mathilda for supper. He'd called, but I'd let the calls go to voice mail. I knew without listening to them that it would be empty air, him just waiting for me to speak. But I had nothing to say. No plans made, and I was afraid that my feelings for him weren't as innocent as I'd once believed. I knew I'd hurt him once, and I was in no hurry to do it again.

I didn't worry about what I might find in the attic, because I knew there was no rush. Finding the ring there wouldn't tell me anything—not how it had been removed from Bootsie's finger, or who had done it. Maybe she'd simply lost it, an easy enough thing to do, and it had long since been buried in the yard, or accidentally discarded.

I stepped out into the garden, a waxing moon with its clever smile looking down on me, its angle in the sky making it seem as if it had asked me a question. And was waiting for an answer. All of Chloe's plants were thriving, and soon it would be time to start harvesting them, before the vegetables got too big and pulled the plants over. The hardest thing would be getting her to eat the lima beans, especially cooking them with fatback. Cora said she had some great healthy recipes she'd share with us, and as long as the idea came from Cora, I had no doubt we'd be happily eating lima bean soup and lima bean salads.

We still had plenty of time to grow more summer vegetables, and maybe even a few flowers for all of Bootsie's empty pots. I'd already started thinking about what we'd plant in the fall, but had stopped when I realized that I might not still be here, and Chloe probably wouldn't either. I'd been unable to think beyond that. It seemed that years of inertia had stolen my forward momentum, my ability to want something enough to make a plan. During the seven months of my pregnancy I'd made concrete plans, thought ahead as to the life my baby would have, and the marriage and family life I wanted to build. But ever since my miscarriage I'd been walking up a down escalator, keeping busy while getting nowhere. Even without the pills, I couldn't seem to push my thoughts forward.

The light was on in Tommy's workshop, and I pictured him with the blue enamel watch, examining the tiny pieces with his patient hands. I'd always loved that about him: his ability to take his time to get things right. He was that way with his fields, too. Waiting for the right moment to plant, even when his neighbors had already jumped aboard and started planting. Except for his love life, his patience had always proved right. Even the way he'd always promised us that our mother would one day be coming home for good.

My cell phone rang, the sound incongruous in the sleeping garden. I'd brought it with me to keep track of the time, telling myself that I needed to stop my wandering by three in the morning. As if I could fool my body into thinking it had to be asleep by three-oh-five. Sometimes it even actually worked.

Mark's name appeared on the screen and I felt suddenly cold. But I'd known it would be him as soon as the phone rang. Nobody else would call me with no regard to the time of day.

"Hello, Mark," I said, not bothering to lower my voice, since I was away from the house, and the drone of the air conditioner would block out any noise.

His voice sounded chipper—happy, even—two words I wouldn't have immediately used to describe my ex-husband. He also sounded as if he'd been awake for hours. "Good afternoon, Vivien." I heard what sounded like an announcement on an intercom in the background.

"Where are you?"

"Funny you should ask, since that's why I'm calling. We've decided to cut our honeymoon short. Actually, Tiffany has. She's been feeling a little homesick and wants to come home and do some nesting."

I thought I could feel my heart slowing its beat. "Nesting?"

I could hear him grinning through the phone. "Yeah. We're expecting."

"Tiffany's pregnant?" I asked, not sure if I'd heard him correctly.

"That's right. I'm going to be a daddy." He actually sounded happy. "You're already a daddy, Mark. You have a daughter, remember?"

He couldn't even pretend to be embarrassed by his gaffe. "Yeah, well, this is the first baby I've wanted. We were actually trying to get pregnant. Just didn't think it would happen so fast."

I struck out blindly with my hand, unable to see past the red that seemed to be coating my vision, my womb tightening on its emptiness. My hand made contact with one of the green chairs and I fell into it.

"Okay." It was the only word I could think of. *Congratulations? How exciting?* It would be like throwing confetti at a funeral.

"'Okay'? Is that all you can say?"

I looked up at the sky and the questioning moon and somehow found the courage to respond with the truth. "Yes, Mark. It is. Because I wanted our baby. And you have a twelve-year-old daughter who never needs to know that you didn't want her."

The sound of blown air reached me. "Yeah. Like you can criticize my parenting. Like you're a contender for the mother-of-the-year award—you and your pill popping. What makes you think that all of a sudden you know how to be a good mother?"

Being here. The thought came to me in the warm breeze that swept across the fields and past the cypress trees and around the old house and into my garden. It brought with it the memory of Chloe and me on the Indian mound, staring up at the stars and listening to the night music, and an earlier memory with my mother in the same spot as she held my hand and said a prayer I couldn't hear.

"I don't know how to be a good mother, Mark. But I'm trying. I've been clean ever since you told me I needed to get clean to keep Chloe here." My voice was shaking and I prayed he couldn't tell.

"You know you only wanted Chloe to spite me. You've always been spiteful like that, Vivien."

I wanted to throw the phone as far as I could if it meant I never had to talk with him again, but I held on to it, knowing I needed it to move forward. If there was ever a moment for that, this was it.

I took a deep breath, remembering what I'd learned in my short-lived acting classes. I'd taken them after giving up my dreams of being a TV journalist, because I'd met Mark and he thought I should be in the movies. "I'm sorry, Mark. And you're right: I wanted Chloe here to make you mad. I'm sorry. That was wrong of me. But I'd like to ask you to allow Chloe—"

Mark cut me off as another announcement came over the intercom. "They're boarding first class, so I've got to go. I just wanted to let you know that we're flying directly to Atlanta and spending the night and then we'll fly to Mississippi to get Chloe."

Panic bubbled in my throat and I forced myself to keep calm. "But that's what I wanted to ask you—if Chloe—"

"Gotta go. I'll text you my flight information."

"But I'd like to discuss—"

Once again I was met with dead air. I wondered if he'd been like that when we'd been dating, or even in the early, heady days of our marriage. I didn't think so, because surely I wouldn't have married him. But I had. Despite what Tripp had said, that no one's past was written in stone, mine was. I had married badly, and still bore the scars to prove it and always would.

I ended the call, seeing the photo I'd put on my background screen: of Chloe and the unnamed dog in the middle of the cotton field on the day she'd spent with Tommy. He'd texted the photo to me along with "Does she always ask so many questions?" I'd almost laughed, because Chloe had once been so sullen that one day her total word count had been ten. When Tommy had brought her home and I'd asked her how it had gone, she said it hadn't sucked. But later, Tommy told me that she'd said it was one of the best days of her life.

The photo faded as the phone went black, and I recalled Tripp's words again. *Nobody's past is written in stone.* Yes, I'd married badly. But it had put Chloe in my life. Sweet, angry, lost, lovable, surly Chloe. She was all those things, and all the things that made me warm to her. Maybe that was what Tripp had meant. That no past mistake is unredeemable.

A soft sound, like sniffling, made me look up. I stood, wondering if there was some animal in the garden with me, and prepared to make a leap on top of the chair. But another sound, like a moan, told me that it was human, and my heart slammed against my chest when I realized it was Chloe when the white dog stepped out from behind her. If she'd been wearing the oversize white nightgown I would have seen her. But she wore the new navy blue nightshirt, the one with Justin Bieber's face plastered on the front, and she'd been almost completely hidden in her corner of the garden.

"Chloe," I said, walking carefully over to her, not wanting to crush any of the plants. "What are you doing out here?"

"Leave . . . me . . . alone," she said between sobs.

At the same moment I realized that she'd heard every word of my side of the phone conversation, I knew what she was doing in the garden in the middle of the night. She'd been tending her babies, making sure the deer and rabbits stayed away. I'd told her that I'd done that as a little girl, when the gate was broken on the enclosure and I hadn't wanted to lose any of my babies. That was what I'd called them, and she'd laughed.

"Chloe, sweetheart. What you heard . . ." In my mind, I went back over everything I'd said, and I cringed. I started again. "Chloe, your dad's on his way to come get you. But I wanted to ask him if you could stay here until school started, and then maybe come back for regular visits. . . ."

"Go away!" she screamed at me. She struggled to stand, stumbling into the middle of her garden plot, her foot landing on the newly sprouted plants. "That's not what you said. You don't want me here. You only did it to piss off my dad."

"No, Chloe. That's not it. If you'd just let me explain . . ."

But she'd already started her blind run from the garden and to the back of the house, the dog running after her. In the glow of the back porch light I watched as she paused to wipe her feet, something Carol Lynne and I did without thinking, thanks to Bootsie, and that one action cut my heart into a thousand little pieces.

I raced after her, reaching her bedroom door just as it slammed in my face. I knocked on it gently, calling her name, but all I could hear were her muffled sobs as she cried into her pillow. I sank to the floor and stayed there until morning, watching the sunlight steal through the windows and creep stealthily across the ancient wooden floors.

🌿

Chloe didn't come out of her room the entire day, but we could hear her slamming drawers and stomping across the floors, so we knew she was still in there. When I heard a big thud coming from the hallway, I'd run upstairs to find her packed suitcase ready to go outside her door.

Several times I'd knocked on her door, telling her we needed to talk, but after the third attempt, a note had been slid under the door with the words "GO AWAY!" written on it.

Cora and my mother watched me with quiet, worried eyes, and every once in a while Carol Lynne would ask who was making all that noise. I finally had to shut myself in my own room so I wouldn't lash out at the wrong person. It was always easier than yelling at myself.

Cora brought trays of food up at each mealtime, but they remained untouched out in the hallway. I brought up dog food and a water bowl, and she let the dog out of the room so he could be taken outside. I tried to keep him with me, to entice her out, but he would run to her room, pawing at the door until she let him back in.

After Carol Lynne had been settled into bed and Cora left for the evening, I began pacing the house, knowing sleep would be impossible. The stomping around in Chloe's room had stopped, and I used the key she didn't know I had to peek in on her. She was sleeping in one of her old outfits, including the combat boots, on top of her bedclothes, black eyeliner and tears streaking her cheeks. The dog slept beside her, his head on her pillow, and I thought how we'd have to name the dog before she left, and then I wondered if there'd be any point if neither one of us would be here to take care of him. I watched her sleep for a long time, studying the steady rise and fall of her chest. Then I let myself out of her room, locking it quietly behind me.

I was standing in the middle of the kitchen at midnight, feeling a lot like my mother when she walked into a room looking around her in confusion and wondering why she was there. For the first time I could empathize with her, understand a little bit of what it was like to wander through your life as if you'd suddenly been thrown into the middle of somebody else's. My cell rang. I saw it was Tripp and for a moment I didn't want to answer, didn't want him to witness another one of my spectacular failures.

"Vivi?"

I realized I'd answered the call but hadn't spoken. "Hi, Tripp. How did you know I was awake?"

"Tommy just called—said the lights were still on at the house. He said you're a mess."

"Situation normal, I guess."

He was silent.

"Is there something you needed?" I asked, hoping he couldn't hear the tears behind my words.

"I'm on my way over," he said, then hung up. For the second time in as many days, I listened to dead air.

I was sitting in the porch swing when he drove up, and he sat beside me without saying anything, pushing off with his heels.

"So what are you going to do?" he asked eventually.

"There's nothing I can do. Mark's coming to take her back tomorrow and there's not a thing I can do about it."

He continued to move the swing without saying anything.

"There isn't, Tripp. I can't do anything to stop him. And I don't think Chloe wants me to, anyway." I swallowed, and told him about the phone conversation she'd overheard.

For a long time he didn't say anything, and then: "Yeah, that's a big mess." He paused. "You'll figure it out, because that's what you've always done." He put his arm around me. "Right now you should try to sleep a little. From what I know of your ex-husband, you're going to need a clear head. And sometimes it's easier to sleep sitting up and leaning on something when you're finding it hard to sleep." He patted his shoulder. "Come on; give it a try."

There was nothing soft or pillowlike about his shoulder, but it offered warmth and comfort, and I immediately began to feel drowsy.

"See what I mean?" he asked softly.

"Um-hmm," I murmured. "Why are you always being so nice to me?" The words were slurred, and I wondered if I'd said them out loud, because I was already half-asleep.

"Because I love you. I don't think I ever stopped."

I didn't respond, because I knew I was dreaming.

*

I awoke on the parlor sofa, covered in a blanket, the smell of eggs and bacon wafting out of the kitchen. I sat up with a jerk and looked for my cell phone for the time, vaguely remembering leaving it on my bathroom counter. I threw off the blanket and stumbled into the kitchen, where Tripp and Carol Lynne sat at the table eating, blinking at the large clock over the sink. I'd somehow managed to sleep until nine o'clock.

Tripp stood and pulled out a chair for me, then grabbed a mug and filled it with coffee. Placing it in front of me, he said, "Looks like you could use this."

I nodded gratefully. "Is Chloe up and dressed? We'll need to leave soon for the airport." I choked on the last word and hid it with a sip of coffee, scalding my tongue.

Tripp nodded. "She's already on the front porch with her suitcase."

"Thanks," I said, grabbing my mug. I spotted Chloe's gardening journal on the counter and picked it up before heading outside. Chloe sat on the steps, her suitcase on the ground beside her, looking pretty much like the girl who'd arrived on my doorstep a little over a month before. And no less angry at the world. I thought I'd changed that about her. But I'd failed. Again.

I sat down next to her. She didn't move away, but she didn't acknowledge me, either.

"I'll take good care of your garden," I ventured. "And the dog. I'll keep him here, but that means we're going to have to come up with a name for him."

She kept staring down the drive, as if willing a taxi to appear so she could leave.

"I thought we'd call him Cotton Two, after Tommy's dog. Would you like that?"

She didn't answer, just squinted into the morning sun.

I wanted to tell her that what she'd heard that night hadn't been true, that what I really wanted was to talk her dad into letting her stay. But I knew she wouldn't believe me, even if she stayed long enough to hear everything I wanted to say. From my brief experience with children, they learned by what they saw adults do, not what they said. I'd been doomed before I'd even opened my mouth.

As if it were conjured, I saw dust from an approaching car, and then a limo emerging from the alley of trees into the circular drive before stopping behind Tripp's truck.

"Who's that?" I said, my chest constricting.

"My dad. I told him I didn't want to sit in a car with you for two hours, so he said he'd come get me."

I wanted to cry. I'd pictured those two hours alone with her as the time I needed to explain things. To tell her I wanted her to stay. That I thought my heart would break if she left without plans to come back. That I'd made mistakes that I didn't want to be permanent. But that opportunity was now gone.

As the limo pulled up, the front door opened and my mother and Tripp came out onto the porch. The driver turned off the engine and opened the windows, anticipating being there for a while, then opened a back door of the limo. I watched as Mark exited the backseat and then came around to the other side to help out what looked to be a human Barbie, with large pink sunglasses that stood out against her suntan and a silk scarf tied in her hair. She didn't look much older than Chloe.

"Hello, Chloe," Mark said. He gave her a perfunctory hug while she stood motionless.

"Hello, Chloe," the Barbie doll said, smiling with frosted lips.

The limo driver approached and put Chloe's suitcase in the trunk while Mark turned his focus on me. "Hello, Vivien." He studied me for a moment before tugging at his two shirt pockets. "Looks like you could use a little lift."

I heard heavy footsteps behind me and had a horrible feeling that Tripp was about to punch Mark in the face. Instead, he was holding out his hand to shake. "Hello, Mark. I'm Tripp Montgomery. Pleased to finally meet you."

Mark accepted the offered hand but frowned up at Tripp. "Are you the Tripp Montgomery who's been sending me notes with the lab reports?"

"The very same. I hope you enjoyed all the little extras I included on those reports." He smiled widely, and even I had to admit he looked like a redneck who by some miracle of fate had kept all of his teeth.

Carol Lynne, in her Jackie O costume, came down the steps, her arms held wide. "Welcome to my home. Won't you come in and have some tea?"

The dog, who'd been frantically pacing as if he knew he was about to be separated from Chloe, began growling at Mark. Tiffany, with a protective hand over her abdomen, ran to the limo and slammed the door.

"Get that mutt away from me and my wife," he said, and I hoped Chloe hadn't noticed that he'd omitted her name.

"That's Cotton Two," she said. "He's mine. Maybe he can come live with us. . . ."

The dog continued to growl at Mark, showing his teeth, and Tripp had to step forward to take him by the collar.

"That dog's not coming within two feet of me or my family," he said.

"Come on in," Carol Lynne said, as if this were a normal visit and she was the grand hostess, standing on the porch in her high heels and motioning for everybody to join her.

Mark looked at her as if he'd just entered a circus tent. He rubbed his hands together. "Is that all your stuff, Chloe? If that's it, go ahead and get in the car. Maybe we can catch an earlier flight."

She began walking toward the limo, then turned around. I took a step forward before I realized that she was running toward my mother to hug her.

"Where are you going, JoEllen? Are you coming back soon?"

"I don't think so," Chloe said, her words full of tears. "Thanks for teaching me how to French-braid my hair."

"You're so welcome," Carol Lynne replied with a smile, as if she'd remembered doing so. As if she remembered teaching me the same thing when I was twelve.

"Chloe," I called, stepping toward her, but she ignored me, turning briefly to offer a wobbling smile at Tripp before getting into the limo.

"Nice job," Mark said. "She couldn't even take two months with you."

I opened my mouth, wanting to tell him that the only reason he'd bothered to drive two hours to pick her up was to make me look bad. But it didn't matter. He'd won. Again.

"Let me know if you need another prescription for your happy pills. I can have my office call it in to your nearest drugstore. Assuming they have them here."

I had to remember to breathe so I wouldn't pass out in the dirt as I watched Chloe turn her head away from the open window.

"That's it?" Tripp said softly. "You're just going to let her go?"

Breathe. Breathe. The engine started, and I heard the driver shift the gear into drive.

"Wait," I shouted. "You forgot your gardening journal." I ran to the porch and grabbed it, shoving it through the window for Chloe.

She turned away. "I don't need it. I don't have a garden."

I bent my head so she couldn't see me cry, and the limo started forward. My gaze fell to my hand clenched around the journal, to the finger with the wire and bead ring that I'd worn every day since Chloe had made it for me, even though it turned my finger green. Because I'd wanted her to know how I felt. But maybe showing her hadn't been enough.

"Chloe!" I shouted, jogging after the car, the windows still open. "I love you. You are my daughter, and I love you. I always will."

I stopped running, the limo too far ahead. I stared after it until it turned out of the drive, with Chloe's face watching me from the rear window.

Chapter 44

Adelaide Walker Bodine Richmond
INDIAN MOUND, MISSISSIPPI
APRIL 19, 1927

The rains continued, tensions rising as high as the river. We'd barely seen the men for three days, the call for hands—both black and white—to help with sandbagging coming from up and down the river. The men slept in tents on the levees in the rain before awakening in the morning and moving farther upriver to do it all over again. I prayed for their safety, and that John remembered to keep his neck warm to ward away a chill.

On Mrs. Heathman's most recent visit—disguised as a visit to see me, even though I knew she mostly wanted to hold Bootsie—she mentioned she'd stopped by Peacock's to resize a ring for Sarah Beth, and she'd said how nervous Mr. Peacock had been about making sure he had time to secure his merchandise. It seemed the entire downtown was moving everything from the lower floors, preparing for the worst. Even she and Mr. Heathman had decided to leave and had already made plans to go to Vicksburg.

I was packed and ready to go at a moment's notice. The impending flood made it easier, my packing no longer suspicious. But the longer we had to wait, the more nervous I became that something bad would happen. I kept reassuring myself that if the rain and possible flood interfered with our plans, it would also interfere with the plans of others.

There had been no arrest in the Angelo Berlini case, and I wondered if they'd been able to return his body to New Orleans with so many roads and bridges overrun with water. I didn't want to think of him in a wooden box, waiting indefinitely to be shipped home. I thought of Bootsie's ring, and wondered what had happened to it, then immediately chastised myself. A man was dead. A baby's ring was so insignificant in comparison.

I was sitting in the parlor, mending a pair of John's socks while Aunt Louise was at church praying for an end to the rain. I looked up at the sound of a car in the drive and then frantic knocking on the front door.

Mathilda, who'd been crossing the foyer, answered it. Sarah Beth stood on the threshold without a coat or hat, despite the rain and unusually frigid temperature. I stood, the sock falling to the floor, as she rushed into the room and flung herself at me. She seemed unaware of her sodden state, or that she was making me—and the chair I'd been sitting on and the floor beneath her—almost as wet as she was.

She was trembling and sobbing into my neck, holding so tightly that I could barely breathe.

"What's wrong, Sarah Beth?"

Mathilda appeared with a blanket and I helped her wrap it around Sarah Beth before leading her to the settee by the fireplace, where the last of the dry wood burned. I sat down beside her.

"I go get somethin' warm her up some," Mathilda said.

"Thank you, Mathilda. Coffee, please."

I took Sarah Beth's icy hands in mine and began rubbing them, trying to bring the blood back into her long, delicate fingers. Despite her matted hair and smeared makeup, she was still beautiful. Like what I imagined the sirens of my fairy tales might look like: not quite of this world, her eyes appearing darker and wider in her pale face.

Her lips trembled so much she could barely speak, and when she did she had to talk very slowly so I could understand.

"Where . . . is . . . Willie?"

"Uncle Joe's on the levee guard. He took Willie and John to help with the sandbagging. They've been gone for three days."

Her head sagged along with her shoulders, making me think of a drowned bird I'd seen in the yard that had fallen from its nest. "Angelo. He's . . ."

"He's dead. I know. John and I read about it in the paper."

She lifted her head, and I saw she wasn't wearing the emerald earrings. I remembered the look on Willie's face when he'd seen the earrings the night he and Chas had come here drunk, and it occurred to me that Sarah Beth hadn't wanted to wear them where Willie might see them again.

"Were you and Angelo . . . ?" I almost said "lovers," but I didn't want to hear her confirm what I'd believed to be true for a long time. I still remembered Sarah Beth as a young girl, and I hated to see what she'd become. But in my heart, I knew. I'd seen her wearing the emeralds.

"He's . . . gone," she said, her lips trembling hard now, as if it weren't just the cold that made her nerves shiver.

"Did you love him?" I asked, unable to look her in the eyes, imagining his body floating in the pond, alone. I remembered the secrets she and I had shared as children and wanted to ask her if she knew how he'd died, wanted to tell her that John and I thought it was his business associates, and that we were going to Missouri to be safe. But I couldn't. We were past the age where a secret told was a secret kept.

When she didn't respond, I lifted my gaze to hers and saw eyes that had grown cold.

She didn't answer my question. Instead, she said, "When will . . . Willie be . . . back?"

I shook my head. "I don't know. Not until the rain stops or the danger of flooding is over. Do you have a plan to get somewhere safe? You can't go back to New Orleans—all the roads are flooded."

She threw back her head and laughed. "I know . . . that's . . . where I just . . . came from. There's no . . . safe place."

I rubbed her arms again, trying to get the shivering to stop. "I heard your parents have refugeed to Vicksburg." Their house had been built on the highest point in the county, but I supposed that wasn't safe enough for the Heathmans.

Sarah Beth nodded, her lips staying pressed together.

"You can't be at your house alone. You must stay with us until it's safe, and you can evacuate with us if it comes to that."

She looked at me with those empty eyes and didn't say anything.

Mathilda returned with a coffee tray and poured coffee for us, and I pressed a cup into Sarah Beth's hand, but she put it down on the coffee table with a thud, a drop of the liquid spilling over onto the polished wood. With trembling fingers she pulled a small flask from her garter and poured a generous amount into her cup, emptying the flask. With a shaking smile, she picked up the cup with both hands and drained it, not noticing the hot coffee as she gulped it down.

She seemed to have warmed up after that and stood, clutching the blanket around her shoulders as she moved closer to the fire, her back to me.

Her voice only trembled slightly when she spoke again, her gaze on the bright orange flames. "I need your help."

"Of course. I already told you that you can stay here. I'll get the guest room—"

"I'm going to have a baby."

My next words vanished, their importance and meaning erased by Sarah Beth's.

I remained sitting, trying to digest what she'd just said. "You're pregnant?"

She faced me, a weak smile on her face. "Aren't you supposed to say 'Congratulations'?"

I tried to keep the shock from my voice as I stood and approached her. "Of course," I said, hugging her. "The news of a baby is always good."

Her jaw twisted. "Not always. Not when there's no wedding ring involved."

"But I know Willie's crazy about you. He always has been. He'll marry you in a heartbeat, Sarah Beth. I know he will."

"I'm not so sure." She returned to staring into the fire. "Especially if he knows I'm already pregnant."

"But all the more reason for him to want to marry . . ." I stopped, her odd mood suddenly making sense to me. "Is he not the father?"

She shook her head, and the blanket sank to the floor without her notice. I took her hand and we returned to the settee, and I could feel her fingers trembling in mine.

"Angelo?" I whispered the name, as if the dead could hear.

"Yes." She squeezed my hands painfully. "He said he was going to marry me. That his engagement to Carmen was just to make his boss happy. Don't you see, Adelaide? That's why you have to help me. Willie must marry me now, or I'll be ruined."

"But what could I do? Surely Willie will know it's not his."

She avoided looking at me. "It might be."

I sat back, trying to hide my shock but knowing I was failing miserably. I understood Sarah Beth's attraction to men and their attraction to her. And even accepted that she might have a lover. But not those two men, and not at the same time. "Oh," I managed. "Then you should tell him that it could be his, and I know he'll do the right thing by you."

"I already did." Her gaze slid away. "Right before Angelo was killed."

When she looked back at me it was as if she were trying to tell me something with her eyes, something she wanted me to know without saying it aloud.

"What is it?" I asked, dread filling me.

"Willie says he won't marry me. And I need your help desperately. I need you to tell your aunt and uncle that I'm in the family way. They're good people, and I know they'll make Willie do the right thing. They trust you and won't ask any questions. And if he tells them stories about how he might not be the daddy, you can back me up and tell them it's not true."

"I've never lied to them before. And this is such a big lie." I looked at her, an idea springing into my mind, my earlier thoughts about secrets easily forgotten in the turmoil of her predicament. "John and I are planning on going up to Missouri for a while. You can come with us. Have the baby there. Maybe by then Willie will have changed his mind. And when he sees that baby, I know he'll do the right thing then."

Her words were stiff. "And if he doesn't?"

"Then the baby can be adopted. Like you were. And raised by a loving family."

"No!" she shouted, and I leaned back, never having seen this new emotion in her before. She was like a cornered bear, lashing out at those who would save her, because she didn't know what else to do. "My parents will disown me if they ever find out I had a baby without being married. You have no idea what would happen."

She put her hand over her mouth, pacing over and over the same patch of carpet, her heels digging into the wet wool. "I've thought about getting rid of it, going to some back-alley doctor and getting it taken care of. But I'm as likely to die as the baby."

I stood again, trying to reason with her. "Sarah Beth, if I didn't see any alternatives, I might agree that forcing Willie to marry you would be the best thing. But lying is never the answer. I'm sorry; I am. But I won't lie for you. I'll help you, but I won't lie for you."

Her face was so contorted I barely recognized my old friend. "But I need a husband's protection; don't you see? Somebody who's not afraid to take matters into his own hands if the baby's born . . ." She stopped, her mouth closing quickly, as if she were afraid that the word would fall out on its own.

"If the baby's born what?" I tried to finish her sentence. "With dark hair and eyes like Angelo's? But you have dark hair and eyes, too. People would just say that the baby looked like you."

"I thought you were my friend!" she screamed at me, and I suddenly realized that it wasn't so much the disappointment that I wasn't going to help her do what she wanted me to. Her anger was all about her not getting her way. I saw with new eyes that she'd never grown up, not really. She still thought and behaved like a spoiled child.

"I am your friend. That's why I won't lie for you. I'll help you get through this, but I won't do what you're asking. Because I'm a *real* friend. Please, Sarah Beth. Come with us to Missouri. Everything will be all right."

She picked up her empty flask and threw it into the fire, hitting one of the andirons and making it bounce back into the room.

Leaning down, she picked it up again. "You'll be sorry, Adelaide. I will make sure you're sorry you didn't help me when I needed you."

I watched her run toward the front door, her damp dress clinging to her slight frame.

"Please, Sarah Beth. Don't leave. Let me help you."

She paused in the open door. "It's too late," she said, then slammed the door behind her.

I heard a deep intake of breath and turned to find Mathilda still in the parlor. She'd been so silent and still, standing in the corner by the window in the shadow of the clouds outside. I knew from her eyes that she'd heard everything. But I saw something else there, too: something that looked a lot like fear.

My eyes dropped to the collar of her dress, which was buttoned up to the neck. But I could see the small round lump beneath the fabric, and knew it was the pearl necklace that Sarah Beth had lied about to Willie, saying she'd given it to Mathilda.

The baby began crying upstairs, awakened by the slamming of the door.

"'Scuse me, Miss Adelaide," Mathilda said as she made her way past me to the stairs.

"Mathilda," I called after her.

She stopped without turning around.

"Who gave you that pearl around your neck?"

Her hand reached up to her throat. "Miss Sarah Beth. She done give it to me."

I sucked air in through my nose, knowing she was lying to me. Lying to corroborate Sarah Beth's story. A story Sarah Beth had made up to protect Mathilda.

The baby's cries became more strident, and I wanted to stop asking my questions so one of us could go to her and pick her up and tell her that everything was going to be all right. But I remained where I was. "Why would Sarah Beth want to protect you?"

Mathilda began climbing the stairs again. "I gots to get the baby now."

I watched her run the rest of the way, knowing I was through with my questions, remembering something she'd said to me that night Robert, Mathilda, and I had brought a drunk Sarah Beth up to her bedroom. *I be real good at keepin' secrets.*

I returned to the parlor and picked up the sock, unable to concentrate on pulling thread through fabric. I put away the sock, then went into the dining room to finish packing up the rest of the china and silver to move to the attic in case the bottom floor flooded. The wind and rain pushed at the house as my mind continued to churn over my conversation with Sarah Beth while I prepared for disaster.

❧

APRIL 20, 1927

The storm continued to rage with barely any respite, the temperature plummeting. The firewood was too wet to burn, and we moved about the house bundled in coats and woolen underthings. Bootsie, who was now crawling, grew impatient with the extra layers that hindered her scooting along the floors, and her chubby knees were raw from moving about uncarpeted wood. But she remained mostly cheerful, despite the change in her world and the tension among the adults.

Uncle Joe had sent word that they were barely keeping up with the level of the river, the need for sandbags constant. The only way they could come home would be if the levee broke and sandbags would have no effect against the expected torrent. We could only hope and pray that the crevasse—and there would be one—would happen downriver of us.

He told us to go ahead and load supplies into a mule wagon and prepare to head to the old hunting cabin on the highest point of our property.

Mathilda, Aunt Louise, and I, along with a couple of the field hands that Uncle Joe had left behind, loaded up the wagon, including the suitcases I'd packed for the journey north. I couldn't go without John, so temporarily moving to higher ground was the only thing I could think to do while I waited for him to return.

I had tried to salvage part of my garden, but when I'd gone out the day before, during a five-minute period when the rain had slackened to a drizzle, I'd realized it was all gone. It saddened me, but excited me, too. The rains would stop, the floodwaters recede. And those of us who returned would replant our fields and our gardens, and live our lives like they were brand-new, and with the knowledge that we'd survived yet again. It was the way of the delta.

Mathilda was waiting for me in the kitchen when I returned, placing my muddy shoes inside the door instead of out, knowing they'd float away if kept outside.

"I'm afraid we're going to have to start over once the water goes down."

"Don' worry, Miss Adelaide. I puts your seeds in paper bags and puts them in the wagon."

"Thanks, Mathilda. I'd forgotten all about them. My mind is in such a turmoil these days."

"Mama says I remembers everythin'." She smiled and I smiled back, wondering why her words sounded so prophetic. Maybe when I was old and gray and arguing with John about a lost memory, I'd have cause to ask her to remind us.

"I'm glad," I said, reaching for Bootsie, who'd just pulled herself to stand using the skirt of Mathilda's dress.

The fire whistle began to sound in the morning hours of Thursday, April twenty-first. Even though we were prepared and had been expecting it, it still sent my nerves jangling. A neighbor, on his way to Vicksburg with his family and what possessions they'd loaded into their truck, stopped to make sure we'd heard the whistle, and to let us know that the crevasse was in Mounds Landing. It was the worst possible place, only forty-five miles north of us. Most of our land and part of the house would be underwater.

Aunt Louise ran from room to room to make sure nothing had been left behind. I'd decided to place all the photographs and books I could grab into the attic, along with the china and silver. If I could save those things, I could handle the loss of everything else.

On my way down from the attic, the telephone rang. I was surprised it was still working. I'd tried calling Sarah Beth several times with no luck getting through, and I liked to believe she'd tried, too. Service had been spotty for weeks on account of the rains and thunderstorms, and it had been so silent that I think we all believed that the telephone wires were already down.

I was standing by the phone in the foyer and picked it up before it rang twice.

There was a moment of silence as the call was connected. "Hello?"

"Mrs. Richmond?"

The voice was familiar, but odd-sounding, like he wasn't opening his mouth wide enough to get the words out.

"Yes, this is she."

"This is Mr. Peacock. John asked me to call you. The phones are so unpredictable right now, you understand."

I was confused as to why my husband hadn't called me directly, but I needed to know about John. "Is he all right?" I asked.

"He's on his way here, to the store. To help me pack up all the jewelry and move it to a safe at the bank."

"He's on his way now? Downtown? But the whistle has sounded—we're evacuating."

"Yes, of course." A pause. "He, uh, he said he would evacuate with you, to the place you discussed previously, up north, he said. But he wants you to meet him here instead of evacuate with your family."

John must have heard something—something that made him believe that we needed to go north now. I felt a shiver of fear. I thought of our suitcases in the wagon, and knew I didn't have time to get them. If I had to sell my watch for supplies, then I would.

"All right. Are the roads between here and downtown still passable?"

"Yes. Muddy, so you'll need to be careful, but still passable. But you need to leave now."

"Of course. Thank you, Mr. Peacock. I should be there in no more than thirty minutes, depending on the roads."

I hung up the phone and saw Aunt Louise watching me. "You're going with us, Adelaide. To the hunting cabin."

I managed a smile. "Later. Right now John wants me to meet him at the jewelry store. He's helping Mr. Peacock secure his merchandise."

She looked at me as if I'd lost my mind. "The levee's been breached, Adelaide. There's so much water coming in. One of the field hands just told me that a refugee just passed by from Greenville—water's already up to the bottom of the doors on the shops downtown, and that's less than forty miles from here."

"I know. But I have to go. John needs me."

"What about Bootsie?"

"She stays with me."

Her brow furrowed. "I don't understand. . . ."

I hugged her and kissed her cheek. "I'll explain it all later. I promise. But right now we need to leave."

I bundled Bootsie up and dressed myself in an extra layer as Aunt Louise fussed and pleaded with me over and over, trying very hard not to cry. I wanted so badly to tell her, but I remembered what Angelo had said—about how I might put others in danger if I told them where I was going. But I trusted John, and knew that he would bring us back soon, and I held on to that thought so I wouldn't start crying, too.

Aunt Louise kissed Bootsie hard, and then kissed me again and said good-bye. Mathilda kissed Bootsie, too, her eyes wet, then stood silently watching. I gave her a quick smile before I ran outside in the teeming rain, the sound of the whistle almost obliterated by that of the wind and rain pelting the ground and the old yellow house. I placed Bootsie on the seat beside me, then looked back at the front porch, where Aunt Louise and Mathilda stood, their faces drawn in identical expressions of worry.

I waved, and they waved back; then I put the car in gear, making sure I didn't look in the rearview mirror. Mathilda had once told me that looking behind you when you left a place meant you'd never come back. But as I made my way down the long drive, I hit a fallen limb— almost invisible in the mud—and when I looked up again I saw the reflection of the old cypress in the backyard, its leaves weighed down by the rain, its limbs drooping as if in mourning. I quickly looked away and focused on the road in front of me, praying that this would all be over soon.

Chapter 45

Vivien Walker Moise
INDIAN MOUND, MISSISSIPPI
JUNE 2013

For two hours the dog ran up and down the long drive, whimpering and pawing at the ground, looking out toward the highway. I was afraid he'd keep going, running down the paved asphalt all the way to California. I'd heard of dogs doing that, finding their owners after traveling for long distances. But each time he came back to the porch, where I sat on the steps, dry eyed, and put his head in my lap as if to tell me that he knew running away wasn't going to get him where he needed to be.

Tripp had taken my mother inside to calm her down. She'd grown agitated watching Chloe leave, her confusion mixing with the sure knowledge that something bad was happening, though she couldn't figure out what it was.

Cora had finally put her back to bed, and after making sure she was settled, Tripp came out on the porch and sat next to me. We sat in silence for a long while as the sun got higher in the sky and turned the brunt of its heat onto the front steps where we sat.

"You're going to get more freckles," he said.

I closed my eyes, remembering the day at the lake, and how Chloe had been so happy and for the first time in my life I'd felt like I'd done something right. "Good," I said, tilting my face up toward the sun, hoping I'd burn.

"I just want you to know that I would have punched that son of a bitch in the face if I thought it would improve matters. But I know he's a surgeon and wouldn't have risked his hands even if he knew how to punch back. That would have made me feel like a bully, and gotten me sued, to boot."

I didn't respond—couldn't. It was as if the morning's events had scooped out my insides and scattered them in the fields, leaving me an empty shell.

As if he were unaware that I was within a strong breeze of falling over, he continued. "Of all the things my mama and daddy taught Claire and me, there's one thing that's always stuck out. When we were hitting our heads against a problem, they said to find one true thing about the situation. And following it would be like unwinding a ball of yarn, leading you to the heart of it. And you know what? They were right."

I slid away from him, angry that he'd be telling me stories about his parents when I could barely breathe. Could barely summon the energy to stand up and go inside the house.

"This is bigger than just a problem, Tripp. Everywhere I look, I see one self-inflicted disaster after another. It's like I'm sinking in quicksand and I don't know how to get out of it."

He was thoughtful for a moment, and I braced myself. "That one true thing is your rope you're going to need to pull yourself out."

What I needed was a time machine to take me back before I'd made the first in a string of bad mistakes, not stupid platitudes from a guy who spent a lot of time with dead people. If I'd had the strength, I would have pushed him, or hit him, or yelled at him. But all I could do was sit with my face toward the sky, hoping I'd burn.

He stood, blocking the sun, making me blink up at him. "I heard what he said, about the prescription. It's not the answer, Vivi. And it sure as hell won't pull you out of the quicksand."

"Go away," I said, angry that he'd read my mind. That he knew that as soon as Chloe had gone, I'd been wanting to pop a pill to take away all of my hurt, to take away my dreams of being somebody other than who I'd become.

I turned my head, but I knew he was still there because I felt his shadow on my face.

"Something else my mama told me. She said that it's those who are hardest to love who need love the most." He stood and slowly walked down the steps, stopping but not turning around. "She told me that when you left."

I listened to the crunch of dirt and rocks as he made his way to his truck, then the engine starting and the truck making its way down the drive and out to the highway, following the path of the limo. Just one more person I'd pushed out of my life. Just one more mistake I couldn't stop repeating.

The dog began to pant, and I knew he wouldn't go inside without me, so I managed to pull myself to stand and lead him into the kitchen, where he headed straight for the water bowl, making me feel worse than I already did.

He followed me up to Chloe's room, where her made bed—complete with lumps and untucked sheets but otherwise made—sat empty, the unused dog bed on the floor by the side.

The closet door was slightly open, and when I walked over to close it, I saw that all of the clothes I'd bought for her were hanging haphazardly on hangers. The floral tops and jeans, her plaid skirt, the purple leggings. I stared at the clothes for a long time, and finally I began to cry, something I hadn't been able to do since Chloe left. At some point I moved to the bed and was sobbing into the pillow, the dog up on the bed with me, licking my face as if he really believed that would make it all better.

I cried until I had no more tears left, the pillow damp beneath my head. I found myself staring at the plastered ceiling, at the small brown spot of water damage near the light fixture that needed to be fixed. It was like that small spot had become the proverbial straw, and I felt as if the whole ceiling were now pressing against my chest, making it impossible to breathe.

I sat up, my mind racing as I panted for breath. I knew in the far reaches of my conscious mind that I was having a panic attack. And that one pill was all I needed to make it go away. I remembered the single pill in the bottom of my purse, remembered leaving it there as if even then I knew that I wouldn't be able to stay off them for long.

I scrambled from the bed, trying to remember where I'd left my purse, tripping and stumbling in my need to find a way to forget. I made it to the hallway, pausing to catch my breath, to quell the dizziness that threatened to pitch me forward and down the stairs. I closed my eyes for a long moment, trying to remember how to count backward. *Twenty, nineteen, eighteen . . .*

I managed to make it to one, although I had no idea if it had taken me one minute or thirty. I slid to the floor, trying to catch my breath, trying to recall why I'd been so frantic. I put my head in my hands when I remembered, wishing I had more tears to cry.

My breath still came in shallow gasps, and I concentrated on filling my lungs as my gaze stumbled along the hallway, looking for something on which to focus. Bleary-eyed, I stared at the portraits of long-dead family members, relatives whose names I didn't know but should. I imagined I could hear Bootsie's voice telling me about her mother and the flood, and growing up on the farm with Emmett, and how at Christmas they would collect magnolia leaves for the mantels in the house.

I found myself wishing I could go back in time so I could listen more carefully, so I could write it all down so that her words wouldn't be forgotten forever. But Emmett had once told Tommy and me that wishes were like the fish we never caught: too slippery to hold in our hands, and pointless to chase after when we already had a bushel of fish in the boat. He'd been right, of course. I'd just been too young and stupid for too long to understand he'd been talking about chasing ghosts.

My gaze settled on the closed attic door across the hall from me, the light from Chloe's room reflecting off the crystal doorknob and making it shine like a beacon. I needed a distraction that would keep me busy for long enough to forget about Chloe being gone and what was sitting in the bottom of my purse.

I figured now would be a good time to ignore the spiders and sort through the attic for Bootsie's ring, although I was no longer sure what finding it might tell me. But maybe searching the attic would help me reconcile with my past, and even find a way to reconnect with Bootsie and the other Walker women who'd gone before me, to find a clue as to where they drew their strength and wisdom, since my own supply had been on empty for years and I was in desperate need of it now. With deliberate steps, I crossed the hallway and opened the attic door.

The smell of cedar and dust came out first, followed by what I was sure was the scent of dried oranges and cinnamon, reminders of the garlands and wreaths I'd helped Bootsie store after my last Christmas.

I stared into the dark staircase for a long moment, then reached inside to the light switch and flipped it on. The bare bulb at the top of the stairs illuminated the wooden risers and ceiling rafters, and the shadows of trunks and boxes on the periphery looking down at me like spectators at a boxing ring.

I sniffed again, wondering how those old scents could still be contained within the four walls of the attic, and thinking that maybe they just existed inside my own memories. I took a step up, trying to make out the shape of something hanging from one of the rafters. It was draped in an old Hamlin's dress bag, the bottom half unzipped, and when I squinted to where the contents spilled out of the opened bottom, I recognized Bootsie's fox-fur coat.

Before I even realized what I was doing, I was running up the stairs, as if somehow feeling the fur against my skin would bring a part of her back to me, would give me a little of her wisdom that would tell me what I needed to do.

The two-way zipper on the cover was stuck, and I worked frantically to pull it up so I could open it and take out the coat. I sat down on a nearby trunk and pressed the fur collar into my face, remembering how I'd loved being hugged by Bootsie as a child. The coat was musty and carried with it the scent of cedar, but when I breathed deeply I could still detect the Youth Dew perfume she'd worn when she dressed up for church or a garden club meeting. Just touching the fur seemed to slow my heart, forced me to breathe again. Took away the frantic desire for a pill without completely eradicating the need.

The dog stayed at the bottom of the steps, like a guard, while I sat with my grandmother's fur coat pressed against me until I heard the clock strike and I realized I'd been up there for two hours. The dog hadn't left his position and I started feeling guilty, wondering if he was hungry or thirsty.

I stood, my desperation still there but only clinging to the edges now. I carefully rehung the coat, making a mental note to get a longer bag so it would all fit inside, zipping it halfway. Almost to the top step, I looked over at a box to the side of the staircase with its four flaps open. With a quick glance I saw a stack of old magazines, an ancient issue of *Vogue* on top, an image of a green-turbaned Audrey Hepburn on the cover. Not wanting them to get ruined by accumulating dust, I went over to close up the box, but stopped when I recognized several of my mother's old headbands shoved between the books, along with a fringed leather vest that probably should have been thrown away or used as a Halloween costume.

Of all the times I'd been up to the attic with Bootsie and Tommy to retrieve and then return holiday decorations, we'd never stopped to look in the boxes. I'd always been too eager to decorate the tree, and then after Christmas, I'd been too eager to get the boring job of dismantling the holidays over with.

But I remembered the year I was sixteen and my mother had come home for good, and how she'd packed up her things in her bedroom and brought a box to the attic as if she could pack up her past and store it away like it had never happened. I'd heard her struggling up the stairs with the box and hadn't offered to help. And never once, in all of these years, had I thought of it or what it might contain.

I stepped out of the light from the overhead bulb and there, sitting in a corner on top of what looked to be a Greyhound bus schedule, was a red bound journal with the word "Diary" in cracked embossed gold on the front. I wasn't sure how long I stared at it, torn between closing the box and picking it up. But eventually I leaned in and took it, then sat down on a trunk with the diary in my hand.

I recalled my disappointment upon my return in April, when I'd discovered that my mother's memory was gone, that she would never know enough to remember why she needed to tell me she was sorry, that I would never hear her story that would explain what was missing in me that made her want to leave.

As Bootsie used to say, all things happened for a reason. Maybe that was why I'd stumbled into the attic and seen her coat. And found my mother's diary. It was almost as if Bootsie were there beside me, prompting me to read it.

With a deep breath, I opened the cover, pausing at my mother's signature on the first page, and it hit me with a pang of nostalgia that I'd never seen her handwriting before. Would have no idea whether this was hers except for the name scrawled on that first page. *Carol Lynne Walker Moise, Indian Mound, Mississippi, August 5, 1962.* Her seventeenth birthday. I hadn't remembered that her birthday was on the fifth of August. And I'd never asked.

I slid down onto the floor of the attic and rested my back against the trunk. Then, with my mother's story in my hands, I bent my head and began to read.

It was the dog's bark that eventually drew me back to the present. I wasn't aware of how long I'd read or how long I'd been sitting on the attic floor with the book on my lap as my mind worked its way in and out of my mother's story—where it intersected with mine, and how my own past had suddenly been rewritten.

I still felt empty, and Chloe remained gone from me, but I imagined I could see a sliver of light, as a window was slowly being eased open.

Carefully, I made my way down the steps with the diary still clutched in my hand, holding tightly to the railing because of my lightheadedness. The dog was gone, and I wondered if he'd been barking to tell me that we both needed to be fed. My stomach growled as I realized I hadn't eaten all day.

I paused halfway down the front stairs. Carol Lynne, wearing her old jeans and blouse, sat on the bottom step, two suitcases waiting by the door. She looked like she might still be waiting for Jimmy Hinkle to come pick her up and take her away from here, like a ghost doomed to repeat the same action over and over.

"Mama?" I'd called her that when I was a little girl. I'd forgotten that I had, and was glad she'd written it in her diary so that I'd remember.

She looked up at me and smiled. "Yes, baby?"

"Where are you going?"

Her eyes moved to the door, and then to her suitcases, then back to me. "I don't know."

"Why don't you stay here awhile? I think I'll stay with you, if that's okay."

"That'll be nice."

I put my arm around her, and she rested her head on my shoulder. I thought of all that I'd just read. We'd faced the same demons, yet had somehow found a way to fight them again and again, had found the grace we sought in the walls of this old yellow house, and the people and memories who lived under its roof. Like migrating birds we'd come back, eternal optimists who believed this house held all the second chances we'd ever need. Or maybe we were both just too stupid to ever admit defeat.

The hollowness still echoed inside my chest as I thought of Chloe, and how here I was, back where I'd started, with nothing to show for the journey and no idea where to go next. We watched as shadows moved across the walls, and I wondered if those same shadows walked inside her head.

"We've been a long time gone, Vivi."

Tears pricked at the back of my eyes. "Yes, Mama. We have."

There was still so much pain between us, too much to be completely erased by the words in a diary, but they were a start. And we were here. We'd both come back. Maybe that would be enough for both of us for now.

I breathed in deeply, smelling the lemony scent of her skin, and I was eight years old again and we were lying on top of the Indian mound, counting stars.

The door opened and Tommy walked in, taking in our mother and me sitting on the stairs together, her suitcases by the door.

"It's all right, Tommy," I said, standing. "Mama and I were just deciding that she's going to stay a little while longer."

"That's good to hear." He looked at me, his expression somewhere between confusion and excitement. "I'm sorry I missed Chloe this morning. Tripp said it was hard."

I grimaced. "That's one way to put it."

"I got your watch working." He held it out to me, and I placed it on my wrist.

I compared the time to the face on the grandfather clock in the hall. "It's dead-on."

"Thank you."

I looked at his face, trying to read it, but couldn't. "What is it?" I asked.

He stuck his hand in his pocket and pulled out a tiny slip of paper, no longer than an inch and less than a quarter of an inch wide. "This is why it wasn't working. This was shoved into the back."

I took it and then, squinting to read the tiny handwriting in black ink, read the two words: *Forgive me.*

"Do you know what that means?" he asked.

Droplets of ice slipped their way down my spine. "No." I scrubbed my hands over my face, weariness pulling at my bones and settling behind my eyes. "But I think I know who might. I just need to go lie down for a little bit so I can think straight." I handed him our mother's diary. "I think you should read this. It will explain a lot of things."

He studied the cover, then looked at me closely. "Are you all right?"

I shook my head. "No. Not yet. But for the first time in a long while, I'm beginning to think I could be."

"Anything I can do?"

"I don't think so, but I'll let you know."

Our mother was attempting to drag her suitcases up the stairs, and Tommy stopped her, lifted the bags, then followed her upstairs.

I heard Cora in the kitchen talking to the dog as I slowly went up the stairs to my room. I was nearly swaying on my feet with exhaustion, but I dug into my purse and found the remaining pill. I quickly dropped it into the toilet and flushed it before I could think twice.

Then I dragged my suitcase out from under the bed and began dumping all of my trophies and awards and high school photos inside. Like my mother before me, it had taken me a long time to realize it was time to grow up. To stop looking toward the vanishing point where horizon met sky, and instead look around where I stood, and finally see all that I'd been given.

I left the remaining books on the shelves, thinking that if Chloe ever came back she might want to read them, then zipped my suitcase closed. Panting from the exertion, I lay down on my bed and closed my eyes; the last thing I remembered before sleep claimed me was the tiny note pulled from the watch. *Forgive me.*

"Forgive me," I repeated, the word whispered to my mother and Bootsie; to Tommy, Chloe, and even Tripp. To all of those I hadn't had the courage to say good-bye to.

Chapter 46

Vivien Walker Moise
INDIAN MOUND, MISSISSIPPI
JUNE 2013

I slept for fourteen hours straight, my head feeling clear for the first time in months. I'd kept my phone held close while I'd slept, in case Chloe called, but wasn't surprised when I saw that I hadn't missed any calls. I hit speed dial and her phone went straight to voice mail. I hung up and tried again, but this time I left a message—telling her my side of the story until I was cut off, then calling her again to tell her the rest until I was finished. She might delete them all without listening. But she might not. I had licked clean the pot of fresh ideas, and could only hope and pray that Chloe would listen, and not hate me for the rest of her life.

I had breakfast with my mother, half expecting her to ask about JoEllen, but she didn't. When I left I kissed her on the cheek and told Cora I'd be back around lunch, and then I called Mathilda to let her know I was coming. Even if she pretended she was sleeping or feeling poorly, I would sit in her old recliner and wait.

She was sitting up in her chair when I entered, an afghan spread over her birdlike legs, the television tuned to Kathie Lee and Hoda, the volume set almost as high as it would go. Her hands were cupped together in her lap and she smiled as I entered.

"It's Vivien," I said.

She lifted her cheek for me. "Hello, sweet girl."

I kissed her papery cheek. "Hello, Mathilda. It's good to see you again. I hope I'm not interrupting your show."

She waved her hand. "Oh, no. I jus' like to hear Kathie Lee laugh. I think it scares the roaches away. Just go ahead and turn it off, if you don' mind."

I hunted for the remote and flipped off the TV, then pulled up a chair next to her.

"You brung me somethin' good to eat?"

Despite myself, I smiled. "I'm sorry—I forgot. I promise I will next time."

"I blind, but I ain't deaf, and I can hear a world of sadness in your breathin', Vivi."

Her sightless eyes settled on me, and I wished I remembered what they'd looked like before, how my mother and Bootsie and Adelaide had seen them.

"I found my mother's diary and read it. It started when she was seventeen and ended when she came back that last time." I stood, hoping to ease the unbearable ache around my heart that had begun the night in the garden with Chloe. As if changing my position could possibly help. I stopped at one of the plants in the window, noticed it needed water. "She mentioned you a lot."

Mathilda nodded, her hands remaining cupped in her lap. "I 'spect so. I knows her since she was just a tiny baby. She like my own."

I looked at her sharply, recalling that I'd had more than one mother, too. "She wrote that you were real good at keeping secrets." I walked slowly back to the bedside chair, trying to think of what I needed to ask. "It was your room she went snooping in when she was a little girl, wasn't it? She took something, and when you found out you asked her to give it back."

She lifted a hand and held it out to me, and before she dropped the little ring onto my palm, I knew what it was. I stared at it, then tried to put it on my own pinkie finger, but it was too small.

"You've had it all this time."

"For such a little thing, it be a heavy burden."

I stared at it while I spoke. "I asked you before if you knew what happened to it."

"You asked just to know the answer. I didn't want to tell you till you askin' for the right reason."

I didn't understand, but knew she'd wait until I'd figured it out. I ran the ring between my fingers, a symbol of a mother's love for her child, and I had to force the next words from my mouth. "How did you come by it?"

She began to pluck at her blankets in agitation. "Can I have some water, please? All this talkin's makin' me thirsty."

If I hadn't been so agitated myself, I would have laughed, seeing as how she'd only spoken a handful of words. I picked up a water pitcher by her bed and filled a plastic tumbler and stuck in a straw like I'd seen Cora do.

She took a sip. "I found it."

"Where?"

"In William's room—though Adelaide and them calls him Willie. I went lookin' for it right after Mr. Berlini got kilt."

I frowned, remembering the name from the newspaper article Chloe had pulled from the archives. I'd read it thoroughly, taking notes, thinking it would be an interesting story for one of the pieces I was supposed to write. "The man who was found in the pond at the Ellis plantation with supposed mob connections?"

She nodded, her eyes focused on me in a disconcerting way and I had to remind myself that she couldn't see.

"I don't understand. Why would Adelaide's cousin have the ring— and why would Mr. Berlini's death have anything to do with it?"

"Why you wants to know? So you can bury that sweet girl with a clear conscience? Or because you think you might find the answers to you own problems? Because ain't nobody can do that for you but yo'self."

I remembered the sliver of light I'd imagined when I'd read my mother's diary, and I couldn't stop myself from clinging to the hope that if I heard Adelaide's story it might throw the window wide-open, illuminate the path in front of me that I couldn't see no matter how hard I looked.

"Please, Mathilda. I need to know. I do want to bury her and honor her life. But I think her story might help me in some way, too. Is that too much to hope for?"

"No, Vivi. I just don' want you disappointed you don' get the answer you want."

"I'm ready. Really, I am."

She nodded and took a sip of her water, then began to talk.

Her story began when she first met Adelaide when Mathilda came to help her mother at the Heathmans'. She told the story of a New Year's Eve party when Adelaide had saved her, and a night when she and Adelaide had brought in a drunken Sarah Beth and put her to bed.

I walked around the room while she spoke, watering her plants, trimming them and loosening the soil. My fingers gravitated to the care of all growing things, and I found it helped me focus on what Mathilda was telling me, as if by nurturing something I could buffer the bad parts in her story.

She told me of Adelaide meeting John, and their wedding, and all their lost babies until Bootsie was born, and how she was the shining light in both their lives.

She paused to take a drink, and I was afraid that she'd stop, so I pressed on. "Even though he was involved in bootlegging, that didn't affect their relationship?"

"It did, and the man he work for, Mr. Berlini, he don' want Mr. John to quit even though both him and Miss Adelaide wants him to. I don' know why for sure, but he kept workin' for Mr. Berlini, and Miss Adelaide, she put up with it. She love him that much."

"So where does Willie come into all this?"

"I knows he messed up with the Klan—and I think Miss Adelaide, she know this, too, but don' want to upset her uncle, who be busy with the farm and all that rain we had. My Robert, he was at Ellis the day they kills Mr. Berlini, workin' one of the stills for his uncle. They don' see him, but he saw everythin', which would get him kilt for sure if they knew. He told me it was the Klan with they robes. But Willie, he take off his hood so he can look in the dead man's pockets and Robert say he took something. I had a good idea I knows what that be, 'cause I remember seeing Miss Adelaide give him something right before Miss Bootsie stops wearing her ring. That why I go look in his room."

She paused, her eyes moving as if she were watching the play of events inside her head.

My head swarmed with questions. "Why would the Klan have killed him? What would they have to gain?"

"They kills him because Willie know Miss Sarah Beth's sweet on Mr. Berlini, and she be in the family way."

I sat down to digest this little bombshell, remembering dates in the newspaper articles and on my family tree. "With Emmett. So Emmett was Angelo's baby."

She shrugged. "Sarah Beth made sure it could be both. That girl always knows how to takes care of herself."

"But Berlini had the ring—why? And how did Willie know?"

"Miss Adelaide, she give it to him—I saw her do it, and so did Willie. I don' know why till later. But Mr. Berlini, he has a soft spot for Miss Adelaide, and Robert say Mr. John in a heap o' trouble 'cause he ain't workin' with the bootleggers no more. See, Mr. Berlini asks Robert to help him, say he trust Robert, and when the time right, he gonna give the ring to Robert to show to Miss Adelaide, let her know she can listen to him. 'Cause Mr. Berlini try to help them get away somewheres until there's no danger for them. She gives him the ring to keep her family safe." Mathilda shook her head slowly. "She wouldn't part from that ring for nothin' less."

I stood again and picked up the water pitcher to pour more in her glass and get one for me, and I saw that my hand shook. "But when you found the ring, you didn't tell Adelaide."

"No." She looked down at her neatly manicured hands, at the pink nail beds and yellowed tips. "She would ask Willie how he got the ring. She not used to lyin', and even though she try to protect me sayin' she took it, he would have known she lyin'. I don't think a day pass afore I end up in the pond, too, or worse."

"So you kept the ring all this time, and didn't tell anybody."

Her milky eyes settled on me, and I shivered. "I never say that."

"Then who did you tell?"

She took a deep breath, and a small pearl on a chain popped out from the neck of her nightgown, teasing my memories of her leaning over my bed when I was small. "You wants to tell my story or you wants to be patient and let me tell it the way I remembers it?"

I squeezed my hands together, feeling the ring, trying to force myself to be patient. "I'm sorry, Matilda. Please continue."

"Only if you stops squeezing your hands together so tight. You likes to stop the blood goin' to your heart."

I stared at her in surprise. "How did you know what I was doing?"

"Because Bootsie and Carol Lynne both do that when they's agitated-like. You do it, too, when you's little. Don't take no workin' eyes to see sometimes."

I slid the baby ring onto the tip of my little finger and forced my palms flat on my thighs. "All right. I'm listening."

She told me of the rain, and the flooded fields, and Adelaide's garden, and how Adelaide saw it all as just an opportunity to start over. She spoke of Sarah Beth's last visit, and how Mathilda had stayed in the room and listened to every word.

"So that's how you knew that Adelaide and John were planning on going away to Missouri as soon as they could."

Mathilda nodded. "And Sarah Beth, now she know, too. I never see her so angry, and I know it a matter of time afore she makes Miss Adelaide sorry. She in a bad way, and even Miss Adelaide don' know how bad."

"What do you mean . . . ?" I stopped when her eyes settled in my direction.

She took another sip of her water, and I would almost have accused her of enjoying herself, but I saw that her hands were no steadier than mine.

"I had to just wait and sees what I can do to help."

Her hand moved up to her neck, where her stiff fingers pressed against the single pearl glowing like a star against the dark skin. I held my breath, wanting to ask about it, but afraid she'd stop talking if I did.

"I wish Robert never gives this to me. I thinks everythin' might be different. But maybe not. Everythin' happens for a reason."

"Why?"

"Because it made people notice me. Because Sarah Beth, she had to lie and say she gives it to me, even though we both know Robert steals the pearl he found on the ground and gives it to me."

I didn't know anything about Emmett's mother, but from what I'd heard so far, Sarah Beth didn't seem the type to defend a servant. Or lie for her. "Why would she do that for you?"

She turned her sightless stare on me, and I forced myself to lean back in my chair, resisting the urge to fist my hands together in a ball.

"Because we knows a secret about the other." She began to cough and she took another sip of water. "The day of the flood Mr. Peacock calls, and say Mr. John need Adelaide to come to the store right away, and Miss Adelaide, she thinks it's so they can go north, so she brings that sweet baby with her."

I could tell it was getting hard for her to talk, that her emotions were welling in her throat, her words slower now.

"We can stop now, if you like," I said. "Maybe continue another time." I held my breath, hoping she couldn't tell.

With her head down, she shook her head slowly. "I can' promise I be here tomorrow to finish. And maybe my soul rests a bit easier if this all out."

"All right," I said, leaning back in my chair. "Whenever you're ready." I unclenched my fists and forced them to lie flat again.

"I watch Miss Adelaide leave with that sweet baby, and they's nothin' I can do but pray she and Mr. John and Bootsie get to Missouri likes they plans."

She was silent so long that I finally spoke. "But she didn't. Somehow she was killed and her body buried in her own yard, and her baby ended up with Sarah Beth." I took off the blue watch and stared at it, reading the inscription on the back. *I love you forever.* "And so did her watch. She gave it to Emmett and said to make sure Carol Lynne got it when she was older, but I don't think she told him why. It didn't work, and he tossed it in his spare-parts box." I clipped it back on my wrist, my fingers rubbing the smooth enamel. "It didn't work because she put a note inside of it that read 'Forgive me.' What did she do, Mathilda, that she needed to be forgiven for?"

Mathilda was silent for a long moment, and I stood up, agitated again, wondering why it was so important that I know, wishing it had more to do with letting Adelaide rest in peace instead of my need to validate my own past.

She continued. "I don' know what happen at the store. Mr. Peacock, he die that day, too—found his body in Indian Bayou ten days later, and dead men, they don' talk. But my Robert, he at Ellis with his still. The Klan done clean them out, but they's not goin' to let the Klan win, so they's back and runnin' just as soon as the Klan done tear everythin' up. He there with his wagon, loadin' up jugs of moonshine to save them from the flood.

"He hear a baby cryin' and then he sees Miss Adelaide drivin' her car, and a man he don' know in the backseat holdin' that baby. Afore he knows what's goin' on, he see the man lean forward and then Adelaide, she cryin' and beggin' for the man to let her baby be, to do what he wants with her, but to let her baby be. Then he reach up to her, and she falls over, her head restin' on the window, and Robert sees blood all down the front of her dress.

"Another car pull up next to the other car—Robert say they city folk, because they stop in the mud and the man gets in, but the car ain't movin', 'cause it stuck. So they drag Miss Adelaide and her baby out of her car and leaves them there and they gets in that car and drive away.

"Robert pick up Miss Bootsie, and sees Miss Adelaide, she already gone, and that baby cryin' and cryin' likes she knows her mama is dead." She stopped speaking, pausing as if we both could see the young mother in the sodden grass, her inconsolable baby lying nearby.

"He see her blue watch, the one she set such store on, lyin' in the mud, and he pick it up. He put Miss Adelaide in the back of the wagon and sits up front with the baby and goes to the Heathmans', 'cause it closest, and 'cause it built on high ground. Miss Sarah Beth, she there all by herself, drinkin' and smokin', and she don' believe Miss Adelaide is gone till Robert show her.

"He say he bring her inside, and Miss Sarah Beth bathe her and lay her out like it be her funeral, then wrap her in sheets till they can bury her, and Sarah Beth, she can hardly breathe, she be cryin' so bad. But she takes care of Miss Adelaide, and then take care of that baby."

Mathilda began speaking faster, as if to cleanse herself of the story, to unload a burden carried for decades.

"The waters come, more than ten feet in places, and they stay at the Heathmans'. It so cold outside, they leaves the body on the back porch. Robert makes a boat with Mrs. Heathman's dining room chairs, then goes and finds a real boat, and they goes to Miss Adelaide's home and bury her afore anyone come back. The water didn't stay so long up there, that part of the yard being higher than the rest. Sarah Beth say that where Adelaide belong, and where she want to be."

I was sobbing now, remembering my dreams where I was lying in the hole and somebody was shoveling dirt over my face. Even knowing that Adelaide was already dead, I still couldn't stop thinking of her young life taken, and the daughter who would grow up without her. I stood and walked toward the window, staring out without really seeing anything, but unable to look at Mathilda.

"But why bury her like that? Why didn't Sarah Beth call the police?"

There was a long pause before Mathilda spoke again. "Because it what Sarah Beth done that get Adelaide kilt." She was shaking her head, as if Sarah Beth were there and she was trying to scold her.

"She don' mean to hurt nobody. She want to make Miss Adelaide worry some by havin' them mens mess with Mr. John a little. Robert say Sarah Beth tell Mr. Berlini's fiancée that she think Mr. John had somethin' to do with Mr. Berlini being in the pond, and that he plannin' on headin' north. She promise to help the fiancée teach him a lesson." Mathilda shook her head. "As smart as Sarah Beth think she is, she ain't. She don' know it, but she messin' with the wrong people, people who don' give warnin's. People who know how to hurt a man is to hurt those he love most. Robert say it must have been them that makes Mr. Peacock call Miss Adelaide, and they kills him, too."

I pressed my hand across my mouth, trying to find the right words. "All because Sarah Beth was pregnant and Adelaide wouldn't lie for her to make Willie marry her." I shook my head. "I don't understand. Why wouldn't Robert tell anybody what Sarah Beth had done? So she could be punished?" I swiped away the tears that ran down my face, hoping she couldn't hear them in my voice.

Very softly, she said, "He don' 'cause of me. 'Cause Sarah Beth and me, we was kin. Blood kin."

I turned around slowly, recalling what Mathilda had said earlier and what I was only beginning to understand. *Because we knows a secret about the other.* "What?"

"Her daddy and my daddy—they brothers. Our uncle Leon, he in charge of the stills at the Ellis plantation. Sarah Beth's real mama, she half-white, and she die in childbed. But that baby was born beautiful and just as white as cotton, on account of her daddy, Gerald, being a light-skinned Negro. Her daddy, he ain't got no use for a white baby and no mama, so they left her on the Heathmans' doorstep on account of them having no babies, even though they buried five of them."

"And Sarah Beth knew that?"

Mathilda shook her head. "Not at first. Her mama and daddy never knows, though I think they's ashamed she found on they doorstep. They never put her name in the Bible 'cause of that, 'cause she ain't worthy to be a real Heathman, and I know it hurt Sarah Beth deep. But that friend of Willie's, Chas, he knows where she come from. He got in a fight with Leon about the price of his hooch, and somehow it came out. Chas told Sarah Beth, tryin' to get some of what she already givin' to Willie, but she say go ahead and say what you want, 'cause nobody believe it. And she right. But she knew. She go to Leon and ask him and he tells her the truth. That's when I found out, too. We was first cousins—her just as white as can be and me darker 'n a raisin."

I pressed my forehead against the window, needing the coolness of the glass against my skin. "That's why she wanted Willie to marry her. If she had a mixed-race baby with dark skin, Sarah Beth would at least have a husband's name and protection." I shook my head. "But poor Adelaide, she didn't know. Otherwise she might have done things differently."

I sat down on her bed, not wanting to be close to her, feeling even more drained than I had when I'd arrived. "Have you known all this time?"

"I figure some out on my own, and what I don' know Robert tol' me on his deathbed. Until then I happy thinkin' she die by accident in the water. When Robert pass, Sarah Beth, she gone, too, so I told myself it be better to let people believe what they already do. I see Miss Adelaide's haint, though. That's why I put up my bottle tree. I just don' know for a long spell who it was."

She turned her head toward the window. "We all do what we thinks is best at the time. I couldn't bring Adelaide back, so they no sense in taking more lives. Things don' always work out the way we think, and there ain't no way to pay for mistakes except to learn from them."

My hands were clenched again, and I didn't have the willpower to pull them apart. "So three generations of us Walker women grew up believing that the only way to find ourselves was to leave this place, regardless of who we left behind." I felt a glimmer of anger, something

I welcomed over the gaping emptiness. "So what happened . . . after the flood?"

"Miss Louise and me raise Miss Bootsie, and Sarah Beth some, too. She and Willie get married—I think they's guilty 'cause of what happen' to Miss Adelaide and feels it's they right thing, and Emmett born six months later. Willie, he stay drunk most of the time, and dies when he stumbling drunk and slips on the marble floor in the Heathmans' house and hits his head. Miss Sarah Beth, she get real involved in her church, and when the crash came, she help feed the poor until her daddy lose his house, and she come live with Willie's mama and daddy.

"She take real good care of Miss Bootsie, like she was her own, and then Miss Louise and Mr. Joe when they gets too old to carry on. Guilt can sure change a person."

"And John?"

Her face softened. "That man always a gentleman. He run his own watch store, and he treat Emmett like a son, teachin' him things about them watches and clocks, and how to judge the weather by the clouds. He love Bootsie, too, but he leave her raisin' to us womenfolk. I think she look so much like Miss Adelaide it hurt him too much to look at her. He only live 'bout twenty more years. His car crash into a tree one night and he gets kilt. No other car, and he don' drink, so nobody know for sure what happened, but I thinks he just gets tired of livin' without his Adelaide. I figure it a blessin' he never know the truth."

"And the mob left him alone?"

"I figure they thought he be punished enough, and then Prohibition was over and they's no need for him. He was finally free."

I held the ring tightly, the little letters on top warming my skin like a mother's touch, too exhausted to decide whether to stay or leave.

"They crows still come back to that cypress tree?"

I looked up at her, surprised that she knew that. "Yes. They do. Even after the tree fell over, they still came back."

"You knows the story of the crows?"

"You mean that nursery rhyme you used to sing to me? It's kind of hard to forget."

She shook her head. "No. I means the real story. How they mates for life, and generations of they same family come back to they same nest every year, with everybody takin' turns to feed they babies. Sometimes one of they chil'ren leave the nest and don' come back for years. But then they do, and the family welcomes they back like they always been there."

"I didn't know that," I said, remembering the crows and my apprehension of them—no doubt fostered by Mathilda's nursery rhyme.

"You needs to plant another tree for they crows, so they have a home."

"Funny," I said. "Chloe told me the same thing—but because she thought I'd need a place to sit under with my grandchildren."

"Um-hmm," she said, nodding as if I'd just explained the miracles of the universe. "So, you done chasin' ghosts?"

"I have no idea. I thought knowing the truth would somehow set me free. Would validate my life in some way. It's like for generations our whole lives have been based on a lie."

She reached out her hands and I sat beside her again, her fragile bones settling within mine. "No, Vivi. All you Walker women has more love in your hearts than I see in most people—and I seen lots in my days. It take a lot of love for a mother to let go of her own chil'ren. Mos' don' have the strength for that." She squeezed my hand with surprising strength, the ring digging into my palm. "That what your life be. That what be in your blood."

I took a deep breath. "I've got to go. Thank you for telling me the truth. It was hard to hear, and I know it was hard to tell it, but I'm glad to know what happened to my great-grandmother. I think we can bury her now—properly."

"Come back to see me, Vivi."

I leaned down and kissed her forehead and forced a smile, even though she couldn't see it. "I will."

"And don't forget to brings me some food."

"Promise," I said, gathering up my purse and car keys and letting myself out of the room.

I took my time driving home, stopping first at the Ellis plantation, now a total ruin and barely accessible from the road, then past the old Heathman mansion, converted since I'd been gone to a bed-and-breakfast. Then I returned to the old house Adelaide had loved and where she'd borne her daughter.

As I climbed the stairs inside, I paused by the watermark that showed how high the water rose during the time of the flood, running my fingers over the plaster as if it could conjure ghosts. Then I went up to my room, where I placed another call to Chloe that went directly to voice mail. I lay awake, staring at the drooping butterflies on my wallpaper until I fell into a deep sleep, where I dreamed I lay on the ground beneath the cypress, the limbs so thick with crows that I couldn't see the sky.

Chapter 47

Vivien Walker Moise
INDIAN MOUND, MISSISSIPPI
JULY 2013

I spent most of my time in the weeks after my visit with Mathilda in the garden with my mother. Tommy had gone ahead and cut up the old tree and had already fixed my gate and rebuilt the fence. He was now repairing his roof, and promising me that with the wood that was left over, he'd start rebuilding Bootsie's old greenhouse and the garden beds for the larger vegetables that took more space and had longer growing times—melons, pumpkins, squash, and sweet potatoes. And I had plans to plant tomatoes, peppers, eggplant, and definitely sweet corn. I had an almost physical craving to be growing something, to be useful. To help fill the emptiness left by Chloe.

Carol Lynne would help me sometimes, pulling weeds or trimming dead leaves, but most of the time she'd sit in one of the green chairs and watch me with a look of anticipation, as if I needed somebody else to remind me that it was time for the second act.

I'd taken over for Cora, and helped my mother get up in the morning and dress so that we could have breakfast together at nine. Tommy and I had even managed to get her to see a doctor, who'd prescribed some pills that might help her memory, and might slow down the loss of what she still had. It was the best medicine could offer right now, and I finally accepted that she really would never get better. I remembered the resentment I'd had of her and her illness when I'd first returned. The shame burned, but it also made me determined to make it up to her. To make sure we both were here in the moment, appreciating what we had. What we'd always had but had been too busy looking elsewhere to realize.

Our roles had been reversed, and I was now the mother, and she my child. I reasoned it gave me purpose, and when people began to assume I was staying to take care of her, I let them believe it. It was so much easier than explaining that I had no place else to go.

Sheriff Adams had visited Mathilda to hear her story, and when she was finished he'd declared that he could close the case. The final results from the crime lab had come in, letting us know that Adelaide had been five feet, seven inches, about one hundred and thirty pounds, and one foot was slightly larger than the other. No cause of death could be determined, but we no longer needed the bones to tell us how she'd died. I'd felt numb when the sheriff called to tell me, feeling no closure or sense of accomplishment. But it had inspired me to purchase a cypress sapling, bringing it home strapped into the trunk of my Jaguar.

I left voice messages for Chloe every day, having perfected the two-minute message so I could finish before being beeped off. I gave her a travelogue of sorts, telling her what was going on in her plot of the garden, and what Cotton was up to—including how I'd cried when he had to get his shots, and how funny he looked with the cone of shame on his head when I'd had him neutered. More important, I let her know that he had no microchip and nobody had responded to any of the flyers I'd put up everywhere. I told her about Carol Lynne, and how sometimes she'd remember random things, like how mosquitoes liked me but not Tommy, and how when I was four I'd gone trick-or-treating as Dorothy from *The Wizard of Oz*.

I didn't know if she ever listened to my messages, but I kept calling, having nothing but hope to go on. According to the restraining order, I wasn't supposed to. But if Mark decided to take me to court, I could always mention that he'd allowed Chloe to stay with me for more than a month while he was on his honeymoon.

The dog had become my shadow, and I welcomed his company.

Cora had cut back on her hours, since I was there now to see to my mother's needs, and when Tommy wasn't working, he was spending time with Carrie Holmes.

The flowerpots were now all filled with flowers—flowers I'd purchased at a nursery with a muttered apology to Bootsie and a promise that I'd grow my own next year—and I'd decided it was time to start making some of the repairs to the house that had remained undone since Bootsie's death. The house needed repainting, and it would remain yellow. I couldn't imagine it any other color. The gutters needed cleaning, and a few windowsills needed replacing. And the leak in Chloe's ceiling needed fixing. I was almost afraid to stop moving, to stop doing, knowing that if I did I'd start thinking about how Chloe was still gone.

Every evening Cotton would lie down on the front porch until the sun set, his gaze focused on the front drive just in case Chloe reappeared. After a while, I started to join him out there, too, leaving my mother inside in front of one of the TV shows that she seemed to enjoy. Even though I tried to look at everything except the front drive, that was where my eyes always seemed to be fixed when the night finally stole the last light of day.

It was near sunset on a weeknight toward the end of the month when we heard the sound of an engine. I knew it wasn't Tommy—he was driving Carrie and her kids to a Little League baseball tournament in Memphis. Cotton's ears perked up as I sat forward in my rocking chair, knowing it couldn't be Chloe but unable to stop myself. I put my hand on Cotton's collar, then stood and waited until I recognized the white pickup.

"You change your phone number or something?" Tripp asked as he exited his truck.

"No. Why?"

"Because I keep calling and you never call me back."

"You haven't left me any messages."

He didn't respond as he climbed up onto the porch and scratched the dog behind his ears.

"You didn't," I repeated.

"I know. I didn't think I needed to."

He sat down without being invited.

"How've you been?"

I sat back down in my chair. "Great."

He looked at me with a raised eyebrow.

"I am."

"I didn't disagree."

I sighed, not wanting to have this conversation with him. Because it would lead to dark places where I didn't want to go, to thoughts of the quick fixes that offered me oblivion every time I felt the hurt of Chloe's absence, or when my mother forgot to put on her shoes.

"I enjoyed your article in the newspaper last Sunday. About the blues singer Robert Johnson. Most people don't remember him anymore. Good to know there're a couple of biographies we can check out when the library opens."

"That's the point. I'm supposed to be getting people excited about the new library opening with my articles. The editor says that it's so popular he might make it into a permanent thing. Which is good, I guess, because the more I work organizing the archives, the more interesting things I'm finding."

"Can't you take a compliment?"

I blinked at him, trying to remember what it was he'd said that could have been a compliment, and then bit my lip as I realized that I barely knew what one was anymore. "Thank you," I said. "If that's what you wanted to tell me, you could have just called."

"But you wouldn't have answered, so we'd be back at square one. If I didn't know better, I'd think you were avoiding me. But then I thought, 'Why would Vivi be avoiding me?' I can't imagine. Unless she's afraid I'm going to ask her questions she doesn't want to answer. Kind of like it's always been between us."

I moved to stand but he put his hand on my arm. "Don't worry. I really just came over to give you this. I cleaned it up so you can wear it if you want." He reached into his shirt pocket and pulled out a long chain with a little ring dangling from the end. "I thought you might want this back, now that you have the matching one."

I raised my eyebrow in question.

"I went to visit Mathilda and she told me. I wish I'd been there with you. I'm sorry—I knew it would be a sad story, but I didn't quite expect that."

I held out my palm and the ring touched my hand first, like an anchor, the chain pooling on top of it. "Thanks," I reached around to the back of my neck and unhooked the chain where I'd been wearing the other half of the ring. While Tripp watched, I matched them up so that we could read them together for the first time. *I love you forever.* I slid the ring from my small chain and put it on the bigger chain before hanging it around my neck as if it had always belonged there.

Tripp slid back in his chair as if preparing to stay a while. "Jessica from Butler's Funeral Home called to let me know they'd be handling the arrangements and to have the crime lab send them the remains. You could have called me directly, you know."

"I guess. I've been . . . busy."

He pushed back and forth on his rocker, silent as always.

"I have been," I said, wishing my voice didn't sound so defensive. "I've signed up for a couple of classes at the junior college. Thinking maybe I'd like to be a landscape architect. Might as well have something to do while I'm here taking care of Mama."

I fell silent, and the two of us seemed to be waiting each other out. My hands gripped the arms of the chair, my knuckles whitening as I listened to the soft creaking of the chairs and the sounds of the cicadas saying good night.

Tripp finally spoke. "Have you talked to Chloe?"

I stood. "I have to go in now. Thanks for stopping by. . . ."

Tripp stood, too, and took my arm. "Vivi, stop trying to run every time you feel uncomfortable."

"I'm not running. See? I'm here."

"I see. And I'm glad to know you're staying here to take care of your mama, and I'm glad you've found some peace with her. God knows you both deserve it. And you're doing your gardening and you're writing your articles and you're taking classes—and that's all great. But are you happy?"

For once I had no answer, and I reversed our roles, standing there without saying a word.

"Do you remember what I told you?"

"Please, Tripp, just go."

"You can run all over this earth and never find what you want until you know what it is you're looking for."

I turned, and the dog didn't turn with me. He stayed next to Tripp, as if picking sides. As if I could take one more loss.

"Tommy gave me your mother's diary to read—said it would help me understand you a bit better."

I frowned at him, promising myself I'd have words with my brother later, but Tripp didn't look apologetic.

"That and what I've learned about your family ever since that tree fell down tells me one thing for sure: You didn't come from a line of quitters. They made lots of mistakes, but they always came back. And they fought hard to come back. Look at your own mother, Vivi. How many times did she fail to stay clean? And she kept trying until she could. And even Bootsie. She was beaten so badly that she had to go away for six years and find her way back for her daughter. It's never been about their leaving. It's all about the fight in them that brought them back. That's who you are. That's your people, Vivi."

I remembered Mathilda saying the same thing, and for a moment I thought maybe that was where he'd heard it. Or maybe I was just the only one stupid enough not to have figured it out.

He moved down the steps, Cotton following him with his eyes as if he wanted to go with him. I grabbed the dog's collar just in case.

"Call me if you need me. You've got the number. But I don't think I'm going to be calling you anymore. You've got to figure out what you want, and nobody else can tell you what that is."

I just stared after him until his truck disappeared. It felt like I'd already spent a lifetime standing here on this porch or in the drive looking back, watching people disappear from my life.

The touch of my mother's hand on my shoulder startled me. She was looking at the fading puff of dust from Tripp's departing truck. "I miss her."

Chloe. "I miss her, too."

"Is she coming back?"

I shook my head. "No. I don't think so."

"Why not?"

I tried to think of something to say that was close enough to the truth. "Because she's very far away."

"Then why don't you go get her?"

I met my mother's eyes, prepared to argue with her logic. To tell her that it wasn't that easy. But Tripp's words hounded me, battered at my brain and made it impossible for me to open my mouth with any argument at all. About the one true thing. About who my people were and all they'd given me. About being happy. And suddenly it was as if that window where I'd only been seeing a sliver of light had been thrown open, the whole world suddenly shimmering with possibilities.

I looked at my mother again, seeing for the first time the girl she'd once been, the woman who'd failed so many times but hadn't quit. The mother who'd waited so long for me to stop chasing my own ghosts and come home. I hugged her tightly. "Thank you, Mama. Thank you so much."

"You're welcome, Vivi." She pulled back, her eyes searching mine. "For what?"

"For teaching me more than I ever realized."

She touched my cheek, and for a moment I thought she recognized me, who I was right then, and she smiled at me. Her real smile, the one I remembered. "I love you, Vivi."

"I love you, too, Mama."

And then the look was gone and she was just smiling at me. I grabbed her hand and led her inside, while behind us the red ball of sun melted into the rich alluvial soil of the Mississippi Delta.

❦

AUGUST 2013

I struggled up to Tripp's front door, juggling a flowerpot full of sunflowers and a peanut-butter pie. I was trying to figure out how to ring the doorbell with my elbow when the door opened and Tripp stood there with wet hair dripping and wearing only a towel knotted at his trim waist. I tried to avert my eyes, but they seemed to be working independently of my brain.

"Sorry to have caught you at a bad time. I can just leave these here on the steps and call you later. . . ."

He was already taking the pot out of my hands and moving into the foyer, giving me an eyeful of his nicely muscled back.

He set the pot down on a hall table that held a photo of him holding his trumpet and wearing his high school marching band uniform. "Not a bad time at all—I went for a longer run, so I'm just playing the rest of the morning by ear. But when I heard a car door and saw you from the bathroom window, I figured it had to be a fire or something. Seeing as how I haven't heard from you in a while."

I blushed. "Nope, sorry. No emergency. And I promise I won't make you any later. I just wanted to bring by some peace offerings."

He took the pie and raised his eyebrows. "Is this what I think it is?"

"Bootsie's peanut-butter pie. I've been making them by the dozens, trying to get it just right. I'm thinking about selling them to start a little nest egg. Maybe start selling my services as an unofficial landscape architect, too—at least until I can make it official." I glanced over my shoulder at the wasteland of grass in his front yard. "I'd recommend that you become my first client."

He didn't ask me why, and I couldn't roll my eyes, because he was looking too good standing there in his towel holding my pie.

"I just wanted you to know—I'm going to California to talk with Mark. He won't answer my phone calls, so I made an appointment for a consultation at his office. I used Claire's name—I hope she doesn't mind." I gave him a feeble smile. "I figured he could throw me out, but I'm hoping he'll be so surprised he'll at least listen to me. I'm going to ask him if he would trade in my alimony for joint custody of Chloe. And if he doesn't go for that, I'll come back with another offer—I just haven't gotten that far. I'm banking on Chloe making his life miserable for the last month, in addition to his wife being pregnant. Tiffany didn't strike me as the type who'd be happy with what pregnancy does to a woman's body, so I'm thinking that right about now the whole household is coming unglued at the seams. I'm thinking she might be who I target for my next visit."

He was smiling. "Come on back so I can put this in the fridge and we can talk some more."

I wanted to suggest he go throw a pair of jeans on first, but he'd already disappeared into the kitchen.

He was closing the refrigerator door when I walked in. "Can I get you some coffee?"

"Um, sure. Just one, though. I'm trying to wean myself to just a couple of cups a day."

He raised his eyebrows but didn't say anything as he pulled two mugs from the cabinet.

"It could be a long battle with Mark, and I need to be as mentally and physically fit as I can so he can't bludgeon what little inner strength I've managed to restore. It could take a while, but all I've got is time. Just knowing that I'm trying helps me get out of bed each day."

Something about being alone with him in his kitchen, with him dressed only in a towel, was making me babble, but I couldn't seem to stop myself. "I had Adelaide's remains cremated. I'm going to wait until Chloe is back to have the service. I think she'd want to be here."

I choked on the last word, having no real idea of what Chloe thought anymore. I still left messages on her voice mail every day, but for all I knew she never listened to any of them. And she'd never called me. I sometimes even found myself doubting the wisdom of asking for custody, wondering if it was what she wanted. But all I had to think about was Mark telling me the only child he'd ever wanted was Tiffany's, and I felt more committed than ever to bringing Chloe home with me. To work with her in the garden, along with my mother, the three of us coaxing life from the earth, nurturing our wounded souls among the seeds and sprouts.

Tripp was silent as he poured coffee into two mugs. I wondered if he was this way with everyone, or his silent tactic to get people to spill their guts was something he reserved just for me.

"Tommy said if I wanted to go the legal route, I could get a loan and use the farm as collateral. If it were just my life we were talking about, I'd do it in a heartbeat. But I can't do that to Tommy. Or Mama. So I've had to do a lot of creative thinking instead."

He just nodded, his eyes regarding me carefully. "I like what you're doing to your hair," he said as he made my coffee—one sugar, two cream. Like he'd always known that.

I patted the back of my head. "Mama French-braided it for me this morning. She seems to enjoy it, and I'm grateful each day she still remembers how."

He placed a mug in my hands. "So you're here to tell me I'm right?"

"Excuse me?"

"The pie. The flowers." He took a sip of his coffee, an eyebrow shooting up in question.

"It was more to say thank-you. For not giving up on me. For being nice to me even when I didn't deserve it."

"That's for damn sure," he said, leaning against the counter and taking another sip. "But you also wanted to tell me I was right, didn't you?"

I held the mug with both hands and went to look out the large bay window into the backyard. "You could put a pool back here, you know. Or just do a beautiful outdoor kitchen. I could help. . . ."

The kiss on the back of my head surprised me. "You're welcome."

Something warm and viscous slipped through my body, making me shiver. "I don't deserve you," I said, the first honest words I'd said to him in a long, long time.

I waited for him to say something, but of course he didn't.

"Which is kind of a stupid thing to say, because you're not mine, but I've been thinking, well, hoping, that maybe we could start over—well, not go back to kindergarten, but if you could just give me some time to show you how much you mean to me, and how I can make it up to you . . ."

He reached around me and took the mug from my hand, and I heard it being set on the kitchen table behind us. "You're still finer than frog's hair, Vivi."

I turned to face him, realizing too late how close he was standing. I didn't move away. "You know, Tripp, I don't think that would be a compliment coming from anybody else. But there's something in the way you say it . . ."

His kiss made me forget what else I wanted to say, along with all of the reasons that for years I'd denied my feelings for this man, and how I could have ever believed that I belonged anywhere else but here.

❧

OCTOBER 2013

I fixed the plastic wrap over the last peanut-butter pie before carefully stacking it in the back of my new SUV with the boxes filled with pies, the chain with the two baby rings tucked securely inside my sweater, close to my heart. On each of my three trips out to California, I'd worn it as a form of security, a reminder of why I was there. The love between a mother and her child was an unbreakable bond. It made each time Mark said no less defeating, empowering me to try again.

I'd begun to see cracks in Mark's refusals, suspecting that I'd been right about Chloe's behavior since her return. I hadn't been able to speak with Tiffany, because she'd had such bad morning sickness that she'd been hospitalized and was now on bed rest at home. I wanted the baby to be born strong and healthy, but a part of me couldn't help but hope that Chloe was playing her Marilyn Manson CDs as loudly as the speakers in her room allowed.

I hadn't told Chloe about my visits. This battle was between the adults in her life—and I never wanted her to think that the reason I won was because her father let her go.

Tommy appeared on the front porch with a nursery flat filled with tiny sunflower sprouts. He'd rebuilt Bootsie's greenhouse, and I'd thought it appropriate that the first plant I'd grow in it was her favorite. I'd make sure there was a row of them up against the garden fence in the summer, their faces smiling in the sun and reminding me of her.

"Carrie just called—she's at the festival and says there's already a good crowd. She found a red-and-white-checked tablecloth and she'll have it all taped down by the time you get there with the pies."

"Great—thanks, Tommy. And I think I'm all set here—you go ahead. I know Carrie's been waiting for you to take Bo on the Tilt-A-Whirl."

I winked at him, remembering the Harvest Festivals of our past, when no matter what remedy Bootsie offered, anytime Tommy got swung in a circle, he would get sick. In all those years, I didn't think he'd ever been given the time to digest a single cotton candy or saltwater taffy.

"You got the ring?"

He patted his pocket for Bootsie's engagement ring, which had belonged to Adelaide but had been left at the jewelry store to be resized at the time of her disappearance. I'd found it in the dining room server when I'd been polishing the silver. She must have placed it there the last time she'd polished, then forgotten where she'd left it. It had been like a little wink from both women, and when Tommy had mentioned his intentions of asking Carrie to marry him, I'd known it was a sign. "Yeah. I figured I'd do it before the Tilt-A-Whirl so I don't throw up on her."

"That's probably a good plan." I hugged him tightly. "I'm so happy for you."

"Yeah, well, maybe we can make it a double wedding."

"Or not," I said, although without much conviction. "And one of those pies in the fridge is for you—but only one. The other three are for Cora, Mathilda, and Mrs. Shipley. If one of them is missing I'm going to tear off your arm and beat you with the bloody stump." Bootsie used to say that, usually directed at Tommy and his habit of stealing food and leaving a trail of crumbs.

"I'm scared," Tommy said, and I could hear the grin in his voice, and it made me smile.

The harvest had been a good one, and it had made us both start thinking about the future. I'd always loved the cycle of the harvest, of how each spring we'd plant the seeds and each summer we'd watch the fields fill with creamy white and pink blossoms that soon became white puffy bolls looking like old ladies clustered on a church pew. And then in the fall the fields were emptied again, preparing for the long sleep of winter. The never-ending cycle was a familiar one in the delta, and it brought me comfort now, helping me believe that after the cold of winter, spring would come for all of us.

I looked up, noticing for the first time the white pickup truck parked at the side of the house. "When did Tripp get here?"

Tommy barely paused long enough to shrug before jumping into his own truck. "Must have been when you were in the kitchen getting the last of the pies." He waved, then backed out a little faster than necessary.

I knew Tripp had been on call all day, so I hadn't texted him, knowing he'd communicate with me when he had a spare moment. It must have been an unusually busy day, because I hadn't received a single text or phone call. I'd been just about to text him with a reminder that he was supposed to meet me at my pie booth at the festival at seven.

I began heading toward the house to look for him when I realized that Cotton wasn't at his usual spot at my side. In fact, I couldn't recall the last time I'd seen him. I remembered when Tommy's dog had died, how he'd gone out to the swamp when he knew it was time, and we knew where he'd gone only when the buzzards appeared above the cypress trees.

My heart tightened. I could never face Chloe again if I let something happen to her dog. I began jogging slowly toward the back of the house, hoping he might be at the back door, where I kept a water bowl for him.

Sunset was still about an hour away, but the light had begun to fade, the russets and yellows of the trees in the swamp toned down to shades of gray. I stopped at the sound of voices, trying to determine where they were coming from.

"What the hell happened to my lima beans? And is that a greenhouse? How lame."

"It's not ladylike to swear." Tripp's voice.

"Yes. Sir. But where are my damned lima bean plants?"

I ran blindly to the garden and stopped at the open gate, wondering if the light was playing tricks on my eyes. The dog yipped, alerting the others to my presence. Tripp smiled broadly, but I barely noticed him, I was so focused on the black-clad girl with the lopsided French braid and black combat boots. I could tell that her mouth was fighting between a scowl and a smile, the smile eventually winning. And suddenly Tripp's words popped into my head. *Sometimes it's those who are hardest to love who need love the most.* I knew I'd have cause over the years to remember that, and the thought didn't scare me at all.

"Chloe!" I half shouted, half sobbed. I ran to her and wrapped my arms tightly around her, not caring if she hugged me back. "How did you get here?"

"In a plane," she muttered against my chest as I squeezed my arms around her. She was resistant at first, but I didn't let go, couldn't.

I was smiling through my tears, half-afraid that I was imagining her standing there in my garden. "I missed you so much, Chloe. Oh, sweetheart, I'm so glad you're here."

I finally pulled back, but I kept my hands on her arms, frightened that she might disappear if I didn't touch her. "Do you have any idea how much I love you?"

Her lips trembled, and I could tell she was struggling to hold it together, and had even made half an eye roll before she finally gave in and threw her arms around me. "I love you, too, Vivien. I'm sorry I never told you."

And then she was hugging me, too, and we were both laughing and crying and talking at the same time about everything and nothing at all, each of us clinging to the other as if we never wanted to let go.

My mother appeared in the kitchen door, peering out, no doubt attracted by the noise. "Hello?"

Chloe pulled away from me, then stepped through the gated fence so my mother could see her.

"JoEllen!" she shouted, spreading her arms wide, and I laughed and cried some more as Chloe ran into them and hugged my mother hard.

Carol Lynne held Chloe at arm's length. "Let's go inside and fix your hair."

Chloe looked at me, her smile not completely eradicated by her practiced twelve-year-old nonchalance. "Wendy texted me and invited me to hang out with her at the festival. She said there's a hayride and there'll be some cute boys. I know it's lame and all, but it's too dark to work in my garden, so . . ." Her voice trailed off as she looked at me expectantly.

"Sure. I can drive you, but you'll have to hurry. And all your clothes are up in the closet if you want to change. Not that you have to," I added quickly.

"Whatever," she said with a heavy sigh, and all the months of missing her and worrying about her disappeared, making it seem as if she'd never left. Which was exactly how I'd wanted it to be when I'd allowed myself to dream.

She followed my mother into the kitchen, but paused to turn back and speak. "I got your voice messages. And I listened to every one." A corner of her mouth quirked up. "Thanks."

"You're welcome," I said, wanting to do cartwheels across the lawn, but contenting myself with just smiling stupidly as the dog bounded into the kitchen past Chloe, and the door shut behind them.

I turned to Tripp, my arms held out from my sides in complete wonderment. "How?"

He wrapped his arms loosely around my hips. "I figured Mark kept telling you no not because he didn't want to say yes, but because he didn't want to tell *you* yes. So instead of going dove hunting like I told you a few weeks ago, I took a little trip out to the West Coast and made me a little appointment for some cosmetic surgery."

I closed my eyes, trying to imagine what that meeting must have been like.

"I wish I could say that there was lots of arguing and tears, but there wasn't. He seemed almost relieved. I told him we wanted her every summer and every other Christmas and Thanksgiving. He threw in birthdays, too."

"Does Chloe know about that part?"

"No. All she knows is that you and her father came up with an arrangement, and he gave her a return ticket here for the weekend as an early birthday present."

"She's only staying for the weekend?"

"She'll be back for a whole month at Christmas. And I told Mark I wanted it in writing, just to make sure."

I kissed him gently. "What did I ever do to deserve you?"

He shook his head slowly, pretending to think. "I have no idea. But I expect you to spend the rest of your life trying to show me."

"I don't know if that's going to be long enough."

He kissed me back, and then arm in arm we walked toward the ancient yellow house, with its peculiar turret and the old black bed my mother had recently vacated, stating that it was mine now, and that it was time for me to start having babies. I hadn't shared that yet with Tripp, but I would. Soon.

A pair of crows flew to the new cypress sapling that I'd planted, which looked odd among its taller pine neighbors. I remembered what Mathilda had told me about how crows stay together for generations, all of the adults feeding the young, the wayward adults welcomed back to the nest whenever they returned. I hoped it was a mating pair, and that they would bring their children and their children's children back to see the tree grow. And to watch as I brought my children and grandchildren to sit beneath it.

I have decided that when I repaint the inside of the house, I will keep the watermark on the wall, a reminder of those who've gone before us who connect us to this house and the land. We are all separate boats on this river of years, never expecting to see the boat before or behind us except when the current of time unexpectedly pushes us together, touching but never altering our course. We are born to fight the bends and curves of our own rivers, pushing back that which will not give, understanding where we are meant to be only when we let go and let the river take us back to the place where we began.

A Long Time Gone

KAREN WHITE

QUESTIONS
FOR DISCUSSION

1. "Home means so many different things. . . . It's where your people are." The author creates such a dynamic sense of place for the reader through sensory details and evocative objects such as the heirloom black bed, the watermark from the flood, and the lost diary. What things or memories evoke "home" for you?

2. Does Vivien get the closure she needs with her mother once she returns home? How do Bootsie's death, Carol Lynne's dementia, and Vivien's reliance on prescription drugs complicate things?

3. What is the effect of Carol Lynne's dementia on those around her? As a reader, what was it like to encounter Carol Lynne only through her diary?

4. In one of her diary entries, Carol Lynne notes, "There's something in the ways of mothers and daughters, I think, that makes us see all the bad parts of ourselves." Do you think this is true? How does this apply to the Walker women? Does each woman grow emotionally from this realization?

5. "Because it was something I'd been born with, a poison in the blood I'd inherited from my mother and she from hers and way on back before anybody alive could still remember." When they left home, what ghosts was each Walker woman chasing? What made each woman return?

6. Carol Lynne's diary also reveals the following sentiment: "[Boot-sie] just smiled and told me to wait until I become a mother, and then I will understand that my real destiny will be decided by those not yet born." What does Bootsie mean by this? How do children shape the futures of the Walker women?

7. Did you suspect the identity of the body earlier in the novel? How does this "ghost" affect the lives of the Walker women?

8. How does the author use objects or heirlooms such as the watch and ring to unite the characters' stories across multiple generations? Is there an heirloom you've inherited that is loaded with meaning or inspires curiosity about the past?

9. Did you have any trouble shifting between time lines, which run from the 1920s to the present day? Which era or woman's story was your favorite?

Read on for a preview
of Karen White's next novel,

The Sound of Glass

Available in May 2015 from New American Library

Prologue

One need not be a chamber to be haunted,
One need not be a house;
The brain has corridors surpassing
Material place.

—Emily Dickinson

BEAUFORT, SOUTH CAROLINA
JULY 1955

An unholy tremor rippling through the sticky night air alerted Edith Heyward that something wasn't right. Like a shadow creeping past a doorway in an empty house, or the turn of the latch on a locked door, the movement outside Edith's opened attic window raised the gooseflesh along her spine. Her breath sat in her mouth, suspended with anticipation as icy pinpricks marched down her limbs.

Her gaze moved from her paintbrush and the tiny drop of red paint she'd drizzled onto the chest of the doll's starched white cotton nightgown, to the sea-glass wind chime she'd made and hung just outside the window. The stagnant air of a South Carolina summer had stifled any movement for months, yet now the chimes seemed to shiver on an invisible breeze, the frosty blue and green glass twitching like a hanged man from a noose.

She jerked her gaze to the locked door, wondering whether her husband had returned. He didn't like locked doors. The bruises on her arms, carefully placed and easily hidden under long sleeves, seemed to press against her skin in memory. Edith dropped her paintbrush, barely aware of the splatter of red paint on the dollhouse-size room she'd been re-creating, eager to unlatch the door and make it down to the kitchen and her mending basket before Calhoun had cause to wonder where she was.

She'd barely slid from her stool when the sky exploded with fire, illuminating the river and the marshes beneath it, obliterating the stars, and shooting blurry light through the milky glass of the wind chime. The stones swayed with the shocked air, singing sweetly despite the destruction in the sky behind them. Then a rain of fire descended like fireworks, myriad balls of light extinguished as soon as they collided with water into hiccups of steam.

Smaller explosions reverberated across the river, where the migrant workers' cottages clustered near the shore like birds, their roofs and dry postage-stamp lawns easy fodder for the hungry flames that fell from the heavens. A fire siren whirred as Edith leaned out the window as far as she could, listening to people shouting and screaming, and smelling something indiscernible. Something that smelled like the tang of wood smoke mixed with the acrid odor of burning fuel. She recalled the hum of an airplane from when she'd been working on the doll, right before she'd thought the earth had shifted, and imagined she knew what was now falling from the sky.

A thud came from above her head, followed swiftly by the sound of something heavy sliding down the roof before hitting the gutter. Then the sound stopped and she pictured whatever it was falling into the back garden.

Edith ran from the room, ignoring the shoe-size bruises on her hips that made it hard to walk, sliding down half the flight of stairs to the second story, where her three-year-old son, C.J., lay in his bed, blissfully unaware of the sky falling down around them. She scooped him into her arms, along with the baby blanket he'd worn thin but wouldn't give up, feeling his warm, sweaty skin against her own. Ignoring his whimpers, she moved as quickly as she could with the boy in her arms down to the foyer.

Edith threw open the front door to stand on her wide columned porch and stared past her garden and across the street to where the river seemed to bleed in reverse with rising steam. Her neighbors streamed toward the water, as if all the trauma were occurring somewhere else and not in their own backyards. She made her way to the street, but instead of following her neighbors she turned around to inspect her roof, expecting to see it lit with flames.

Instead she was met with the same sight she'd been seeing since she'd moved into her husband's home on the Bluff nearly eight years before, the dark roof outlined neatly against a sky that seemed dwarfed in comparison.

With her little boy tucked against her shoulder, Edith stepped gingerly through the garden gate at the side of the house by the driveway, looking for anything that might have fallen from the sky, wondering what she'd do if she found something on fire. Wondering whether she'd try to put it out with her son's blanket. Or throw it into the house and watch it burn.

She studied her flower garden, her only hobby that Calhoun approved of, smelling the tea olives and lemon trees that almost eradicated the odd smell of fumes that wafted toward her in waves. The full moon guided her along the white-stoned path, past her roses and butterfly bushes that nestled closer to the house and where she imagined whatever had fallen from the roof had landed.

Her foot kicked something hard and solid, reminding her that she was wearing only her house slippers. She started at the sight of a disembodied hand, its fist enclosing a rose. She pressed her hand against her chest to slow the heavy thud of her heart as she realized it was the arm from the marble statue of Saint Michael. He'd watched over her since she'd placed him there when she first realized she needed protection.

She spotted the rest of the statue lying faceup on the path among broken branches from the oak tree, his sightless eyes hollow in the moonlight. When she stepped forward to assess the damage, her foot collided with something hard and unyielding, hidden in the shadows beneath the fragrant boxwoods.

More sirens joined in the cacophony of sound that had invaded her quiet town, but as Edith knelt on the rocky path, she hardly seemed to notice, her attention completely focused on the brown leather suitcase that sat upright in her garden as if an uninvited visitor had suddenly come to call.

C.J. began to stir as Edith deliberated what she should do. Unwilling to separate herself from either her son or the suitcase, she pressed C.J. against her body with her left arm, ignoring the throbbing from the bruises that ran along her rib cage, then grabbed the handle of the suitcase. Gingerly she lifted it to test the weight, finding it lighter than it appeared. Walking slowly, she carried the suitcase up the back steps and into the empty kitchen.

After placing C.J. in the playpen, Edith returned to the brown suitcase, noticing for the first time the large dent in the bottom corner, the hinge badly damaged but not broken. Judging from the relatively good condition of the suitcase, she realized the canopy of oak limbs had broken its fall before it landed on the roof. A name tag dangled from the handle, practically begging her to touch it.

She should call the police. Let them know that she had a piece of whatever disaster had happened in the sky that night. Perhaps some survivor would be looking for this exact suitcase that now rested on her kitchen floor. Still, she hesitated. She wasn't sure why she felt the need for secrecy, but the thrill of the forbidden teased her senses, brought forth her rebellious spirit, which she'd learned years before was best left hidden.

She pressed her lips together with determination. She'd push the button on the latch to see whether it opened. It was probably locked anyway. Or the lock could be too damaged from the fall to open. Then she'd call the police.

She heard a sound from the playpen and saw C.J. watching her with his wide blue eyes. "Mama?"

She smiled. "It's all right, sweetheart. You go on back to sleep, all right?"

"Suitcase," he said around the ever-present thumb Calhoun had been demanding she make him stop sucking.

"Yes, darling. Now go on back to sleep."

He remained standing, watching her intently. She knew his rebellious streak came from her and she was reluctant to stifle it. "You can watch for a little bit if you like. I'll be right back."

Edith kissed his damp forehead as she walked out of the kitchen and to the front door, which she carefully opened to peer out. She was more afraid of her husband's return than of the band of angry people she imagined marching toward her door to find the errant suitcase. The smells and sounds were stronger now, the sky glowing orange across the river over the fields of okra and watermelon as sirens screamed into the night.

Edith retreated into her house and closed the door, turning the key in the lock, then returned to the kitchen and the suitcase. After a quick glance at C.J., who remained sucking his thumb and watching everything with his father's eyes, she reached for the luggage tag and tried to read the name and address. Moisture must have seeped beneath the plastic cover and the cardboard name tag, making the ink run like tears. The address was nearly illegible, but she could read the name clearly: Henry P. Holden. When she flipped up the handle, she saw that a monogram had been boldly stamped in gold: HPH. She imagined a middle-aged man in a dark suit and hat, with a wife and kids at home, traveling on business. She thought of where they were now, and how they might be notified of the accident. Wondered whether it was possible to survive such a thing as falling from the sky.

She pushed the button and the latch popped open. It was a sign, Edith thought as her hands moved to the two latches on the sides of the suitcase. One opened easily, but the one on the side with the dent took a few twists and tugs.

Without pausing, she opened the suitcase wide on her kitchen table. She unlatched the separators on each side and folded them up, revealing neat stacks of starched and pressed dress shirts and suit pants, bleached white undershirts, boxers, and linen handkerchiefs. Everything had been packed so tightly that there'd been little room for movement as the suitcase had tumbled to earth.

Edith recognized the scent of the detergent that wafted up to her as the same one she used, as if the clothes had come from her own washing machine. It had so obviously been packed by a woman that Edith almost laughed at the predictability of it, then sobered quickly as she pictured the faceless woman walking down a dark hallway to answer the ringing telephone.

She stared down again at the clothing, taking note of the quality of the thread count in the shirts, the soft linen handkerchiefs, the fine gabardine of Henry Holden's trousers, the thickness and brightness of the undershirts. Each handkerchief had a perfectly stitched monogram on the corner in bright, bold red: HPH. It all made sense for a man traveling on business. But as she stared at the suitcase's contents, something bothered her, something she couldn't quite put her finger on.

Calhoun had once told her it was her analytical mind that had first attracted him to her. As the only child of a widower police detective, she'd never known any other way to be. So when the handsome lawyer Calhoun Heyward had come to her small town of Walterboro to try a case, she hadn't known that she would have been better off pretending to be a simpering female without opinions. Because in the end, that was what he'd really wanted.

C.J. was sleeping standing up, his head cradled on the top rail of the playpen, his thumb in his mouth. Edith glanced nervously at the round metal clock over the sink. Calhoun could be home at any minute to find a locked front door and a man's suitcase on the kitchen table. She didn't stop to think where he'd been or with whom, or if he'd seen the airplane explode and had thought to worry about her and their son.

She quickly refastened the separators, the fasteners slipping through her fingers because she was going too fast and her hands shook. It was then that she realized what had been bothering her. The dopp kit. The ubiquitous men's toiletry kit was missing. No man traveled without one. She pulled the cloth separators back again, looking at the neatly packed clothes, studying the side where the clothes had shifted slightly more than on the other. She reached in to shove a stack back to the side, revealing a small pocket where a dopp kit would have fit during the packing. She pursed her lips, thinking. Could Mr. Holden have removed it before boarding his plane, believing he might have need of something inside it during the flight?

Edith smiled to herself. These were the questions her father had taught her to ask until her inquisitiveness had become a part of her. During the years of her miscarriages and Calhoun's growing disappointment in her, it had become her saving grace. It had been what had made her ignore the censure of her friends and husband and reach out to the local police department and offer her services as an artist with an unusual talent. It had kept her whole.

Forgetting the time and the sound of an approaching siren, she reached into the suitcase and carefully began to shift the clothing, searching for the missing dopp kit. She searched the top half of the case first, and then the bottom, almost giving up before her fingers brushed against something that didn't feel like cloth. Careful not to disturb anything further, she gently pushed away three pairs of neatly rolled-up dark socks to find a crisply folded letter.

She hesitated for only a moment before taking it out. It was expensive stationery, thick, heavy linen, the Crane watermark visible when Edith held it to the light. It wasn't sealed but had been tightly folded, as if the writer had pressed his or her fingers along the creases many times. When she flipped it over, a single word was written in thin black ink with elegant penmanship.

Beloved.

She paused, wondering how many boundaries she could cross, quickly deciding that she had already crossed too many to worry about one more. With steady hands she unfolded the letter and began to read the short lines written in the same elegant script as the word on the back.

She stared at the words for so long that they began to blur and dance off the page, until the letter fell to the floor as if the weight of the words were too much for Edith's fingers. She let it go, watching as it slipped beneath the new white refrigerator that had been delivered the previous week as an apology from Calhoun. She didn't try to retrieve it, wishing that the words could disappear from her memory just as easily.

She wasn't sure how long she stood there, staring at the small crack between the black and white vinyl floor tiles and the bottom of the new appliance, but she jumped when the hall phone began to ring. With a quick glance at the sleeping boy, she ran to answer it.

"Edith? It's Betsy. I'm so glad to hear your voice. We all ran to the river, but Sidney and I got worried when I saw that you and Calhoun weren't with us. Is everything all right?"

Edith was surprised at the calmness to her voice. "I'm fine. Calhoun is working late, so I was here alone." It never surprised her how easily the lies spilled from her mouth anymore. "I didn't want to leave the house because of C.J. He's been sick and was sound asleep. Didn't even wake up at the sound of the explosion."

"It was an airplane," Betsy said, her voice higher pitched, a tone usually reserved for neighborhood gossip. "They're saying it exploded—just like that. Sidney said it was probably an engine catching on fire. You know how dangerous airplanes are. I took a train to visit my parents in Jackson last Christmas even though Sidney told me I should fly instead, so he can't tell me I was wrong now, can he? It's just tragic, though. All those people . . ." Her voice trailed off.

"How awful," Edith said, her hands still remembering the feel of the stranger's clothes, the image of a ringing phone in a dark hallway. The elegant handwriting in the letter. Her throat felt tight, as if the fingers of the letter writer were pressing against her windpipe. "Are there any survivors?"

"Sidney said he didn't think so. He was outside walking the dog when it happened, and he says it was pretty high up in the sky. But the authorities are handing out flashlights to all the men to go search the fields, the river, and the marsh for survivors. A solid beam for any sign of life, and a flashing light to indicate a . . ." Her voice caught. Betsy Williams was Edith's bridge partner, and they were neighbors. And Sidney Williams was their family lawyer. That was where their common interests ended. Betsy was content to live on the surface of life, to avoid any sharp edges that might force her to open her eyes a little wider. Betsy would tell people that she and Edith were best friends, but she couldn't tell them anything about her except for Edith's favorite flower and that she disliked chocolate.

"A body," Betsy continued. "That was a while ago. Sidney sent me home, but I'm too restless to do anything. I thought maybe you could use some company."

"No," Edith said, a little too quickly, thinking of the suitcase in her kitchen. "I'm exhausted from taking care of C.J., and I think I'm just going to go to bed. I'm sure Calhoun is out there searching, too, and can fill me in on the details when he returns."

There was a brief pause, and Edith pictured Betsy's small mouth tightening with disappointment. "All right. But call me if you get nervous and need me to come around."

Edith said good-bye and carefully replaced the phone back in the cradle, suddenly aware of the sound of voices from her front lawn. She'd already started back toward the kitchen when the doorbell rang. She stopped, unsure what to do. It wasn't Calhoun. He would have banged on the door when he'd discovered it locked. With an eye toward the closed kitchen door, Edith smoothed down her skirt and carefully tucked her hair behind her ears before opening the door.

Two police officers stood on her front porch, their hats in their hands. She wondered if she would be sick all over their polished black shoes that reflected her porch lights or if she could make it to the side railing. How had they known about the suitcase?

"Mrs. Heyward?" The young officer on the left spoke first. She thought she recognized him, but she was having a problem focusing.

She smiled, forcing the bile back down her throat. "Yes?" She struggled to suck a breath into her lungs, the air now thick with the scent of rain. While she'd been in the kitchen, the moon and stars had disappeared as if ashamed to illuminate the scene beneath them. The splat of raindrops hitting her front walk and the leaves of the oak tree that shaded most of the front yard almost obliterated the sound of her heart thrumming in her ears. "Can I help you?" She knew she should invite them inside, just as she knew she could not.

A figure moved from the shadows of the porch, and she recognized the police chaplain as he stepped inside the arc of light. She blinked in surprise, wondering why he was there with the officers.

A flash of lightning lifted her gaze from the three men to the scene across the river, and she found herself holding her breath. Dozens of blinking flashlights came from the shore and from boats on the water like hovering fireflies, spots of light marking the souls of the departed.

"Edith?" The chaplain stepped closer, so she could now see his kind eyes and the deep creases around his mouth placed there like scars during the war. "I'm afraid we have bad news."

"Mama?" C.J. called from the kitchen.

Edith turned to the chaplain in a panic. "I'm sorry; I have to see to my son. . . ."

He reached out to take her hands, his fingers as icy as hers. "There's been an accident. Calhoun's car was found off of Ribaut Road up against a tree. An eyewitness said it looked like he was distracted by the explosion." He paused. "He . . . he didn't survive."

She felt as if she were free-falling from the sky, the lack of oxygen making her light-headed and strangely calm. She felt nothing. Absolutely nothing. "Was he alone?"

The men shuffled their feet in embarrassment, but it was the second officer who finally spoke. "Yes, ma'am."

Edith nodded, feeling inordinately relieved that they hadn't come because of the suitcase. Her son called out from the kitchen again, distracting her from the sight of the blinking lights. She knew she needed to say something, to pretend that she cared that Calhoun was dead, to pretend that she felt anything except relief. She thought instead of the feel of her mother's cold hand in hers, and her father's voice saying something about her being free from pain. Edith let out a sob, then pressed her knuckles against her mouth.

The chaplain spoke again. "Can I get you anything? Or can I call someone to come stay with you?"

She shook her head, blinked back the tears. "No. I'll be all right. I just need to be alone right now with my son. I'll be in touch in the morning to see what needs to be done. Thank you, gentlemen." She closed the door on their surprised faces, her last glimpse that of the chaplain's knowing eyes.

The storm outside intensified as she pressed her forehead against the closed door, feeling guilty that instead of thinking of Calhoun dying alone on a darkened road, her thoughts were occupied with the letter under her refrigerator and the woman who'd written it. Edith felt an odd kinship with the unknown woman, the bond of a secret the other woman would never know she'd shared. A secret Edith knew she'd take to her grave.

Before she turned from the door, a gust of wind pushed at the house, unfastening a shutter on an upper story and slamming the limbs of the old tree against the roof of the porch. As she began walking slowly back toward the kitchen, she heard the wind chime cry out into the troubled night like a prayer to accompany lost souls to heaven. She shivered despite the humid night, then closed her eyes for a moment, hearing only the sound of glass.